Selected Praise for *The Harlot*
A 2011 CRW Award of Excellence nominee

"Take one gorgeous rogue seeking vengeance
and a desperate woman charged with witchcraft,
toss them together with a healthy dose of lust
and you've got an enticing tale of revenge, justice and magic."
—*RT Book Reviews*

"Fans of wanton heroines, revenge plots,
hot love scenes and reluctant heroes are going to *love* this book…
rich writing, erotic love scenes, and intriguing plot line."
—*The Romanceaholic*

"This novel is one more delightful addition to Ms. Walker's
literary portfolio and is one of those books that entertains
as it educates. A reader cannot help but be better aware
of the culture of those bygone days, yet the timelessness of the
power of love to overcome the greatest of prejudices stands tall.
I liked this novel a lot and wholeheartedly recommend it
for the lovers of historical romance fiction."
—*Book Binge*

"This is an exciting, enticing eighteenth-century romance
with a touch of whimsical witchcraft…. Readers will appreciate
Saskia Walker's bawdy historical with a bewitching nod
to *Memoirs of a Woman of Pleasure*."
—Harriet Klausner

"Definitely recommended for historical romance lovers,
especially if [you like] your historicals with a twist of magic."
—*BookingIt*

"Scorching hot! The story of Jessie and Gregor is very well written.
Saskia Walker should be commended for creating characters
that a reader can actually root for."
—*Sweet Reads*

The danger isn't over for the Taskill siblings!
Watch for *THE LIBERTINE* and *THE JEZEBEL*,
coming soon from Harlequin HQN

the Harlot

SASKIA WALKER

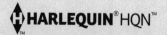

Recycling programs
for this product may
not exist in your area.

ISBN-13: 978-0-373-77736-5

THE HARLOT

Copyright © 2011 by Saskia Walker

Printed in U.S.A.

HARLEQUIN®
www.Harlequin.com

the Harlot

For my wonderful agent, Roberta Brown.

For my exceptionally talented editor, Susan Swinwood.

And for my rock,
the man who supports me every step of the way, Mark Walker.

chapter One

Dundee, 1715

The first thing that Gregor Ramsay noticed about the harlot was her delectable buttocks. It was hard to avoid the sight, revealed as it was while she engaged in a ferocious catfight with another wench on the sawdust-strewn floor of a squalid Dundee inn. It was not, however, the sight of her attractive rump that made him consider her the ideal accomplice for his task. That notion came later on in the course of events, but the vision certainly caught his attention, forbidding him to walk away.

Gregor had sought only a swift draft of ale, to begin with. The noise that emerged from the inn indicated trouble was afoot, and he almost turned away. But when he caught sight of that view—that perfectly rounded womanly cushion with its enticing cleft—he pressed on through the raucous crowd.

"Stand clear," someone shouted, as the two women rolled across the floor, intent on tearing viscously at one another, skirts flying, bodices torn, breasts all but completely bared to the onlookers.

Coins were being passed to a man who stood on the far side, the crowd laying wagers on which woman would win.

Meanwhile, on both sides of the challenge, insults were flying. The wench with the attractive arse seemed to relish the fight, taunting her opponent.

"Scrawny hoor," she accused, tossing back her unruly black hair. "A man likes a woman he can hold on to." She slapped her hip and chortled.

The redhead hissed. She was much less to Gregor's liking.

His attention kept roaming back to the raven-haired woman, who was determined to get her opponent on her back and keep her there. Once she had done that, she pinned the redhead down with the weight of her body, legs kicking. Then she rested her knees either side of the redhead's thighs, bent over her opponent and bit her shoulder. As she did, her skirt and petticoats flew up again. The sight of her bared thighs and bottom—as well as her plump mound and dewy cleft—brought another cheer from the onlookers. It was indeed an enticing sight, and it made Gregor wonder what it might be like to plow her furrow, to ease his cock into that alluring niche. One glance at the men gathered around the scene assured him that he was not alone in that thought. They gaped and lathered at the view.

"What is the quarrel about?" Gregor inquired of a nearby patron, a toothless man in a dirty shirt and torn breeches.

"Eliza," he said, nodding at the redhead, "accused Jessie—" he pointed at the raven-haired woman "—of luring a customer from her. Jessie, oh, she's a wild one." He lowered his voice. "They call her the Harlot of Dundee." He gave a significant nod and paused before he continued with his explanation. "She said she would fight Eliza for the man's custom."

"The Harlot of Dundee," Gregor repeated. "And what has she done to deserve such a grand title?"

The man chortled. "'Tis on account of her spirit. She's not

one for just lying there and collecting the coin, if you understand my meaning."

A spirited wench. How intriguing. Perhaps it was luck that had brought him to this particular establishment? Here by the harbor the inns were full to heaving, and he could easily have gone elsewhere. His trip to Dundee had been necessary in order to see off his ship, the *Libertas,* without him. A strange task and one he had not done before. The nature of the venture ahead and the absence of his familiar world made him tense, and ale was needed before he crossed the Tay back into Fife.

Now he was glad he had paused, for the spectacle was most entertaining. The Harlot was fierce in her attack, with apparently no regard to her appearance. Straddling her victim's thighs, she locked one hand around her opponent's bared nipple, and with the other she poked and tickled her puss through her skirts, prodding at her between her thighs. Gesturing with her hand as if it were a cock, she moved her hips back and forth, a lewd reference to fucking the woman who she had on her back. She was shameless. Gregor's attention was already loosely harnessed, and it was then that an idea began to form at the back of his mind. A whore with a winning smile might be a pretty lure in his game. His enemy never could resist a shapely lass, and was rumored to have bedded half the local lassies. Perhaps when the whore's tussle was over, he would approach her with a proposition.

The crowd roared their approval, and the woman on her back turned vicious, scrabbling with clawlike hands at her opponent. The Harlot dipped and swayed, avoiding the redhead's attack rather adeptly.

"Who is taking coins?" Gregor put his hand into his pocket as if readying to place a wager. He was curious as to who held the power here. Life had taught him that was the key to any situation. In his opinion, the darker-haired woman, Jessie—the Harlot, as he now knew her to be called—would win.

"Ranald Sweeney holds the purse." The patron gestured across the crowded room as he slurred his reply.

Ranald Sweeney was a weasel-faced man who did not inspire Gregor's trust. He had a dirty grin on his face and a palm full of coins. While he was watching the two women, he exchanged comments with a man beside him. Gregor scanned them both quickly. The pimp was dirty and smug. The other man, who he assumed to be the one whose custom the women were fighting over, wore a heavy powdered wig. His coat was embroidered silk and his necktie made of the finest cotton. Despite his ostentatious garb, he seemed quite at ease in the wharf-side inn—a wealthy man who liked to step alongside the gutter when the urge took him. If he were in the same position, Gregor reflected, he would be less obvious about his wealth. Some men were not as circumspect, and reveled in such displays.

Gregor made his way through the rabble toward the counter, where his presence barely distracted the landlord from the show. "Ale," he requested, and pushed a coin across the wooden counter.

Without taking his eyes off the scrabbling women, the landlord nodded and sloshed ale from a jug into a tankard.

It was a rough brew and Gregor coughed out the gritty residue in his mouth after he had slaked his thirst. A squeal issued behind him and a body butted up against his side. Shoving the tankard back across the counter, he turned and stared into the eyes of the woman who had careered his way. It was Jessie, the raven-haired woman who had caught his eye.

"Pardon me, sire." She looked him up and down, and planted her hands on hips. Her eyes flickered with interest.

Gregor nodded at her. Her hair looked as if it had never

known a comb, and even though she was in need of a good scrub, he couldn't help noticing that her lips were eminently kissable. Behind her, her opponent loomed. Judging by the expression on the redhead's face she was in a fury. Gregor nodded again at Jessie. "Your opponent approaches."

Jessie stepped aside.

The other woman landed against him, having missed her target. He gave her a moment to steady herself and then turned her around and urged her back into the fray with a shove. Jessie laughed heartily and batted her eyelashes at him most enticingly before she resumed the fight.

Gregor surveyed the crowd as he downed the rest of his ale. Eleven years he had been away from Scotland. He had traveled far and wide, and he'd come home three weeks ago to a country that had been unwillingly united with the English. The prevailing humor was bad because of the union. In many ways, however, it did not seem so very different from the place he remembered. The people of Dundee had survived decades of war and hard times, one and all. Yet still the city thrived around the harbor where the world's ships came and went on the Tay, his vessel included. Eleven years earlier he'd left Fife a bitter lad without coin. His life as a mariner meant he was able to return with money aplenty. He now had a stake in the vessel he'd worked on.

A shriek went up from the skirmish at the center of the crowd. The onlookers jostled as if eager to back away. Gregor sought the cause of the shift in mood, his curiosity baited. Apparently he should have placed his bet, for Jessie stood triumphant, her opponent lying slumped at her feet.

Eliza was fast recovering, and cleverly saw a chance for a reprieve. Pointing with a suitably shaking hand, she cursed her opponent. "Witchcraft! She used witchcraft on me."

"Hush, Eliza," the accused woman declared, her cheeks

flushing with anger. "I am the one who helped you through this winter last, and I won this fight fair and square. That is the truth of it."

"Witchcraft, 'tis witchcraft," Eliza spat. "She will poison us all with her strange brews and her foreign words."

The atmosphere grew tense, the crowd whispering one to the other.

"I saw her," an onlooker confirmed. "Her eyes rolled and then Eliza choked, as if on air." Two men pounced and held the accused, one on each arm, and she twisted and turned in their grasp, spitting and cursing.

Gregor glanced back at the woman on the floor, Eliza, the redhead. She had her hand at her throat, as if she had been winded. If it was true, it had likely been a trick with a fine piece of thread or a hair. Gregor had seen clever tricks the world over, and it was his way to investigate how it might have been done.

Someone was already out on the street and calling for the bailie of the burgh to arrest the whore-witch, Jessica Taskill. Amused at the turn of events, Gregor leaned against the wooden counter and considered the black-haired vixen, who would soon have half the town gathering with torches, eager for a hanging and a burning. When he'd been a lad at home, the stories of witches and their sins reached them in Fife from time to time. The ministers would lecture the bairns about the evil ways of those in league with the devil, and then horrify them with tales of hanging and burning. Gregor did not believe a word of it, for he did not give credence to such ludicrous claims. Much had changed about his birth country and yet some things had not altered at all, for the accusation of "witch" could still bring about a violent reaction. If the bailie took the word of those who spoke out, this woman would be dead within the week.

She was attractive—a canny lass with a trick or two up her sleeve. It would be a shame to see such talent wasted to the noose and the flame. The idea of making her vanish from the baying crowd entertained him. He and his good friend and fellow mariner, Roderick Cameron, had once liberated a drunken shipman from a cell in Cadiz on a wager.

Gregor reminded himself that he should be on the road by now, back to Fife, where he had taken up lodgings. But the performance was not yet over. The woman called Jessica Taskill wriggled like an eel, cursing and glaring at her captors. Her plump breasts drew his eye, and her spirit entertained him. Once again Gregor considered her as a candidate for the task he had in mind. If he could get her out of her current situation she would be grateful to him—indebted, too. He would have to teach her some manners, but she would clean up well enough, and her aptitude for brazen behavior was unquestionable. There would be pleasure in grooming her for the task, especially if it heralded his enemy's downfall.

The bailie arrived and quickly gathered the information he needed. "Take her to the tollbooth," he instructed. When she argued, the official shook his head, though with a regretful glance at her bared breasts.

As they took her away Gregor observed her angry, flashing eyes and pictured her on her back. It was an image that pleased him. A pretty lure she would make for his enemy, indeed. If Gregor found a way to free her, she would be in his debt and glad of the work. It would be worth the risk.

Jessie Taskill rubbed her hands over her face and glared at the bars of her cell. It would be simple enough for her to undo the lock and slip away by means of an enchantment, but it was the accusation of magic that had landed her here. What annoyed her most was that she had not even used her magic, not this night. Foolishly, she had tended Eliza with a Betony brew to cure her ails when she was sick the winter before, and in doing so had made herself vulnerable. As Jessie had often found out, that was the way of it for her kind. "What use is this gift," she muttered, "when it brings such a burden?"

Her moods had swung wildly since she had been thrown into the tollbooth, from fury to misery and back again, and no amount of pacing the meager space of her new abode would help. There was no chair, not even a cot. The only light that reached her came from candles that were set in sconces farther down the passageway. Apart from the putrid pail in one corner, old straw filled the floor.

Wrapping her hands around the cold bars, she pressed her face between them and peered along the narrow passage to where the guard sat. He was chomping on a chicken leg, and when he saw her look out at him he licked his greasy lips, taunting her.

Her belly growled. If she used magic now, she could collect the remains of his chicken supper on the way. It was tempting, too tempting. Fighting the urge to use her secret talent was growing harder each day, but if one more person witnessed her making magic the bailie would have her strung up before dawn, without a trial. There was still hope, for she knew the man frequented the whorehouses, and he would not want that news passed about. She had to bide her time and be clever about it. Dropping to a squat, she wondered if they had brought the straw here directly from the barn. The dismal hovel she shared with six other women was preferable to this place, and that was not something she had ever thought before.

Eliza was one of the women she lodged with. They had shared good times and bad, and yet Eliza had turned on her, calling her out for her craft. That saddened Jessie. They'd often argued, but not this way. They usually made friends again afterward. The customer had been Eliza's, but he'd shown a liking for Jessie, as well, and Ranald had leaped at the chance to draw attention to his girls by means of a fight. Perhaps Eliza had taken it bad, and if that was so, Jessie wished she had noticed.

Something had distracted her. It was a man, she recalled. Someone she had not seen before—a stranger with a scarred face and dark, hooded eyes. He was tall and watchful, and she'd found herself distracted by him. *Fool.*

She scrubbed her hands over her face again. Ranald would not be pleased about this. She knew him well enough to guess that he would turn his back on her. He held her earnings, and if she did not return soon, they would be his.

It will not happen, she vowed. Even if she had to use her magic, she would not let go of her only hope, her dream. It was a long time since she had last used her secret talent, not since Eliza was sick, and that meant Jessie had begun to sleep better. Magic itself was not the enemy. It was the reaction it brought about in those around her, the trail of devastation that followed that she could not stomach. That went back years, too, for she had been shown how dangerous it was to be gifted when she was a bairn. And yet she had felt her magic burgeoning these past few months. It was as if her secret craft yearned to be nurtured and explored. The change was akin to that of a young girl becoming a woman.

Voices from the corridor caught her attention and she moved to her hands and knees, creeping toward the bars. Cautiously, she glanced along the corridor. There was another man with the guard now—a minister, judging from his garb. Jessie sank back onto her haunches and sighed. No doubt he was here to deliver a lesson in all that was pious and holy, serving it up for the good of her soul. She put her elbows on her knees and rested her chin on her hand. Her beliefs ran in an entirely different direction. Like all those in her mother's line, her soul was attuned to nature, not the kirk.

Once she gathered a few more pennies she would be able to travel north to the Highlands, where her kind was not viewed quite so harshly. There she could let her craft blossom and grow as she longed to. Magic was rising within her, a powerful legacy she could not deny. Each day she had to rebuild the dam that held it back, lest it flood her. In the Highlands, she could live without fear. *Home,* she silently chanted, *home and brethren.* It was her dream.

Her eyes closed. Memories from her upbringing haunted and pained her. A dream it was, a dream that might never be fulfilled if the events of this day were any indication. She would meet the same fate as her mother if she did not escape, and that meant she had to take the risk. She had to use her magic once again.

Footsteps sounded in the corridor.

Once the minister was gone she would decide upon her course of action. Rising to her feet, she stalked into a corner, where she stood with her arms folded across her chest. When the guard rattled his key and shoved it into the lock, she looked at it longingly. She could easily make it drop from his belt as he walked away, but she could not take the risk right at that moment, especially not with two of them watching her.

"Luck is on your side, Jessica Taskill," the guard said. "The minister has risen from his bed to pray with you awhile."

Jessie pressed her lips together while she battled the urge to tell them her beliefs did not match theirs. She managed to resist sparring out of bad humor, because she knew if she kept quiet and acted penitent, he would be gone all the sooner.

The minister stepped into the cell and the guard locked the door behind him, then gestured with the candle he held aloft. "If she gives you any trouble you be sure to call out, Minister. I will hear you."

Jessie looked at the minister for the first time. He wore a wide-brimmed hat and his head was lowered, which made it difficult to see him. Squinting in the gloom, she ducked a little, trying to catch sight of his face. Then the guard set his candle in a sconce outside the cell. The light filtered in and she was able to properly assess the build of her caller. He was a large man, tall and bulky around the shoulders, unlike any minister she had ever seen. He wore the long somber cassock of the church, true enough, and it was buttoned from collar to hem, but she spied a fine ring snaked around his little finger, and expensive leather boots on his feet—silver-buckled boots.

"Thank you," the minister replied. "I will say a few prayers with the sorry lass, and I'll call you when I am ready to leave."

The guard nodded and lumbered off.

The other man kept his head lowered until the sound of the guard's footsteps scuffing along the hallway faded. What little candlelight fell into the cell from the hallway beyond was not aiding Jessie's quest to study his face, and she leaned closer, her curiosity rising by the moment. His jaw was solid, and when he turned his face to listen to the guard's retreat, she saw his mouth. Wide and passionate it was, and scarred from one corner to his cheekbone.

Recognition flared in her. "That guard is a fool," she whispered. "No minister would wear fancy boots such as those."

"You have sharp eyes and an astute mind." The man lifted off his hat, fully revealing his features.

Jessie's interest grew. "I know you. You were at the inn when they came for me."

"Yes, and I can get you out of here, in exchange for a favor."

"A rescuer," Jessie said, with a soft laugh. In truth, she did not need anyone's help, but it suited her well. If he thought he could get her out of here, then there would be no need to use her magic.

He inclined his head. "With a price."

"Ah, I see." She would readily offer him her favors in return for such aid. Besides, he was an uncannily attractive man, despite the hard, assessing glint in his eyes and the scars on his face. His body was fit and strong, and he held himself well. He had the look of someone who had traveled abroad, as she often saw when the ships came in and the travelers alighted. The man whose custom she had been fighting for earlier was rich, but this one was also handsome, and looked potent, as if he could give a woman a good seeing-to.

Nevertheless, Jessie considered him cautiously for a moment longer. He had some money on his person, of that she was sure—and she would find out how much soon enough. Why was he doing this? He did not need to be gallant and rescue an accused woman in order to gain her attentions. There were easier ways to procure carnal gratification, especially for a man of his appearance. Why did he want her? Perhaps there was a secret thrill in the act for him, something to do with the nature of their current situation. He had put himself in danger, coming here in such a costume, especially when the bailie might return at any moment to question her.

At that very moment he glanced down the corridor, watchful for the guard's return. Yet he did not seem overly concerned, and when he looked back at her it was with humor in his expression. Was he a man who liked a challenge? If so, she was the woman to give it to him.

With her hands on her hips, she approached him. In the

candlelight his angular features were cast in leaping light and shadows. "I'll pay your price, in exchange for my freedom."

Before he had a chance to respond, she dropped to her knees and rested her hand over the bulge at his groin. He opened his mouth as if to speak, but paused, his eyebrows lifting as he realized her intention. She couldn't help smiling. His plan must have been to take the tumble after the rescue. That would be safer, but rebellion pumped in her blood. Would he chastise her? Knock her hand away and hush her?

He had not stilled her hand, and his handsome mouth moved in a suggestive smile. She knew the signs well enough, and it appeared this man was not deterred by their surroundings. Anticipation for a taste of him made her blood pump faster. She would pleasure him right here in the tollbooth. Tightening her grip on his bulge, she gazed up at him. "You do not fear discovery?"

"I was aware it was a dangerous undertaking when I came here," he responded, "although this was not quite what I had in mind for the order of proceedings."

She'd been right about his intentions. Well, if he liked danger, he would surely like this. Shaking back her hair, she slid her hands beneath his cassock and ran them up the outside of his breeches as high as his belt, weighing his purse briefly in her hand as she did so. It was impressively heavy, even more so than she might have guessed from the quality of his boots.

"You're a wild lass," he commented.

"That I am." Again she ran her hand over his groin, her cunny tightening when she found his bulge had grown bigger and was now hard and ready for her within the confines of his breeches.

"You are large, sire," she whispered, a teasing note in her voice.

"And I grow larger by the moment under your skilled

fingers." His gaze was on her breasts and his body was taut with lust.

She laughed softly and moved her hands around his thighs, measuring and squeezing them. The muscle was strong. He could easily lift and carry her. Working her way down around his boots, and then back up, she returned to her goal at the front of his breeches. His cock was now long and fully upright beneath the fabric. Between her thighs she grew hot and wet. With a hum of approval, she clasped him firmly. "How satisfying it would be, to mount such a fine weapon."

He cursed beneath his breath, glanced quickly down the corridor one more time, then his lips tightened as he watched her unbutton his cassock to gain better access.

Jessie noticed then how he towered over her, and how self-assured he was. Virile, wayward and mysterious, he was a tempting man. She wanted to pleasure him. She wanted that and more. When his cock bounced free, she embraced it and found it hot to the touch. Reaching below with her other hand, she cupped his sac. His ballocks responded, lifting. If he were on his back she would happily straddle and ride him. Everything about him made her feel lusty, had her core clasping needily. She wanted to hold fast to the bars of the cell while she begged him to rut her from behind. Her hand slid around the shaft and she measured its girth with an impressed sigh, her cunny damp to the tops of her thighs.

Quick as a flash his hand closed over hers, locking her in place. For a moment she thought he was about to stop her. Then her heart beat wildly when she caught sight of the dare in his expression.

"They will burn you thrice over, witch-whore," he commented, "if they see you making lewd with a minister."

Jessie's breath caught in her throat, her spirit flaring as she met his challenging stare. The sinful glint in his eyes made him look less like a minister than any man she had ever seen.

Her hand tightened on his shaft and she licked her lips. "If I am to burn, I would prefer it be for a good reason."

chapter Two

As soon as her pretty mouth closed over his cock end Gregor knew it would not be enough. He would have to delve between her pale thighs and possess her. As she knelt before him and worked him with gusto, it only made him eager to sample more of her talents. Was that her intention?

If so, he doubted her sanity. They were both in danger of incarceration, with her so flagrantly disregarding his disguise. The fact that the guard was but a few strides away only seemed to make her bolder. It was madness. Raining kisses on his shaft, she clutched his ballocks and sucked his crown into her hot, damp mouth.

His cock reached, and when it did she ran her teeth along its underside, an act that almost undid him there and then. When he cursed beneath his breath she growled in her throat, which vibrated along his length as she did so, adding a new element to the experience. She was an impetuous lass and he knew he should put a stop to it, but her forthright, lusty manner only made his need for release greater.

She glanced up at him and the flickering candlelight caught the desire that burned bright in her eyes. Gregor saw why she had gained such a notorious title—a harlot indeed, for she surely did enjoy her trade. He could no more stop this than he could melt the bars that contained them. It was an unfamiliar experience to have his plans complicated by a woman. Gregor attempted to caution himself. It was his enemy he wanted her to distract, although her tenacity showed she would be good for the task he had in mind.

Even so, the urge to pin and have her grew with each stroke of her tongue along his length. The guard was no threat, for he'd readily believed Gregor's claim to be a visiting minister assisting the local kirk. If they remained quiet, perhaps it would be possible. With his hands on her hair, Gregor clasped her head while she milked him with her mouth. "You know no shame."

Her eyelids lifted and she pulled free, sighing most contentedly as she did so. "That much is true, but I sense no admonishment in your comment, sire."

There was humor in her tone. While she spoke she held his straining cock in one hand, and then she dipped her head and ran the tip of her tongue beneath its crown, where the skin was tight, teasing him quite deliberately.

"There was no admonishment, but we must be on our way soon, and quick about it."

The shadows danced around the small cell as if a draft had blown down the corridor, and he heard the groaning of the drunken sot in the cell beyond. When he concentrated harder he could hear the guard humming to himself as he enjoyed his supper. All these things—and Gregor's impending release—made haste imperative.

Again she licked the underside of his crown. Then the hot, wet clasp of her mouth on his engorged cock forced him back against the wall. Cursing beneath his breath, he rested his shoulders against the hard surface while the woman kneeling at his feet squeezed and tugged his ballocks with one hand, the other tightening around the base of his rod as she worked it up and down. She was good, too damn good.

Glancing down, Gregor could see she was aroused herself. Her hips rocked from side to side, her body undulating. If he wasn't mistaken, she wanted his length inside her. The thought affected him, harnessing his need. From the depths of her throat, she gave another loud growl of approval as his cock leaped and lengthened.

Pulling free, the woman stared up at him. Her strange blue eyes glittered in the candlelight as she teased him with her fingers. "You would have me rush the task?"

"No." He snatched at her arm, hauling her to her feet, and quickly turned her around so that she was braced against the wall instead of him. "But I must take charge of this situation, lest you bring the guard here with your sighing and exultations." That would happen soon enough, but he had to be ready to break them free, not midvault, with his breeches at his knees.

Delighted laughter escaped her mouth.

Had she no sense of fear? Silencing her with his lips seemed the only viable option, and he could do that while running her through with his length. He hauled her skirts up and thrust his hands beneath her shapely bottom, lifting her from her feet. She gasped, then gave an approving murmur and wrapped her legs around his hips, inviting him in.

"You are a noisy wench."

"What of it? Are you one of those men who despise women who find pleasure in the act?"

"Quite the contrary." It took immense control to answer her levelly. At the base of his spine a deep, unremitting throbbing had taken hold of him, signaling the urgent need for release. If the guard came now, they would both be damned.

"Good." She flashed those strange eyes at him and then

peeled down the rim of her stays, lifting her breasts free of their confinement in order to toy with her nipples. Between thumb and forefinger she arrested the hard nubs and tugged, hard. She let out a garbled moan as she did so.

Gregor pursed his lips. The way she acted made him want to graze those tender nipples with his teeth, in order to hear her cry out more loudly—an act that would be suicidal under the circumstances. She was taunting him with her bawdy behavior, the vixen. This was something he would have to keep in mind in the days ahead. "You are trouble, my dear, of that I am now sure."

She laughed softly, and yet there was both hunger and longing in her expression as she met his gaze. The practiced glance of a clever whore, to be sure, but his body answered nonetheless, his cock eager to be buried inside her. He bent his knees, and when his erection slid against the folds of her damp puss, she shuddered visibly.

"Ah, yes, this is what you need. This is why you know no fear."

"Perhaps," she responded, and her eyes narrowed to dark slits as she regarded him. A chuckle rose in her, and he stifled it with a kiss. His tongue thrust into her mouth, as he would soon thrust into her body.

With her arms around his neck she pulled free of his kiss and leaned her shoulders against the wall. Her loosened breasts swayed in front of his eyes as she arched her back and manipulated her hips so that his cock slid readily inside her as soon as he found her hot, slippery hole.

Gregor shifted his weight, eager to find his rhythm. Forcing himself deeper, he reveled in the tight clutch and give of her core. She was so eager, and he was equally keen to satisfy the lust in them both. The intense connection captured him, making his thoughts like mud. At the back of his mind, he wondered if he'd taken leave of his senses.

She whispered encouragement beneath her breath and then stifled a cry by pushing her hand against her mouth when he drove deeper, shoving her up against the wall as he did so.

To see her that way gave him great pleasure. He placed his feet wider, gaining leverage and using it. Her sleek, hot cunt grasped at his distended cock eagerly with each thrust, and he cursed beneath his breath, ruing the inconvenience of their current whereabouts.

Then she wrapped her hands around his neck, whispering against his ear, forcing his release much more urgently. "Harder, sire."

Gregor had to close his eyes and gather himself a moment. His ballocks ached, the need to find release becoming all-consuming. The rocking of her lower body and the suck and pull of her damp flesh on his shaft soon urged him on. "I would not allow you to rush me so, if we were under different circumstances."

Her eyebrows lifted. "A man who knows his own prowess… I am most impressed."

That comment led him to shove her more firmly against the wall. He was so bound up in the need to thrust and drive that he was in danger of forgetting the perilous nature of their situation. Then he fixed her and ground deep, and she gave a barely stifled moan. As swiftly as he could, he covered her mouth with his, again muffling her.

"Are you always this noisy," he asked when he pulled back for breath, "or are you trying to lure the guard back here?"

She bit her lip and looked at him from under her lashes. "Forgive me, sire, I am finding your assault most pleasurable."

With that she shoved one hand between them, to the place where he was buried to the hilt in the tight fist of her puss.

She enclosed the base of his cock with her fingers, squeezing him hard there while she paddled her folds with the flat of her hand.

Thrusting vigorously inside the moist fist of her cunt, he cursed under his breath. Her hand there was most advantageous, and his ballocks were high and primed to off-load their burden. Vaguely, it occurred to him that he would be unable to stop now. Even the threat of the guard's appearance was nothing compared to the desperate need for the pair of them to come off.

Meanwhile, her mouth opened and her eyes closed. Never before had he seen a woman so eager and ready for pleasure. However, she was about to cry out again—he knew it. Gregor closed his mouth over hers yet again, silencing her. Her puss quivered around his length, and he barely pulled free in time to spill his load elsewhere. How he wished he had been inside her for her completion. As his cock jerked and spent itself, her hands closed tighter around its head and her lips moved under his, parting. When her tongue stroked his, he felt as if he had captured her cry in his own mouth, the sensuous kiss an indication of her pleasure. Unexpectedly, the kiss arrested him, and he lingered a moment, enjoying the soft pull of her lips and the inquisitive stroke of her tongue for as long as he dared risk it, before pulling back.

Sated, she looked as supine and regal as a contented cat. She arched her neck in the wake of her release, as if savoring every morsel of pleasure. Fascinated, he observed her as her breasts rose and fell with her labored breathing. A most sensuous woman indeed, he decided.

When she opened her eyes she gave a soft growl and looked at him from under her lashes, as if her eyelids were heavy with pleasure. "You are a fine lover, sire. I trust you found I warrant the risk of breaking me out of here?"

Her voice was softened by what had passed between them, and he knew that if they were elsewhere he would soon be hard again and ready for another tryst.

Setting her on her feet, he stepped back and secured his breeches, while taking a quick look down the corridor to assure himself that the jailor had not been roused from his supper. Luck was on their side, for he was still occupied with picking bones.

Once Gregor had buttoned up the cassock, he responded, "Well worth the risk. Now step behind me and be ready to run when the moment comes."

He watched as she pulled her clothing into place, arranging her torn bodice. She folded her hands piously across the front of her skirts and adopted a chaste look, as if he truly had influenced her in a much more holy manner.

For a brief moment, he shook his head and wondered what madness had led him to this. Then he reminded himself of his purpose. She had proved her worth and would be good bait for his enemy's downfall. Gregor cleared his throat and nodded at her, snatching up his hat from where it had fallen to the floor. With another quick glance through the bars at the guard, he called out and then gestured to indicate he was done. "Guard, I am ready to leave."

The jailor approached, glanced in at Jessie and, seeing her quiet and apparently contrite, lifted the key at his belt and opened the cell door.

Gregor stepped out, gripped the door in one hand and gave the guard a swift thump in the stomach with the other. When the man bent forward to clutch at his belly, Gregor knocked him backward, until he teetered and collapsed in a heap in the corridor. Gregor stooped to check that he would stay down for at least a few moments. The fellow was stunned, but would come to quickly enough.

"Apologies in advance for the ache in the head," Gregor murmured, then waved at the woman to follow him.

They weaved their way down the corridors and out into the night at the back of the tollbooth. The moon was high in the sky, a blessing. At the end of the alley, where it opened out into the cobbled lane, he heard voices and paused, his arm out to stop the woman. Easing them both back into the shadows, he put his finger to her lips.

Two figures walked past, holding one another up as they went. Once they had passed and the lane was quiet, he removed his finger from her mouth and nodded.

She dusted down her clothing. "Thank you for your help, sire. I'll be on my way now."

Gregor frowned and grasped her firmly by the jaw. "You will not. You agreed to undertake a task in return for your freedom."

"And I fulfilled the task." She jerked her head free.

She seemed to be under the impression that he had put his life at risk for one of her carnal favors. Gregor gave a wry laugh and shook his head in disbelief. "That was not the task I had in mind, my dear. That was something you brought about."

She put her hands on her hips and glared at him. "Whatever do you mean, that was not the task you had in mind?"

Gregor felt the urge to shake her, but quelled it when he saw another figure moving down the street beyond. Hauling her into the shadows once more, he held her upper arms. "Be silent now, or someone will hear and you will find yourself back in that cell quicker than you can flash your eyes at the next passerby. The guard will awaken and raise the alarm soon enough. We must be on our way, and quick about it."

She wriggled like an eel, growled at him and gave him a nasty jab in the shins with her foot. He pressed his lips together and tightened his grasp, drawing her to him so that her feet all but left the ground.

Alarm flitted through her eyes, and then they narrowed while she lashed out at him, her fists pummeling his sides. "You cannot keep me."

The woman could fight, and her punches made Gregor's blood pump. Even though she was pitted against him, she seemed wanton in her every act, moving in his grasp like a lush, unruly siren.

"Think on it," he growled. "Do you want to hang?"

"Let me go." There was a distinct warning note in her low tone as she issued the instruction, and her eyes glittered strangely in the moonlight.

"No. You agreed to the terms in exchange for your freedom, so will hear me out and come along quietly." He jerked his head in the direction of the tollbooth. "I, for one, do not want to join you in the cells for my part in your escape. You'd do well to follow my lead and hasten away from this place."

It occurred to him that she was too much trouble to bother with and he'd be wise to cut his losses and let her go. However, something about holding the wench while she glared and struggled made him harden. Perhaps it was because of the exceedingly good job she had done pleasuring him moments before.

She delivered another blow to his lower ribs.

Gregor grimaced. Perhaps their earlier tryst was also the reason that he dredged enough patience to hold her and protect her from discovery, instead of letting her run free as she so obviously wanted to. Whatever the cause, he was enjoying lewd thoughts about her writhing that way beneath him on a bed. That was far too much of a distraction while they were in danger of being discovered. The truth was he did not want to let her go. "You have your freedom," he reminded her, "and that is because I risked my own neck to salvage you. Now pay your debt."

The comment forced her to cease her physical attack, but she pouted and glared at him still. "I did not need your help. I was about to leave the tollbooth of my own accord."

This time he laughed aloud.

The wench's eyes narrowed. "Believe it, sire. Did you not hear what they said about me at the inn?"

"Aye, witchcraft. Clever trickery, more like."

She peered at him, and never before had Gregor felt scrutiny like it. Nevertheless, his comment seemed to settle her somewhat, so he continued.

"Come now, you do not expect me to believe that. You are a canny woman and that is what drew me to you, but do not attempt to use any of your fancy illusions on me. I have traveled the world, seeing places you have not even heard of. There are clever folk everywhere who claim a special gift known only to them—although I would be interested to know how you did it. You can tell me over a mug of ale when we reach my lodgings."

She considered him carefully, as if seeing him in a new light, and she seemed pleased by his response, as if accepting the fact he was not one to be fooled. "In that case I am grateful for your assistance, but you have already received a good reward for your efforts."

Gregor's frustration was building. He was beginning to wonder if he had made an error. The wench should be in his debt. "And you will have a good reward, a full purse for a few days of your time, a better wage than you could make any other way, by far."

She looked him up and down as if considering the offer.

"Come now, you owe me at least a few minutes to listen to my proposal."

She shook her head, then glanced uneasily toward the activity in the lane beyond. "I do not tie myself to one man. Danger lies there."

Her remark made him curious, for it was something he'd never heard a woman offer as an opinion, but he had to think of the task in hand. "You will not be tied to one man. That is not the kind of task I have in mind."

Their encounter had been so much more pleasant when it involved carnal gratification rather than conversation. That was not his purpose in pursuing her, however, difficult though it was to keep that in mind. Moments after she had brought him off he was ready to mount her again, and the image of doing just that kept pushing to the forefront of his thoughts. He huffed a laugh.

"I am listening," she said. "Tell me what it is I would have to do."

Gregor kept an eye on the street beyond, as did she. "I need someone to get close to an old enemy, to bed him and to listen to him in order to discover information for me. Someone who is not known to that enemy."

She cocked her head, as if considering his words. Her pretty mouth lifted. She wasn't averse to the proposition, indicating she truly was a woman who relished her sensual nature. That assured him that she was a good choice.

"The task would need preparation. I will have to educate you in his ways, his desires and his whereabouts. I would purchase you some clothes and ready you, and then perhaps require a few days for the task itself. You would be on your way with a full purse soon enough."

"How long?"

"As long as it takes." Gregor's mouth twitched. He was eager for them to be safely across the Tay. "You wish to feel the weight of my purse?"

She folded her arms across her chest. "I can see how heavy it is."

She had also weighed it when it was tied at his belt; he was aware of that. He would have to keep an eye on her or she would pick over his goods and be gone. "The offer is not tempting?"

She glanced away to the north and he saw a fleeting look in her eye that made him wonder what her plans had been before she was thrown in the cell.

"It is tempting." After a moment, she nodded. "Give me a few coins on account, for the pleasure I afforded you this night. Then I will know that your word is good." Mischief glittered in her eyes.

Gregor shook his head, but opened his purse, hefting it in his palm to impress upon her its worth. Then, delving into the deepest part of the pouch, he pulled out two shillings. Her eyes rounded.

After she took the payment and dropped it down the front of her bodice, she spat on her palm and offered it to him as a man might. Gregor shook her hand, gave her a slight bow and gestured along the path to get her moving.

At first she kept up with him, willingly.

Then they reached the kirk.

"Stop here a moment." He still had to return the borrowed cassock. Glancing over the wall, he saw that no one had missed it. He clambered over the barrier and looked back at her. "Don't even consider running off. Not unless you want to go back to the tollbooth."

In four strides he crossed the vegetable garden, which was laden with crops, it being the height of summer, and then arranged the garment over the tree branch where he had found it and the hat hung out to air. Luck had been on his side when he'd sought the kirk earlier that night, for he hadn't had to blackmail the housekeeper for a loan, as he had planned. As he returned the garments he left a few coins in a pocket, for the collection plate. Ducking down, he lifted his bundle from where he had left it, between the roots of the tree. When he got back to the wall he found his new cohort peering over the stacked stones with great curiosity.

"So this is where you got your costume."

"It is. Can you think of a better place?"

She shrugged and then eyed the bundle he had retrieved.

"Stand clear," he instructed. She moved away as he mounted the wall, but once he was on it she closed in again, stepping between his dangling legs. Settling her breasts against his thighs, she jiggled them, and then reached behind him to give his bundle a grope.

"As much as I am enjoying your attentions," he commented, nodding down at where her breasts pressed upon his cock, "we have little time to waste. We must raise the ferryman. Once we cross the Tay we can travel faster. My mount is stabled outside the city walls at Saint Andrews."

Still she stood there between his thighs, and seemed not to be listening. Apparently he was going to have to remind them both of their goal. He had hired her to lure his enemy and aid his downfall, not to dally with Gregor himself. He nodded at his bundle, pulling it from her grasp. "Let me save you some time. You will find nothing there worth stealing, my dear. Just a bunch of papers and a wizened apple."

She jerked away as if annoyed.

"Some of your customers may be fools," he commented as he dropped to the ground, "but I am not, and you would do well to remember that fact." He grabbed her by the arm. "Come, let us leave before word of your escape is put about."

When he began to march her off, she pulled away, standing her ground. "Wait. Where is it that we are going?"

"Fife." He would give no more specific location than that, not until he knew he could trust her.

"Fife?" Her eyes rounded again.

"You'll be hidden away from witch hunters and resting safely within a day," he informed her, thinking it would put her mind at rest and hush her mouth. "I have lodgings some ten miles beyond Saint Andrews." It was there that he had taken rooms at an isolated staging post on the way to Craigduff, the village where he had grown up. He had made himself comfortable partway between his enemy and the gateway to his life in the outside world, the harbor at Dundee, where his vessel, the *Libertas,* would come back to collect him in six months' time.

"Ten miles beyond Saint Andrews," Jessie repeated, frowning.

Perhaps she could not quite fathom that distance. He assumed she had never been out of Dundee, or if she had traveled about, knew little of assessing the distance covered. "We will be there by sundown tomorrow."

She would be safe and out of public view, and he could prepare her for her task. For a moment he pictured her on the bed there and had to remind himself that she was not a distraction for his own pleasure, but a lure for his enemy. Gregor had no doubt he would have to remind himself often.

Still she stood her ground. "I thought perhaps we were Highlands bound, or at least heading to the north, when you took this road. Is that not the case?"

"No. It was only to return the borrowed garments." He felt that might reassure her, but the news did not seem to please her, either.

"I only agreed because we were headed in this direction." She had her hands on her hips now and once more looked as if she thought she had been duped.

"Jessica Taskill, you would do well to remember you owe me a rather large favor. I am at the mercy of the gallows now, too, since I have put myself at risk to rescue you."

She glared at him, her mouth an angry pout.

Gregor's patience had worn thin. "Consider this. You have no other option. You cannot go back to Dundee, not if you want to see another sunrise."

Cursing aloud, she glared at him as if *he* had put her in this mess. "I will have to go back when this is done, for my savings are there. Everything I have earned this past year."

"You will not need your savings after you undertake this task for me."

"'Tis my money," she shouted angrily. She appeared to want to vent her ire on him.

Gregor's last thread of patience snapped. "To hell with you."

He shook his head and turned his back on her, striding off. If she wanted to risk remaining here, that was her choice.

Within moments she was hastening behind him.

He resisted comment, though the urge to do so was fierce.

"They torture and kill witches in Fife," she grumbled, as much to herself as to him as she walked alongside him.

"Then you must stop pretending that you practice witch-craft."

Her head lifted and she peered at him in the gloom. "And there was me thinking it was one of my 'fancy tricks' you wanted me to play on this man who has upset you so."

Gregor grasped her by the upper arm and hurried her on, annoyed at the inferred curiosity about his private business. He was paying her to do as he said, not speculate over his motives. She was canny indeed. Given her curiosity, could he honestly hope to keep her at arm's length while preparing her for the task ahead? *Perhaps, if I resist her charms and keep her solely for my enemy.*

Apparently his task grew more complicated by the moment. He'd possessed her. With any other woman that would have been enough, but it would take some will on his part to resist this shapely wench if she were there for the taking.

"Your *fancy tricks* led me to believe you might have a bit of sense in your head," he muttered, "but I am beginning to doubt it. It was your bare arse that made me think you were worth having, and nothing more, and don't you forget that."

"My arse?" She wrenched free of his grip.

Her face bore such an affronted expression that the tension he carried broke and Gregor laughed aloud. "Yes, your arse, the one that you were exposing to the whole of the inn while you tussled in the dirt. What, did you not know that your rear end was on display to the entire gathering?"

Obviously she had not, for the news silenced her.

Gregor gave her a sharp slap on the behind in order to keep her moving along, and to drive his point home.

Her mouth opened and she looked astonished, but she said nothing. Instead she rubbed her bottom and stared at him ruefully.

Finally. She seemed bereft of words.

Gregor stored away that fact. A sharp slap on the rear end might be needed from time to time with this one, if he was to keep her in line for the duration of their time together.

Now why did that seem to signal even more trouble?

chapter Three

It was the sound of conversation that woke Jessie. When she looked about the place she found herself in she did not recognize it. Sitting bolt upright, she rubbed her face. The light that edged in through the thin curtains at the window made her blink, and she peered around the room with curiosity. She barely remembered arriving here the night before, but she did remember the arduous journey, and that her rescuer had forced her to climb up behind him on a horse—a horse!

She had been so high from the ground she felt quite ill, and had to cling to his back whimpering, with her eyes tightly shut. He, of course, found that greatly amusing, which only increased her annoyance about being obliged to stay with him. So distressful had the journey been that she was greatly fatigued by the time they finally reached their destination.

The room was sparsely furnished. She'd been sleeping in a narrow cot, in her shift. Her torn dress, petticoat and stays lay on the floor, together with her shoes, where she recalled depositing them after he'd ushered her into the room. The cot had a serviceable blanket and was reasonably comfortable. In the opposite corner of the room stood a pail, covered over with a piece of wood. Nearby, a bowl and cloth and a jug of water stood on a wooden washstand. It was more appealing than the cell she had last rested in, as well as the hovel she lodged in with six other women in Dundee.

Sitting up on the cot, she poked open the curtains and peered through the window. Green hills rolled away from the building, a sweeping view. Instantly she felt the age-old desire to be out there, to smell the wild grass and walk barefoot over the ground. And this was Fife, a fertile region that could just be seen from the highest part of Dundee. Often she had gazed across the Tay and wondered about it. It looked pretty enough, but she had been put off venturing here even when she thought she should leave Dundee, because dreadful stories came from the villages of Fife—tales about the torture and hanging of those who practiced the craft. The very thought brought back painful memories for Jessie, memories of her mother.

Forcing her attention back to the present, she saw that the door to the adjoining room was slightly ajar. She got up, used the pail to relieve herself and then peered into the jug suspiciously. Two mint leaves floated on top of the water. She picked them out, then lifted the jug in both hands and drank deeply. Doing so was risky, for it might hold disease, but she was always thirsty in the summer and there had been little sustenance while they traveled the day before. Wiping her mouth with the back of her hand, she set the jug down.

She was about to go to the door when she remembered the coins she had asked her new sponsor for in Dundee. It was important to hide them, and quickly. Inside her stays she had stitched a pocket where she dropped her earnings, and she removed the coins and sought a hiding place for them in the room. She wedged the two shillings in between the floorboards and then stood on them, embedding them there. Tugging a few stray threads from the hem of her shift, she covered the coins over. Satisfied they were safe, she crept closer to the door and listened.

"You did not say you would be keeping company." It was a woman who spoke.

"A change in circumstances."

Jessie recognized the man's voice, for it was the one who had come to the tollbooth for her. She did not yet know his name.

"You do not need to concern yourself," he added, "I will pay you well."

Jessie could not withhold her curiosity. She tugged her torn shift across her bare breast, knotting it and tucking the bunched fabric into her armpit before she opened the door and peeped out. Her rescuer was seated at a table in a much larger room, a private parlor of what was clearly substantial living quarters. It housed a table and chairs, and a winged armchair by the fire that flickered in the hearth. There was a good stack of peat nearby. Through a doorway directly opposite she saw another room, a bedchamber. A large, comfortable-looking bed stood on the far side, with heavy, half-drawn curtains around it. Next to it, Jessie noticed a trunk with a hefty lock and key. At present the lid was open, and when she craned her neck she spied clothing and papers heaped inside.

The woman her rescuer was conversing with stood by with a tray of food in her hands, the contents of which drew Jessie's attention. She had not eaten in two days.

"As I pointed out when I first took rooms here," he continued, "I wish to keep my business private. That still stands, and it is of the utmost importance."

Jessie noticed how handsome he looked, with his hair wet and his shirt open, revealing a broad expanse of chest. His face was clean-shaven.

"My word is good, Mister Ramsay," the woman responded.

So Ramsay was his name, Jessie noted, and then yawned loudly, announcing her presence as she stepped into the larger room.

"Ah, Jessie." Mister Ramsay looked amused at her arrival and her skewed garment.

The woman glanced Jessie's way with a frown. She was a mature matron who wore a drab brown dress and an apron. Her head was swathed in a cap.

"This is the alewife here at the Drover's Inn, Mistress Muir. Jessie is…my cousin, and she will be residing with me for the next few days, at least. She is my ward."

Jessie listened to his explanation, mightily amused by her elevated status. As the cousin of a man with a good purse, she would be well treated here. Perhaps this would not be such a tedious task, after all.

The alewife looked Jessie over and then set her tray on the table. She made ready to leave, as if pacified by his explanation.

"Oh," Mister Ramsay added, "could you arrange for more hot water to be brought? My cousin had a long and tiring journey."

Water? Jessie shuddered.

The alewife shot her a dubious glance and then nodded and took her leave.

"What if I do not want hot water?" Jessie quizzed, once the woman was gone. Rebellion often stirred her blood and that trait had been roused by the situation she found herself in.

"You'll have it and be grateful."

"The water might carry disease." The smell of the food had reached her and she wandered over to the table.

"It might. You'll have to take your chances with the water, much as I took my chances with you." A wry smile passed over his face. "One thing I am sure of is that I would like a closer look at the woman I have bought, and for that we need to be rid of at least several layers of dirt."

Jessie pouted. Then she noticed the plate of bannocks on the tray and it made her mouth water with anticipation. There was broth, too.

"Sit," he instructed. "Eat."

She pulled out the second chair at the table and took a bannock. It was still warm and she ate hungrily, then pulled the bowl of broth closer, snatching up the spoon. It was tasty, and there were good-size shreds of mutton in it. Her belly responded gratefully, rumbling loudly.

Mister Ramsay watched her eat for a moment. He was most likely amused by her uncouth ways. Perhaps he thought her a simpleton who needed to be pitied and cared for. He had mentioned tutoring. That annoyed Jessie. She did not need tutoring on the subject of how to seduce a man. However, she supposed that if he was willing to pay her keep for the duration she would simply have to set him right in good time.

He turned his attention to the bunch of papers he held. Jessie took the opportunity to study him from under her lashes. His heavy frown made his stern looks seem even darker and more threatening than before, and the scar that ran from cheekbone to mouth was stark in the morning light. It had been an ugly wound. Where had he gained it? she wondered. And how fared the man who had given it to him?

She did not know her sponsor well yet, but she was willing to bet the other man had paid. Perhaps even with his life. "I am much elevated, sire," she commented, as she finished the meal, "finding myself your cousin now."

"Would you rather I told her you are a whore, one currently being hunted down under a charge of witchcraft?" The glance he afforded her was slight, and disapproving. "I'm sure she would have welcomed you with open arms, had I told her your true circumstances."

Jessie shrugged. The comment annoyed her, but only because he had so obviously not welcomed her conversation. The rest was only the truth, and Jessie never shied from that.

"Taking a whore into your quarters is not so unusual, believe me." She gave a dry laugh. "Not unless the innkeeper is particularly pious and can afford to select her customers based on their morals, which, judging by the circumstances, she cannot."

"It was for my protection as much as yours. My business must remain private." He set his papers down on the table. His tone was surly, and he raked her over with a look that suggested he wasn't altogether happy about her presence, or the sound of her voice.

That annoyed her immensely, especially since he had forced her to come here. She pushed the bowl away and glowered at him. "How long have I committed myself to? I am not happy about being plucked from Dundee."

The longer she left her earnings with Ranald, the more grounds he had for keeping them. She knew him too well. He would deny all knowledge of them if she did not get back soon.

Mister Ramsay blinked at her knowingly. "You were about to be tried as a witch. In case you did not realize, that means certain death."

Jessie winced at his choice of words, swallowing down the memories as fast as she could.

"You had little alternative but to leave."

She bit her lip, but he waited for her response, eyebrows lifted expectantly.

"I would have left there, yes," she blurted, "once I had collected my belongings. You did not give me that opportunity."

"Why would I? You might have been caught, and I did not rescue you for that." His eyes narrowed. "Most women would be grateful that I had come for them, under the circumstances."

This was a man who did not expect to be questioned and denied. Jessie's skin grew unaccountably hot, so intense was his stare. Raw lust shone in those eyes of his, but there was resentment there, too, as if he regretted bringing her here. The fact that she felt both emotions did not help.

"That may well be," she snapped, "but it does not overrule the fact that you tricked me into forging a pact with you, when I knew so little of what I had agreed to."

She pushed back her chair, but once she got to her feet he slapped his hand around her wrist, pinning it to the table, tethering her there. His grip was merciless, and he put his full strength into it, as if to acquaint her with the seriousness of his intentions.

She glared at him. His mood, which had been restless at best and irritable at worst, had changed again. There was thunder in those eyes.

"You are a hellish, belligerent woman, but you made a good point—you agreed to the pact. So spare me your complaining."

The subject was not open to negotiation. He was used to being obeyed. She attempted to pull free, but he held her tight, and his expression was both mercenary and forbidding.

There was no choice but to tell him the nature of her concern. "If I do not return to Dundee, Ranald, my master, will keep hold of my earnings." She hated to reveal her situation, but she had to. "I do not intend to lose what I have worked hard for this past year...." She took a deep breath. "I cannot afford to."

"I will equal the amount, in addition to your fee." His tone had leveled, but still he held her, with his hand and his gaze.

Jessie swallowed. She felt oddly adrift, even though she was so firmly pinioned by him. Once again lust shone in his eyes, and it made her wish he would kick the table aside, pin her over it and take her. Her blood raced and her breathing hitched. That look he gave her was so devouring, so all-encompassing, that it made her cunny ache with need for the thrust of him there.

Before she had a chance to respond there was a knock at the door and two servants—a thin lad who gaped at them most blatantly, and a buxom young woman with an apron, who sidled them a glance as she passed—carried a large pail into the room Jessie had awoken in. When they had deposited the container the young woman paused to curtsy before she left again. "I will bring more hot water."

She smiled as she took in Jessie's position—latched to the table in her undergarments by her supposed cousin and guardian—then shot off behind the lad. A moment later the pair could be heard in a fit of giggles outside the door.

It must have been obvious the roles were a sham.

Mister Ramsay freed Jessie's hand.

The laughter outside the door faded away, and soon the servant girl returned with a second, smaller pail of steaming water. Mister Ramsay ignored the activity. Instead, he looked at Jessie with undisguised appraisal. It was then that she realized the thin stuff of her shift was all but transparent as she stood in the light from the window, and he was peering at her as if assessing her potential to bed his enemy.

He truly wanted to use her to bring down another man, something she had never before encountered. The situation offered her some level of security. Nevertheless, she balked at it. And something about the way he looked at her made her wonder if he had doubts about her ability to seduce this other man. The gall! She clearly had much to clarify for him.

She took a deep, steadying breath and lifted her chin, eager to conclude their earlier discussion. "I accept your promise of a second purse, sire. I do not enter into a pact lightly and I assure you I am good for the task you have named."

Amusement kindled in those unfathomable eyes of his, making him look roguish and wild. Her curiosity about what he was thinking grew, and she also wondered what might have happened had they not been interrupted by the servants.

The lad had not returned, but the serving girl lingered. She had her sleeves rolled up and a linen cloth hung over one arm, as if she planned to assist. Jessie felt unaccountably awkward.

Mister Ramsay gestured. "Go. Clean yourself up. Be quick about it."

He was making plans for their time together, Jessie realized. Well, so was she. Her curiosity about his situation was building. Besides, the sooner they were done with this, the sooner she could get back to Dundee to claim her earnings from Ranald, and then escape to the north. With both purses.

Meanwhile this man seemed intent on proceeding with this ludicrous instruction. If there was one thing she was sure of in this world, it was that she was able to turn a man's head. Her year of whoredom had taught her much in that respect. But she would attempt to go along with his plan while collecting his coin. As Jessie strode off, she couldn't help but wonder again what kind of man his enemy was.

The serving girl awaited her. Unsure what to do, Jessie pulled off her torn shift. The girl gestured at the large pail and Jessie stepped into it. "I will aid you, miss," said the young woman, pushing up her sleeves.

Jessie was mortified at the idea of being scrubbed by another woman. On the rare occasion she'd afforded a full wash, she had shared the experience with women, but never had she been bathed by another person before. She knew that ladies of wealth had such things done, but she was not one of those. "I can do this myself."

The young woman continued with her task. "I would rather be scrubbing yourself, miss," she said in a forthright manner, "than scrubbing the floors downstairs."

Jessie shrugged. That was understandable, but neither was she going to stand there in silence throughout. "What is your name?"

"Morag, Miss."

The water was still warm and she wriggled her toes.

Morag picked up a cloth and began to sluice the water up her legs.

Jessie's cheeks flamed. "Tell me about this place. Is the Drover's Inn well frequented of an evening?" She vaguely recalled the reek of stale ale when they had reached the inn. Two men had slumbered over a table in one corner, fists still tightly locked around their tankards, when she'd walked through the place.

Morag picked up a jug and filled it with water from the pail. "Tip back your head, miss." Jessie did so and the girl poured it through her hair and over her shoulders. "Most days we are kept busy, and especially so when it is market day in Saint Andrews. The farmers stop here on their way home. They spend some of their earnings if they have had good sales."

Jessie found herself thinking that might be a good source of custom, before she reminded herself that was not why she was here. It was to Mister Ramsay that she answered. Just then she noticed that he was pacing back and forth outside the door, glancing in as he passed. "And who else lodges here?"

Morag was armed with her washcloth. Unceremoniously,

she lifted each of Jessie's arms and scrubbed her pits. "People come and go." She shrugged and pushed her sleeves higher. "Mostly they only spend the one night in order to break their journey and rest their horses in the stable."

That did not sound very interesting. Jessie shot the girl a conspiratorial look. "Mister Ramsay is the only gentleman who has taken rooms for longer?"

"There is one other gentleman, Mister Grant. He stops here for longer. He's an excise man." Morag paused and her eyes rounded. "Oh, we aren't supposed to put that about."

Jessie chuckled. "An excise man never is a well-loved person. Do not fret. I will not pass the word along."

"Thank you."

Mister Ramsay was now standing in the doorway, his shoulder resting against the frame, arms loosely folded across his chest as he stared blatantly at her naked form. Jessie noticed that his shirt was made of good quality cotton, and it fell softly about his collarbone, where his skin was tanned. The column of his neck and his jawbone were both strong and distinctive. The fine leather breeches he wore drew her gaze. It was the first time she had been able to appreciate him in a good light. The fact that he wanted her for another man was a damn nuisance.

This was the first time he had seen her entirely naked, she realized, and he was no doubt checking the goods he had purchased. His gaze was cool and assessing, and yet it kindled heat in her, making her wish he had bought her for his own pleasure. Still, she could make the best of it. Despite her better judgment, she wanted Mister Ramsay to dally with her as he had in Dundee, not give her lessons.

When she saw him admiring her breasts, she lifted her wet hair and turned this way and that. His eyes grew darker for a moment, and he clearly lost track of his thoughts. It was good to know that she could distract him if she wanted to. These things were important. Her plans ticked on.

"Your cousin seems very fond of you, miss," Morag commented beneath her breath as she worked.

Jessie laughed softly. She liked the maid, she decided. The young woman was a practical sort. "He certainly seems to appreciate the view."

Morag smiled and pushed her sponge lower, between Jessie's thighs.

Mister Ramsay's stare followed.

Jessie ran her hands over her breasts. When the sponge moving back and forth between her legs stimulated her cunny, she let her head drop back, and sighed loudly.

To her surprise—for he had looked as if he were enjoying what he saw—he strode over, plucked the linen from the washstand and wrapped it around Jessie from behind, covering her up.

"You dally, my dear," he whispered close to her ear, his voice like velvet, "and we must begin work."

Jessie swayed when she felt his warm breath against the side of her face. Then he rubbed at her with the linen, his large hands measuring her at waist and hip. The desire to couple with him swelled at her center. She recalled how easily he had lifted her. How good it had felt when he had rammed her up against the wall of that cell and his sturdy length had thrust inside her.

Morag rose to her feet, drying her hands on her apron.

"Do you have clothing you could lend my cousin?" he asked. "Her own was torn on the journey."

Morag nodded.

"Please fetch it."

She curtsied and shot off.

They were alone. Jessie turned to face him expectantly, her desire simmering. "How thoughtful you are, sire."

One corner of his mouth was lifted, but he shook his head. "A used sack would have been preferable to the filth you were wearing. Now dress and be quick about it. You are here for a purpose and there is work to be done."

He spoke with absolute authority, then draped the linen over her shoulder and turned away, leaving her to finish the task.

Jessie stared after him with a pout. He was a strange sort, and she found it hard to predict his reactions. Given time, though, she was sure she would know him well enough to do so. It was her goal.

The borrowed clothing arrived and Morag helped her into it, lacing the stays and the bodice of the dress tightly, for Morag was larger than she. When she had tied back her hair, Morag went out onto the landing and shouted for help. The lad reappeared. The pair of them cleared away the pails and took their leave.

As soon as Jessie joined him, Mister Ramsay dragged a chair away from the table, scraping it noisily across the wooden boards, and set it in the middle of the room.

Jessie stood by expectantly.

Resting his hands on the back of the chair, he began. "I need you to be committed to this task. Are you willing?"

Her mouth twitched with annoyance. Of course she was not willing. "You have not yet said much about it."

"I need you to insinuate yourself into a wealthy man's house and gain his trust by seduction."

"For what purpose?"

"To aid me in bringing about his downfall." Ramsay paused. "Retribution for a past injustice."

"I understand."

"Does the nature of the task offend you?"

"No." She laughed softly. "Did you expect me to balk?"

"I need to be sure."

For some reason her sponsor suspected she had doubts about the act of seduction, and his reasons for needing it to take place. That was not what riled her; he did. "Have you forgotten what I am? A whore takes custom where she can. There will be little difference for me, except I will be paid by you instead of him."

He nodded, the question apparently settled to his satisfaction. Meanwhile Jessie's curiosity raged about the old enemy he had mentioned, and what their history was. Folding her hands in front of her, she met his gaze. "If you want me to play a part, my performance would be much richer if you would tell me why I need to do so. What is your grievance with this man?"

The slight flicker in his cheeks revealed his annoyance. "All you need to know at this stage is that you are to gain a position of trust within his household."

Jessie wondered why Ramsay did not want to tell her more. "When you say trust, do you mean that he must trust me with his secrets, or with his silver?"

He gave a wry smile. "I knew you were a canny lass, the moment I saw you…performing."

That pleased her. It was not often that people gave her the chance to show she was good for more than opening her legs. She had a sharp mind, given half a chance to prove it. "And the answer to my question is…?"

"Both. I want you to have access to his silver and his secrets." He moved to take the chair he had positioned, facing her. "I want you to listen to what is said, and to observe his business arrangements."

Jessie nodded, admiring the way Mister Ramsay looked

when he sprawled in the simple wooden chair. His long legs stretched across the floor toward her, crossed at the ankle. All of that strength and virility had been hidden under his costume when she had first seen him. What a pleasure it had been to discover it that night, and to observe him now.

"For that you will need to lure him and gain his trust." With one elbow resting on the back of the chair, Ramsay gestured fluidly with the other hand. "Tell me, for example, how you might go about offering yourself to a man of wealth, in your everyday occupation."

There was curiosity in his expression. She was sorely tempted to tease and taunt him, but she did not want him to withdraw his assessment of her wit. Once he accepted that as fact, she would offer more of her opinion. Meanwhile, she would reel him in—just to show him exactly how able she was to seduce a man.

"My feeling is a woman has to be more cautious in her approach and allow a man of wealth to believe he has plucked a freshly ripening fruit, one that is perhaps not as soiled as the other wenches he might have encountered on the street."

Thoughtfully, Ramsay nodded. "Yes, you are right there."

Jessie could not help herself; she rolled her eyes. "Are you thinking of yourself now, or this enemy of yours?"

He lifted a brow. "I was thinking of my enemy. He has taken many an innocent maiden without regret."

"And you—is innocence your preference, too?"

"This is not about me. Please keep that in mind." Nevertheless, he was amused. His gaze raked over her. "Since you have asked, I prefer women who enjoy the carnal act."

Her blood raced. He had enjoyed their tryst in the cell. She thought he had, but afterward, when she'd learned his reason for rescuing her, she wasn't so sure.

"There is more pleasure in mutual exchange with a woman

who knows what she is about," he added, "than in the corruption of innocence for the sake of it."

Jessie was beginning to get a better picture of both him and his enemy. Had the man stolen Mister Ramsay's sweetheart? she wondered. "I'm sorry, sire, I did not mean to interrupt your…instruction, with my question about your preference."

He laughed softly, and she had the feeling he read her better than she could presently read him, which was rather annoying.

"You are a distraction, Jessie, I'll admit that, but that is why I sought you out for the task." With a flick of his wrist, he gestured at the floor. "Imagine that you have secured a position as his servant. I have thought on it, and this seems the best way to gain access to the information I need." His eyebrows gathered. "Although I'm not quite sure how we will gain you that position. It needs thought."

"That is no great challenge."

His expression lifted. "You have an idea?"

It pleased her that she had brought about that change in his mood. "Perhaps. Is it a large household?"

"Yes, I estimate a dozen or so servants, plus stable hands and groundsmen."

She nodded thoughtfully. "It is easy to make work in such a place, and an extra pair of hands is welcome when chaos occurs. Leave that to me. It will be done."

That requirement would easily be helped along with a touch of magic, and if that hurried the task, it might be worth the risk. She would keep that part to herself, though. For some reason he had dismissed the ousting he had witnessed, and that suited her well. Changing the subject, she asked, "You want me to pretend to polish the floor at your feet?"

"Aye, but do it in a way that I…he, might find alluring."

Ramsay's gaze lingered on her when she smiled in response to his error.

Each and every time he looked at her that way desire simmered expectantly in the pit of her belly. There was a mighty tug between them. Why then was he apparently able to sit there so easily? Yes, he wanted her for another man, yet the way they had coupled that first night proved they were well matched when it came to pleasures of the flesh. Even though she had her own destiny to follow, she would take anything she received from him along the way. Jessie had never been rescued from the gallows before, and that experience—after such a fine mutual tumble—was beginning to settle well in her memory now. As she lowered herself to her knees before him, she vowed to make him claim her again.

At first she was dazzled by the late spring sunshine behind his head as she tried to see him. His figure, dark and looming, was absolutely still. She put her hand to her eyes to shield them while she grew accustomed to it. Then she took a deep breath and let it out with a sigh.

"Forgive me, sire. I must polish the floor here, Mister Ramsay." She said his name to let him know she had caught it earlier.

He did not reply. Yet the mood in the room altered.

Something she had said or done had made it do so. Jessie noticed how quiet it was, the only sound a distant bird singing. She went about her chores, pretending to polish the floor, humming to herself. Occasionally she looked up at him from under her lashes, suppressing a smile, and jiggled her hips and torso as she worked, to be sure she caught his attention.

Tension swelled from the place where he sat.

What was he thinking?

He observed her silently. Nevertheless, the rising air of expectancy made her blood heat. The notion that he was sitting there assessing her allure made her want to act very differently—to slink over to him and beg him to pleasure her the way he had before.

A moment later he rose to his feet and stood before her. Reaching down, he put one finger beneath her chin, lifting it. "Your head at this angle, when you are kneeling. It displays your bosom to good advantage."

The very sound of his voice vibrated along her nerves. Deep and low and seductive—and deliciously demanding—it aroused her, making her want to hear more of it. He had blocked out the sunshine, and she was able to see him. As she looked up at him she was forced to remember her first taste of him, back in the tollbooth in Dundee, when she'd knelt at his feet for an entirely different purpose. Then she'd thought only of him. Now, he would have her think of another man, an enemy.

His finger remained under her chin while he scrutinized her. His gaze was all-encompassing, his handsome mouth slightly pursed while he considered her. It occurred to her that in a roomful of gentlemen, he would be the one who caught attention. Handsome and yet scarred, rough and so darkly secretive, the man lured her in every way.

"Sire," she whispered, "what else would you have me do?" She wanted him to order her to strip, to bare herself to him. She wanted him to demand she sit on his cock and ride him until he came off.

A curious look flitted through his eyes, and he stroked his thumb over her lower lip. Jessie could not help herself—she shivered with arousal.

"Remain kneeling." Slowly he straightened up. He did not, however, return to his seat. Instead he walked around her, pausing occasionally to study some detail of her appearance.

Jessie could not resist glancing over her shoulder. With

her head cocked she could see him out of the corner of her eye. Even though he did not touch her, her blood raced. She wondered if he was aware of the effect he was having on her.

When he was directly behind her, he inserted one foot between her feet and pushed them farther apart. "Place your knees wider and arch your back."

She did so, pulling her skirts a little higher to aid the maneuver. With her knees parted that way her thighs were wide apart. He had instructed her into a position that would enable her to be easily taken from behind, should someone choose to lift her skirt. Her cunny prickled with arousal and her core began to throb unbearably.

"That is more agreeable," he said.

Agreeable for whom? Jessie had to shut her eyes for a moment. The new arrangement was doing nothing to aid her concentration. She wondered how long she could bear it, for her cunny was poking out like a ripe fruit, ready to be taken. She was wet with wanting, and meanwhile he was standing there as calm as could be, instructing her to pose lewdly.

"Now polish the floor."

She was sure she heard disguised humor in his tone. Was that amusement at his enemy's expense, or hers? Frustration began to get the better of her. With a deep intake of breath, she shifted and pretended to polish. The position he had arranged her in made her rear end wobble and dip as she worked. Flipping her hair back over her shoulder, she shot a disgruntled glance his way as she did so.

"If I did not know better," she blurted, unable to hold her tongue, "I would think you were trying to shame me, sire."

"Shame you?" There was definitely humor in his voice. "Shame the Harlot of Dundee? An impossible task, surely?"

Curses. He knew of her notorious title. Jessie pressed her lips together hard, for it annoyed her immensely. He was a stranger, a man who had lately been away at sea, and yet he knew what they called her. That was a great pity.

She sat back on her haunches and peered up at him, folding her arms across her chest. Who had he spoken to about her? What else did he know? That title was a dubious honor. Many times, in anger, she'd called it the bane of her life. That was far from the truth. Her secret gift was her true burden, but still, the title did not please her.

However, it was when she broke off following his instructions that she noticed the soft chamois leather of his breeches was strained at the buttons, his manhood lifting inside the confines of his clothing. That he was stimulated by their play was obvious, and the sight pleased her. "Your instruction, sire. Please continue."

"It is good to see you are becoming more amenable."

She buttoned her lip.

One corner of his mouth lifted. "I want this man to lust after you, but he must not know that your purpose is to get close to him. I need you to attract him, but for him to think he is the seducer, in order not to arouse his suspicion. What would you do, under such circumstances?"

Jessie's mind quickly wandered into various lewd scenarios, but the only man she could picture at that moment was him. "I would first play innocent in order to convince him I am chaste, and then perhaps allow him to see that he had stimulated me."

Ramsay nodded. "How would you do that?"

"I could show that I am desirous of a man's touch, but at a loss for one. I would go somewhere where he might find me, where he could observe me desperate for relief…and attempting to handle myself."

Mister Ramsay considered her at great length before he replied. "That may indeed stimulate his ardor."

His comment was measured, and there was a brooding quality to his posture. Had she unsettled him? Jessie hoped that was the case. It was only fair, after all. He'd put her in such a state of longing that she *would* be forced to handle herself, and soon.

"Demonstrate your meaning," he instructed, "so that I can be sure."

Staring at him, she shook her head. "Demonstrate?"

"Do it. Play the innocent woman burdened with her lust, the woman who must somehow find relief." His eyes glittered.

That made her breath catch. He wanted her to bare herself, to touch herself, while he watched. The idea excited her. Secretly thrilled by the turn of events, she silently dared him to resist what he was about to see. As she rose to her feet, renewed anticipation assailed her.

She moved to the chair nearer to the window, where the fall of light would assist her display. "Allow me a moment to picture myself there, in *his* home, in order to do it well."

"Go ahead." Ramsay folded his arms across his chest and leaned against the wall. His pose was one of leisure, but his eyes were narrowed and his lips tightly pressed together as if he was concentrating.

That pleased her immensely. She would soon have him needy for her. Meanwhile, she could happily look on his handsome, scarred face as she plucked and teased at the seat of her pleasure. After a moment's consideration, however, she decided that would not aid her quest to look innocent. "Please stand further in the shadows, sire. That way I can pretend I don't see you...I mean *him*."

Curiosity flitted across his face. He lingered, staring at her as if challenging her somehow. It made her heart flutter, for although she was sure she could do this, his attention made her feel more vital and alive than she ever had. When he moved away from the light the shadows only served to make his presence more looming, more exciting. Without warning she remembered the thrust of his cock inside her, and it was as if an echo of that moment haunted her intimate places, and she was back there in the tollbooth again, with his strong arms holding her. Her cunny tightened in response to the memory, her sense of frustration building. Determined to succeed in arousing him to the point of madness—as he had her—she rubbed her hand around the back of her neck and sighed with longing.

Even with her eyes averted, she could not banish his presence. If it were him that she had to seduce, she would have no trouble in mustering the urge. So she imagined it *was* Mister Ramsay who she had been sent to seduce, Mister Ramsay who unwittingly harbored her in his house, unaware of her true purpose. That quickly presented a vivid picture for her to think on as she stroked and squeezed her breasts through her bodice and stays. In it, he was her master and she was his servant. As master of the house he had shown interest in her from afar. She had gone looking for him and had spied him, perhaps at his washstand, naked. Aroused to a state of anxiety by the image of his strong, manly form in a state of undress, she had crept away into a linen cupboard to ease the fevered desire she felt.

While Jessie lifted her skirts to access her cunny, she imagined she might become aware of him watching her—peering in at an open door, perhaps, standing in the shadows. Ah, yes, it was Mister Ramsay she had to get closer to, and she was succeeding. Jessie bit her lip, struggling with the urge to look directly at him. She would eventually, because she had to know how her performance had affected him, but not yet.

The lurid nature of her imaginings urged her on. Resting

one foot upon the chair, she hitched her skirts to her waist and pinned them there with her elbows. With two fingers she delved into her cunny, and quickly discovered exactly how damp she was. It came as no surprise, but made her sigh with longing nonetheless, and she quickly worked the fluid over her sensitive places. Within moments her hips began to weave back and forth, the friction making its own demands on her, causing her body to react. Her core ached for him, for the solid, gratifying thrust of his engorged shaft. Again her body shivered as she remembered how it had felt, and her cunny clamped, eager to be filled again.

As the moments passed, she grew desperate to come, for his presence only heightened her need, but she resisted the urge to tip herself over the edge. The tension emanating from the place where he stood was growing by the moment, thrilling her. He was about to pounce, about to order her to bend over the chair and present herself so that he could fill her with his cock, she was sure. It was what she wanted, but she forbade herself to look his way or to encourage him, for she had to prove to him that he could not resist.

chapter Four

Gregor Ramsay wondered how in hell's name he had got himself into this ludicrous situation, because fixing his thoughts on the goal ahead—rather than the current moment—was going to test him immensely.

His vow to resist her had been challenged as soon as she'd stood with the sun behind her and he'd seen her body outlined through the thin stuff of her worn shift. She had a fine, womanly figure, and the urge to explore it made him lose all sense of purpose for several long minutes.

It was a mercy that the serving girl had arrived and Jessie left the room. At first he'd avoided following and peering in at her while she was naked, but that was short-lived. Why shouldn't he?

Then, when she delivered her husky invitation to stand in the shadows to observe her performance, his attention was all hers. Now he was transfixed, because the sight of her abandonment was the most seductive thing he had ever seen. Several times he had to remind himself of his goal, and the effort he had put into reaching it thus far, to keep from letting his baser instincts take over.

She was carnality embodied in female form, and since she had been scrubbed and dressed in a relatively clean garment, she was even more of a temptation. Resisting her was imperative, or else he would fritter away his time bedding her. He had taken these weeks away from his ship to resolve the legacy of the past, not to satisfy his own lust.

It was, however, hard to even remember the task that lay ahead when she lifted her breasts free of her stays and began to squeeze and mold them in her hands. This was the first time he had seen them in full light. The pale skin gleamed, the nipples a dusky rose color that was darkening as they hardened and lifted. Jessie's fingers roved over them, and then she pulled on the nipples until they lengthened and poked out rudely.

That alone would have his cock standing at attention if it was not already doing so. Then she grasped her skirts in her hand and lifted one foot, resting it on the chair she had moved closer to the window, baring her puss. He remembered then how it felt to be inside her. That made him harder still. Torn between the need to satisfy his desire to couple with her, and their more important purpose, he had to fix himself to his post in the shadows.

The sight of her juices glistening on her fingers as she plied the folds of her puss open made his hands fist. He wanted to grip her buttocks in his hands, to lift her, open her and taste her.

The flush on her cheeks indicated that her sensuality and passion brimmed to the surface. He noticed how she coated her fingers in that heavenly dew and then began to trail them back and forth in her furrow—slowly at first and then with increasing haste. Her spine was against the wall and she pivoted, moved her hips back and forth in an agitated fashion.

But then she shifted and the view was obscured.

He moved, but her legs closed, her hand buried between them. Gregor frowned. Her gaze was fastened in the distance, but if he didn't know better, he would think she was trying to provoke him. The vixen!

As if she could read his thoughts, she lifted her head and met his gaze. A vixen she was, through and through, following her own needs and disobeying his instruction, even while he tried to prepare her for what lay ahead.

Gregor shook his head.

A startled look appeared on her face, and she crushed her hand between her thighs. "Oh, sire, forgive me for my improper behavior. I did not see you standing there."

She began to drop her skirts, but her eyes flashed with mischief and he knew then, with the utmost certainty, that she was toying with him, which meant she was not giving this her full attention. That enabled him to concentrate on the goal that had driven him these past eleven years.

He closed the space between them in three strides. "Do not stop. Touch yourself again as you would for him, and let me see you."

"But sire…" Her head rolled and she cast her eyelids down. "I am thoroughly ashamed."

The smell of her arousal was intoxicating. She was close to coming off. He had been so absorbed by the way she looked that he felt sorely deprived, but he would make her earn it. "You are not ashamed. You are nowhere near ashamed enough!"

Her head jolted up, her eyes wide.

"You have forgotten your first rule, the one you so cleverly stated earlier. This man must think you innocent and untouched, and yet I see blatant lust in your eyes."

She shook her head vehemently, color staining her cheeks. "No, I…I did not mean to."

He placed his hand over hers, crushing it to her puss. "Do it, but do it properly this time."

She staggered back against the wall and looked up at him with round eyes, her cheeks flushed. Her hand began to work again and she bunched her skirts higher, tucking them under her elbow. "I am so ashamed, sire," she whispered. "I cannot help myself. It is you that makes these fevers of longing come upon me."

His cock was so hard it was painful, the need to plow her rising all the while. Through gritted teeth, he issued another instruction. "Try harder!"

She gasped, and when she moved her hands inside the cup of his, she swayed, her eyelids lowering. "Oh, sire, you are able to feel how dreadfully wet and wanting I am. I cannot bear the shame."

Gregor inserted one of his fingers between hers and nodded at her, encouraging her. She moved her hips back and forth again until his finger slipped easily into her hole.

He inhaled a ragged breath.

She was so deliciously slippery that his cock pressed insistently at his breeches. Then her flesh tightened around his finger and her mouth opened. He thrust his digit deeper and moved it around, learning her—learning the shape and texture of her, the intense heat, and how sensitive and responsive she was.

Her body welcomed his hardness, and their hands began to move as one, until she rocked her hips, and the embrace of her flesh on his finger became crushing, and she grew wetter still as she neared her peak. She panted aloud and moved to steady herself by resting against his chest, her forehead against his shoulder. Her body trembled. "Oh, oh…"

Her hips rolled, and she worked herself up and down on his finger, passionate and wholly feminine, sensual and lush. Gregor had no doubt that she could claim any man, no matter where his tastes lay. More skilled and lushly feminine than a courtesan she was, and devoid of shame.

That did not excuse the fact that she thought herself beyond his instruction. She was about to come-off, but she had forgotten her task.

With his free hand he gripped her by the chin, forcing her to look at him. "Not innocent enough, my dear. Not by any means…"

"But sire—"

"You look too brazen, too greedy and eager for a man to satisfy your needs." And didn't that make him all the more hard for her?

"I cannot help it." She wriggled and shifted, attempting to play the part and break the easy stride she had gained. Instead she acted as if she was unsure what she was doing. Her cheeks flamed, but it was not shame nor innocence, it was sheer, demanding lust.

"No." Gregor withdrew his hand. "You must not break with the picture you have created!"

She stared at him in disbelief, her lips parted.

With a wry laugh, he shifted her away from the chair. "Now you will see how serious I am."

Sitting down on the chair, he pulled her quickly to him, forcing her facedown over his lap.

"Sire. Mister Ramsay!"

With one hand between her shoulder blades, holding her in place, he hauled her skirts up and slapped her arse. The twin globes of her bottom bounced up in response, her body jolting.

"You are a cruel man," she exclaimed. "I am on fire." Any attempt she had been making to play the part had now fully departed, for she glared at him.

He slapped her again, several rounds on both buttocks in

quick succession. When he paused, the attractive curve of her rump and the heat coming off her made him realize that there was, apparently, no easy remedy to this, for everything he did only seemed to pleasure her more and make his own situation more dire. Only the thought that his enemy would be totally unable to resist her forced him on.

"I see no blushing innocent here," he declared, with no small amount of relish as he delivered another stinging slap to her soft flesh.

She clenched her fists and pummeled his thigh angrily, but her arse lifted higher still. He landed another smack on each buttock, noting with satisfaction how her pale flesh showed the imprint of his hand, and how her moans grew more wanton.

"Still you sound brazen and demanding. You are like a bitch in heat."

"Damn you," she cried over her shoulder, "I am trying, but you are making my situation even worse."

Gregor restrained comment, and for a moment he considered leaving her on the edge of release for the rest of the day, in order to make her earn it by getting it right. But for some reason he couldn't quite muster that level of persuasion. Instead, he stroked his hand over the soft curve of her buttock.

The flesh trembled and her head lowered, her posture submissive once more. Gregor smiled to himself, for he sensed they had reached a level of understanding at last.

"This?" He slapped her again, making sure she felt it where her puss was pushed out between her open thighs, as if begging for attention. "Is this making your situation worse?"

"Yes. Please, sire, I must…" she whimpered. "Please help me."

With his hand a hair's breadth from her arse, he paused. He ground his teeth, counting time. When she wriggled closer, he moved his hand away. The tension between them had grown too large and unrelenting. This must be done or they could not move on.

"What will I get from you in return?" he demanded. "Think about your answer carefully."

Silence filled the room, the tension between them sharp as a drawn dagger. He could almost hear her thoughts racing. Nonetheless, she kept still, and he noticed that she had her fingertips on the floor to balance herself.

Breathlessly, she replied. "I will try harder to get it right, next time."

"That was the correct answer." He moved his hand down to the cushion of her puss. "Here? Is this where you need a man?"

She kept still, her head hanging down, her hair trailing the floor. "Yes."

Her breath was scarcely above a whisper, as if she did not trust him to relieve her of her burden. Finally, she had recognized who was in charge here. He smiled, and stroked his finger the length of her slit. A muffled moan issued from below.

She would do better next time, and she would not tease or question him. Stroking back and forth from damp hole to swollen nub, he marveled at how her moans rose in response, how he was able to play her like an instrument. When his finger on her clit started her panting breathlessly, he concentrated on that part of her. Never before had he found such a sensual, responsive gem. Gone now was his need to teach her she could not lead this situation. Instead, he wanted to make her come. His desire to feel it happen was binding. He stroked her to the brink of completion and then eased two fingers inside her. The sigh of relief she let out when he thrust them deep was satisfying.

He rested his free hand on the base of her spine, and moved

his fingers in and out of her hot, wet sheath. Her flesh responded instantly, closing hard on him, releasing, and closing again. All the time her juices flowed, coating his fingers. It required every ounce of his self-control not to take over there and then, not to thrust his cock inside her to ease their mutual need. Instead he forced himself to learn the make of her, to explore her and enjoy the way her inner muscles grasped at his fingers.

When her body stiffened, he found his fingers crushed and then swimming in her juices. She shuddered from head to toe. When she wilted over his thighs, he pulled his fingers free. Rolling her over, he lifted her and sat her up on his lap.

She rested against him, her breathing unsteady.

"I'm sorry," she murmured against his shoulder, as soon as she could speak, "that I did not do it right."

Gregor did not trust himself to reply. He rested his arm around her back, tucking her against him. It would take some time before his erection subsided, but it had been a necessary lesson for her to learn. And him? Perhaps. It wasn't as if he didn't know she was a temptress. That was why he'd rescued her. What he hadn't bargained for was that she would tempt *him* quite so relentlessly.

She looked up at him. Her lips had darkened to red and her eyes were shining. Tendrils of her hair had escaped the ribbon that held it and her eyelashes were damp and glistening. How strange that it had affected her so. Was it the pleasure she had been afforded, or the unwilling submission to him that had brought that about?

The urge to kiss her, to feel those soft lips under his own, was great. To have her body—supple and pleasured as it already was—under his on the bed, where he would bring her to release again and enjoy her more specifically from the inside.

"Will I do, do you think? If you tutor me some more?" Her eyelids fluttered.

Was this genuine submission, or a ruse to make him rest easy? He gave a wry smile and cupped the back of her head. "You'll do."

Her expression grew even more serious. "You think your enemy's attention will be secured, if I act that way and do it well enough?"

Her comment reminded him most firmly of his purpose, that which had driven him these past eleven years. For a moment there, he'd forgotten it. That reassured him she was a good choice for the task. She would lure Ivor Wallace's attention completely. That was what Gregor needed to know, after all. He reassured himself that the lesson had been valuable.

Still she gazed up at him, her lips parted as she awaited his answer. Unable to resist, he inhaled her sweet nectar from his fingers, and licked them. She tasted good. He would allow himself to enjoy more of that. Not yet, but before his enemy had her.

Jessie watched what he did, and then her teeth bit into her lower lip, her eyes darkening once more as she observed his actions. Her breasts lifted and lowered more quickly, and he knew she was already growing ready for coupling.

"You are undoubtedly suitable for the task," he eventually replied. "With practice."

chapter Five

Mister Ramsay went out onto the landing to call for service, and after he returned, Mistress Muir appeared at the door. He ordered food for one.

Jessie observed the exchange with curiosity. Wasn't he going to feed her? She was not overly concerned, for she'd had a good meal that morning and her mind was still on what she considered the unfinished business of earlier. While she had been over his lap, the heavy bough of his erection pressing against her had made her dizzy with lust.

Jessie was surprised he had not used her to satisfy his own needs, those that were so readily obvious. The bulge in his breeches barely subsided for several long minutes afterward, and not until he set about studying papers he pulled from his trunk. Why did he resist?

When he'd had her across his lap, she'd been willing him to turn her so that she was splayed and ready to be probed with that sturdy length. The hiding he had given her only seemed to arouse them both to a state of frenzy. Yet now his whole attention was given over to the papers from his trunk. Were they so important, and what else had he in there?

When he caught sight of her eyeing the trunk, he got up

and shut the lid. "Tidy yourself up," he instructed, with a frown.

That interested her. He did not want her to see what was inside his precious chest. Languidly, she laced the bodice of her borrowed dress while she speculated about what he might have in there. Patience had never been within Jessie's grasp for any length of time, but she attempted to sit by quietly, waiting for him to resume instructions. She was sure that when he continued to order her about, as seemed to be his wont, things would move forward to a mutually satisfying result.

However, when the alewife brought a plate of pigeon pie and a mug of ale on a tray, Mister Ramsay gestured at Jessie, indicating it was for her. The look of the baked pigeon and pastry lid made her appetite grow. There was easily enough for two, and she would enjoy feeding it to him. But he was busying himself, as if preparing to leave. He had strapped a sheathed dagger to his belt and was now putting on his frock coat and hat. Confused, she stood by the table, picking at the pastry crust with her fingers.

"You are not hungry, sire?" she asked as she lifted a morsel to her mouth.

He did not look at her when he made his reply. "I have business to attend to this afternoon. Take the food and go to your room."

He gestured at the small room in which she had slept. She thought it rather odd, but the food was now her main concern. It was by far the best meal she had tasted recently. She lifted the plate and carried it with her.

Gregor followed her to the door. "I will be back by sunset. Behave yourself while I am gone."

With that he closed the door.

Jessie stared at it. Did he truly expect her to stay in here while he was away? She chuckled to herself, then sat on the edge of the narrow cot and picked up the fork. As soon as he was gone, she could explore her surroundings.

It was then that she heard the key turn.

He had locked her in.

Jessie stared in horror, then thrust aside her plate. "Open the door!"

Darting over, she pounded on it with her fist.

"Hush. I do not want you wandering about in case you are seen."

Angered, she stomped her foot. "You cannot keep me locked in here like an animal."

The only response was the sound of his boots fading into the distance.

Apparently he did not trust her.

It did not matter. No lock would hold her, not unless she wanted it to. She had informed him of that in Dundee, but he honestly had not believed it. Jessie shook her head, amused by that, and returned to the cot and the meal.

Most people feared her when they got any sort of hint she may know witchcraft. Not Mister Ramsay, and he'd seen a whole inn shouting for the bailie to condemn her. He had traveled, and there was a worldliness about him that attracted her. It was no excuse for him to lock her up, however.

Her thoughts wandered back to that night in Dundee, and for the first time she addressed how close she had come to her end. Since she had cured Eliza the winter before, it seemed that the women around her had secretly feared her. Jessie had tried to help someone, which meant her outing and condemnation were only a matter of time—all because she had healed with her witchcraft.

Jessie's mother had warned her and her siblings that people would fear them, because those who did not understand the craft thought it evil. It was beyond their grasp to offer tolerance. Her current protector was above that. Mister Ramsay did not seem at all threatened by the possibility of magic, and there was great comfort in that for Jessie.

For a few days she need only do as he asked, and she would be safe and well fed. Not to mention pleasured. Her cunny was warm and heavy still, and her bottom tingled most satisfyingly. That made her smile. Mister Ramsay was an intriguing man, and the way he had pushed her and bent her to his will was most arousing. It was not what she was used to, and despite her annoyance at being locked up, she found herself anticipating his return.

When she had finished the meal she wiped her mouth and rubbed her hands together. First, she would remain quiet and rest awhile in order to ensure that he had gone from the place. Then she would use the time to find out what he kept in that precious trunk of his.

Gregor urged his mount to a fierce gallop, grateful for the wind in his face and the distance from his new cohort. He sought freedom—freedom from the pressing need to plunge into the wench's sweet softness and do nothing but enjoy her.

Not only was she the most delicious honey pot he'd ever wanted to ease his cock into, but she seemed determined to make him lose his mind. The fresh air eventually pacified his lust, at least for the time being. With distance between them he was able to conclude that her performance had all but turned him into a demented fool. He was more certain than ever that he had to keep some detachment from her in order to be able to think straight.

The horse was making short work of the distance. Freshened by the canter, Gregor slowed his mount to a more sensible pace. He was able to move a lot quicker without the burden he'd had the previous day. Jessie had turned their escape from Dundee into one of the slowest journeys he had ever completed, what with her arguing and recriminations. Then, when they finally reached Saint Andrews, she had stared aghast at the horse, and when Gregor hauled her up behind him, she'd clung to him like a limpet. With a disturbed bleat, she'd locked one arm around his waist and the other over his shoulder.

Once they were on their way, he'd glanced over his shoulder as he urged the horse to a trot. "Is it necessary to cling to me quite so tightly?" he had asked. "I can scarcely move the reins."

She grumbled beneath her breath.

"Apparently it is." It amused him, though, because she had been surly toward him when they traveled by foot, her arms folded across her chest, the occasional angry stare thrown in his direction. Once up on the horse it seemed she could not get close enough to him.

Her body had been warm, and her breath huffed against the back of his neck, instantly kindling his carnal interest. Occasionally she had whimpered, and he assumed it was the horse she was afraid of. Her grip did not loosen, and after they had been traveling awhile she'd requested to walk beside the horse to ease her cramped limbs. It was an excuse. He knew it was.

Gregor smiled as he remembered. Just when he thought she was as tough as an old boot, she'd showed fear and fatigue. Today all of that was forgotten as she returned to her former mischievous self. One thing he was certain of was that he would never forget Miss Jessie Taskill. Even though he had known her only a day and a half, he was sure of it.

As he neared the landscape he knew so well his thoughts became more subdued. The ground beneath the horse's hooves was good land, fertile. The hills rolled away from him toward the sea. On the horizon, he saw a boat. The sea here was teeming with herring, the catch that kept the folk along the coast in coin.

The sight of the boat also made him think of his ship, the *Libertas.* It wasn't the first ship he'd signed up on, but he had spent nine years aboard the *Libertas,* a trade vessel under the command of a Scottish-born captain. The crew was a mix of Scots and Dutch, united by their long-held mutual dislike of the English, who sought to rule the trade routes.

Some called the crew of the *Libertas* brigands, for they allied themselves with no one. But they were more inclined to think themselves free traders. Then, three years ago, their old captain was taken down by gout that had been wrongly treated by a surgeon in Tangier. When the rot set in he'd lain on his deathbed and called for his two most trusted men to take charge, Gregor and his fellow shipmate, Roderick Cameron. The captain had no son or heir that he knew of, and had signed it over to them in good faith. Together they had taken over the running of the vessel, with the captain's blessing. To this day they shared the duties and the captainship.

Gregor and Roderick had treated the *Libertas* crew well, paying them better than they had been before, and maintaining their loyalty. That had enabled them to make their fortune in contraband trade. They carried dangerous and valuable cargo from places others feared to venture.

It was a good life, a life he thrived upon, and Gregor had split with Roderick and the *Libertas* only to avenge his father. His partner had set sail for North Africa, where the goods they shipped could be sold all over Europe. More trade would be picked up along the way.

In six months time he would reset the compass for Dundee. Gregor and Roderick had agreed that they would make contact when the ship returned, and all being well, Gregor would rejoin the *Libertas* when his business was attended to. If he was not yet ready, he would send word.

For the first time in many years he was back in Fife, for as long as it would take.

When he mounted the hill that overlooked the village of Craigduff, he drew his mount to a halt to gaze down at the place of his childhood. The cottages clustered around the small harbor were as familiar as the back of his hand. This was the village where his mother had been born, the place where he himself had attended classes in the mornings and church on Sundays. The place where he had buried both his parents.

Resting his hands on the pommel of his saddle, he studied the sight for some time, then looked away to his right, toward his old homestead. Strathbahn was fertile farmland, two dozen good fields set in a sheltered valley. His jaw tightened. Eleven years ago he'd left the place, and the need for justice was still strong in him. It never faded, as he often hoped and prayed it would.

So much was the same, yet this was a different Scotland than the one he had left, he knew. More importantly, he was a different man. He'd left as an angry young man because his family had been destroyed by one man, Ivor Wallace. Now, on his return, Gregor was older, wiser, with knowledge, experience and wealth at his fingertips. And he was a man who would not be stopped in his quest to redress the injustices of the past. Now was the time.

He urged his horse on.

When he finally rode into Craigduff, he did so warily. He wore his hat pulled low to hide his eyes, and a loose neckerchief obscured the lower part of his face. With caution, he looked about the place as he guided the horse down the steep, cobbled incline of the main street.

A trio of barefoot children bolted past him, their mother

fast on their tail, her skirts lifted as she chased them up the hill. At first glance, little had changed. The stone cottages lined the street on either side, and he saw that the curtains were still the same in the windows at Margaret Mackie's place. His mother's cousin, who had nursed him as a babe, was still alive? He would visit with her soon, once he'd achieved his goal. She had to be a good age, and the sight of her familiar wooden door made the memories run.

He turned away, and on the far cliff he saw the kirk, the building stark and gray against the green hillside. Up there he'd attended Sunday school, and he'd seen his father's coffin lowered into the ground, next to the spot where his mother's coffin had been since Gregor was a bairn.

The lane he was on led down to the harbor, where the gulls cried and dipped in the sky. As the bay opened in front of him, the scent of the sea assailed his senses. Beyond the shale-covered beach he saw the rough rocks and crags that jutted out into the waves, the wild, beautiful terrain from which the village of Craigduff had taken its name. Those rocks were treacherous to the fisherman who didn't study the weather.

Gregor had docked in strange and wondrous harbors and ports the world over, and every one had made him reflect on this place, the one he had left behind. It felt oddly dream-like being here now.

He was much relieved to see the blacksmith's. It stood three doors up from the waterside inn where the fishermen went after selling their haul. There were two boats pulled up on the shale now, the morning catch long gone.

Dismounting, Gregor secured his horse and entered the blacksmith shop. Would his old friend, Robert Fraser, still be here in Craigduff? As he sought him out, the smell of the forge stirred memories. He and Robert had run amok here as bairns, under the watchful eye of Robert's father, the blacksmith. When they got too unruly, he would send Gregor home to Strathbahn.

Gregor expected to find Robert's father standing there at the forge, but it was Robert himself he discovered. Even with his back to him, Gregor instinctively knew him. Working at the forge the way his father had, he wore a leather apron, and his breeches bore smut marks and burns here and there. He had taken over his father's role running the smithy, and he had a young lad of his own by his side.

"Robert?"

The blacksmith straightened and set his hammer down by the forge. Ruffling his thick, ash-colored hair, he turned toward the potential customer. Gregor quickly took in his old friend's appearance, and found him broader in the shoulder, more powerful in the muscles and somewhat timeworn in the face—much as he was. They had both turned thirty this past winter. They were no longer callow youths.

Gregor removed his hat.

It took a moment before recognition lit Robert's expression. Then he blinked and peered more closely, as if he could not believe it. "Good Lord, Gregor. Is it truly you?"

"Robert, old friend, it is."

A broad, welcoming smile lit up that familiar face. Gregor felt raw emotion assail him. Gruffly, he embraced the man he had played with as a child and bonded with as a youth.

"I would rather keep my presence here unspoken." He glanced over his shoulder, wary of causing tongues to wag on the subject of a stranger in the village.

Robert nodded, stared at him for a moment longer and then reached out to shake his hand.

"So you are the hammer man now?" Gregor asked.

"That I am." Clapping him on the back, Robert beamed.

"Come inside." Turning to the boy, he added, "Tell your mother to bring ale."

"The lad is yours?" The similarity in looks attested that he was, but Gregor could scarcely fathom it.

"Aye, the eldest of three. I am married these nine years past. A lassie from Saint Andrews caught my eye and my da gave us his blessing in exchange for my work here."

Robert had wanted to leave the village, to travel and find his fortune in foreign lands, much to his father's disapproval, but his old man had found a way to keep him there. Gregor was the one who had wanted to stay and work the land of his ancestors, but had been unable to. Life had reversed the fortunes they'd sought as youths.

"He got your agreement while your eye was fixed elsewhere?"

"That he did, but it was no bad thing. I am happy here, after all." Smoke curled up from the forge behind him, and Gregor nodded.

Robert led him into the storage room where the tools were locked at night. Gregor took in the familiar scents and sights. They had spent many an hour in here. Robert pulled two worn wooden stools from beneath a counter, and they sat down together.

"You have gained a scar."

"I have. Never fear, the man who gave it me has two."

Robert chortled at that. "You look well, old friend. Where in God's name have you been?"

"Far and wide. I joined a crew in Dundee…and now I own a share in a trade ship. I've been at sea many years now."

"The sea, that explains it. I wondered on it. Just about every day I wondered." Robert shook his head, his eyes bright with emotion. "I'm mighty glad to see you again."

"Please, keep it to yourself for the time being."

"Why?" Robert's earnest expression made Gregor falter.

"I need time." He would have to tell him why.

"Will you be staying?"

"No. But I have come to reclaim what was ours. I have money, plenty of it."

Robert grew serious. "That will be difficult."

Gregor leaned closer. "I appointed a notary to represent me in Saint Andrews. He informed me that some of the land would be up for auction soon."

"Oh, aye. Wallace continued to build up his estate for several years, and occasionally now sells off bits of it that he deems unworthy. But I doubt he will sell it to you."

Gregor reflected on that. It was Wallace's way to buy up or win land adjacent to his own just to swell his estate. Gregor had appointed his notary and established himself with a banker two years before. That was when he began making his plans. The news that part of the estate was being sold was what had brought him back. The time was right to do what had to be done.

Robert continued. "He has half the village calling him 'Laird' now."

Gregor bristled. That was always Wallace's aim, but he was not well liked by the powerful families of the region, those who warranted respect because they treated their tenants well.

"But now Forbes, his eldest, is like a guard dog. Whenever there is a transaction on any of the surrounding land he appears and tries to put a stop to it."

Gregor grimaced. "As bad as his father then?"

"Worse, believe me."

Gregor lifted his eyebrows. He barely remembered Forbes Wallace, who was several years younger than them.

Robert nodded. "Forbes doesn't live up at the house. He disappears off to who knows where, but as soon as there is any business going on he is back. It's as if he has an informer up at the hall. If old man Wallace threatens to unhinge his inheritance, Forbes rears his ugly head, arriving back here from wherever it is he hides himself."

"There is bad feeling between them?" Gregor absorbed the news. Anything that might be useful was worth storing away. If he could install Jessie there, she could easily find out more.

Robert leaned closer. "Ivor Wallace is bitterer even than the rest of us about the union with England. He supports the fight for independence with zeal."

Wallace's motives had always seemed to be selfish. He'd built his wealth out of other people's misfortunes, using trickery, his aspirations to be the most important landowner in these parts driving him. Therein lay great power, political power.

However, what surprised Gregor most of all was that he might have something in common with his old enemy—support for the rebellion against English rule. He considered Ivor Wallace his complete opposite, a man he would have nothing in common with.

War and politics did forge unlikely bonds, it was true.

"Under English law," Robert continued, "Wallace cannot demand favors of men he kept in his pocket for years. Word is that he has committed funds to the independence movement, and the sale of land is his source. Forbes, on the other hand, fancies himself some sort of spokesman for a new order, the Scotland under union." Robert's expression was one of great disapproval. "Some say he has colluded with the English, aided them, but there is no proof."

"A despicable betrayal of his countrymen, if it is true." It was with a sense of irony that Gregor realized Ivor Wallace was receiving some justice in this world already, for if he was at odds with his own son, his only son, it was what he deserved for his past misdeeds.

Just then a red-haired woman entered the storage room with two mugs of ale.

"Fiona." Robert gestured her over and took the mugs.

The woman stared at Gregor warily, but left them a moment later when her husband made no introductions and the conversation ceased. Gregor wished she had not seen him at all. Women were likely to gossip about callers they did not know. Word got about.

Her appearance seemed to sober Robert, too.

"Tell me this," Gregor said, "does Wallace still collect maidenheads?"

Robert gave him an odd glance, but nodded. "Aye, and Forbes is as bad, by all accounts."

That boded well. If Jessie could manage to present herself as an innocent, she could get close to him. The hard part was, of course, imagining her as an innocent.

"What is it you intend to do?" Robert asked.

"Wait, watch. I know that he has left the house at Strathbahn untouched, and that the livestock he grazes on the land can be moved elsewhere." Gregor paused, because the thought of the old farm left to waste aggrieved him. "If luck is on my side, he will put it up for sale and soon."

"You can do it without him knowing it is you?"

"The notary assures me I can, for a price."

Robert chortled.

Truth be told, Gregor wanted more than that, but it was a start. During his first years at sea he would lie in his hammock and plan all sorts of misdemeanors for Ivor Wallace, from sabotaging crops to stealing his livestock and cattle. For a long time Gregor had wanted to go back and fight him, bare knuckled, to inflict the pain he felt. As a more mature man, however, he knew that would only bring temporary relief and, in view of Wallace's status as a wealthy landowner, a spell in jail for himself. The more intelligent way to go about it was to treat Wallace to a taste of his own medicine.

Buying back the land, as much of it as he possibly could, and then presenting himself to Wallace as the mystery buyer, would begin a satisfying quest for supremacy among the local landowners. Once he felt Wallace was suitably embittered by his reappearance, he would find tenants for the land, and then return to his ship. With a foothold and a notary to watch over his concerns, he could continue to buy land from afar.

"If only your father were here to welcome you home," Robert commented, somewhat cautiously.

Only Robert could have said that to him. They had been close, and Robert Fraser had stood by Gregor, advising him to step away when he'd been angry and hotheaded. It was Robert who had suggested he leave Craigduff for the sake of his sanity. Gregor had turned to this man to cheer the good times and to wonder over the bad. Until the end, when nothing more could be done to save their land, their home and their income, and he had lost his beloved father. Gregor had left without saying goodbye, and it had grieved him over the years.

There was wariness in his old friend's expression, as if he was afraid Gregor might still be the volatile young hothead he'd had to advise eleven years before.

Gregor nodded. He sipped his ale and considered his response carefully. "Our land was stolen from him. I owe it to my father's memory to get it back. Hugh Ramsay labored all his life for that, for our line. He brought me up alone and I knew how hard that was, every day of my life. He told me he made the land good for me and mine. He didn't deserve what happened."

Robert studied Gregor and then nodded in turn.

"It was Wallace's whim to shatter my father's dreams. That was cruel and unforgivable and I will not let it pass. The only thing that kept me alive, at first, was the knowledge that I would be able to come back and avenge him."

Robert looked at him thoughtfully. "It might be possible to buy back the land, but that won't bring your father back, old friend."

Gregor's gaze dropped and his hand tightened on the mug. "It is what he would have wanted."

Robert leaned back on his stool and scratched his head. "You have built a new life, and it sounds like a good one. Are you sure this is the right thing to do?"

The old sense of frustration swelled inside Gregor, and he wished he hadn't come here to the smithy's after all. Robert did not know everything that had gone on. He did not know how Hugh Ramsay had suffered.

Eventually, Gregor nodded. "It has to be done."

chapter Six

Jessie stretched and yawned. It was not often she had a hot meal in the middle of the day, and she had drifted into a short sleep while savoring her full belly. All was quiet in the rooms outside her current quarters. Now was the time to find out a little more about her sponsor. After all, she did not know whether she could trust him to pay her as he had promised. He was a fine-looking man and she wanted to believe his words, but he was quite clearly a blaggard. She had seen it herself when he'd presented himself as a minister to gain entry to her cell. The act had amused her, but it also indicated what he was capable of. He could easily double-cross her if it suited him, and she was cautious.

Kneeling by the door, she peered into the lock. He had taken the key with him, which made it a slightly harder task, but a spell would do it. And so long as she regained her quarters before his return, he would be none the wiser.

Resting back on her heels, she recalled that this was the first enchantment her mother had ever taught them, lest they ever got locked in anywhere. Jessie vaguely recalled having climbed into a cupboard on her hands and knees, with Maisie, her twin sister, following. They'd been hiding from Lennox, their brother, who was older by several years. Unable to find them, he had run off to their mother and reported them missing. Presumably it had set her thinking, and so the lessons in magic had begun for the girls. Lennox already knew a few spells, for he was older and their mother said he was more naturally gifted.

All the good memories that Jessie had of her mother were associated with magic. She had drummed into them what she called the important enchantments—the ones they would need to protect themselves. Jessie knew how to gain her freedom, how to cause trouble or avert it, and how to harness a person's attention to an object. The latter was useful when selling wares. Their mother had also taught Maisie and Jessie how to protect themselves from ill health and from becoming pregnant. She'd drummed those things into their young hearts and minds so ferociously that they instinctively knew she regretted giving her affections so easily to their father, a man who had abandoned her when he found out about her craft.

There was so much more to learn and explore than what she knew; Jessie was aware of that. Yet the knowledge had only brought tragedy to her mother, and Jessie, too, found herself in danger because of the gift she had inherited. When tempted to try to expand her skill, she shied away.

In the Highlands she would be safe to explore it, and would perhaps meet more of her kind. Above all, her aim was to be reunited with Maisie and Lennox, from whom she had been wrenched the very day their mother was put to death. Meanwhile, Jessie knew enough to protect herself when needs must.

With a longing sigh, she concentrated her thoughts on the lock and summoned her freedom in the ancient tongue. *"Thoir dhomh mo shaorsa."*

The lock clicked and the door swung open.

She rose to her feet and sidled into the quarters beyond. No one was about. She looked at the door on the landing, which the alewife and the servants had used earlier that day. It was all that stood between her and freedom. She could escape now and be on her way. But she didn't want to.

The mysterious Mister Ramsay had captured her attention that morning. It infuriated her that she was being held, but she could not resist the challenge of breaking his focus while he attempted to teach her about seduction. Curiosity about his enemy and the dispute between them also riddled her. As she glanced about, she spied his bed through the doorway beyond and she approached it. The bolster was bruised by his head and the bedcovers hung down where he had discarded them. She pictured him there, at rest. No, she was not ready to leave just yet.

Glancing around the bedchamber, she noted that this room was much more comfortable than the one she had awoken in. There were heavy damask curtains at the window and around the bed. In the servant's quarters, the curtains were thin and aged, and the cot had only a thin blanket.

The trunk by his bed was locked. He obviously kept the key on his person. She knelt beside it and worked her magic. Lifting the lid, she quickly rifled through the clothing. Beneath it she found several rolls of papers tied with ribbons. Casting them aside, she moved on to what appeared to be more interesting contents beneath—heavier goods wrapped in worn fabric. There were two parcels, and she lifted one out. It contained coins, a hefty sum. She was tempted to purloin a few. After several long moments of temptation, she decided it would not be worth the risk in case he had counted them. *I know where they are, should he try to double-cross me.*

Pleased by that, she rearranged the parcel and lifted up the second. It, too, was heavy, although not as weighty as the coins. When she unwrapped it she found it full of what at first appeared to be bits of broken glass or stones. Of different colors, they would make pretty gems were they not quite so rough. She frowned. Perhaps that's what they were—unpolished gems? Jessie had never seen such a thing and she held one up to the light, looking at it with curiosity. If he had traveled to foreign places, he might have brought these stones back. It made her want to ask him about the places he had been. And the women he had encountered.

There was a small velvet purse as well, and inside it she discovered several small white stones. These she had seen before, and knew they were of great value. "Pearls," she whispered.

Restoring the contents to their former arrangement, she closed the lid and locked it. Reassured of her sponsor's wealth, she decided she could rest easy about what he owed her. If he didn't pay her, she knew where to find recompense.

She sat down on the bed, then rolled across it.

It was so much more comfortable than the narrow cot she had rested on the night before and that afternoon. This was a good horsehair mattress and there were pillows and a sturdy bolster for comfort. Her cot was a piece of sacking nailed to a wooden frame, and she would much prefer this bed. Reaching out for the blankets, she found them soft and well made. Wriggling into the place where he had dented the mattress the night before, she breathed in his manly scent and sighed.

What would he think if he walked in now and discovered her in his bed? *He might punish me again.*

She chuckled to herself. She had never been treated that way before—well, not as a grown woman. The fact that it had happened with a lover, while they were in the midst of a lusty display of her talents, astonished her. His hand on her behind had not only distracted her from playing the part, it had heightened her need for relief. Even thinking about it now made her body ripple against the mattress. She pulled her knees up, feet flat to the bed, and let her skirts gather at her waist. With both hands, she stroked the inside of her thighs, imagining that he was standing there looking at her. He would shake his head at her, and tell her she was doing it wrong.

"Oh, my," Jessie whispered, astonished at how quickly the notion of his chastisement made her lust flare. It was not something she'd ever imagined would happen to her, but when he took her in hand, she was fit for nowt that involved thinking.

As for him, he'd looked like a man possessed. His body was rigid with strength, with restraint. He'd handled her without mercy, allowing her to feel his mood and forcing her to rise to his challenge. As she thought back over it, the need to touch herself went from a suggestion to a demand. Her hands moved down to the creases at the top of her thighs, and with her thumbs she opened up her folds, allowing the cool air to reach her inflamed bud.

Rocking her hips, she imagined him at the end of the bed. Those brooding eyes of his grew darker when he was in a state of arousal, and she knew that he had enjoyed punishing her. Why, he'd moved his hand to her furrow to push her further into ecstasy. That was no punishment, and they both knew it.

If only he had instructed her to sit upon his lap that morning and finish them both. His erection was polelike, and she'd have enjoyed nothing more than following that instruction. The thought made her cunny clench. Deep inside, at the pit of her belly, the ache of longing swelled.

Her bud was swollen, and she swiped her fingers through the juices that were gathering between her folds, and circled it, remembering as she did the way he had licked his fingers

clean after they had been inside her. There was no doubt
he had enjoyed that. Pumping her fingers faster, she bit her
lower lip.

When she reached her pinnacle, it was with the image of
Mister Ramsay striding over to her side, opening his breeches
as he did so. Her breath caught, her cunny tightening until
release flooded her.

As she floated back to earth, a soft chuckle escaped her.
Oh, yes, if that morning had been anything to judge by, she
would be sleeping in this bed soon enough.

After Gregor returned to his lodgings and stabled his
mount, he paused beneath the window that he had previously identified as Jessie's room. He half expected to find it
hanging open, his new cohort having broken free and made
her escape. It looked to be intact, and he made his way inside.

The quarters were exactly as they had been before, and yet
he could not shake the strange feeling that she had not remained where he had deposited her. When he retrieved the
key and unlocked the door to the servant's room, however,
he found her sitting on her cot, untangling her hair with her
fingers. It was then he realized he should have purchased her
a comb. She had no such feminine fripperies, and it might
have kept her amused.

She gave him an admonishing look. That was inevitable.
Her initial angry response had mellowed somewhat over the
afternoon, but he could tell he was about to hear her thoughts
on the matter. He waited expectantly.

"'Tis not right," she snapped, rising to her feet and folding
her arms across the chest as if readying for a fight, "to lock
a person up this way."

Gregor gave a weary sigh. "I may not know you well, Jessie
Taskill, but I have already learned that you are easily bored.

The chance to run amok around the Drover's Inn would be too much of a temptation for you. It is for your own protection that I kept you in here. You need to learn to hide from view until people have forgotten that there is a condemned woman who may be about these parts."

She narrowed her eyes at him. "You rescued me from one cell, to keep me in another."

Apparently, she had not listened to a word he'd said.

Gregor turned away, taking off his coat as he went. A tirade of angry abuse followed him. Gregor bore it all stoically, while considering that it might have been easier to let her run free, and then hunt her down upon his return.

When supper arrived they ate in silence, occasionally glaring at each other across the table.

Eventually, she lifted her shoulders in a shrug, as if admitting defeat. "What plans have you for me this evening?"

Gregor wanted to laugh aloud. She was bored. It was no wonder she got herself into so much trouble. He surveyed her at length. He knew what he wanted to do with her. After this morning's escapade he wanted nothing more than to work off the day's frustrations in a solid bout of bed play. That was not what she was here for, however. It was proving difficult enough to control her, without giving her the free rein that would come from closer companionship.

She stared at him expectantly. "I am most willing to do anything you desire," she added, with a suggestive glance.

Willing? When it suited her. He was reminded of how willingly she'd accepted his hand on her arse that morning—how she had pumped and writhed against it, until her lust reached fruition. He glanced over at the full curve of her bosom and the earnest, erotic look in her eyes. His cock hardened.

It was becoming a matter of dire necessity that he dismiss her, or distance would not be possible to maintain. Besides, the day's events had left him with much to consider. The meeting with Robert had proved fruitful, and Gregor had to make plans for the morrow.

"I am weary after the business I had to take care of this afternoon. I suggest we both go to our beds and sleep." It was far from the truth, but if she continued to sit there looking so lush and provocative, he would be forced to carry her to the bed and seek relief between those delicious thighs of hers.

That was not what she wanted to hear. She pouted at him, and her gaze flitted about as if she was seeking more mischief to get herself into.

"We will continue your tutoring first thing in the morning," he added, in an attempt to shoo her off.

Her expression brightened. "So," she said knowingly, "you wish to observe me attempting to seduce an imaginary man again?"

Lord, the woman was more of a burden than a blessing. The blatant teasing in her eyes made his jaw clench. She wanted to flaunt herself, which was all well and good and helpful to the cause, but he was in danger of being driven to madness by her lascivious behavior. Abstinence was not the easiest task in the world when Miss Jessie Taskill revealed her skills. The inviting look she gave him would melt the strongest man's resolve.

Gregor frowned, determined not to let her influence him. "No. Your table manners need some refinement. We will address that next."

She stared at him, apparently wildly affronted by his comments. "Table manners?"

Gregor suppressed his amusement. She had a lot of pride for a woman who sold her body to survive. He was willing to wager that had caused her a problem or two. He found himself unable to resist teasing her. "Do you know how to say grace?"

Her eyes rounded.

"The Lord's prayer?"

She threw up her hands. "I know full well what you meant. And yes, I do know how to say grace. I just do not understand why I would need to impress *this enemy of yours* with such things."

"It is not only for him that you need to behave properly. If we manage to establish you within his household—"

"We will," she interrupted, clearly annoyed.

"When it is done," he continued, "you will need to convince the other servants that you are nothing but a hardworking, pious young lady who is in need of a position, a young woman who will not be troublesome in any way."

She flashed him a warning glance when he emphasized the word *troublesome*.

"I am capable of all these things," she responded defensively. "I have not always been a whore. I can do plenty of other work, and you do not have to worry about my manners." With that she stood up and flounced off to her quarters, slamming the door behind her.

Gregor stared after her, and for the first time he found himself wondering what else it was that she had done. He knew very little of her previous life. Was she Dundee-born? What of her family?

As soon as she was gone, Gregor missed her presence. Frowning, he wondered how that could be so, when all they had done was bicker. He stood up and reached for the port bottle. It was just because he was not used to having a whore on hand whenever he might want one. He bedded women at every chance, yes, but that was limited to when they reached safe harbor. That event began a wild time of whoring and drinking. Then it was back to managing the sea.

Now he had a provocative and tempting woman close by. Any man would be tempted. The nature of the situation made it difficult for him, that was all. As he tried to explain away the mixed feelings he had on the matter, he recalled how she had looked that morning, facedown over his lap, and he instantly hardened. He swigged straight from the port bottle.

It was just as well that she had gone, he decided. She had a quick tongue and was far too wily, which meant he would have been driven to taking her in hand and delivering another good slap to that fine arse of hers. And if he did, his vow to abstain would be shattered within moments.

He downed enough port to knock himself out, and took to his bed. Her scent seemed to be everywhere, though. How could that be? He tossed and turned. Images of her there on the bed, debauched and willing, filled his mind and his dreams. Dawn eventually arrived, and even though he'd had a troubled night, he was proud of himself for resisting.

However, once sunlight filled the quarters, Jessie strolled out of her room, and she was as naked as the day she was born. Gregor cursed beneath his breath, certain that his vow to abstain would soon be shattered. Her eyelids were lowered, giving her a sultry look, her pretty mouth curving as she approached.

Accepting his fate, he made a new vow—to make her earn it.

"Too knowing by far, Jessie," he said, and reached out and grabbed her.

chapter Seven

Jessie let out a startled cry, thoroughly delighted that he had captured her.

"You have just made this even more difficult on yourself," he said, as he pulled her down onto his bed.

She had woken most eager to climb into his bed with him, and decided she would approach the problem in a much more direct manner—naked. The plan was to startle him with her appearance and then slide under the covers with him before he had a chance to gather his faculties. He would be aroused in moments. How could she fail? It had taken some effort to be brave and determined enough to approach him while in such a state. It was rare that she was ever fully undressed, but she mustered the requisite boldness, sure that he wouldn't be able to resist when she climbed in with him as he awoke.

He'd pounced at her before she had the chance.

Whatever did he mean, she had just made it harder on herself? It didn't seem that way to her. Her body thrilled at the way he had reached for her. He rolled her onto her back, keeping her there with one hand. Pinned down that way, her body was arched over the hard rack of his thighs. Then she noticed that there was humor in his eyes. Was it a jest at her expense?

The way she was fixed was not what she had in mind. Her

breasts jutted out and her intimate parts were on display. She couldn't change her position or wriggle free.

With one hand on her collarbone, holding her in place, he roved over her body with the other hand, handling her roughly, squeezing and testing her flesh in all her sensitive places. Even though she grew wary because of his comment, his actions practically made her melt, her nipples hardening and her cunny fast growing damp.

"You are so masterful," she murmured, unable to hold back her response.

"In that case you should have no trouble obeying me." Sarcasm rang in his voice.

He continued to stroke and knead her breasts until she was gasping with pleasure, and then he stopped.

Jessie's breathing faltered.

"Get up."

When she didn't move, he rolled her over onto her front, pushing her the length of the bed. With her feet scrambling for the floor, she put her hands on the mattress and pushed up, barely managing to straighten up before he was out of the bed and beside her.

"As you are so keen for your instruction this morning, we will have our lesson before I call for breakfast."

Jessie stared at him, confused. "Whatever do you mean?"

He lifted his eyebrows. "You did not pause to dress, my dear. I can only surmise that you are very keen to be moving forward with your tutoring. Most admirable."

"I—"

He put one finger to her lips, silencing her. There was a wicked gleam in his eyes.

It made her gulp. She swiped his hand away. "But—"

"No." He held her by the shoulders.

Then she felt the brush of his upright cock against her

belly and her body thrilled. He did want her. Emboldened, she reached down and trailed her fingers along its length as she flashed her eyes at him. "The task you have in mind is not the one you mentioned last night?"

"It is."

Her hand stilled.

He removed it from his person. "We will begin work now." The look in his eyes forbade her to disobey. "Then we can address the problems that arise." He glanced down at her breasts, where her nipples were hard and poking out rudely.

The heat from that single glance made her dizzy. Even so, she was torn between the urge to disobey and the urge to submit. Her physical response was very different. Heat traversed her body. She felt weak, as if her desire was sapping her strength. If she submitted, would he find her agreeable and satisfy the lust he so obviously felt, as well? She could only hope so. Clinging to that notion, she nodded, and forced out an agreeable response. "Yes, sire. I will get dressed immediately."

She went to turn away.

He stopped her with one hand locked around her wrist, tethering her to the spot. "No. We begin now."

Confusion swamped her. He couldn't mean it.

She glanced down at his groin, where his cock was long and hard and arched up as far as his belly. "But…we are both naked!"

"Once again, a situation you have suggested by your arrival in that state." He smiled most amiably and then led her to the table.

Smarting wildly, Jessie recalled what he'd said the night before about her table manners.

He gestured at her to sit in the chair. "If you can portray humility and innocence in a state of undress, you will have taken a step forward. It will be a fine test of your acting abilities."

"Surely you jest." Horrified at the situation, she nodded at his polelike erection. "I cannot act the innocent, not when presented with such a thing."

Again she glared at his cock.

In all her days she'd never known a man so single-minded that he would deny himself the urge to come when it presented itself. Apparently he wanted to tutor her on how to behave, even though he was as hard as a rock and ready for a tumble. The man clearly wanted to torture her.

Standing opposite her, he rested his hands flat on the table and looked into her eyes. There was a wicked smile on his face. "I am entirely serious, believe me."

"And you accused me of having no shame."

He opened his palms as if innocent of her meaning.

He was mocking her. Jessie grumbled loudly and wriggled on the chair. She was far too aroused to act the part rationally, and her gaze kept roving back to observe his state of readiness for fornication. Besides, she had not seen him entirely naked before, and now he was strolling about exhibiting himself with the utmost detachment. It was unbearable. From his broad shoulders and chest, the latter dusted with dark hair, her gaze traveled down to where his cock sprung out, like a tree from the earth, tufts of dark hair adorning its base. Beneath that, his heavy sac made him look most virile. The shaft was long and rigid and arched up lewdly, the foreskin drawn back, revealing the darkly swollen head. Her cunny clamored for it.

"Eyes up," he instructed sternly.

The tone of his voice was so commanding that she shivered with arousal. She rocked her bottom on the chair as she straightened up and met his gaze, and the hard surface maddened her aroused flesh. "You are insane!"

"Sit up straight while you are at the table."

She did so, but flashed him another angry look.

He examined her with mock disappointment, his own acting ability apparently made more dramatic by the situation. "It seems I have to remind why you are here. As you so rightly pointed out, a man of wealth and opportunity would prefer an innocent maiden. You assured me that you would be able to seduce him under those circumstances."

"Not like this." She glared at Gregor, clutching at the table edge to keep herself from storming off. She didn't want to do as he instructed, but she did not want to leave, not now. Having him looming over her, so darkly handsome while he issued instructions, meant all her thoughts were moving in an entirely different direction. He was an arm's reach away, but he was denying them both. The fact that she was naked did not help her at all. She felt as if she had walked into a trap.

Jessie turned away and closed her eyes, shaking her head in disbelief.

"Do it and you will be rewarded."

The promise made her blood pump ever faster. She squeezed her thighs together and stared down at the tabletop in an attempt to keep herself from breaking his hold on her. It was the hardest thing she had ever done with her body in such a state of arousal, and with him so close at hand and ready to give her exactly what she wanted. But she attempted to force her thoughts together and be what he wanted her to be.

Lifting her head slightly, and at the angle he had suggested the day before, she looked at him from under her eyelashes, and then widened her eyes as if startled. Forcing her lower lip to tremble, she shifted one hand to her throat. "Forgive me, sire, you have caught me while I am at breakfast. I will prepare for my day's chores immediately."

She expected him to lecture her about manners, but he did not. Silence filled the air between them and along with it the tension mounted.

Cautiously, she lifted her head fully and looked at him, keeping her expression most humble and serious and well-meaning. "How best can I serve you today, sire?"

His mouth moved, his lips pressed together as if he was trying to restrain from comment, but his eyes told a different story. Black with lust, they scored her greedily. Her skin flashed hot and her breathing sped. It was he who was doing battle with his needs now.

Be careful, she reminded herself. He could easily send her to her room, if she did not continue to make an effort.

"You have caught my attention," he said, his tone more subdued but also more intimate. "You are a good worker and I wish to keep you here in the household."

"Thank you, sire. I am most eager to please you and gain a permanent position here." She blinked at him, being careful to show nothing but innocence.

"But you turn my head, Jessie."

The statement startled her. For a moment she stared into his eyes, and she knew he wasn't acting. That made her belly flutter, and she battled to contain her reaction. Blinking hard, she cocked her head slightly. "Me, sire?"

"Yes." He stepped closer and touched her hair. "It is your character. Your strange mix of innocence and candor."

Jessie's heart thumped wildly in her chest. It was what his enemy might say, but she knew he was doing this as part of the test. And, as an innocent, she would not notice his erection. Or if she did, she would blush and look away. Steadfastly, she looked only at his face.

She noticed how his expression reflected his mood. Restraint echoed in every part of him. Large and powerful, his naked shoulders overshadowed her. The column of his neck was taut, the muscle standing out. His eyes gleamed darkly.

"Stand up," he instructed.

Jessie did so, her legs trembling under her. She was so weak with arousal that she swayed unsteadily. She kept her eyelids lowered, attempting to hide the emotional state she was in.

He shoved her chair out of the way and stepped behind her. With one hand on her shoulder, he squeezed it. "You are a special girl, Jessie. Do you want to please your new master?"

That question affected her so powerfully that she had to close her eyes. Her lips parted and her head dropped back. Urging herself to respond, she mustered the appropriate words. "Forgive me, but I am not sure of your meaning, sire."

"You have made me want a kiss from your pretty lips." He touched her hair, stroking its length.

"Sire." The one word came out breathlessly.

"You have never had a fellow want to kiss you before?"

"Aye, but I did not let him."

"Then let me show you the path to pleasure, sweet Jessie."

She bit her lower lip, longing to turn around and face him, yet knowing it would be harder if she did.

He moved closer still, and she felt the bough of his erection at the small of her back. For a moment, she wondered if it was another test. But she knew he wanted the reward as much as she did, that he had been holding back ever since she had approached his bed.

Struggling to find the right words, she summoned a response. "I am frightened, sire, but I only wish to please my master."

Silence followed, the tension in the room growing. He was so close that she could feel his breath on her skin.

Eventually, he responded. "Better. Better today, Jessie."

He kissed her shoulder, and the brush of his mouth on her flesh made her want him even more. Then she felt his hand on her waist.

"Bend over the table," he said, his voice low and yet undeniably commanding.

Those words thrilled her, but she took her time, indicating that she was unsure about him, with a shiver and a distraught glance over her shoulder. The look in his eyes convinced her he was no longer tutoring her.

This was all about their mutual need.

Immense relief flooded her. She did as he instructed, resting her forearms and her hands on the surface of the table. Her cunny pounded with anticipation and she licked her lips, her mouth turning dry.

Gregor rested his hand between her shoulder blades and eased her completely flat to the table, controlling her still.

"Oh!" Her tender breasts were crushed to its surface, the nipples stinging wildly at the contact.

Then his hands were on her buttocks, stroking them. For a moment she thought he was going to slap her arse, as he had done the day before. She pressed her cheek flat to the table. *I shall faint if he does.*

What she wanted was what she didn't get the day before, and this time there was no hiding that he was ready to give it to her. She wriggled in response to that thought, her hips swaying within his grip.

She heard him mutter beneath his breath. But he moved his hands lower, stroking them down the backs of her thighs. Trembling under his touch, she squeezed her eyes tightly shut as he easily clasped her slim calves in his large hands. He lifted one foot from the floor and rested his hand along its length. The strange exploration made her aware that her intimate parts were on display because of the position he had put her in. Her cunny tightened as if to hide her naked state, and when it did, a trickle of moisture slid down her inner thigh. Jessie's head lifted and she cried out when he licked it from her skin.

Then his thumbs splayed her open, and she felt cold air against her damp, sensitive core.

"Do you think you have earned this?" he whispered.

So that was his game—dashing her back and forth to measure her ability to respond appropriately, whatever the circumstances. Jessie could scarcely believe it, but she gathered her every remaining resource to carry it off.

"I believe I have done all my chores for the day, sire," she whispered with a distinct tremble in her voice, as if she were fearful about what would occur next.

"It appears that you have. In that case, you will be rewarded."

She could hardly breathe, for the blunt head of his cock was at her opening and pushing inside. Once he had entered her, his hands moved around her hips. Easily, he lifted her upper thighs, shifting her hips to gain better access. In doing so, he lifted her feet from the floor.

The first slow thrust opened her, and he paused before pressing deeper, slowly filling her, measure by measure. In that position she was powerless to move, powerless to do anything but receive him. His member was so large and rigid that it pressed firmly against her aching center, and set loose a wave of pleasure the likes of which she had not experienced before. Her breasts burned, and she scratched at the rough table with her fingernails.

When she gave an ecstatic cry, he pulled back and then thrust deep.

"You are a temptress, all right, Jessie Taskill," he told her.

"Now hold tight, for this must be done." He lifted her hips higher still, and began driving into her mercilessly, the pent-up desire between them manifest in every push and shove, and every thrust was welcomed as her body clutched at his length.

She was already close to coming because he had made her wait, and then she felt his heavy ballocks slap her tender folds, and her breath was caught in a long, low moan. The prolonged arousal followed by the exquisite sensation of his turgid cock filling her cunny made reaching her climax so much sweeter.

"Oh, yes," he murmured when she hit her peak, "I feel you, Jessie." He pressed her down at the small of her back and worked his cock hard, pushing them both over the edge.

He pulled free as his seed spilled, but worked her with his hand even after he was spent, exploring her hot, tender folds while she wilted over the table. It made her pleasure linger and blossom again, and she burned and throbbed from her cunny to her chest as a second wave of release washed over her. When he finally let her be, Jessie was glad the table was holding her up.

chapter Eight

"Is it truly necessary for you to lock me up when you go away in the afternoons?" Jessie put her hands on her hips and eyed him ruefully, standing at the doorway to the small servant's room most unwillingly. She hated to be kept locked up and the thought of another afternoon spent that way made her good spirits plummet.

They had passed an agreeable morning together after their early encounter over the table. Jessie had secretly enjoyed discussing good manners with him, and he'd also spent some time describing the size and nature of his enemy's household. She'd listened attentively and carefully committed each detail to memory. Then he'd readied himself to leave and had ushered her to her quarters. That felt like a betrayal after what had gone before.

"You know the answer to that question," he responded, and frowned. "I have invested time in you and I do not want my investment to run away on some wild notion of returning to Dundee to hunt for a long-gone purse."

The suggestion that her purse was gone frustrated her further, and Jessie folded her arms across her chest, glaring at him from beneath her lashes.

"You are safe here, which should be appealing to you," he

stated angrily, lifting his hands in frustration, "and I want to keep it that way. Or would you prefer to be carted back to your cell and tried as a witch? No? I thought not."

For her own safety. She'd heard that before and it brought back bad memories. Thwarted in every way, she pouted.

Gesturing into the room, he added, "Stay hidden and forget you were ever in Dundee."

Grudgingly, she walked into the servant's room and stood with her arms still folded across the chest, waiting for him to slam the door on her and lock it.

"Smile, my pretty. I will bring you a new garment or two on my return." He gestured at her borrowed dress.

Much to her annoyance, that promise captured her attention, and there was something in his voice that suggested he felt guilty for locking her up. And so he should. She mustered a half smile, although it was hard.

"That's better. Now rest. I will return soon."

Taken by the urge to ask something that had been on her mind, she called out to him as he went to close the door and lock it. "Mister Ramsay?"

He paused, but kept his hand on the doorknob. "Yes?"

"What is your given name?"

He considered her at length, and then sighed. "You take liberties with me that I should not allow."

She clasped her hands together. "I know I do, but I cannot help being curious."

The way he looked at her reflected his doubt on the matter. He wanted to keep her in her place, and he wanted his privacy. Why, he hadn't even once used the name of his enemy while describing his house and land. Would he refuse to tell her his own name?

"Gregor."

It felt like a victory, but she was cautious. She nodded. "Thank you."

Gregor. She repeated it silently while she watched the door shut. The name fitted him well.

The key turned in the lock. She frowned heavily.

His footsteps faded away. Still she stared at the door.

"Gregor Ramsay," she said to the closed door, the very look of it making her anger swell. "Why do you still have to lock me up, Gregor Ramsay?" She'd been well-behaved, she'd shown willingness to learn and they'd shared much pleasure that morning. There was more trust between them, but it did not extend to leaving her alone without a lock and key.

Impatiently, she paced the floor. She would have to escape the room by magic again, but she couldn't risk going out there if he had not left the inn. Being confined this way was something she detested. It went back to her childhood. When she and her siblings were orphaned, she'd found herself imprisoned every night by those who had taken her in.

She wondered if her brother and sister had fared any better than her, as they grew up. They were all three torn apart and kept that way, after their mother's burning. It was for the good of their souls, Jessie was told. The hard knot of grief she nursed ached every time she thought of her kin. She did not even know where they had been sent, but images of Maisie kicking and screaming as she was lifted into a carriage with the curtains pulled closed haunted Jessie. Who had taken her? Someone wealthy enough to have his own crest on the door of the carriage, that's all she knew.

Deep in her heart she felt that Maisie and Lennox would be drawn back to the Highlands, as she was, to the place they were born. If it took her last breath she would find them. She sat down on the cot and let her thoughts continue to wander back in time.

No fancy carriage had come for her. Jessie had stayed in the village where their mother had been stoned and burned. Every time she was forced to walk past the place where it had happened she'd had to fight back tears. The grief was overwhelming, but soon enough she learned to hide it, for it angered her keepers.

A local teacher had taken her in. Mister Niven was his name. It was a charitable act undertaken as a result of pressure from the local minister, rather than willing kindheartedness. But the teacher's wife had been afraid of the witch's offspring. She never left Jessie alone with her children. Mister Niven's wife would not even let her take lessons with them and used her as a servant instead. At night she locked Jessie in the outhouse, telling her it was for her own safety—much as Mister Ramsay did.

For a long time Jessie had been too afraid to use her magic to escape, after what she'd seen them do to her mother. Then the confinement angered her. That brewed for a long while. Ultimately, it was as much boredom as rebellion that had forced her to react.

She would escape by magic and roam about at night, and it was then that she began to learn things. Stealthily, she eavesdropped on the teacher and his wife, and learned just how afraid the wife was of her.

"I heard what they do. Those that practice the evil ways of witchcraft congregate in the woods when the moon is high to plot against us good Christian folk," the woman had said one night, as Jessie listened. The teacher's wife then begged her husband to be rid of the witch's child that had been thrust upon them. "Demon's spawn they are. How can you let one of them get close to our own?" Mister Niven had wearily agreed, but said he could not anger the minister lest he lose his work at the schoolhouse.

Jessie had listened, learning all the while. There were others like her somewhere, and they met in the woods at night! Her heart had filled with hope, hope that still forced her footsteps onward years later, and had done so even during the times when her life in the gutter was so dark there seemed nothing to live for. Oftentimes she'd been ready to lie down and wish herself to sleep forever. Stubbornness had taken root in her, though, and she nurtured it. She had vowed to find them, her kin.

"They're at it like wild animals, fornicating under the moon." That was another thing she had overheard.

It took Jessie a while to learn what "fornicating" meant, but once she had, she instinctively knew it was not wrong to feel desire and to act upon it. That's what people like her did, and they felt no shame. Shame was something that was taught by those who despised nature and did not want to be connected with it.

"Evil they are." The teacher's wife had told her that much to her face, spitting the words at her as if in doing so she would be protected from the evil.

Even as a child, Jessie had denied it. Her mother had taught her different.

We are not evil, we are nature's children. It is they who subscribe to the devil, not us, though they will accuse us of it. They do not understand our ways, that is all.

That was true. Every day of her life had only proved that to her, yet still Jessie longed to find her true path—and still she found herself locked up against her will!

Darting over to the door, she put her ear to it. All was quiet in Gregor's room. Dropping to her knees, she whispered into the lock.

She blew into the cavity and pictured a key as she whispered the ancient enchantment. A moment later light shifted around the lock and then moved inside it in a thrusting, rolling manner, as if her spell had taken form and become bright and visible.

Startled, she drew back, observing. It wasn't anything she had seen before. When the lock opened, it was with a musical chime, and the door swept toward her as if ushering her out.

Astonished, Jessie put her fingers to her mouth.

My magic, it flourishes. Why?

She had felt it burgeoning these past months, and the urge to perform enchantments had come over her more frequently. It was harder to resist courting danger by exploring her craft. It was if she was coming of age. That's how she had explained it away. Much like the time when her body had reached full womanhood and she'd craved the touch of a man to satisfy her. Yet she could not explore her magic, because of the danger.

Magic was and always would be her secret gem, an invisible jewel that she couldn't exchange for comfort, but made her feel blessed. It frustrated her, too, because she could not use it for fear that others would call her out in spite, fear and even jealousy. It was her gift and her curse. She had long since accepted that.

There was something different about this spell, though. It glowed brightly, as if alive—as if her magic was more powerful than it had been the day before. How odd. Jessie shrugged and stepped across the threshold into Gregor Ramsay's rooms, glancing about eagerly for something to occupy herself with.

First she returned to the trunk that stood by his bedside. Once again it was locked. Once again she opened it. Nothing had changed since the day before. Returning it to its former state of security, she sat on the bed. Plucking at her bodice, she gazed around the room. There was so little to distract her. Well, there was so little to distract her when he was not here. She smiled as she thought on that. Mister Gregor Ramsay himself was very much a distraction.

She flung herself back on his bed. Smiling, she moved her hand to feel the dips his body had made, then rolled next to that spot. She closed her eyes and breathed in his scent from the bolster. Savoring it, she remembered the pleasurable tumble they had shared that morning and how pleasant it had been to share breakfast with him afterward.

It was an unfamiliar feeling, but for some reason she missed his presence when he went out. It wasn't just being locked up that irked her today, it was the simple fact that he had once again gone and left her. She'd quickly grown used to the sound of his sardonic laughter and his teasing words, and his brooding glances never failed to draw her attention and stoke her fires. There were brooding glances aplenty when he was around.

The quarters seemed so empty without his presence filling them. Not so long ago she would have been glad of the comfortable, warm rooms to lounge in while food and drink was brought to her. There was promise of a wage at the end of it all, as well. She should be content to wait. It was better than being on the streets seeking a customer.

Yet she could not stop herself wanting to leave the room, and wondering why he could not take her with him when he went out. She was being hunted down in all likelihood, but she could easily have disguised herself. He had proved himself a master in that area, and she might even be useful to him in whatever tasks he was undertaking.

There had to be a reason why he left her here, where he feared she would run away, instead of keeping her safely by his side at all times.

Her eyes snapped open.

Was it another woman he had gone to visit, someone he

would not ask to undertake the sordid task of seducing an enemy? A sweetheart, perhaps, a noblewoman he courted with aspirations to marry?

The thought of it made Jessie's frustration swell and fester. That in turn let loose a powerful need for rebellion.

Sitting up, she stared through the bedchamber and into the room where the door to the landing was located. She sprang from the bed. By the time she was halfway to that door she had already mustered the enchantment that would open that lock, too.

Gregor paced up and down impatiently in the hallway of the most prominent auction house in Saint Andrews. His notary had given him the name of the auctioneer who dealt with most of the major land transfers in Fife, from Saint Andrews as far south as Kircaldy.

The scribe whose desk was located in the hallway where he waited lifted his quill from the papers he was working on and frowned at Gregor. It was the third time he had done so. Gregor forced himself to take a seat.

Although he had left his quarters at the Drover's Inn in a calmer state than he had the day before, he had gradually become agitated. The cause was, of course, the same: Jessie. He should be thinking about his business matters, but no. Once he had engaged in intimate congress with her it only seemed to make his lust increase. What was it about this woman that made it so difficult to stop thinking about her?

Then she'd made him feel guilty for doing what any man of sound mind would do—lock her up for her own safety. The worst of it was that the downturn of her pretty mouth and those sad eyes pleading with him affected him more than they should, unaccountably so. Her crestfallen expression haunted him for the entire journey to Saint Andrews.

He cared too much for her comfort. And he shouldn't have told her his given name. She was a common whore whom he had hired to undertake a task.

Strangely, though, Jessie did not seem to fit that description, at least not to his mind. Never had he met a more uncommon woman. There was something unusual and oddly appealing about her. She had the cheek of the devil, but even when that was the case he couldn't stop himself from admiring her spirit. She was like no other woman he had encountered.

Even as he rode into Saint Andrews and passed down the busy high street he thought of her and her lusty ways. He knew with certainty that she would do well at the task he had set her, so long as she could keep herself in check. When she was in a temper she was harder to control than an entire crew of men who were overdue their issue of rum. It was that cheeky tongue that he had to teach her to harness. He had to offer her more tangible rewards, perhaps.

That thought drove him to visit a seamstress before he even arrived at the auction house. He asked around in the marketplace and was referred to a suitable-looking establishment in a side street of the ancient burgh. Once he had stabled his mount, he located and entered the seamstress's workshop— a narrow cottage with a sign in the window. When he went inside he only meant to procure some items for Jessie to use, things that might keep her occupied.

Once he was in there, however, and he imagined what Jessie would think of such finery, he purchased more than he had planned to. He caught sight of a woolen shawl the very same color as her eyes, and gestured at it. The seamstress lifted the item from the display and took it to a table where she began to fold and wrap it.

"Have you clothing suitable for a serving woman?"

The seamstress paused and then held up the item she had been working on when he arrived. "Aye, here are some samples of our work."

Gregor looked that dress over and another she brought out, and thought them suitable for Jessie to appear in as a decent person in search of employment. When he put his hand around the waist they looked to be about the right size. "I'll take them both."

"These are being made for another customer, but if you would like to order something similar—"

"I need them soon. I will pay highly if you complete those two items for me instead."

The seamstress seemed astonished by his behavior, and at first would agree to none of it, until she saw the amount of coins he offered to secure the items. When he said he would take what was ready and return the following day for the dresses, the woman's eyes nearly popped out of her head. But she spoke with a girl who sat in one corner sewing, and after some whispered debate and several glances at the money, she promised the work would be done.

As he was about to leave, he spied a gown somewhat more extravagant than he was planning to buy, in the hands of the helper. It was a blue silk affair, the sort of thing a lady might wear. He imagined Jessie swanning about his quarters in it, smiled to himself and told the seamstress to add it—and any necessary undergarments.

"This will run to a tidy sum," the seamstress warned.

"That is not an issue. I will return for the goods at the same time tomorrow."

Now that he was waiting to discuss business with the auctioneer, it disturbed him that his mind kept wandering to images of Jessie in the garments he had seen, rather than preparing his thoughts to discuss important matters of business.

Brooding on it, he knew he'd done the wrong thing indulging his lust for her. Too long without a woman of his own, perhaps. The whore was for his enemy, not himself. There hadn't been any denying it that morning, however.

Eventually he was ushered in, which was just as well, for he was growing increasingly angry with himself, and that made him uneasy. It was with relief he turned to matters of business.

The auctioneer was a heavyset man with calculating eyes and an expensive powdered wig that seemed rather too ostentatious for his offices. At a bureau nearby, a thinner man hunched over a stack of papers, his quill barely rising from the page to gather more ink as he worked.

Gregor introduced himself and took the seat he was offered. The auctioneer rambled through a lengthy and irrelevant monologue about the state of affairs under King George's rule, and as soon as Gregor could interrupt, he hastened the discussion in the direction he wanted it to go.

"I am most eager to buy land in Fife, somewhere with sound agricultural prospects. Somewhere I can attract good tenants to work the land while I am abroad."

The auctioneer nodded, his fingers tapping at the button on his velvet coat. That he mistrusted Gregor's intentions was more than obvious. "You have come to the right place," he responded.

Gregor could not afford to be viewed skeptically.

"Notary Anderson recommended you. Please, speak to him about me. He will assure you I am financially solvent and in favorable account with my banker."

Both men were also under strict instructions not to reveal more about Gregor than that he was a merchant trader with some wealth who wished to settle here.

The mention of a common acquaintance eased the discussion somewhat. However, when Gregor asked about specific areas of land that might be put up for sale, the man's expression once again grew shuttered. "I am not at liberty to divulge such information."

The auctioneer should welcome custom. Had the years of war with the English brought such cautious attitudes about? Gregor gritted his teeth for a moment, aware that his impatience was getting the better of him—either that or all that talk of dresses and fripperies had addled his mind.

Buying land was not something he had experience of and he had no idea of the customs. In his line of trade decisions about who to trust had to be fast and instinctive, and a potential deal was always open to negotiation.

"Perhaps I should explain. I am eager to procure some land in this region because I am a seafaring man and want to build up a more solid inheritance for my offspring. I am not from these parts, but my mother's line was and I find it most appealing for that reason."

"The usual course of events would be to show yourself at the time of the sale."

"Of course," Gregor agreed, "and I will be here for as long as it takes. Please be assured of my seriousness on this matter. I have planned for this for many a year, while at sea."

The man contemplated him, stroking his chin as he did so. "It is unusual for us to find a gentleman who has recently traveled abroad so interested in purchasing land in these parts. Especially so in light of the troubles and changes the English have put upon our laws, our government and our people."

He paused and his lips tightened for a moment. "Our custom is usually local, and is made up of goods and chattels. Land does pass through my hands, but not often. Even less common is it anticipated by an eager customer." He mustered a cautious smile.

Gregor relaxed somewhat. "I have faith in my Scottish brothers, and trust that better times lie ahead." He lifted his eyebrows to infer his meaning.

The auctioneer nodded, approving his comment.

He had good reason to be suspicious, although the English were more likely to send their soldiers in to take what they wanted, striking down anyone who stood in their way, than pay for it in the proper manner. However, the more encouraging news was that the auctioneer was not going to turn away a potential customer, merely question his motives.

"There may be land suitable for your requirements at some point in the future."

"In that case I will lodge a down payment with you now. If any property comes up in the region, I wish to buy it. Please consider my bid higher than any other you might get."

The scribe, who had continued working throughout the discussion, paused. The scratch of his quill was notable by its absence.

The man glanced at his assistant and pursed his lips. "I am unable to accept a down payment under those terms. It would not be fair to my client or my other customers. We do not suffer collusion or any attempts to manipulate the bidding in this house. All items have to go in a fair and open auction."

Gregor thought he saw regret in the auctioneer's expression as the scratch of the scribe's quill recommenced.

Gregor had the feeling the man might have taken his bribe had they not had a witness. There was land in the offing, and if Robert's information was correct it was Ivor Wallace's. Gregor could not, however, be sure of that, nor could he take it for granted. That was where Jessie would prove useful.

Once again he attempted to reel in his impatience. Bribery had served him well in the past, both as a means to get what he wanted, and, when he was on the receiving end of a bribe, a way to make money fast. Then again, he had few morals when he had a goal to acquire. The auctioneer was obviously a much more worthy man than he. It was difficult not to insist, however. Gregor had other things to do. Establishing a relationship with the auctioneer should have been quick and easy. He was eager to be on his way and back to the more pressing job of tutoring Jessie for the task ahead.

"Can you give me a date for the next appropriate sale?"

The man shook his head. "There is a sale in the process of being prepared, but the owner has not yet decided which fields he wishes to part with."

Gregor nodded.

"Perhaps I can let you know when the date is set?"

Gregor considered the offer, but could not afford to give details of his whereabouts, in case word got about. News of a stranger with an interest in local land would soon capture the imagination, and he didn't want Wallace to have any idea he was in the area.

"Please, inform Notary Anderson." He rose to his feet. "I hope we can do business soon. I will return later in the month to see if you have that date for me."

The gentleman became most obsequious as Gregor made his way out, encouraging him to return, apologizing that he could not be more forthcoming on this occasion. As Gregor took his leave he was more convinced than ever that it was the right thing to send Jessie in to Wallace's home, Balfour Hall. She was a canny lass and she would listen and learn. He would have the information soon enough.

As he made his way back to the stables where he had left his mount, he wondered how best to handle the exchange of any information she might garner. Originally he had thought he would get her to send word when she found out what he needed to know. That would involve a third person, which might be dangerous for her. As he thought about it he changed his mind. Once she was established in Balfour Hall he would meet her on the grounds at night. That would be necessary in order to find out about her progress, and to guide her if she needed assistance.

With a wry smile, he reminded himself that although they had made progress over the past two days, it would be wise to keep a close eye on her, because Jessie had a mind of her own and she was wayward and difficult to manage. If he was to keep her focused on the task, he would have to rein her in each night.

That notion made his mind wander, and it was with no small amount of irony that Gregor wondered who would rein him in, when she swayed him in matters of intimate congress.

chapter Nine

Jessie pressed her ear against the door to the landing and listened. Somewhere beyond she heard noises, but it wasn't close by. Ducking down, she blew into the lock, wrapped her hands around the handle and funneled her body heat there, whispering an enchantment as she did so.

Once again a haze of light moved into the lock and it clicked open smoothly. An answering burn in her chest reflected the power she had wielded, giving her a sense of satisfaction that she'd never had before. Again she was perplexed by the way the spell unfolded, but she was quickly distracted from wondering over it when the door swung open. It led onto a landing and she peered into the gloom.

There was no candle in the sconce near the door and the only light came up from the staircase on the far side. She could see that there were four other doorways, and darted over to the nearest one. It always paid to know who your neighbors were; many a time she had been saved from trouble with a customer by knowing that. When she pressed her ear to the door she heard voices in the room, but could not make out what they were saying.

Moving along the landing, she kept glancing at the staircase. At the next door, she heard nothing. Sounds from the

inn below lured her—the very place she should avoid for fear
of discovery was calling to her like a moth to a flame. She
knew it was wrong, but she had a good mind to go down
there. What harm would a quick glance about the place do?
The chances of anyone from Dundee being about these parts
were not high, she wagered. No one would recognize her.
However, Gregor would find out she had gone down there
because someone was bound to tell him, and she did not
want him to know that she could get out and about when
he thought he had her under lock and key.

Curiosity was nevertheless getting the better of her, and
she walked to the top of staircase, ducking her head in an
attempt to catch sight of the place below. She didn't get too
close. She had a terrible aversion to heights, and even walking up or down a staircase made her feel quite ill. The discomfort went back to the moment of her mother's death, and
even though she knew she should be able to force herself beyond it, it still haunted her.

The smell of ale and grease rose from the tavern below,
mingling with the aroma of a peat fire. Somewhere in the
distance she heard a voice shouting instructions. It sounded
like Mistress Muir, but then faded away before Jessie could
be certain it was her. The hallway below was stacked with
barrels, sacks of provisions and at least three broken chairs.
She vaguely remembered being marched up the steps on her
arrival. They had passed through an inn where two men
slumbered over tables and the fire was low in the grate, but
the memory was not detailed otherwise.

Just as she was about to take a step down, one of the doors
behind her creaked. Bolting upright, she glanced back. The
door behind which she had heard voices was open a crack,
but no one had emerged. Jessie darted back toward Mister
Ramsay's rooms, moving past the open door as quietly as

possible. However, when she caught a glimpse of what was going on inside the room, she paused and took a second look.

The room was similar to the one she had emerged from. Two men stood by the fireplace. One was fair-haired and looked to be a nobleman, or at least a man who earned a good wage, for he was dressed well.

Jessie determined that this must be Mister Grant, the excise man whom Morag had spoken of the day before. His companion was a handsome, younger fellow with long dark hair. He looked to be a fieldworker. He wore a loose shirt with a simple yoke, and well-worn breeches. The dirty, rough hide shoes on his feet and the dark, threadbare stockings also indicated his status. The wealthier man wore buckled shoes and brightly colored stockings. As she quickly assessed them, Mister Grant cupped the other man's face in his hand in an affectionate gesture.

Jessie was startled. She leaned closer to the gap in the door. How would the younger man react? The fieldworker lowered his head and rested one hand against the nobleman's hip. Jessie's curiosity was well and truly baited and her blood heated, for in an instant she saw their true nature and knew that they were lovers—secret lovers, hidden away here in the middle of nowhere, much as she was. Most fortuitous of all was that they clearly had no clue that the door was ajar, besotted as they were with each other.

Intrigued as to how their meeting might evolve, she flattened her body to the wall. That way she could observe the two men for as long as possible without discovery, and still glance over her shoulder in order to keep a watch on the stairs. The door to Mister Ramsay's rooms was a mere dash away, should the need to make her escape arise.

"I'm glad you came here today. I had hoped to see you again." It was the fair-haired man who spoke, and he did so while he removed his frock coat and began to unbutton his waistcoat.

Jessie had witnessed such encounters before, between men whose appetites were for each other rather than a member of her own sex. She'd seen them in the backstreets and alleyways where her kind sought custom, as well. Some of these men engaged in quiet bartering before slipping away into the night together, while others sought their release immediately, pleasuring each other there and then by hand and mouth on shaft, or up the rear, fast and furtive in the shadowed doorways.

But these two men wanted one another and they had done this here before; she could see it in the way they leaned together and touched with familiarity. It was the urgent flicker of hand and eye that indicated they were lovers who knew one another physically, lovers who sought each other out for another tryst.

The fieldworker pulled his shirt off in one swift move, revealing a body hard and strong from labor. He undid his waistband and reached inside for his shaft, letting his breeches fall to the floor, where he kicked them and his shoes off. The muscles on his chest were made more obvious by the dark hair that grew there, tapering down into a fine line that led her gaze to his groin, where his rod stemmed from a thick, dark patch of hair. There was no doubting he was a willing participant in this encounter. When he held his rod in his hand, offering it to his lover, Jessie observed how ready he was to be touched and used. His manhood stood out like a flagstaff, its foreskin drawn back and the head shiny and swollen. He cupped his large and heavy-looking ballocks as if offering them to his master.

Mister Grant's eyes shone. His hands trembled as he shed his shirt, and he struggled with his buttons. Mumbled words of admiration and need were exchanged as they undressed. Jessie strained to hear, but they were speaking more quietly. Then Mister Grant reached to cup the other man's hand in his own, embracing his heavy sac. As he did, his trews fell to the floor, revealing a pale, slender rear end and surprisingly strong thighs. His prick was up and hard, and it was long and bowed to one side.

The dark-haired man gave a hungry grin as he stared down at Mister Grant's member. He reacted suddenly, grabbing his master around the back of the neck. He planted a possessive kiss on Mister Grant's mouth while his hand stroked the long, bowed cock adoringly. In hurried movements they devoured each other at mouth and hip, hands feverishly exploring. Then they moved as one to the bed. Once they were reclined on it, their embraces grew even lustier.

Jessie peeped in as their bodies rolled together in an urgent rhythm, their hips thrusting, cocks rubbing one against the other. It was a lewd and stimulating sight, and she soon found herself with a nagging ache to frig herself to release.

Who would take whom? she wondered. Ranald would be accepting wagers on it. That thought tickled her and she almost giggled. Putting her hand over her mouth, she quickly contained the sound of her response. She kept her hand there when she observed the darker man turn and reverse his position on the bed, until they were top to toe and he could take his lover's member in his mouth. Her eyebrows lifted as she observed the man underneath do the same, returning the favor. She had witnessed this act between two women before, but not between two men. It was startlingly arousing for her to observe and—as she could clearly see—for the two men to take part in. Her thighs rubbed together as she shifted from one foot to the other, her body growing eager for such ministrations, for the touch of finger and lip to her eager seat of pleasure.

Jessie could not help feeling oddly aligned with their situation. Although hers was very different, there was similarity in the way they must hide and keep their secret. She felt a bond with the pair of them, for they would be cast out much as she had been. Not only were they fornicating with their own sex, but the wealthier man let a mere worker order him about and defile him. The excise man's sanity would be questioned if his tastes were put about.

Condemnation haunted them all.

Muffled grunts emerged from the entwined figures, and occasionally she caught a glimpse of their faces as they devoured each other. There was a bucking of bodies, thrusting and arching, until the fieldworker lifted his head and issued an instruction.

"Make ready for me now." His voice was ragged with lust.

Mister Grant rolled free of his younger lover.

Taking charge once more, the younger man mounted his companion, who lay facedown on the bed. He was a fine-looking man, and now that he had assumed the role of master, he seemed even more attractive. Jessie could not help admiring him, especially when he began to stroke his own member, spitting in his palm before doing so, and coating the head and rigid shaft.

With one knee, he pushed his lover's legs apart and climbed between them. The fair-haired man lifted his head, and she could see how much he wanted this. His hand moved down between his front and the mattress, and locked around his rigid member. But his lover pulled that hand free and planted it firmly on the bed. As he hovered over him, he whispered instructions. Once again he spat into his hand and pushed that hand between his lover's buttocks.

Mister Grant uttered a low curse, and Jessie craned her neck to observe. The fieldworker was manipulating two fingers inside his lover's rear end. Mister Grant's hips rose and fell against the bed, his fingers clutching at the pillows as he welcomed the intrusion, just as a woman would welcome such in her cunny. A moment later, the dark man replaced those fingers with something much, much larger.

Jessie's skin raced. A damp sweat was gathering at the back of her neck and between her breasts as she imagined how Mister Grant would feel—how utterly debauched and thrilling it would be to have a handsome young lover rut him this way, an act most people would consider obscene and morally corrupt.

She could tell the crown of that large member was in place, because it was greeted by more lusty cries from the man beneath. The fieldworker then balanced his weight on his arms and began to drive his length inside the other man.

Jessie's lips parted and she bit on one finger. She did not want to miss a moment. Her body brimmed with excitement, and she clutched at her nipples through her bodice. The sight of that beautiful cock entering the prone man was driving her to distraction. Her thighs were damp and clammy, her dress far too tight at the bodice. With her free hand, she rubbed at the swell of her mound through her clothing.

When the worker had fully embedded himself he shifted position, lying alongside the other man's back and rocking him so that they were like two spoons nested together. Then he reached around and grasped Mister Grant's prick, milking him off as he began the slow thrust and grind of his own milking at the rear.

Mister Grant was delirious with pleasure, his eyes tightly closed, his body willingly enslaved to the dark master who possessed him so thoroughly. Jessie pressed her skirt between her thighs and cupped her mound, squeezing it for relief as she watched the two men shunt and writhe.

A sound echoed up the stairs from below.

Jessie froze, then glanced over her shoulder. She did not want to be interrupted now. They were approaching their peak. Neither did she want the lovers to hear anything, for they might discover the door was open.

Checking on the lovebirds inside the room, she found that the men did not seem to have noticed, so deep in their abandonment were they. She attempted to muster an enchantment to close the door over and keep it that way, but her thoughts were far too muddled by her state of extreme arousal. *Curses on that.* To be so torn made her magic useless.

The sound was of shoes scuffing across the floor below. A moment later she heard another noise, that of a barrel being rolled across the flagstones. Then all fell quiet belowstairs. She returned fully to her watching. Just in time, for they were at their moment of release and she would have hated to miss that. The dark-haired man pitched and bowed at his lover's back, every part of his body tense and gleaming with sweat in the moment of his climax. His hips jerked and his hand tightened on his lover's cock. The fair man grunted loudly and spent himself in his lover's grasp.

Jessie squeezed her hand hard against her mound, attempting to stay still, but it was nigh on impossible in her current state of excitement. She had to find her own relief, and soon.

The man at the rear echoed that most enraptured act, emitting a loud exhalation of breath as his hips jerked several times and then stilled. The sound of their mutual panting was loud enough to be heard quite clearly on the landing, and she also noticed that Mister Grant was opening his eyes and reaching for his lover. It was time to make her retreat.

Darting back to Mister Ramsay's door, she went inside

and closed it quietly behind her. She had to take several deep breaths and force herself to concentrate, in order to undo her previous enchantment and relock the door from inside. She couldn't risk leaving it open a moment longer in case Gregor returned earlier than he had the day before. Dancing from foot to foot, she blew into the lock hurriedly and said the words. She had to repeat them three times before she got it right, cursing herself as she did so, and when she finally heard the lock click she ran across the room, lifting her skirts as she went, and threw herself facedown on Gregor's bed.

Breathing in his scent from the pillows, she put her hand under her skirts and between her thighs and commenced rubbing herself vigorously. Her cunny was slippery with her juices, her bud swollen and protruding—and mightily sensitive to the touch. She thrust her hips against the bed, her mind full of the images she had just seen. Then Mister Ramsay himself stepped into her imaginings, and he was telling her off for her escape, slapping her arse as he had done the day before.

"Oh, oh, oh." She squeezed her eyes tightly shut and stuck her bottom out, imagining she was over his knee again and he not only slapped her sensitive rump, he dipped his hand in between and rubbed at her folds roughly, maddening her. He was chastising her for watching the lewd behavior of the men next door, but beneath her lap she could feel the hard length of his cock, and she imagined him lifting her, spreading her and thrusting into her grateful cunny.

When she peaked moments later, she lay still until she recovered and then rolled onto her back and laughed aloud. "And there was meself thinking I was to have another tedious afternoon of solitude."

The day had brought much entertainment, and now the sun was lowering in the sky. Mister Ramsay—Gregor—

would return soon. She smiled and caught her lower lip between her teeth, anticipating his presence. Although she balked at being held captive, there was pleasure to be found, with a good purse at the end. Perhaps her situation was not so bad, after all, and she rose onto one elbow to look at the window.

The sun was setting on the rolling Fife hills, and she watched it, wondering again where Mister Ramsay was and where he had been. The mood between them had been most enticing that morning, before he had announced he was taking his leave. She would make it so again.

Many of the whores she knew dreamed of having a sponsor like this. A protector of sorts. Someone who kept them as his own woman. It was not something Jessie had ever craved, because she knew it was dangerous territory for someone with her wild nature and her gift for the craft. Her mother had told her and Maisie that often enough. To grow attached to one man could only make things more difficult for them.

Yet when Gregor had turned her away after supper and made her go to her own room, she'd felt a sense of longing that spelled trouble. Especially after the time they had spent preparing, in which he'd aroused her to the point of madness in the name of seducing some unknown enemy. Under normal circumstances she would relish a room of her own. Because he was there, beyond it, the servant's room made her feel lonely and deprived. He had resisted her, for a while. It bothered her immensely that she did not understand why. Especially as she'd put so much effort into breaking down his resistance. Was there another woman in his heart? With careful thought and preparation, she decided that she would find out. That very evening. By fair means or foul, she would discover if it was to another woman he went.

With that vow bolstering her mood she tidied his bed, re-turned to her quarters, relocked the door by means of magic, then sat down to wait.

chapter Ten

Gregor did not suffer the recriminations and vitriol of the day before when he returned that evening. In fact, Jessie seemed delighted to see him. Her eyes sparkled with mischief and she embraced him—which took him quite by surprise—eyeing his stuffed bundle as she did so. Curious, he wondered how she had occupied herself while he was gone. Once again he had the feeling she had not stayed in her room, but there was no evidence that she had forced the lock, and he had the key.

Then it occurred to him that she might be more settled because of what had passed between them that morning. If that was the case, he had a difficult choice to make—keep her satisfied, happy and loyal, or at arm's length for the sake of his sanity. Gregor gave a wry smile as he thought it over.

That morning there had been little choice. It had only been a matter of time before he'd buckled and broke with the tutoring to relieve them both of their lusty burden. He had done his utmost to use the situation to his advantage, but there was no denying it had to be done—regardless of the equally pressing need for a lesson in good manners. As soon as he'd sat her at the table, naked, he had pictured her in a much more carnally advantageous pose. Working off his stiff rod while she was facedown over that table with her arse in the air was an inevitable event.

Now that he was back the table served as a reminder of that most pleasurable session, as did she. He gave her the packages he'd brought her in order to distract himself. "I have hired a seamstress in Saint Andrews. You will soon have new clothing. In the meantime, a handkerchief and shawl by the same seamstress. On my journey back here I also located some decent hide shoes."

Her eyes lit at the mention of the shoes, and when he put them in her hand, she stared at them in wonder. He'd noticed that her own were worn paper-thin.

"That is why you…" She put her splayed hand to her foot, as he had done to measure the length of it that morning.

He'd thought she hadn't noticed. He nodded.

Eagerly, she took the shawl from him and rubbed the soft woolen garment against her face. As he'd thought when he selected it, it matched her eyes. The cotton kerchief was equally welcomed, although it was with some regret he watched her cover her bosom as she wrapped it around her neck and shoved the tails into the front of her dress. With the shawl around her shoulders, she danced back and forth.

"I am decent," she declared, with laugher in her voice.

Gregor had expected her to be delighted. In his experience women usually were when they received gifts. But there was a kind of awe about Jessie that surprised him. She had nothing, he realized.

It was many years since he had been that way himself, but he could still recall the night he had arrived at Dundee harbor, with just the clothes on his back. What he did have was the determination to find work and an ability to work hard. His drive had been fueled by bitterness and anger. It was lucky anyone took a risk on signing him up at all, but he'd found the captain of a frigate whose crew was a few men short. Hard labor was what he'd needed to work off some of his anger and grief, and he'd learned quickly, soon rising through the ranks when he showed a talent for navigation and gauging the winds. His father, Hugh, had taught him how to read the weather as they worked the land together, and his skills quickly adapted and grew.

Eventually he'd become master of his own destiny and accrued wealth. But he saw part of his young self reflected in Jessie's expression, the grateful awe he had felt when he'd received his first earnings and was able to send money back to Craigduff so that his father's grave would have a stone put upon it.

Reaching into his pocket, Gregor handed her the final item. It was a comb, crafted from a fine-grained piece of wood. Jessie took the offering somewhat cautiously, examining the paper it was wrapped in.

"Open it," he urged.

She did so, and gasped when she saw it. "Oh, it is beautiful."

To him it was a plain, serviceable item, but Jessie was delighted by it and immediately put it to use, combing it through the tails of her thick, wavy hair, chuckling to herself as her locks grew longer and straightened under the ministrations of the tool.

She honestly had nothing, he reflected once again. She'd mentioned that her purse was kept by her pimp. What was she saving for? He recalled some mention of traveling north. Did she have a child lodged somewhere? Whores invariably did, but he had seen no signs of childbirth upon her.

When she saw him watching, she blushed and pushed the comb into the pocket on her borrowed dress. "Thank you."

She rubbed her hands on her shawl as if pleased, but he noticed that she looked a little concerned.

"What troubles you? You do not like the shawl?"

She seemed to consider her words carefully before she responded. "Will you take the cost of the clothing and the comb from the wage you promised me?"

Gregor frowned. It hadn't occurred to him that she would think that. "No."

Relief flooded her expression.

She was worried about the money. It was important to her. *Of course it was,* he surmised, with no small amount of self-mockery. *Otherwise she'd be long gone by now.*

"Will you take me down to the inn this evening, now that I am decent?"

Gregor immediately shook his head. "It is too much of a risk. Travelers from Dundee might pass by here."

"I can disguise myself with the shawl." She reached for his arm, imploring him. "I shall go mad locked up in here."

Once again she was taking liberties with him. He felt a nerve in his cheek begin to twitch. "What?" He threw her a warning glance. "You told me you could break free from a cell without my help, and now you are complaining about being locked up here?"

She pouted, but she seemed amused by his remark.

Gregor sighed. "You always want to court danger," he said on a more serious note.

"That is not so. I want to be safe, really I do. But I get terribly restless being in here for so long." Her glance was pleading. "Just for a few minutes."

"Liberties, Jessie, you are taking liberties."

A hopeful smile lit her face. "I promise I will not ask about it anymore, and I will be good and quiet when you…lock me up in my room."

That was made to make him feel guilty, he knew. *Damn woman*.

"I want you to know that I am doing this against my better judgment, and only to avoid seeing you in a mope."

Their arrival in the tavern shortly thereafter did little to convince Gregor he had not made a mistake. Jessie had covered her head with the shawl and walked close beside him, but several men who stood by the ale counter turned in their direction, as if the mere scent of a woman had alerted them to her presence. He touched Jessie around the waist, indicating she was his. It did not stop them from leering. Gregor's humor darkened.

Beyond them, the serving girl, Morag, walked behind the ale counter with a massive jug in her hands. She craned her neck to see what the commotion was about. When she noted it was him and that he had brought his cousin with him, she grinned.

"Sit there," he muttered over his shoulder, and nodded at a rickety table in a dark corner. He ushered Jessie to it and then gestured for Morag to bring ale.

"Good evening, Mister Ramsay, Miss Jessie," Morag said when she delivered the ale.

Jessie grasped the girl's hand. "Feel the fine stuff of this shawl," she said, and offered Morag the trailing hem of it.

Gregor frowned as they whispered together about the garment, and wished he had not bought the damned thing. When Morag bent over the table to study the weave with Jessie, he saw that one of the farmhands at the counter had stepped into the middle of the room to get a better look, staring at the women with a foolish grin on his face.

"Jessie," he warned under his breath.

She immediately stopped speaking and adopted a suitably chastised expression. Morag quickly assessed the mood and left. Still the men loomed, making Gregor wish he had kept her upstairs.

Jessie looked at him expectantly.

"We have work to do." In an attempt to ignore the rabble and their interest in Jessie, he reached into his pocket and pulled out the piece of paper he had brought with him, together with a stub of charcoal. On one side were the notes he had made after his visit with Robert. Gregor turned it over and began to draw the outline of Balfour Hall. When Jessie saw what he was doing, she leaned forward on her elbows to observe. Marking the entrance with a cross, he named it, and then placed an arrow to show the servant's entrance, and named that by writing above it.

Jessie's face fell and she put her hand over the words he had just written. She shook her head. There was frustration in her eyes.

She cannot read. "I am sorry, I did not know."

She shrugged and her eyelids lowered, but he could tell it mattered to her.

"You had no opportunity for schooling?" If so, it was shameful, for she had a sharp mind.

She shook her head. "Although there is a jest there, for part of my childhood was spent living with a teacher's family."

Puzzled, he waited for more of an explanation, but it was not forthcoming. He was about to suggest she put part of her earnings toward learning, for it would be a good investment, but he thought better of it. Once again he wondered what she was saving her coin for.

"No matter, there is always a way." Many seafaring men could not read or write and knew very little of such things. He picked up his stub of charcoal again and drew a carriage at the front entrance, and a woman with an apron at the rear.

Jessie nodded when she saw what he had done, and her expression brightened. They were in tune again, and he went to add some details to the map.

"Excuse me, sire," a voice interrupted.

Glancing up, he saw a well-dressed man. Gregor quickly rolled up the parchment and tucked it into his pocket.

"I feel sure I know you," said the intruder, "but I cannot place your name."

The man was fair-haired and possibly five or six years older than himself.

Gregor's blood ran cold. "No, I do not think we have ever met."

For some reason Jessie seemed amused as she looked from one to the other of them. That did not help Gregor's mood. He gave a dismissive shake of his head toward the man.

"Grant is the name, James Grant. I'm a collector of taxes for the crown. Perhaps that is how we know each other."

There was indeed something familiar about the man, and his name echoed through Gregor's mind. Cursing silently, he knew they should have stayed hidden. It was important that Ivor Wallace did not hear of his return. Again, Gregor shook his head. "I think not. I am a traveler and new to this part of Scotland."

The man looked confused. "In that case, forgive me."

It was his frown and the way he ducked his head that pinned it for Gregor. He did know him from somewhere. Was it Craigduff, perhaps? That was not good. Perhaps Jessie was not the only one who should remain in hiding.

"We never should have come down," Gregor muttered as he watched the man retreat.

"He is our neighbor," Jessie offered conspiratorially, as if imparting knowledge of great importance.

Gregor frowned. That was all he needed, a neighbor at the inn who hailed from Craigduff. Someone who might remember exactly who he was and tell others that he had returned. He didn't want Wallace to be forewarned when he took action. *And how in God's name did Jessie know that if she had remained locked up in her room all afternoon?*

"How do you know that he is our neighbor?"

Her eyes rounded and then she blinked. "Morag told me there was a man by the name of Mister Grant staying in the rooms here."

Gregor grew increasingly unsettled by the turn of events, and she was not helping. He should be hastening this along in order to get it done before news of his presence got about. Instead he was dallying with the woman he had hired to work for him. "Come, it is not safe here."

"No," she bleated forlornly. "No one has even looked at me, covered up as I am."

She was wrong. Every man in the inn was staring. They were practically lathering at the mouth for want of a closer look. He glared at her. "It is not only you who does not wish to be identified."

"Oh."

When he saw her expression alter, he nodded. Now she understood.

"Shift yourself and be quick about it. I have a bottle of port upstairs. We can talk privately." He checked that the papers were secure in his pocket and then swallowed the rest of his ale. The sooner they were back upstairs the better.

Jessie did not relish the suddenness of their departure, however. She looked woebegone when he rose to his feet, as if he had just informed her a close friend had passed on. He grasped her wrist and indicated in no uncertain terms that they must leave.

When he had her halfway up the stairs, she grumbled bitterly to his back, "I had barely sat myself down when you dragged me back up here."

"And I should never have taken you down there in the first place," he retorted over his shoulder.

She was dawdling, clinging to the banister as if she did not want to mount the staircase.

He frowned and gestured her on. "Neither of us needs to be identified."

Once they reached his quarters, he ushered her inside and locked the door. She took the shawl from her head and cast it aside before putting her hands on her hips and glaring at him.

The frustrations of the day had already taken their toll, and his patience had worn thin. He grabbed her by the shoulders and forced her to look at him. "How did you know that gentleman was our neighbor?"

Immediately she turned her face away. "I told you. Morag mentioned his name."

"You are lying to me."

She folded her arms across her chest.

"Has Morag been letting you out?"

"No." She was adamant in that. "Ask her if you do not believe me."

"You really think I am going to quiz the servants about your activities?" He shook his head and stomped off, retrieving the port bottle from the mantel shelf. He sloshed the dark wine into glasses and pushed one across the table toward her.

She followed in his footsteps. "I am no more than a servant to you, and you are quizzing me."

Once again she revealed her annoyance about being beholden to him. "Indeed." He pulled out a chair and sat. "But you are more trouble than you are worth. Perhaps I should have left you to rot in that tollbooth."

The affronted look she afforded him made him laugh aloud.

Her eyes flashed angrily. "Where did you go today?"

Gregor lifted his brows. "You know where I went. To buy you clothes."

"Did a woman help you?"

Lord, she was insatiable in her quest. "A seamstress, yes."

A thwarted expression settled on her face.

Gregor threw back a swallow of his port.

Meanwhile, she paced about, and her luscious figure was outlined in the candlelight, forcing him to observe it. This squabble would only be settled by an apology on her side or a rough bout of carnal congress. Preferably both.

"Notice if you will that I answered you civilly when you quizzed me about my doings. You would do well to learn such manners."

She cursed aloud, her annoyance obvious.

Gregor laughed at the irony. "You are the most contrary woman I have ever known."

She alighted on that, but not in the way he might have expected.

"What about the women you have known?"

She truly was in need of something to think upon.

"Tell me about them," she added as she drew to a halt in front of him. "I want to learn."

There was such a demanding air about her that Gregor suddenly relished the prospect of telling her every sordid detail. "You want to know about the whores I have encountered?"

Her lips tightened and her eyes flashed angrily. "Yes."

Inflamed by her challenge, Gregor put down his glass. "In that case, I'll tell you."

He stood and snatched her into his arms, then thrust her toward the bed with one arm around her waist. Once there, he threw her down on the mattress, relishing the way her breasts spilled from her bodice when he did so. He put one knee on the bed beside her, pinning her there with his weight on her skirts. Steadying himself with one hand as he arched over her, he rubbed the other briskly over the mounds of her breasts as they spilled free.

Her eyes flashed with anger, but she put her hands flat on the bed. Her expression revealed her emotions. She had instigated this situation; now she would have to suffer it. Gregor smiled. He had never known such stubbornness in a woman. Even so, her nipples had crested and were delightfully peaked, and he could tell that the flush in her cheeks was brought on by desire as well as anger.

He threw off his coat and hauled his shirt over his head, tossing it aside.

Resentfully, she cast an eye over his bared chest.

"You see this?" He drew her attention to the small scar that ran down his left side.

As she peered at it, she nodded.

"I gained the wound in a knife fight in Morocco. The prize was a night with a dark-skinned beauty who had a talent for bringing a man off by stroking every part of his body with exotic oils, before mounting his oiled cock."

Jessie writhed against the bed, her hands fisting.

"I won that prize, and enjoyed her immensely. In India I bought a whore who had pictures painted on her skin and precious stones studded through her ears, gems that dazzled me in the candlelight while I fucked her."

Jessie cursed beneath her breath.

"In Italy I drank sweet wine from between a whore's cupped breasts, and ate succulent fruit from her cunt."

Jessie twisted under him, looking at him as if she hated him.

"I have seen a dancer so agile that she could pick up with the plump lips of her puss the coins men offered her."

"Such talent," Jessie snapped, her voice ragged with emotion. "It is little wonder you have been abroad so long."

Gregor laughed, his bad humor mellowing as the prospect of bedding her took hold. "There are temptations aplenty, I'll grant you that. Why, I have seen a woman charm a snake so thoroughly that it entered her cunt, offering its head and length to her, for her pleasure."

"It is a wonder you came back here at all, with such lurid delights available!"

Despite her angry retorts, he could see that his diversions aroused her, too. She writhed against the mattress, her hands clutching at the surface, but when she looked at him he saw resentment in her eyes. Would he ever fathom this woman? The only thing he knew with any sense of conviction was that they both had to find release, and soon. His cock ached to mount her.

"Ah, but women are all different, Jessie, and some have so much more passion than others." *And your passion becomes you so well.*

He tweaked her nipple then, for he was more than ready to enter her. The need between them had swelled, and the way her body moved distractedly against the bed made him want to feel that movement more specifically, from inside.

She seemed to take that last comment particularly badly, however, for she turned her face away and he saw dampness on her eyelashes. Had he taunted her too much? That thought made him pause, his mood leveling. But Jessie was rolling in a different direction.

She let out a frustrated cry and then grabbed at his hand, forcing it to rake over her breast. "Mark me," she whispered. "Make me yours."

Startled by the shift in her mood, he attempted to pull free. But she held on, pressing his hand against her.

Gregor fell silent, astonished by her strange behavior. Moving his fist to the front of her skirts, she pushed down on it, rocking her hips in a lewd motion. "Touch me, use me."

The plea was anguished. "Put it in me," she begged. "Fill me, please, make me feel that I am worth as much as them."

Angry with himself for bringing her to this, he shook his head.

She clutched at his forearms. Her eyes shone with some crazed need. "Please, Gregor."

The sight of her this way made his chest tighten, and it was a peculiar twisted sense of yearning that he experienced when he looked at her. "You are worth as much as them, Jessie. More."

She looked at him from under her eyelashes as if she did not believe him. But it was the truth. There was a passionate fire in her that he had never found before. "I have never broken into a jail dressed as a minister for a woman, before I met you, Jessie Taskill."

His words seemed to calm her and she swallowed her tears. "Come now, what foolishness is this?"

"You have driven me to madness with your wild stories," she accused, her expression most ashamed. "I need a man inside me because of it."

"And you will have this man. That was always my purpose, my dear."

She looked deep into his eyes, and he smiled and touched his finger to the end of her nose. "You asked, did you not?"

She nodded.

Gregor stood up, unlacing his breeches. "Lift your skirts. Open your legs for me and I will show you exactly where I want to be."

She took a deep breath and then exhaled it shakily while she did as he instructed. Pulling up her skirts, she opened her legs to him, feet flat to the bed.

He was captured at first by the sight of her bared puss. Between the shadowy enclaves of her soft thighs her slit glistened enticingly. Her bud protruded, swollen and ruddy, and the plump lips invited him to pivot against her, right there in that most tender spot. She held her skirts in one hand, resting the other on the soft curve of her belly, fingertips against the place where soft dark hair feathered over her mound. He nodded toward it. "Show me more. Open yourself to me."

Jessie moaned, and he could see by the rise and fall of her breasts that she was struggling with her needs. That knowledge made his ballocks ride high, ready for action. At that moment Gregor could think of no other woman he would more willingly claim. He took his cock in his hand, fist closed hard around the base, while he looked down at her.

The anticipation in her eyes when she looked at his erect length made his cock jerk within his grasp. The way her lips parted expectantly and the damp tears on her lashes glittered only made him want her more. Then she moved her hand and plied her folds open with her fingers, revealing her most intimate place to his eager gaze. How that dark, juicy opening captured him. The prospect of easing his rod inside its hot, tight grasp and stretching her open was all-encompassing. He climbed over her, staring down into her eyes as he directed his distended cock to her.

Her sweet furrow was sleek and ready and he worked his crown into her, watching her expression alter as he filled her. The stories he had told her had enflamed her all the more, for she cried out and her hot puss snatched eagerly at his length.

"Hellfire," he whispered, and gave himself over to the overwhelming need to drive and thrust into her. She clung to him, whimpering as he rode her, her hands stroking his shoulders and back, her body arching up from the bed. Her responses made him want to hold her in his arms all night long, and he would.

The sounds of her pleasured moans ran fever over his skin. She had locked her legs loosely around his hips, and their thrusts became faster. Each time he rubbed her deepest places her body bucked beneath his, rising to meet him. Gregor relished the grip of her muscles and the heated look in her eyes, and he marveled at how different she was from all those other whores. All those women had impressed him with their tricks and their diversions, and yet never had he found such passion, such sensuality as he did in this woman.

As he pressed home, driving them both over the edge and into the ecstasy of mutual release, that knowledge settled deep inside Gregor Ramsay. Whatever happened, he knew that he would never forget this woman.

Gregor awoke that night when she cried out in her sleep. Stirring, he glanced about to get his bearings. A stub of candle still flickered in its holder beside the bed, and he blinked and looked at the warm woman who nestled against his chest in slumber. He rubbed his face with his free hand. All was dark at the window. It was past midnight, but nowhere near dawn. He was about to settle down to sleep once more when her body stiffened against his and she cried out again. The sound disconcerted him, for it was a mewling noise, like that of a distressed animal.

In the gloom he could see that she held her hands in loose fists, and her fingers furled and unfurled. Her eyelids flickered and her mouth opened. Bad thoughts had come upon her in her dreams. Should he wake her? He rocked her gently in his arms, and her body relaxed. She moved closer against him and seemed to settle in his embrace.

After a few minutes had passed her breathing grew more regular and peaceful. He decided against waking her. However, he could not return to sleep so easily, because he could not help wondering what it was that had disturbed her dreams.

When had she gained her title as the Harlot of Dundee? he wondered, and how long had she pleasured men in order to keep herself from starving? These were not things he had thought about before, but Jessie had kept hidden the unhappiness he had witnessed tonight. Even when she was in a fury with him she was neither afraid nor dispirited.

What had happened to her, and when had Jessie Taskill lost her innocence? Had it been stolen, or had she given it freely? She did not talk about her beginnings. As time went by, Gregor began to wonder about them.

chapter Eleven

The following morning they went about their ablutions and dressing in a cautious silence. Gregor saw that she was humbled and perhaps left somewhat tender by what had happened the night before, and he let her be. After they had breakfasted, she tidied the things and then stood up.

"How may I assist you today, Mister Ramsay? Have you a lesson in mind for me?"

Her demeanor was so different that he found himself amused by her efforts. But she had reverted to addressing him formally. He reached out his hand and drew her nearer to where he was sitting. She looked at him cautiously from under her eyelashes, as if she half expected to be admonished again. That was the last thing on his mind.

"I know I have been hard on you, Jessie, and that you are not used to being kept this way. But you have shown yourself willing, and you were a fast learner. I have great faith in you, and am sure that you will help me in my quest for retribution and justice."

Her chin lifted.

"You had begun to call me by my given name. That was a liberty you took, but I have grown used to hearing it on your lips, and you may continue to do so."

A smile lifted the corners of her mouth. "Yes, Gregor."

"That's better. Now, I have business to attend to today. But you are right. We should make use of the situation. There is little time to waste. Bring my boots and assist."

With neither argument nor question, she darted off.

Gregor shook his head. She was a puzzle indeed.

When she returned, he instructed, "Your master has asked you to put on his boots and polish them. I want you to show me that you would do so willingly, eager to please, and that you will be devoted to your task. But you must find a way to lure his eye all the same."

Jessie went about the job eagerly. She knelt at his feet and straightened his stockings. When she reached for the boots, her hips dipped and swayed and their curve was displayed to good effect.

"Please be lifting your foot now, sire," she whispered, and looked at him from beneath her lashes as she did so.

Gregor restrained his amusement. With some vigorous tugging and no small amount of panting and wriggling, she got both boots on. Gregor stood up.

She remained kneeling at his feet, with her hands on her thighs, and stared directly up at him. Her face was close to the front of his breeches and he was reminded of their first encounter.

"I shall put a shine to them, sire, before you step out, if that pleases you."

Gregor noticed how her eyes gleamed in the morning light. Her lips were dark this morning, the lower one damp and inviting. His cock hardened, and he quickly gestured for her to continue, lest he request she do something else instead.

She is ready. The thought occurred to him as he looked down at her. Yes, if he had been her master it would have been far too tempting to redirect the course of events. *Or have I lost all sense of judgment on the matter?*

Gregor frowned at the waywardness of his thoughts.

Meanwhile, she hurried away and returned with a cloth, then set about producing a high gloss on his riding boots. Her breasts jiggled and she arched her neck, sweeping her hair back when it trailed down across the pale skin of her throat and collarbone. Gregor could think of nothing he wanted to do more than carry her back to the bed and lose himself between her thighs.

When she stood up, he mustered an appropriate response. "Very good, you have developed an appropriate and pleasing manner."

"Thank you, Gregor," she replied, with a demure smile. "I am so pleased that you believe I can seduce a man in the appropriate manner now."

Gregor's attention hitched. Was there a teasing note in her voice? If so, he decided to ignore it. "I will be collecting your new garments today. Tomorrow, I want you to be ready to come out with me."

"Come out?" she repeated, her expression delighted.

"Yes, tomorrow we will travel to my enemy's abode. We will not approach, but I want you to see it in order to be prepared for what lies ahead."

She nodded, and he could see how much she longed to be out of these quarters. *Yes, that is what she wants,* he reflected. To be done with this and on her way, as did he.

When he looked at her upturned face, however, he found it difficult to move.

"If you are ready to leave," she said, "I will go to my room."

"Yes, do that."

He watched as she left willingly. He should have been

pleased by her agreeable behavior, and he assured himself he was, but he could not shake the notion that she did not stay in there anyway, and he might as well let her have the run of the place. She had taken liberties enough, though, and now that they were on an even keel he could not afford to let her become unruly again.

He followed her to the door.

She was seated on the cot, and when he nodded her way, she smiled.

For the first time, when he turned the key in the lock, Gregor felt incredibly guilty.

It was with a sense of achievement that Jessie realized she had made her way into his bed, and it had happened almost by accident. The night before had been a strange one indeed. He'd had a foul mood on him after the incident with Mister Grant, but what had passed between them later melted that away.

Their tumble had been most unusual, and as she thought back on it Jessie became wistful and lingered on the memory. She did not, however, want to linger on thoughts of how his talk of whores and exotic places had made her feel, and so she pushed that aside. It also bothered her that he did not seem convinced by her promises that she would not run away. Would she? No, she did not want to. She would earn her purse honestly, and then her journey north would be a comfortable one. Besides, she enjoyed being with him. What woman wouldn't?

Instead of thinking on the bothersome things, she stood by the window and thought about his promise to take her out with him the following day. There would be new garments, too. Jessie was feeling so uplifted about it that she even decided she would be good and stay inside her room that afternoon.

As the hours ticked past, however, her old enemy, boredom, reared its head. She paced up and down, trying to resist the lure beyond the locked door.

When she turned at the window, she caught sight of Mister Grant's secret lover coming across the hilltops on the horizon. A striking figure he made, tall and burly, covering the ground easily with his long stride. Would he come up to Mister Grant's quarters, she wondered, or did Mister Grant meet him belowstairs? Curiosity got the better of her. She would not venture out, but she wanted to observe the fieldworker's arrival.

Moments later she had worked her magic on both the first lock and the second, and had the door to the landing slightly ajar so that she could see who came upstairs.

Impatiently she watched, bobbing her head. She thought she heard a sound nearby, and then another, and after a moment she opened the door a little wider to take a peek along the landing—just in time to see Mister Grant's door swing shut.

Surely he could not have got up here that quickly, and without her seeing? No. She shook the notion off. It was just the door closing. The two men had to be downstairs, perhaps chatting over a tankard of ale. Having determined that, she crept toward the top of the staircase, listening for voices below as she did so.

An uneasy sense of awareness crept over her. She paused.

Then she was grabbed from behind.

"I told you there was someone skulking about. I felt it yesterday and I heard something again on my way in."

Struggling to break free, Jessie twisted around and saw that it was the fieldworker who had grabbed her. How had he got past her? It was not possible for him to cover the ground and climb upstairs before she got to the door, no matter how fast his strides. Perhaps there was another entrance or stairway? But where?

Beyond him Mister Grant stood, an unhappy frown on his face. "Be careful with the girl," he said.

The fieldworker continued to hold her, peering at her with a disgruntled expression. "What were you doing, lurking here?"

"I was doing nowt." She managed to pull herself free, but it left her perilously close to the top of the stairs. The room began to spin. With a squeal she fell back into his arms.

"Sorry, sire." She stepped away and straightened her skirts. Both men looked at her as if she were mad. "I was merely looking out for my…" *What was he supposed to be?* "Cousin."

"It is true," Mister Grant said. "She was with a man who has lodgings here. I saw them together yesterday."

Wriggling her shoulders defiantly, she darted for her own doorway. "Yes, and he is due to return at any moment," she declared.

Stepping inside, she quickly leveled her head enough to redo the spell, relocking the door, then returned to her room.

Impetuosity had got the better of her, as it so often did. As a result she had been seen out there, and if either of them was loose-tongued, Gregor might hear of it. That was bad, for they were on good terms now. Nevertheless, the likelihood of a secret entrance soon filled her mind, and she hurried to the window, pressing her cheek to the tiny panes of glass, peering out at the building.

After a moment she became aware of a presence. Gregor was standing beneath her window, arms folded, looking up at her with an accusing but wry smile.

She jerked away, biting her lip, and then chuckled. He had packages at his feet. It was with a rush of excitement that Jessie realized it must be the clothing he had promised her.

chapter Twelve

It had not taken long for the mischief to resurface in Miss Jessie. Gregor looked at her with amused suspicion. "What were you doing, planning your escape?"

He was quite certain she would have been gone by now, if that was her intention. Gregor warned himself against being curious about her deeper motives and emotions. He had spent the whole afternoon reminding himself that she was a simple whore. The fact that he became aroused by her was merely incidental. He could not afford to let his sympathy for her situation to grow. He had enough problems to deal with.

"No, I…" Her voice drifted off and she looked over at the packages he'd put on the table rather forlornly.

Did she think he was going to punish her by depriving her of the clothing?

"I was just wondering how many other guests lodged here. I hear voices when you are gone."

"You have uncannily good hearing." Why did he get the feeling he was missing some important point of fact here? "Were you intending to leave?"

She shook her head vehemently. "Oh, no. I am dedicated to the task."

Gregor accepted that much. She had also confessed her

boredom, the evening before. He realized he must hasten the lesson and move on to the task in order to keep her occupied. "I need your dedication, Jessie. We are almost ready, and we will proceed with haste."

He gestured at the table. "You will find two dresses that the seamstress assured me would be suitable for a serving woman of good standing. Please, be certain that they are a good fit and begin wearing them. You must be suitably humble when you arrive on the doorstep."

Jessie nodded and then proceeded to unwrap the packages with curiosity.

Gregor settled in a chair to observe while she examined the items with murmurs of appreciation, her eyes growing round in the most delightful way. She commented on the quality of wool that had been used for the dresses, and the softness to the touch, things he had not even noticed. After the day before, he knew how much new clothes meant, and he'd added a trinket or two on the spur of the moment, items that were not entirely necessary.

The sheer delight in her eyes when she shook out the blue evening gown made him smile. It was an indulgence, but well worth it. Besides, he wanted to see her in it.

"This is a mistake. You said you had purchased two dresses for me. This one is for someone else?" Her expression darkened as she questioned him.

Was that jealousy he saw? She had questioned him about women the night before. "I said two dresses suitable for a serving girl. The third is for the Harlot of Dundee to wear for her current provider, here and now."

Her eyes flickered with a myriad expressions, emotions that he could not accurately gauge. For a moment he thought she was unhappy with the purchase, then she sighed and held the dress up against herself, fingering the silk in awe. "'Tis too good for the likes of me."

Something about the way she handled the fabric made his cock harden. "It will not be too good later, when it is pushed up around your hips so that I may access your sweet puss."

He hadn't meant to say that aloud, and he hadn't meant to indulge his desire for her again. But there it was. Living in such close quarters, it was inevitable. She was a lusty wench with a fine appreciation of a good tumble.

"Mister Ramsay," she admonished playfully. But her eyes darkened and the corners of her mouth remained lifted. He wondered what went on in her mind at such times. If he had to put a wager on it, he would be unsure where his money was safest. With a rueful smile, he acknowledged that was part of the appeal.

"Look in the pocket," he suggested.

She pulled out the pretty trinket he had bought, a necklace. Nothing fancy, but it was set with a couple of blue stones that were of a similar color to the dress. Ideally, he would have had a craftsman work some of the exotic stones he had, but he had decided they might bring her unwelcome attention in the future.

Again there was much cooing and appreciation.

"You will find the appropriate undergarments to wear with the gown in my bundle. The seamstress and her assistant assured me that it was all in order and you would be able to adjust the items to fit."

Jessie darted to the table and untied the sack he had left there. A moment later she had retrieved a petticoat decorated with lace and a boned corset, which she examined at length.

"I've only ever had linen stays." She looked at him aghast. "How will I manage? Will you assist?"

Gregor's experience was limited to removing such items.

Besides, he knew that if he got his hands on her it might take all evening, for he would be easily distracted by her soft skin and the pleasure in her expression.

"I will call for the serving girl," he suggested, and went to the landing.

When Morag arrived the two women moved into his bedchamber, but left the door ajar. There was much whispering and laughter, which sounded good to his ears. It was not something he was used to hearing. He'd been aware that the two chattered when Morag came with food or to exchange the pails and washbowls. That was why he'd thought it was she who freed Jessie when he was away.

After a while he shifted his chair into the bedchamber so that he could watch them. It was almost sunset. The remaining light from the window beyond the women lit Jessie's outline as she arched most provocatively to allow Morag to tighten the corset, reminding him of a rather immoral illustration of a woman at her toilette that he had once seen and enjoyed. Except that this was real, and for his eyes alone.

A deep sense of pleasure kindled in him as he observed the feminine ritual. A sense of entitlement, too, and meshed with that was the knowledge that he had brought this about.

He could almost picture Jessie the mistress of her own home—a house not too grand, but with a fair patch of land, enough to provide security. A house he should have had by now, had it not been for that contemptible charlatan, Ivor Wallace—a man who made money out of others and affected grand airs. With effort Gregor excluded Wallace from the pleasant picture he was currently enjoying.

The corset was much admired by both women. Had Jessie ever had such a gift before? He doubted it, although she was a strange, mysterious woman. The more he thought he understood her…well, the more she took him by surprise.

The two of them strained and chuckled, intent on adjusting the luxurious undergarment. Every penny had been well spent, Gregor mused, as he watched Jessie's breasts surge up from the edge of the corset as it tightened. The dip between her breasts was shadowed and enticing, the two hillocks of flesh swelling in such a way that his hands itched to rove over them. His cock was hardening, but the sight alone was to be savored, and he aimed to temper his reaction, to string out each morsel of pleasure the situation might offer.

"Is it a pleasing sight, Gregor?" Jessie called out at that moment, as if she could tell where his thoughts had wandered.

"It is indeed most attractive." Gregor granted her a nod and a smile. He did not want her to fix on impressing him—she was devious enough in that respect already, and needed no further encouragement—but he could not deny her the compliment when she looked so radiant.

Morag had taken the blue dress and was lifting it over Jessie's head. When it fell into place, the maid moved around her, pulling it quickly into place. When the fastenings were done and Morag was applying her final tweaks to the delicate lace along the bosom, Jessie turned to face his way. Looking at him from beneath lowered eyelashes, she ran her hand along Morag's waist, stroking the other woman while Morag fussed over the neckline of the gown.

Gregor's curiosity sharpened. He'd presumed the dress would absorb her complete attention for some time, but she was definitely taunting him. Had she been watching him all along? He lifted one eyebrow, quizzing her.

She responded immediately, acknowledging their silent connection. A mischievous smile appeared, and then she took action. She wandered over to him as if parading the dress. When she got close, she dipped down and whispered, "You said you believed my powers of seduction were good this morning."

"Indeed."

"May I entertain you some more…in that respect?"

Curious as to her meaning, he nodded.

She paraded back to Morag, her hands on her hips as she surveyed the way the dress swung as she walked.

"It is beautiful, Miss Jessie," Morag said.

"It is." Arresting the buxom servant's face in her hands, she kissed her cheek. "Look, Morag, Mister Ramsay is enjoying the sight of us together."

Lord, but she is a vixen.

Nodding in his direction, she drew the other woman's attention to him. Morag gave a gruff chortle and her cheeks colored. She did not, however, blink or look away coyly, which fascinated him, for he'd assumed her a shy, pragmatic sort.

"In fact," Jessie added, in a seductive tone, "I am sure he would offer you a few coins to watch us together." Her glance sidled over to meet his, and there was a challenge in her eyes.

Now that was an interesting proposal, but once again she was taking liberties. Gregor's brows lifted. He should put her back in her place. However, his curiosity about her intentions and the thought of seeing the two of them "entertain him" were most enticing. He was already growing hard, and now his cock was straining the cloth of his breeches.

He wondered briefly if she was doing this because of what had passed between them the night before. Was she trying to impress him with her own abilities?

Aside from his state of arousal, the proposal intrigued him. How skilled was Jessie? He already knew how she could affect him, but if she was to infiltrate Ivor Wallace's manor house, it would be good to know she could charm anyone who might stand in her way. That seemed justification enough to let the two of them cavort.

"Together?" Morag quizzed. "Whatever do you mean, Miss Jessie?"

"Well now," she responded, her fingers teasing the other woman's hair, as if they were discussing nothing more than the latest fashion for one's tresses, "would you let me embrace you?"

How confident she was, Gregor noticed. The gown, perhaps.

Morag thought for a moment, her expression stoic. "I suppose so."

Jessie hummed aloud as if pleased, and stroked her hands around the outside of Morag's ample breasts. "And would you let me undress you?"

The maid didn't respond, but she had not run from the room in horror. In fact, her cheeks were rosier than before, and her eyes wide and fixed, as if she was enjoying Jessie's caresses immensely.

"Undressed?" she exclaimed as Jessie stroked her. "T'would be for him, Mister Ramsay, to look at me?"

"Aye."

Reaching into his pocket, Gregor pulled out some coins and rolled them in his palm, as if ready to count them. Morag's eyes widened with interest, and her body leaned instinctively into Jessie's touch.

"I suppose I might."

Jessie glanced his way and nodded at him. "I'm sure Mister Ramsay would also like to see me stroke your cunny while I kiss your breasts."

Gregor inhaled sharply. He waited for Morag's reaction. She was eyeing the coins in his hand and had wrapped her arms around Jessie—who was slighter than herself—as if holding her close for comfort.

Amused and fascinated at the turn of events, Gregor resisted a smile and counted out five coins. He stacked them on the edge of the table.

Both women craned their necks to count them.

He made a second pile, of equal height.

Jessie's eyes lit up. "Now that looks fair."

Morag nodded, and Jessie took the servant's hand and led her to the bed. As she walked, Jessie rested her free hand on her hip and glanced back at him. Her black hair tumbled over her shoulder and her eyes glowed beguilingly. In that moment Gregor knew he should never have doubted her ability to seduce anyone. She could win over the whole wide world, he was convinced. She was controlling the lassie easily, seductive yet subtle about it. Had she been having a jest at his expense, allowing him to tutor her in the manner of being coy? He shook off the notion. No, her more circumspect approach was the result of their time together. That she could be brazen was no surprise.

Jessie patted the bed. Morag sat down and then reclined on it. Standing beside the bed in such a way as to give him a clear view of everything, Jessie ran her fingers down Morag's neck and across the tops of her breasts, teasing her.

Morag chuckled.

She unlaced the serving girl's bodice and lifted her ample breasts free from her stays and shift. With a soft, seductive hum in her throat Jessie examined the bared globes, squeezing the soft flesh in her hands until Morag's nipples stuck out in hard nubs and she panted audibly.

When Jessie tugged on the nubs, Morag's feet moved restlessly against the mattress. "Oh, my, that does feel good."

"You like that?" She tugged again.

Morag nodded frantically. There was no doubting she was aroused.

Gregor shifted in his seat.

Jessie ducked down and sucked on one nipple, exposing her teeth as she did so. Gregor was riveted. He watched her run the sensitive nub against her teeth, and found he wanted to try that trick on her.

Morag cried out. She had pushed her head into the bolster, and her fingers gripped the blanket beneath her, clutching and releasing in time with Jessie's actions. "Lord. My paps."

She wriggled and wriggled and her skirt rode up. Then she stilled and gasped loudly, her body shuddering.

Jessie straightened, a proud smile on her face. Without any further ado, she tugged off her victim's hide shoes and then pulled her skirts and petticoats as far as her waist, tucking them tightly there so as to leave her lower body exposed.

Morag had on odd woolen stockings, and one had a rather large hole over the knee. Her legs were as sturdily built as the rest of her, and they rolled apart readily when Jessie walked her fingers up from ankle to thigh, once again humming under breath as she did so.

Gregor looked the serving girl over, but it was Jessie who persistently drew his attention. He marveled at her sensual, easy way with the other woman. She was fully aware of him the whole time, but it was not obvious. Just as she had been aware of him watching her when she'd pleasured herself that first morning. She was connected to him even while she teased and amused another person. Rightly so, he surmised. He was her employer, and this demonstration was exhibiting her talent and her value. The connection nonetheless kept his attention. It also initiated a longing in his loins to possess her. He found it increasingly difficult to deny himself frequent and lengthy access to her intimate places.

Jessie flashed her eyes at Morag when she stroked one finger in the furrow between her full lips. "Oho, you are a minx. You are quite wet already. I think you are enjoying this."

Morag chortled appreciatively. "I liked what you did to my paps. I will do that to meself later."

"Do you pleasure yourself often?" Jessie asked the question while she stroked her finger up and down the woman's glistening slit.

"I do. Every night, if I don't have a good man to satisfy me."

When Jessie paused and glanced his way, her look was so provocative that Gregor had to remind himself to stay seated, lest he miss the performance. He would never forgive himself for missing such a show, no matter how much he would prefer to stand up and drag Jessie aside to give her a good seeing-to. His hands itched to slap her rump until it was as pink as her cheeks, and she had surely earned it for that incendiary look she'd sent his way.

Jessie closed in on her victim. "Tell us what you do. Do you rub yourself?"

Morag rolled her head from side to side on the bolster. "Aye, I do. I do it all the time."

Jessie pushed a finger inside her hole. "Tell us all about it. We want to know."

Gregor gave a brief moment's pause to wonder if she played him this well, before allowing himself to be distracted by her ongoing antics.

Morag's head went back against the pillow, and she opened her mouth as if gasping for air. Clutching at the blanket with her fingers, she nodded. "I rub myself at night, rub it hard. Sometimes I do it up against the door handle in my room, imagining it's a man's...you know, his cock."

"The door handle," Jessie repeated, and glanced Gregor's

way again. Licking her lips, she lowered her gaze to the bulge in his breeches.

"Demoness," he hissed under his breath, for her benefit alone.

That only seemed to delight her. She returned her attention to her current victim. "Well now, the door handle. There's a trick I had not heard of. I must try it myself, perhaps when I'm locked up and alone in my room of an afternoon."

The image that filled Gregor's mind at that point was lewd to the point of obscenity. Three days now he had locked her in that room, and he would be unable to do so now without being haunted by the image of her lifting her skirts to press her mound against the door handle and use it well, in his absence. His cock was now so thoroughly distended it was growing painful.

Meanwhile, Morag continued with her explanation.

"The door rattles when I thump myself against it, right there at the end when I am dizzy with it." She emitted a gutsy laugh, and then gasped for breath as Jessie manipulated her fingers.

"Do that, aye, do that."

"But you did not know that your breasts were so sensitive, did you?"

"Oh, no, that was good." She slapped her hands over her own bared breasts, palms flat, then stirred the lolling mounds, moaning loudly as she did so.

Jessie plowed the serving girl's furrow, three fingers grouped like a man's phallus. Morag cried out, her feet lifting from the bed. Her hands left her breasts and grappled for the iron rail on the bedstead, holding tight for purchase as Jessie slid her fingers in and out of her wet hole. With her arms upright that way, the maid's breasts squeezed together. Jessie pinched one nipple with her free hand, while she rode her fingers in and out down below. Planting her thumb on the swollen nub, she nudged it back and forth.

It did not escape Gregor's notice that Jessie was rubbing herself up against the bed, one knee lifted to aid her as she pressed her hips to the edge of the mattress. At this point he had to place his feet wider to accommodate the size of his cock and ease the ache in his ballocks. What aroused him most of all was how she was affected by what she was doing. It was then he realized that he was more eager to know how wet she was than to imagine himself easing his cock into the wet hole of the other wench, the one so readily displayed.

Jessie had captured his attention fully, but that was no surprise. She was a sensualist of the highest order, more so than he ever would have guessed that first night—and more so than any woman he had ever encountered on his travels.

"Oh, my," Morag shouted.

Jessie had lowered her head and stuck out her tongue to tease the woman's nipple, turning her head in profile so that he could see it all. Gregor was so hard he was in pain. Was she trying to pleasure him or torture him?

Meanwhile Jessie thrust her fingers in and out ever faster. When Morag reached her peak, her feet lifted from the mattress and her arms grew rigid, her hands locked around the bedstead. He thought Jessie might climb into the bed with her, but with the deed done, she turned her attention to him.

Gregor's ballocks ached for release when she glanced at the front of his breeches. She gave an appreciative smile and met his stare. Her eyes were dark, her lips wet. He rested his hand briefly over his cock while they exchanged glances.

Within a heartbeat she'd left her place by the bed and stalked over to him, lifting her skirts as she did so, briefly displaying herself to him. Seeing the pale flesh of her thighs made his need to be between them desperate. The soft, dark hair that feathered over her intimate places only drew his attention to what it concealed.

He was about to shift and rise from the seat so he could touch her there, when she shook her head. She didn't have to say anything. He knew what she wanted, because she was staring down at his bulge, and her skirt remained half lifted in order to mount him. He opened his breeches.

As soon as his cock bounced free she sighed.

Momentarily he considered that her talent might be his undoing. It would be easy to allow himself to be thoroughly distracted by this. Mad things he'd done in the few days he'd known her. He'd rescued a condemned woman and dallied in the jail for some of this.

"You enjoyed what you saw?"

"Perhaps." He gestured with his hand, eager for her to lift her skirts again. "Show me more and I will decide."

She pulled her skirts up as far as her waist, revealing herself fully to him.

For a moment Gregor could only stare. The soft, feminine curves of her body made him want to keep her naked so that he could observe her that way all the time. The place where thigh melted into hip made him eager to run his fingers along that line and claim it. The plump cushion of her mound was an invitation to invade her sweet puss. The delicate brush of hair that fanned out from her glistening slit made him harder still. He forced his gaze back to hers.

Her eyes glittered and she nodded down at his erection. "I think you have decided you like what you see?"

Still she made mischief. He was used to being obeyed, and she should be eager to please, and yet she taunted him. "Are you suggesting you made me pay for a tease?"

"Why no, I was merely making certain you were pleased.

I assure you I am eager to ride a good cock, and that is what I see before me."

Oh, yes, she surely did know how to play him, and now his need was so great his patience had gone. "You know it is true, now carry on. I believe you were about to demonstrate how much you needed to ride a good cock."

"Demanding now. Tsk. And there I was thinking you wanted me for another man."

Gregor snatched at her wrist. "Right now you will mount *me,* or our agreement will not stand."

Jessie smiled, and her eyes were bright with lust and with victory. "Our agreement, the one you have invested so much in already...you would cast it aside for the want of a tumble?"

He gritted his teeth and gestured for her to approach.

She made her skirts swish and sway, eyeing his cock all the while. "Let me warm your bed again tonight and I will make you come as you never have before."

"Cheeky wench, you are in no position to make demands."

"I believe I am." Straddling him, she climbed over his knees, her thighs spread. With one hand she captured her skirts at her waist and with the other opened up the lips of her puss. It was succulent as a ripe peach, swollen and damp with her juices.

Morag had shifted and was watching, agog. When Gregor caught her eye she sat bolt upright. "Pardon me, but should I leave you now?"

Before he replied, Gregor moved his hand to Jessie's crotch, easing two fingers inside her, his thumb resting over her swollen nub.

Jessie gasped, her eyes closing for a moment while her puss clamped hard on his fingers.

His cock jerked. "That, my dear," he said, in answer to

the serving girl's question, "is entirely up to you. This will happen either way, so if you do not want to see it, leave."

Jessie glanced over her shoulder at Morag and laughed softly. With her hand on his shaft she directed it to her and eased his crown into her hole, grasping it tightly enough to make him stamp his foot.

Pausing, she smiled and then lowered herself onto it, taking a portion of him inside her and squeezing it, as if to drive him to distraction.

The hot, damp clasp of her body on his aching cock was both pleasure and torture, and she knew it. "More," he instructed. "I need more."

Arching her neck, she sighed aloud and took him deep.

A groan escaped him when she sheathed him to the hilt. The succulent grip of her cunny on his cock made him grateful to be alive. That was not a familiar feeling, and he wrapped his hands around her bottom beneath the skirts of the special gown he had picked out for her, squeezing the soft, rounded flesh of her buttocks each time she rode his length.

She shifted one hand and pushed her fingers into his hair, clasping him around the back of his head as she rode him. Her moves were as agile as a dancer's and she took everything he had to give. "Am I good enough to seduce your enemy?"

"Good enough to seduce the king himself, I warrant." Gregor dug his fingers hard into her backside.

She cried out when he gripped her, and rolled her hips forward, which bowed his cock inside her.

"Hellfire." The rhythm of her body and the slippery, hot embrace around his shaft made him exhale loudly. "Now I know why they call you the Harlot."

Throwing back her head, she laughed joyously. "I'm not ashamed of enjoying this."

"I noticed. Your skills are exceptional. You could seduce

anyone you desired." Instinctively, he reached one hand to cup her face and hold her.

"Aye. Probably I could." She turned her cheek toward his hand and kissed his palm. "But I wanted you and I could see you watching, and all the while my desire for this grew fiercer."

Her eyes glittered, and for a brief moment he knew that she had him—he could so easily become addicted to this. Fighting it, he glanced away toward the woman on the bed, who now lolled on her front, watching them while she sucked on her fingers.

His hands tightened on Jessie's bottom and his lower back thudded intensely.

"Ride me hard," he instructed, desperate for the release.

Gripping the chair back, she rode him vigorously, her breasts swelling from the edge of her gown, her hair tumbling down her shoulders. Her cunny tightened.

His balls throbbed and fire shot the length of his spine.

"I wanted to do this most of all," she whispered, and then cried out. The grip of her puss on him grew rhythmic and tight at her peak.

That undid him, and he urged her to break free so that he might spill elsewhere. He barely made it, and it was with regret that Gregor came in her hand instead of her sweet puss.

chapter Thirteen

That night Gregor was awake and looking at Jessie when the nightmares began. After Morag had gone, they'd shared a bottle of wine that he procured from belowstairs, and then conversed into the night about Morag's stoic yet brazen ways. Once again, Jessie had startled him. He'd discovered that she was observant to a fault. It was no bad thing, for he wanted her to observe his enemy, above all.

As the passage of the moon across the sky bathed the room in light and shadow, he watched her sleep, admiring her. In repose she could pass for a Madonna, a classical statue of great worth. With decent food and clothing she was an unquestionable beauty. Any man with half his faculties would find her bewitching. And yet Gregor missed the ribald character that usually lit that face, the unique traits and wild-eyed glances that made her the bawdy wench who had caught his attention.

Wryly, he attempted to address the fact that he had grown so curious about her. How had that happened? She was meant to be a cipher, no more. For many years no one had even entered into his thoughts this way. He preferred it like that. Thinking only of avenging his father's tragic end and securing his land, Gregor had moved through the most exotic places in this world with little thought of women and companionship.

Was it because he was so near his home that he had started to feel again, or was it Jessie who had broken the pattern?

He was addressing the conundrum when her head went back against the bolster and a low, pained cry came from her mouth. Gregor lifted himself onto his elbow and was about to wake her when she spoke.

Her eyelids flickered but did not open. "No," she cried. *"Màthair."*

Gregor was surprised. She was calling for her mother in the Gaelic tongue. Was she a Highlander? More to the point, she had not mentioned any family, and it made his curiosity grow. Would she say more?

Sweat had broken out on her forehead and her breathing was labored. Her limbs moved restlessly in the bed. She was obviously in great distress.

Gregor could not bear it.

Kissing her cheek, he whispered her name, calling to her gently, willing her to wake easily and not carry the bad dreams with her. "Jessie, wake up. Come now, you are here with me at the inn. You are safe."

Her eyes flickered open and her hand moved to cover her mouth, but not before she cried out again. Her eyes were wide and troubled, and when they locked on him, he drew her into his arms.

Her hands opened and closed on his shoulders, needy and fretful. "Gregor, hold me."

"What is it that troubles you so?"

She stilled and then shivered.

Silently cursing himself for asking, he drew back and lifted her chin with one finger. He needed to view her face.

He didn't expect the sheer terror he found in her eyes. She did not seem to see him at first, but looked beyond, as if at some other thing that disturbed her. "Jessie?"

Although her eyes showed recognition in response to his voice, she buried her head in the curve of his neck as if not wanting to see more. "I cannot say. You would scorn me if you knew."

"No. Never. Hush now, Jessie. Come closer, my wild little creature, come closer."

Her hand fisted against his bare shoulder. "You promise you would think no worse of me than you already do?"

"I do not think badly of you."

"But I am a whore." The great regret in her voice made him want to calm her more than ever.

"And I have been a thief and some would say a blackguard, in order to survive. I have lied and cheated, and pretended to be what I am not, in order to get ahead. I did not plan for it to be so. It was not the way I was brought up, but life sometimes takes choices away from us."

He shifted, lifting her chin again so that she had to meet his gaze. "Neither of us are holy souls, my dear. I think we understand each other well on that account."

For the longest moment she stared into his eyes, with raw emotion in her expression. Then she nodded. "When I was a wee bairn, my mother was put to death. I saw it all. They made me watch."

"They?"

"The villagers, the people who condemned her." Jessie took a deep breath. "We had come south from the Highlands, because my mother wanted to find my father. He'd run off when she fell pregnant a second time. But when we came to the Lowlands she never found him. Instead, she found her end. Stoned, hanged and burned."

"It was a charge of witchcraft?"

Jessie nodded.

Gregor's mind ticked over fast. "That woman in Dundee,

Eliza. Did she know what had happened to your mother? Is
that why it was easy for her to accuse you of the same crime?"

It explained it well enough.

Jessie did not respond for a moment, and then gave a slight
nod. "Perhaps that was the reason."

In a few moments he had learned much about her. He
rubbed her back. "And you are a Highlander by birth?"

It explained the Gaelic tongue, but he could not help being
surprised.

She shot him a glance. "That information was not meant
to offer you the chance to mock me."

He wrapped his hand around the curve of her bottom and
nudged her closer. "I was not mocking, merely surprised.
You have an uncanny knack that way." He placed a kiss on
her bare shoulder. "You surprise me every day."

When he met her gaze, he saw her spirits lift, and she almost smiled. "Aye, well, yes, I'm a Highlander by birth, and
I remember it still." She looked wistful. "When I have my
purse, I intend to go there."

"You do?"

She nodded. "They do not persecute people for their beliefs in the Highlands."

It made sense for her to leave and head north.

She stared at him thoughtfully. "You do not charge me
with witchcraft, Gregor Ramsay."

He laughed softly. "I have seen no evidence of it."

It made him think on it, however. However wrongly
given, the accusation that she had been charged with would
follow her if she remained anywhere close to Dundee. In
time, perhaps, she would be able to return, but it was for the
best that she leave soon.

She glanced wistfully toward the moonlit window.

He traced his finger across her lips. "You're a strange one, though."

She looked up into his eyes. "You do not shun me?"

"Why would I? You have given me no reason to do so." He cupped her breast and ran his thumb over her nipple. "You are far from being an ordinary woman, for I have never known one quite as lusty and shameless as you, but that is why I wanted you." He was about to mention the task, and thought better of it because of the tender look in her eyes.

She sighed and gave a faltering smile.

Then she wriggled onto her side, looped one hand around his neck and pressed herself to him. His cock had been at half-mast because she was warm and naked against him, and it reared up expectantly when she moved closer and pressed her breasts to his chest.

"You are recovering?"

She nodded, lifted one knee and brushed it along his thigh invitingly. "Fill me, Gregor. Push the bad dreams away."

What man could resist?

Mounting her, he eased his cock inside her hot channel.

Moving slowly back and forth, he worked his way to her deepest point. The sleek, tight clasp of her body on his length made him pause. He stared down at her, looking deep into her eyes. They glinted in the moonlight and seemed strangely lit, as if from inside.

When she noticed him studying her, she lowered her eyelids.

She was vulnerable, he realized, from her nightmare.

Gregor eased back and forth slowly, taking his time with the act, fascinated by the way each thrust was reflected in her expression. Her lips moved, her breath rasping. Her eyelids flickered and a soft cry issued from her throat each time he bedded the head of his cock at her center.

"Look at me," he encouraged.

It took a moment before she did. She swallowed and drew a deep breath, then met his gaze. Her breath hitched, and her eyes shone with withheld tears.

He held her gaze while he rode her.

Making it last as long as he could, Gregor thrust slowly and easily until neither of them could fight the release any longer and they both shattered. Then she clutched at him gratefully, whispering his name, and he rolled free and drew her into his arms, tucking her against him for sleep.

chapter Fourteen

Gregor let her slumber on the following morning because her sleep had been so fitful. He rose quietly and prepared for the day ahead. When she stirred and sat up, she held the blanket to her chest and peered at him with sleep-heavy eyes.

He strolled over to her. "I will ask the alewife to send up some breakfast for you. When you are dressed, come downstairs and we'll be on our way."

He reached out and caressed her cheek.

She nodded, and then covered his hand where it rested against her soft skin.

"I have things to attend to," he said as he drew away and reached for his hat. The truth was he needed to clear his head.

He had slept even less than she did. He'd watched over her, concerned that the nightmares would return again. Then he'd wondered why he was doing such a thing. It had taken several more hours for his muddled reasoning to subside and his thoughts to alight on Balfour Hall and its owner. That was what he was supposed to be thinking about. Jessie was taking his attention away from that goal. The *Libertas* would return in less than six months and everything had to be in place for that moment. They had to move forward.

Once he was outside he took a deep breath and headed

to the stables. The morning was fair, which boded well for their journey.

When Jessie appeared, she was wearing the pale gray dress he had purchased for her, and had her shawl tightly knotted over her bosom. Her hair was neatly secured and her face seemed freshly scrubbed. She looked rather pale, as if being indoors for so long had not served her well.

Why did that make him feel guilty and concerned for her? Why was it that he'd rather have her unruly and passionate, with high color in her cheeks and her hair tumbling down over her bare breasts?

Lust, that's why.

Sure enough, it could drive a man to madness. He had never experienced it this intensely before. Rubbing his head, he doubted his sanity for a moment. For eleven years he'd concentrated on earning good coin in order to come back his own man, a man capable of buying land and seeking retribution for his father. Gregor had taken women here and there, of course, but never had he enjoyed…what? What was this? It was something quite apart from the desire between them, the hearty nature of their fornication. Companionship, he supposed.

As she approached him, he noticed that she looked upon the two horses with a troubled expression. Pushing the lingering thoughts of intimacy from his mind, he recalled the way she'd acted that first day when he'd had her mount the horse behind him. She'd clung to him like a limpet for the entire journey. At the time he'd dismissed it and assumed she was trying to work her female charms on him. Now he wasn't sure that was the case.

Remembering how she had been when he teased her, he vowed to handle her with as much caution as he could. Their recent discussions had been fraught enough. He was not sure how much more revelation he could take, and he needed his faculties clear when they got to Craigduff.

He nodded at the horses. "We will travel quicker with two mounts."

Her hands knotted together, unraveled and then knotted again against the front of her skirt, yet she forced herself to nod in response to his statement. Then she glanced at him and away, her gaze flitting about as if she was planning something. He had become familiar with that particular habit. What was she up to? Was it horses she disliked? Was she unwilling to mount?

The stable boy lingered to assist.

"This one is meant for me?" She pointed at the smaller of the two, a tan-colored mare.

Gregor nodded.

The horse lifted its nose, scenting the air as she approached it. She ran her hand over it. "Hello, my beauty."

Then, in a much lower voice, she spoke in what sounded to his ear like Pictish. Intrigued, Gregor watched. He had already heard her speak a few Gaelic words, and apparently she knew some Pictish, an ancient Scottish tongue, too. One of his seamen, Jacob Carr, would lapse into the language when he had too much rum, a habit he swore was passed down from father to son in his family. What Jessie murmured to the horse sounded to be of similar origins.

The horse nuzzled her uplifted hand.

"It is a beautiful morning. Just look at the view," she commented. She gestured at the hillside. He looked in the direction she pointed, scoured the pigpen at the edge of grounds and the tufted hills on the horizon, but saw nothing as compelling as she seemed to indicate.

When he looked back at her, he found her attention was once more on her mount. The beast had lowered its head in submission, and she rested her forehead on its mane. Her eyes were shut. Gregor watched, bemused, as her lips moved as if in a silent prayer. When she opened them they seemed more vital, bluer than ever before, and strangely vivid.

Even as he noticed it, the effect was gone.

For the first time, his mind flitted back to that night at the inn when he had first seen her, and the accusations that were made while they waited for the bailie to appear. Someone had declared they had seen a strange look in her eyes.

A feeling of unease crept over him while he watched her, and he thought about what had been shouted about her that first night in Dundee. Now he knew about her mother, too. He rubbed at his jaw, and then rapidly shrugged off the notion. Once again his thoughts were wandering.

Jessie was smiling his way, and that made it easier to ignore the accusations that had surfaced in his memory.

"Does the horse meet with your approval?"

"She's a beautiful creature. I know we will fare well together." With that she marched alongside the horse, and with the help of the stable boy, mounted.

Gregor noted she sat astride, but did not question it.

When Jessie noticed, she shrugged. "I feel more comfortable riding this way."

Once again Gregor had the feeling that she had never ridden a horse before, but now that she was mounted and they were on their way, he was not about to confront her about it. They had reached a fair level of compromise, and he wished only to move forward.

Mounting, he lifted the reins and urged his horse on.

Behind him, he heard Jessie making encouraging noises, then a slapping sound. A moment later her horse galloped past his. When she reached him she was laughing in delight, one hand on the pommel of her saddle, the other on the mane of the animal. She was being jolted along at a rapid and most dangerous rate, and she did not seem to be holding the reins. How could she possibly be in control of the horse?

Concern flooded him. He hastened after her, convinced that she was pretending she could ride to please him, and that she was about to fall and injure herself. However, he soon saw that her shapely bottom was still firmly seated in the saddle. He could not fathom how she did not fall off.

Gregor urged his mount to a gallop to keep up with her and to lead the way. He had not planned to cover the distance at quite such a pace, but if that suited her, that is how they would undertake it.

"Gregor, it is glorious," she called out at one point. She said it with pure delight as she peered out across the rolling landscape of Fife.

"It is." An odd sense of pride rooted in him, even though he currently had no claim on the land she was admiring.

Once they neared Ivor Wallace's stronghold, Balfour Hall, however, Gregor found his own mood descending. One look at the rooftops of the manor house and the urge to march in there and flatten Ivor Wallace stirred in his blood. He'd thought that reaction long gone, and he quelled it, knowing that there was a better way to go about things.

He pointed at the rooftops in the distance. "That is the place."

Jessie frowned. "You do not intend for us to ride up to the door, in order to show me it?"

"No, here is where we leave the lane." He gestured off the worn dirt track and up into the woods that flanked the manor house on the far side. Beyond that was the path to his old homestead, and he'd often played in those woods as a child. He knew them well. Taking her reins, he led her horse, keeping it close alongside his own.

Once they were off the lane and the land rose away from the house, he indicated the forest atop the hill. "We will be able to rest the horses up there in the woods. It is a good vantage point. It is well above the house but the trees will give us good cover."

When he pointed things out to her, she looked and nodded. But he noticed that when he fell quiet, it was the forest that attracted her attention. As they began to wend their way through the trees, under the canopy of summer leaves, she became most excited, glancing about happily.

"It is beautiful here, Gregor."

"It is, especially so in summer." He smiled. "I played here as a young lad."

She peered at him as if trying to picture it, and chuckled to herself.

When he drew up the horses and indicated that she should dismount, she scrambled free of the horse, dropping to the ground with a big show and much grumbling. Gregor shook his head. There was definitely something about horses that unsettled her, and yet she had seemed amenable to the beast when she'd mounted it. When he turned back, however, it was to the sight of her running off between the trees, touching the bark of each she passed as she went. Bemused, Gregor watched her strange antics.

She danced from tree to tree, her hands pressed to the bark, looking around eagerly. In the long grass, she took to examining the brambles around her, pushing them between her fingers and inhaling the scent. Gregor found himself entranced when she began to twirl under the canopy of branches, arms outstretched.

Eventually she drew to a halt and let her head drop back. She seemed to be breathing the place in. "Ah, 'tis grand."

Gregor wondered at her strange behavior, but her joy forbade him from questioning it. Once she seemed more settled, and smiled his way, indicating that she had recalled his presence, he headed over to her. "Come, if we skirt the edge of the woods, I will be able to point out the details of the house to you so that you will be prepared."

She nodded and took his hand, but still trailed the fingers of her free hand through the buds and dangling foliage as they passed. "Foxgloves," she declared, pointing over in delight. "And just look at the hawthorn and the ferns!"

Gregor looked where she pointed and then smiled at her, wondering about her again. At the brow of the hill, and with the forest at their back, he nodded ahead. "We are safe to observe from here. The trees give good cover. We are now at the rear of the building."

Jessie peered down, agog. "It is a grand place. Is your enemy a laird?"

Gregor frowned. "A bonnet laird, no more."

"What is that, a bonnet laird?"

"He craves the title and the power, but in truth he does little more than farm his own plot, for he is selfish and cannot win the respect or the loyalty of tenants."

Jessie watched him closely while he spoke, and he noticed that the look in her eyes seemed uncannily keen and assessing. Eventually she nodded and pointed down at the building.

"That is the servant's entrance that you marked on the drawing, yes?"

"It is." He quickly indicated the stables and outhouses.

She studied the building at length, and while she did so Gregor watched her covertly. She was keen and eager, and that pleased him. Nevertheless, doubts had begun to circle in his mind about whether it was the right thing to do. Why? He was about to address the question when she turned to him decisively.

"I will go down there and find my way around."

Startled, Gregor shook his head. "No. If you are seen lurking there you will not be able to go back and ask for work."

"They will not see me, and if I go down there now I can easily make sure there will be too much work for them to manage. I will be able to secure a position in the house before the week is out."

She seemed quite serious, and she stared down at Balfour Hall with determination.

Gregor's thoughts clouded. It was too soon. He hadn't intended for her to approach the house, not today. The eager expression on her face concerned him. *She wants to be on her way and done with this,* he realized.

Unable to help himself, he reacted. He grabbed her into his arms and ran his fingers along the edge of her dress, where her bosom swelled so enticingly. "They will not see you? How will you manage that?"

"Trust me, I will see to it."

"You will turn their heads." She had turned his.

"Is that not why you employed me?" Her eyes sparkled.

"It is." He couldn't keep the rueful note from his voice. His cock hardened and he pulled her against him so that she would feel it.

She lifted her head. "You are not having second thoughts about my ability to do the task, I hope?"

After she spoke, she pressed against him, assuring him she was aware of his stiffening rod. He was about to respond when she danced from his grasp.

With a soft chuckle, she nodded his way. "For a moment there I thought you were about to sacrifice your cause for the sake of your own pleasure."

He reached out to hold her a moment longer, but she hurried off.

"I won't be gone long," she called back. "Wait for me here."

He stepped out from the cover of the trees, but paused. Whatever happened, he could not afford to be seen there, not now. Studying her outline, he glowered after her, fretful that she might be discovered.

A few minutes later she disappeared from view. Much like with her mount, she had a way of taking over *his* reins, nudging *him* off course. What if she was seen? She was not fully prepared. She looked far too…womanly today.

Gregor paced up and down between the trees.

His mood became darker and more unsettled the longer she was away. That was not good. He would have to leave her for several days, if she managed to find employment there. *It is only because I am not prepared.*

Desire kept nudging into his thoughts, making a mockery of his intentions. Jessie's womanly wiles had got the better of him. *She's a whore,* he reminded himself, trying desperately to force his thoughts onto the grand plan he had been building these past eleven years.

After what seemed far too long, he saw her wending her way back to him, hiking up the hill toward the woods. Never had he met a woman more sturdy and determined. Yet it was that very thing that also made her headstrong and wild, difficult to manage and rebellious. How easily she had broken free of him. At the present moment, they were attuned in purpose. With her, that could change at any moment.

Drawing to a halt before him, she put her hands on her hips, panting and puffing from her climb. Those blue eyes of hers were gleaming like gems. Her chest rose and fell, her breasts swelling enticingly from her bodice, the color in her cheeks high. What had she done down there?

After she caught her breath, she locked eyes with him. "What is his name?"

Was it time to trust her with more details? She would have to know soon enough. "Ivor Wallace."

She considered Gregor at length. "Tell me what he did to you. I want to know."

Curses. It was the last thing he expected her to say. Women had to know everything. It did not suit him to share more than he already had. He shook his head. "No. I cannot explain."

"You must, Gregor. I need to know." She stepped closer. "I need to feel your anger and your fire in order to help you with this."

He studied her and found her expression serious—serious and sharp, as sharp as he had known she would be that first night. For all her mischief, her disobedience and the bawdy games, there was much to Jessie Taskill. In that moment he knew that he had only begun to explore the deeper parts of her, the parts she did not show to everyone. Why did he want to be the one to discover every secret she held?

"I *want* to help you with this." With one hand she reached out to touch him, wrapping her fingers around his upper arm through his frock coat, squeezing him as if encouraging him. "I've been down there and it will be easy for me to return and gain entry, but you must help me determine my true cause—your cause. I am bonded with you, and I can take your fire and use it."

That statement was delivered as if it was a simple fact, and yet it carried so much meaning, more weight than she perhaps knew.

With a rueful smile, he drew her closer to him with his hands around her back. "The heavy purse I offered you is not enough of a motive?"

She lifted her shoulders in a shrug and rested her hands on his chest, looking up at him most earnestly. "It is enough, of course it is." A frown gathered her slender eyebrows together. "How can I explain?"

She glanced away and then back, and he could tell she was thinking hastily. This was important to her. He stayed quiet, allowing her to find her way.

"I can take the purse, just as I can bed a man and take his money. But if that man causes me to desire him…" She walked her fingertips up to his collarbone, then pinched his chin and widened her eyes at him. "I can enjoy it, and thus make more of it for us both." She chuckled, pleased with her point of comparison. "And then, of course, I'd take his purse for what I am owed."

Gregor moved his hands to her waist, which he clasped possessively. Amused, he shook his head. How easily she could distract him. "I find that your explanation clouds my judgment."

His lust was rising, and he was fast forgetting his cause. "I take your comments as an indication that you enjoy what we have had together?"

She nodded.

"In that case it is more of this mutual pleasure that fills my head now."

Jessie slapped her hand against his arm. "Oh, hush now. You know that much is true, or you'd be a fool not to."

She paused a moment and eyed him up and down. "Now, tell me what went on that has driven you to this. It will help me. Please. I told you my sorry tale, and you accepted me into your arms still. It cannot be any worse than that, and even if it was, I need to know."

Did she need to know? Perhaps she did.

Unbidden emotions knifed through him.

Could he put it into words? He did not want to share his grief with her. Yet she had hit upon a truth. He needed to face what had happened. He needed to feel it again, in order to press on with this. Lately he had felt his purpose falter, as if he had been distracted from it by the elements of the task itself.

Yes, it would do him good to remember, to feel the anger once more. He looked down into her eyes, and there was such an earnest appeal in them that he grabbed her against him and kissed her forehead, then gazed over her head toward the place beyond the forest, the valley where Strathbahn lay.

"I'll show you," he responded gruffly, and before she had a chance to respond, he grasped her hand and led her back to where they had left the horses.

chapter Fifteen

Gregor fell silent as they rode onward.

Jessie respected that, remaining quiet despite the vast number of questions that popped into her head. All the while she observed him in sidelong glances. He remained inscrutable. It unnerved her. Moments before they had been together in thought and goal—hand in glove, and twice as intimate. Now that he had agreed to reveal more of his motives, it was as if he had set her apart from him.

She could explain that to herself easily enough. He was taking her away from his enemy's stronghold so that he could tell her what had happened without that looming manor house intruding on their discussion. She could understand that. It was not a happy home. That knowledge she'd gleaned quickly during her hasty foray around its boundaries.

Cautiously, she had circled Balfour Hall, studying the make and mood of the place and observing its many doors and windows from the bushes and shrubs in the fancy gardens. It was easy enough to see what went on where, with the drawing Gregor had made for her lodged in her memory. At each hidden observation point she created a spell, marking the spot by drawing a cross in the dirt with a stick.

"Bheir mi-gniomh dhan taigh seo," she'd whispered, draw-

ing chaos to the places she had marked. When anyone passed those signs in the dirt, trouble would break out within the household.

Each time she laid the spells she was increasingly awed at the growing strength of her magic. The places she had marked glowed, intense heat coming from them as she whispered her enchantments. Instinctively, she knew that it was because of her involvement with Gregor. The bond she felt with him and the pleasurable tumbles they had shared fed her ability. Every day that passed she noticed the change.

The knowledge made her more confident, and she took pride in her work. She had been thorough and had woven a web of such spells all the way around the building. Soon enough, they would need extra hands to manage the house, and then she would arrive on the doorstep, readied by Gregor for her task.

Balfour Hall was a grand place, grander than any she had ever been inside. But its walls were laden with its unhappy history and the legacy of tormented souls within. She did not relish the thought of abiding there, and that, above all, was why she needed to know Gregor's reasons for this task.

Jessie wanted to feel what he felt on the matter. For that, he apparently needed to take her beyond the forest. He was not happy about it, but he had agreed. As soon as they were out from beneath the soothing cover of the canopy his mood turned dark. She sensed that even without speaking to him. He had been unsettled when she returned from the manor house, and now it was as if any shred of good humor had vanished. It was to be expected, for she already knew his reasons were deep, complex, and obscured by fancy talk of business and retribution.

The hills rolled out before them, lush and green in the summer sunlight. The landscape was unbroken by either lane or passerby, and Jessie noticed that the grass was greener than any she had ever seen. It lured her, and she felt the urge to stop her horse and dismount, to roll on the ground and absorb the glory of nature into her body. It was only the fact that she knew Gregor would not approve—especially in his current disgruntled mood—that she resisted. There would be other times.

Here and there they passed stone boundaries and clusters of sheep. Gregor glowered at the poor creatures, as if they were his enemy.

Eventually they came within sight of a tumbledown farmhouse and outbuildings—a shell of a house nestled in the pretty valley. Jessie was about to comment on it when she noticed the set of his mouth.

More than that, it was the pain in his eyes that struck her. Her chest tightened.

This was the place he was bringing her to.

Peering at the remaining stones, she could see that the house had been uninhabited for many years. The door frame was charred as if by fire, and the roof was stripped bare. The patch of land that had once been a garden was barren.

"What is this place?"

He continued to stare over at the sparse wreckage for several long moments before he replied. "Strathbahn. My home."

She looked at it again, then back at him. This was going to be difficult. His reluctance to speak had grown along the way. Now misery and fury marked his expression in equal measures. Jessie was beginning to feel the true depth of his need for revenge.

The horses wandered the last few feet, and when Gregor dismounted, she followed. He did not even stop to secure the animals, and she hurriedly gathered their reins and tethered them to a post at the boundary wall of the old farmhouse.

It was as if the place called to him now, and he walked as if drawn by a rope. She hurried after him. By the time she caught up, he had ducked his head and gone through the doorway.

Inside, the place was just as desolate and uncared for, with weeds growing through the walls and dried bracken in the corners where it had been blown in windy weather. Two remaining beams overhead showed signs of fire, the charred logs stretched precariously across the open space. Gregor stood staring fixedly at the hearth, or what remained of it.

Jessie picked her way carefully across the rubble. "You lived here with your mother?"

He shook his head. "The cough took her from us when I was four years of age. Agatha was her name. My father used to take me to visit her grave every Sunday after the service. Aside from that I scarcely remember her. However," he added bitterly, "I'm glad that she did not survive to witness what happened to us."

The bitterness he felt seemed to give him some strength. He forced his head up and she noticed he glared at the charred beams with hatred. His handsome mouth was tightly shut, his eyes narrowed as he stared at the place. Had his enemy done this? Had Ivor Wallace burned down their home?

"It was my father who brought me up."

Jessie could feel the depth of his emotion, the pain and sorrow that swelled within him, filling the broken-down house with bad feeling. "Your father?"

"Yes. Hugh Ramsay was his name. He was a good man, and he brought me up well, teaching me everything he knew. But sometimes good people are vulnerable, because they are kind and try to help others."

Jessie could scarcely breathe. His words and the tense set

of his shoulders boded badly, and she feared she had done the wrong thing, forcing him to explain.

"This land had been owned and worked by our line for three generations. Every day he told me that he worked it so that I could be proud of it, as he was. Then, one day, he stopped saying that."

"I was eighteen or so when I realized that he was worried." Gregor continued to speak, but it took effort and he spoke slowly. "The best of our cattle died, you see. He did not tell me until much later that they had been poisoned."

Gregor paused. Jessie realized how hard that must have been.

"I worked the land with him, but he kept secret how badly he was suffering. At first he was forced to sell Wallace part of the far fields. That's what he really wanted, the land. Wallace's goal was to own the whole area, and he would turn people out of their homes if he had to. Bad deeds were done at his hands."

Gregor had wandered closer to the hearth and put his hand on the stone mantel above it. "His methods to obtain the land of others were underhanded. He destroyed crops and stole cattle. Then Wallace would come in like a benevolent neighbor and offer coin where it was needed. We were not the first, but with my father he was particularly cruel, for they had been friends once."

"When he forced Da to sign over the remaining land and our home, he told him that he had arranged the whole pitiful downfall. Laughed in his face, he did."

Jessie ached for Gregor. She went to reach out to him, but it was as if she was not there. His reflections had taken him back to that time, far away from her.

"My father could not live with the shame. Nor could he face me. He'd lost all we had to Wallace. I came home from

Craigduff that night and it was all over. He left me a letter, explaining what had happened, and he left me an apology for letting Wallace ruin our lot." Gregor lifted his hand, pointing to a burned beam overhead. "I found him here." His voice had dropped, scarcely above a whisper. "He'd hanged himself."

"Oh, Gregor, no." Jessie reeled with shock.

It was as if a veil had been lifted, and now she could understand him—and understand him she did. This was what had driven him to make enough of a fortune to come back here and seek his revenge. As a bairn she had not been able to be strong for her mother, and she could see that Gregor carried a similar burden, only his was much greater. She'd been a helpless child when her mother was put to death. He'd been older and perhaps could have helped, had he known. She stared at the charred beam, imagining how he might have felt, seeing his beloved father hanging there.

"I thought perhaps your enemy had torched the place," she murmured.

"No. I did." His voice had turned to ice. Steely determination shone in his eyes.

A dark tremor ran through her.

"After I buried him, I came back here and set fire to the place. I decided that if Wallace wanted it, he would not have it the way we'd left it." He shrugged. "It was not until years later that I realized he did not care for the house. He didn't use it or offer it to tenants. It was all about power to him."

"The more land he had to his name, the higher his position in life?"

Gregor nodded, but still did not look her way.

Jessie's heart ached for him, and her belly churned as she felt all his grief. Beyond that, she saw all too clearly what it had done to him, how the anger had controlled his life. He needed this to be over, to gain retribution so that he could truly bury his father.

It was as if he was back there; she could see that in his eyes. As if he was the one who had to let down his father's corpse. She saw him there with his father's crumpled body on the floor at his feet, grief blinding him, the loss building into something that would take him many years to control, to understand and to vow to revenge. Would the revenge he sought ever be enough to heal those wounds? she wondered.

Jessie had grown fond of him, and it was in her nature to reach out to those who were suffering, even though that often brought trouble her way. *I will help him with this. I will make it right.*

"Gregor." She squeezed his arm.

Turning to face her, he stared at her vaguely at first, as if he did not recognize her. When he finally focused on her, his eyes narrowed. "Are you happy, now that you know?"

He was angry.

Jessie peered up at him with deep concern. "I had to understand your quest for vengeance. I have thought of such things myself, often, after what happened to my mother. The truth of the matter is that revenge on your enemy will not change history."

That was quite clearly not something he wanted to hear, for he glowered at her. Jessie had not faced a challenge such as this, not ever. She reached for his arm again, eager to calm his thoughts and comfort him.

"You wanted to know," he muttered, and jerked his arm away. "Now you can do what you promised you would do. Gain his ear, inform me what land he is selling and I will buy it. This will be over once I claim back what is ours."

It was as if a door had been slammed in her face.

"Gregor, wait."

But he turned away from her, walked out of the house and strode rapidly across the walled area to his horse, mounting quickly and slapping the beast on the rear. Jessie watched in dismay as the horse galloped off, back in the direction from which they had come. Grabbing her skirts in her hands, she followed, cursing herself for having quizzed him. He had not wanted to come here, and yet she had to know, even though it had put him in a foul mood. And now she had to get back on her own mount without assistance.

Flustered, she tried to repeat the enchantment she'd made earlier, the one that kept her rear end in the saddle, whatever happened. It was the only way she could bring herself to ride, so great was her fear of falling. She knew that for most people the distance to the ground was pitiful, but for her it took her back to an unhappy moment. The moment when she had been forced to stand on a stone wall outside the village kirk and watch her mother be put to death.

The horse was restless, eager to be gone with its companion. As she looked beyond it, she saw Gregor and his mount about to disappear beyond the hilltop. Panic struck her, for she would have to find her own way if he did not slow down and wait for her.

"I will not fall," she chanted under her breath, eyes closed and forehead pressed against the flank of the horse. "And I vow that I will not let Gregor down, whatever foul mood I have brought about through my wretched curiosity."

chapter Sixteen

Gregor had ridden ahead of her for the entire journey back to the Drover's Inn, and he made it obvious he did not want to converse with her. In their quarters once more, he sat in surly silence, his eyes on the window, his thoughts far away.

Jessie guessed at his emotions. If she had to return to the place of her mother's death, she, too, would be crippled by the experience. What she did not understand was why he had turned on her, as if it was her fault. They had grown to understand each other, or so she thought, and yet he had scowled at her and turned away when she'd reached out to him. That stung. She tried to keep her feelings inside and make allowances for his reaction, retiring to the servant's room until later.

When supper arrived, however, he pushed the plate away and ordered her back to her room.

"Gregor, please." She rose to her feet.

To no avail. That night he told her to sleep in her own bed.

The following morning she found him seated as he had been the night before. Slumped, but not sleeping.

After another full day of silence, where he did nowt but glower into the distance with a bottle of port in one hand and a glass in the other, she began to doubt his sanity.

He was fixed on his task, and he had put a distance between them. That made it easier for him. Did it make it easier
for her? No! His encouragement might. Instead, he had become cold and silent. She would do anything for him. Foolishly, she had grown to care what he thought of her, and now
he acted as if this had been nothing but a business arrangement. She had been warned that danger lay in affection for a
man—and yet she had left herself open to this one.

Foolish, yes. A man such as he could never truly care for
a woman like her, a whore. For a day or more she had betrayed herself, allowing herself to believe that they shared
each other, if only for a few days. Soon she would be gone
from his life, and that made her greedy for the time they had
left, resentful of his withdrawal.

The hours passed and the sun set. By then she was nurs-
ing her own raw temper. Hurt by his silence, she considered
how sorry he would be if he knew he had underestimated
her and that she'd been inside his precious trunk and had
breached the locks on his doors. If he had only listened to
the folk in Dundee, he might be afraid she could procure
another protector at will and walk away from him and his
quest for revenge.

She put on her new hide shoes and combed her hair. Then
she presented herself to him. "If you will not speak with
me and continue to prepare me for the task ahead, I will go
downstairs and entertain myself there."

His eyes blazed and for a moment she thought he might
forbid her—that he would snatch her back into his arms and
hold her to him.

"Do as you wish." He stood up, turned his back on her
and walked away.

Astonished, she stared across the room at him. Her statement was intended to force him to address her, to wake

him from his trance. However, he no longer seemed to care where she went.

Crestfallen, Jessie watched as he poured water into the dish on the washstand and then pulled his shirt over his head. The sight of his naked torso only made her more annoyed, because she ached for his embrace. *Fooled myself.* He cared nothing for her. She was just a convenient whore he kept to do his bidding, knowing she was under the continued threat of condemnation and death, a woman who he thought should be grateful for protection and for the crumbs of affection he threw her. And what about the afternoons? she silently raged. When he went who knew where? To another woman, his real woman, perhaps. Someone he would never ask to do the sordid task of seducing an enemy in return for a full purse.

Infuriated, Jessie turned on her heel and stomped out of the rooms before he could stop her, racing down the rickety stairs and into the crowded inn.

Gregor stared down into the basin of water, then cupped his hands and filled them. The splash of cool drops barely registered. He cupped his hands again and doused the back of his neck. Then he dipped his head into the bowl, wetting his hair. He flicked it back, ran his fingers through the wet strands, then pressed his hand to his forehead. Several long moments passed, and then he realized that Jessie had gone.

Frowning, he looked around.

He walked to the sitting room, rubbing his jaw, and vaguely realized his beard was unruly. The door to the landing was ajar. He recalled her badgering him. He scarcely remembered what she'd said, because he had been deep in thought.

Picturing her face, he knew that she'd been upset.

It was wrong to blame her for the visit to Strathbahn, but he could not help himself, his temper was so bad. It was her fault they had gone, and her fault that he had begun to feel things more deeply again.

He'd also had the uneasy feeling that the claims about her practicing witchcraft might have some credence. There was that odd thing about her riding after she had seemed so unwilling, and then she'd said she could easily make too much housework for the servants to manage, and she truly believed it. Would it happen? Soon enough they would know.

What he could not forgive himself for was that he was concerned for the welfare of a whore. He had lost sight of his target, because of a woman he knew nothing about. Now he was almost willing to believe the claims about her, and that set loose another round of doubt. Hours had gone by in these rooms when he did not even think of his goal, because he wanted to claim her and bask in her glow instead. Was this the result of witchcraft? The unfamiliar doubts and feelings nagged at him until he grew grumpy and frustrated, and he'd snapped at her whenever she came near.

Here in these three small rooms he'd managed to lose his sense of purpose. He had to hold on to his focus to fulfill his goal, to live again. He owed it to his father.

Even so, the thought that she was down there, where the men leered at her and she could quickly find another sponsor, began to bite into him, and it was not a pleasant sensation. Over the last day he'd become numb. Not anymore. Anger shot through him, turning to ice in his veins.

The longer he stared at the open door and heard the sounds of laughter and cheering rising from the tavern below, the more tension and possessive anger built inside him.

She was a whore, but until he ended it she was *his* whore.

★ ★ ★

The clamor of voices and the smell of ale and bodies was a familiar experience to Jessie. She pressed into the crowd, even though she did not want to be here at all. She would not satisfy Gregor by returning to his side, however. Perhaps some time alone would wake him from that trance of his and they could move forward again.

The inn was heaving with drunken farmers and she overheard talk of the market in Saint Andrews. It was just as Morag had described. As Jessie made her way to the counter, where the alewife was busily working, she saw that Mister Grant was once more in residence, presumably after a long day of tax collecting. Several of the farmers reached out to grab at her, but she easily danced free of their grasping hands. Pausing alongside the excise man, she leaned forward to speak to the alewife.

When Mister Grant turned to look at her, she smiled his way.

The man's cheeks colored. Then, when he noticed that Mistress Muir had appeared, he gestured at the jug of ale she carried. "A glass for the miss here…" he paused, blushed again "…and another for myself."

"Thank you, sire." Jessie stepped closer, glad of the conversation. It would keep her from running back to Gregor.

"Consider it an apology." Her neighbor inclined his head, most gentlemanly. "My friend treated you quite poorly that day on the landing. He had no idea that you were lodging here, and feared you were a thief."

"That is perfectly understandable, under the circumstances." As she spoke to him, her mind flitted back to the more intimate moments she had witnessed, and she picked up the tankard that was set out for her to hide her secret smile. "I am guessing it is market day in Saint Andrews," she remarked conversationally after she had wiped the ale froth from her lip.

They conversed rather awkwardly for some time, and Jessie was chuckling at one of his remarks when her laughter faded away because she felt a shiver run up her spine.

So bad was the feeling that she feared it was the bailie or some other soul from Dundee who had come for her. But when she glanced over Mister Grant's shoulder, she saw that it was Gregor who filled the doorway beyond. Jessie's heart beat faster when she saw the wild glint in his eyes, and a dire feeling came over her.

He had come for her, which should have pleased her. But the look on his face was thunderous. That he was in even worse humor finding her here conversing with the excise man was quite obvious. How long had he been watching? She recalled that she had touched Mister Grant upon the arm once or twice. Well, it shouldn't matter. Gregor was training her for another man, after all. Nevertheless, Jessie had a feeling of dread when she met his black stare.

His hair was wet and clung to his skin, as did his shirt. The dark circles of his nipples were visible through the fine linen. He had washed himself, but hurriedly. The dark shadow of beard on his jaw made him look wilder still.

He was staring at her with the other man, and there was such fury in his expression that she was stunned. Covering the floor in a few strides, he claimed her. With his hand at the back of her neck, he pushed her toward the doorway. Once beyond it, he snatched her hand and took the rickety wooden stairs two at a time, dragging her behind him.

"Gregor, no." Her arm was being wrenched from her shoulder and her feet stumbled on the steps. She bashed her elbow on the banister, and as she twisted in his grip, she looked back down and grew dizzy. Her free hand snatched at the grubby stairs, but that only made her topple, and she landed heavily, scraping her elbow.

He paused, then grabbed her by her sleeve, hauling her up the final few stairs without further ado. The possessive nature of his approach astonished her—and in some perverse way also delighted her. He was brimming with dark, unruly masculine power and that made her want him all the more.

Once inside their quarters he set her loose, then slammed the door so that it rattled on its hinges. Jessie staggered free. He stared at her, eyes flickering.

"You are filthy," he muttered, examining her arm, where her sleeve was torn and dirt from the stairway smeared her skin.

What would he do with her? If he locked her in that miserable room with its sad little cot, she would feel wretched. But he didn't take her there. He grabbed her elbow and took her into his bedchamber.

"You attempt to ruin my careful preparations," he muttered, as he stood her by the washstand where he had been earlier.

"No. I wanted conversation, that was all. My spirit is wretched to the core, locked up as I am within these walls."

His lips pressed together tightly in response to that. Without hesitation he began to undress her, tearing at the laces of her bodice.

She heard the fabric rip. "Gregor, you are tearing it."

On he went. Once he'd loosened the laces he wrenched the fabric off her shoulders, forcing her to step out of the gown as it dropped to the floor. Kicking the garment aside, he set to work on her stays.

"I have put my faith in you and you betrayed it," he growled at her.

"I've done nowt wrong."

"I salvaged you and brought you here, giving you food and clothing and the promise of a good reward, and how do you repay me?"

Confused, Jessie tried to work out his intentions. Then she saw it. When he had her down to her shift, he pushed her closer to the washstand.

"Take it off."

"No."

He reached out and tore the garment, ripping it down the front with his bare hands. Astonished, she cried aloud, "My shift!"

"You should have done as I said." He lifted a cloth, dipped it in the water and then scrubbed her arm, holding on to her with his free hand.

However, he did not stop at her arm, determined, it seemed, to humiliate her. The water was cold. Furious, she struggled against him as he scrubbed her, glaring at his handsome face, hating him for this.

"Mister Grant did not want me and you are a fool to think so," she seethed. "He did not even touch me."

Disbelief flashed in Gregor's eyes.

"It is the truth."

A rueful smile lifted the corners of his mouth. "I saw it with my own eyes."

"A casual gesture, nothing more," she spat.

"While you are with me, you are mine and you do as I instruct. You agreed to this at the outset, and yet you dare to dispute me." He shook his head. "Your wayward actions are threatening to destroy our agreement."

On he went, turning her to face away from him as he scrubbed her back and buttocks until her skin was raw and tingling, and the brusque treatment he doled out had became entwined with her desire for him.

"I have invested time in you, Jessie." He delivered a sound slap to her buttocks.

Pain flashed through her, her flesh heightened to sensation from the scrubbing as it was. Tossing back her head, she glared at him over her shoulder. "Throw me back in the gutter if that is all you think I am worth. I have pledged to you that my word is good."

"While you are with me you will follow my instructions. If I discover you dallying with that cursed fop again our agreement will be annulled."

How wildly handsome and possessive he looked. Jessie could not help herself; she laughed in his face. "You're a fool. He was not interested in me. If you opened your eyes you would see that he prefers a man in his bed and would no doubt rather it was you he sat with down there instead of me."

Confusion altered Gregor's expression and he paused.

Jessie, however, did not. The ability to hold her tongue had completely gone. "And tell me this while you are doling out the punishment here—why weren't you upset with Morag? You do not want to see me with another man, but you wanted to see me with her."

"That was different." His frown deepened.

"It was no different. I could just as likely find favor with Morag and decide to run away with her."

That appeared to rile him even more, for he grabbed her to him and his lips were tightly compressed as he looked down into her eyes. "You will run away with no one."

"I will if I choose to. You are not my keeper." Even as she said it, she wished he were. That had been the problem when she left the room, and it was still her problem now. "It is no worse than the fact that you want me to seduce your enemy," she snapped. "Aye," she added, when she saw him jerk back. "Think on that, Gregor."

Fury lit his eyes. "That is vastly different. I am preparing you for a task, a job you are being paid for."

"Yes, a task I am being paid for. It is what I do, Gregor. I am a whore." Her eyes smarted. The emotions that she had kept deeply buried were unraveling. "You will never scrub that fact away."

He glared at her.

She shook her head. "You are willing to pay me to be such, but you cannot stand the notion that I might toy with another man out of choice. What sense is there in that?"

The cloth in his hand fell to the floor. "You wanted that... that fop?"

No, I wanted you, you fool. Mired in vexation, Jessie found that her true and deeper emotions—the ones she would not reveal to him—were barely in check.

"What if I did," she spat, and then turned her face away from him, hating that she cared what he thought of her, hating that she knew he was blinding himself to the truth. They both were. She was a whore, and he would try to forget that while it suited him—while he wanted her to warm his bed. It was what men did with whores. He was no different. In fact, he was worse, because he chose to blot out what he was training her for, as well.

An ominous silence surrounded them.

She tried desperately not to shiver, but she couldn't help it.

Gregor moved to her back.

Jessie kept her gaze averted.

"Turn around."

She did so. He pulled off his shirt and rubbed her dry, his lips tightly compressed. Fury poured from him still, but his verbal admonishments seemed to be shelved for the moment. The small amount of heat that he rubbed into her bones made her shiver all the more. He wrapped her in the linen, lifted her into his arms and carried her to his bed.

As he did, she noticed how fast he breathed, and felt the barely restrained tension in him. His naked chest was hot to the touch, luring her. At her center, her body flamed for him. It made her want to kiss his feet, to beg for him to hold her as he had before.

"This must be done," he informed her, then dropped her onto the bed.

"Gregor—"

He put his hand over her mouth, silencing her.

Jessie swallowed.

Looming over her, stripped to the waist, he gazed at her, his eyes glittering darkly in the faint light from the candle that flickered nearby.

Her cunny turned molten.

Pulling the shirt from beneath her, he twisted it tightly in his hands, turning it to rope.

Jessie watched, her heart racing.

He captured and held her wrists in one hand, then wrapped the twisted material around them and tied her hands to the wooden plinth at the head of the bed.

Breathlessly, she followed his movements.

Opening his breeches, he took his cock in his hand.

Reacting, she rolled away, jerking against the restraint.

"Do not defy me!" He snatched her back, forcing her to lie flat. Climbing onto the bed, he shoved her legs apart with his knee.

Roughly, he splayed her thighs and directed his erection to her opening. With a fumble and a bitter curse, he found his way and thrust inside.

The sudden fullness captured her senses and strung out

her emotions. "Gregor," she cried out, unable to help herself. "'Twas you I wanted."

A warning flashed in his eyes. Her confession had angered him, and once again he put his hand over her mouth. He did not want her words, his expression warned her that he did not trust them.

I will show you, Gregor, she silently vowed, locking her gaze to his. *You will trust me. I will make you.*

She stared up at him, willingly him to know her.

His eyes narrowed and his hand tightened as he rode her fast, hard and with no mercy.

The pressure of his palm over her mouth, controlling her, made her all the wilder for him. She thrashed and arched, her body cleaving to his, the restraint heightening her need and emphasizing the exquisite pleasure of every movement he made, every touch, every thrust and grind, inside and out. To be so thoroughly undone, so unmercifully taken and used by him, made her dizzy with pleasure.

Never before could she have enjoyed such servitude, but in this moment she was lost to all it afforded her—the thrust at her center, the weight of him over her and his hand silencing her mouth. The way he rode her was like a man driven, as if the need to lose his seed inside her made him ferocious, every muscle in his body tight as rope as he loomed over her.

Cursing aloud, he lifted up on his arms, his body pivoting against hers as he neared his release. But still he rode on. He bellowed and tossed his hair back, his movements direct and swift as he lifted her legs from around his hips and draped them over his shoulders, bowing her body against the mattress, pressing deeper still within the swollen, sensitive channel of her cunny.

Jessie moaned, for each time he thrust deep against her center carried her into ecstasy. Her body clenched in release and hot juices dampened her thighs. Still he worked her, until she felt blissfully ragged with use, waves of ecstasy washing over her repeatedly. Then he shot his load, and he did it deep inside her.

Panting, he hung his head down over her and his hair brushed her face. Her cunny clenched once more, and he pulled free, turning away.

He sat on the edge of the bed, silent and unmoving.

Jessie stared at his back. It was so finely muscled, so damp with sweat from his exertions. Aching to reach out and soothe him, she whimpered and jerked her hands within their restraints, her legs stirring against the mattress.

He turned and stared down at her.

The faltering stub of candle barely lit the side of his face, and she ached to see him more clearly, hoping that when she did his mood would be more forgiving and mellow.

It was not.

Once he untied her, he walked away. After her breathing had settled and she felt her legs might hold her upright, she followed him to the fireside. She stood next to his chair, absorbing a little comfort from the flames, longing for him to hold her as he had before, when she had woken from her nightmares. "I am sorry that I left your side," she whispered.

He reached for her hand, drew it to his lips and kissed the back of it.

Lifting her head, she looked at him.

He did not meet her gaze.

Frustration simmered on inside her. She had expected him to claim her, mount her and ride her roughly and possessively. What she had not expected was for him to treat her as if she had been sullied, as if she was some precious thing that had been touched by another, and that stirred a deep ache in her chest. Yet still he was withdrawn from her.

He was staring into the fire, and his face seemed more harshly chiseled than ever, gaunt almost. His eyes looked haunted, and that struck her oddly, making her crave him. She dropped to her knees at his side and laced her hands around his neck, clinging to him.

"I'm not immune to your tricks, Jessie," he murmured. "I doubt any man could claim such a thing. You know that already. From the moment we met you have known that." There was reprimand in his tone, and disappointment.

He did care. He was possessive of her. But this mood of his was not good. It was as if he was done with her. Her chest ached. Her goal had been to make him react. She'd wanted to feel his attention focused on her before it was too late. She had taken a risk to have him claim her, and he surely had done so, but this was making her hurt. He had put even more distance between them. Her heart sank. She had stirred up bad feelings in him. She could see it in his eyes. That haunted look spoke of pain and betrayal.

"Forgive me for my foolishness," she whispered, and dropped a kiss on his cheek, close to the corner of his mouth. She paused, hoping he would turn his mouth to hers, but he did not.

The flames from the fire reflected in his eyes as he stared blindly at it. "I am your employer. I should have kept it that way. That would have served us both better."

Wretched to the core, Jessie swallowed hard. She had imagined more between them because they had shared so much of their history, but he regretted what had happened. Regretted that they had shared his bed and whispered across the pillow as they grew closer.

Still she wanted to reach out for him with all her heart and soul—reach out as the woman he had put his faith in, even if he did not care for her in any other way. "Yes, you are my employer, and I will not let you down, I promise."

He glanced at her then, but it was brief. "Be ready to leave for Balfour Hall in the morning."

Lowering her head, she nodded and turned away.

chapter Seventeen

The following morning Gregor remained subdued, but he began to speak with her about matters at Balfour Hall as they breakfasted. He repeated the plans they had forged over the past week, reminding her she was to listen for any talk of sales or business. Jessie quickly showed him that she remembered, and that she was thinking about her task.

By midmorning he seemed satisfied. When he went about putting on his boots and coat, she realized they were done, and went to her room to prepare.

When she emerged, he turned and stared at her. "Are you ready?"

It was the first time he had inquired after her. Jessie met his gaze and forced herself to nod. She didn't trust herself to say more.

As they descended the stairs together, she stepped close behind him gratefully. Out in the stable yard Gregor reached out to squeeze her upper arm. "I know you dislike horses, so I requested a pony and cart for us so that you do not have to ride."

Jessie pressed her lips together. It was not horses she disliked, but heights. He did not wish to understand her, but it was touching that he had made an effort. Was it guilt that drove him to it? Guilt after the way he had treated her the day before? Or was it simply that he was trying to win back her loyalty?

Staring up at his handsome face, she longed to see his frown soften. That haunted look she saw in his eyes from time to time was something she now understood. His pain over what had happened to his father had made him harsh and bitter, and his need for justice ruled him. There was no denying that he could be affectionate when he wanted her service, but underneath it all he was fixed on his revenge. She was just a weapon to be used in his task.

It shouldn't matter. It shouldn't make her melancholy, but it did. She had come to care for him, and that was a mistake. She pulled free of his hand, tied her shawl at her bosom and then put her bundle on the cart. It contained only the spare day dress and the comb he had given her.

At first the journey made her ill. The cart jolted and swayed. It was far worse than being on a horse, she decided. It took all her will and a little magic to quell the urge to beg him to halt and let her climb down.

Then she noticed how well Gregor handled the pony, how masterful he was as he directed its path with his hands on the reins. His brows were drawn low, his mouth set determinedly as he concentrated on his task. She could not help wondering if this was how he might look at the helm of his ship. The notion made her wistful. She would never know. She would never even have been part of his life had he not needed her for his revenge. It was a strange pact they'd made, but she didn't regret it, not even after the bad feeling that had passed between them the day before. She shouldn't have taunted him, not when he was distressed.

The sidelong glances she took lingered. He was a fine man, and it pained her deeply to think of how wounded he must have been as a young lad, finding his father that way. How good it would be to remove that shadow from his eyes. Would his quest for revenge bring him the relief he sought? She hoped so. Ivor Wallace was a despicable man to have ruined his neighbor that way. The more she thought on it, the more she vowed to bring Gregor peace on the matter.

Once they entered the forest, Gregor secured the pony and cart and they went on by foot. The walk passed in silence and it was only when they got to the brow of the hill overlooking Balfour Hall that he paused and spoke to her.

"I will come back tomorrow, at midnight. Meet me in the grounds where the flower beds flank the path."

"I'll be there." The reason was obvious. He wanted to know of her progress. Nevertheless, Jessie's spirits lifted. *Fool. I must rid myself of this attachment to him.*

Sleeping with his enemy would no doubt take care of that, she thought with no small amount of self-mockery.

It was with determination that she turned away from him and walked down the hill toward Balfour Hall. She knew he watched, for she felt his eyes on her, but would not allow herself to look back. Instead she thought only of the task ahead. Her goal was now twofold. For herself, the purse and her journey north. For Gregor, the retribution he needed to lift the dark cloud that hovered over him and made him so ill-tempered. She wanted to ease his troubled soul.

It would be most uplifting to see him in a better humor before they said goodbye to one another. The ache that rose in her chest when she thought about saying goodbye forever was quickly pushed down, lest she get upset.

Jessie went over the immediate plan as she closed on the house. She knew where the servants' entrance was, but she was to go to the main entrance, as if she had no knowledge of the grounds. Skirting the gardens, she crossed to the lane that ran up to Balfour Hall from a nearby village, and joined it.

The mansion looked more imposing when approached from this direction. The gray stone and gaunt windows seemed ominous. Peering up at the attic rooms, where the servants' quarters would be located, she swallowed down the thought of the stairs, and willed herself to be strong. *I will win my way in.*

Five wide marble steps led up to the main door, which was large and topped by a stained-glass window. She took a deep breath and dropped the heavy knocker against the door. Smoothing down the simple dove-gray dress that Gregor had bought for her to wear on this occasion, she adopted a demure, humble expression, and when the door handle rattled she gave a hopeful smile, eager to be held in favorable account from the outset.

It took some time before the door swung fully open. From beyond it, she could hear raised voices and instructions being issued. By the looks of it there was turmoil in the house. That was a good sign.

"We are buying nothing," the woman who stood there said. Her sleeves were rolled up and she had a heavy frown on her face. She wiped her hands on her apron, and appeared to be both grumpy and out of breath.

Jessie assumed her to be the housekeeper. "I am not selling anything, mistress. I am visiting my cousin in these parts and I heard that you might wish to engage the services of a good worker."

Craning her neck, Jessie peered into the grand hallway beyond. Never before had she been inside a place built with such vast coin. She reminded herself that the master of the house had gained this coin through wrongdoing, but still it was an impressive sight. As she glanced into the entrance hall a serving girl staggered down the staircase, a teetering pile of linens in her arms. As she reached the bottom of the staircase she missed her footing and dropped the stack.

Apparently Jessie's spells were still functioning. She was pleased. It had been quite the challenge, and to see them working so well made her proud. It was because of her involvement with the man she had grown to care about. Her passion for Gregor was making her magical abilities blossom. If necessary, she could use her magic again. It would be a risk, but that would hasten things along, and the reward would be to see him unburdened.

"We only take servants from the village," the woman at the door responded. "It is the rule of the house, set out by the mistress." She looked Jessie up and down. "Mistress Wallace prefers to hire those that she knows, people who can be trusted."

"I could begin now, Mistress…?"

Jessie silently chanted a spell, willing the housekeeper to let her pass over the threshold.

The woman continued to look dubious for a moment longer, then relinquished. "My name is Mistress Gilroy."

"I could begin now, Mistress Gilroy." She smiled and curtsied and made herself appear bright and amenable. "It seems as if you could do with the help." She nodded her head at the serving girl beyond, who was now on her hands and knees, scrabbling for the linens strewn across the hall floor. From somewhere beyond, shouting erupted, and a large wolfhound scampered across the hallway and up the stairs, a young lad at his heels.

The housekeeper looked at the chaos within and back at Jessie with a frown. "Come in. The mistress has one of her headaches, but I will ask if she'll take a look at you. Lord knows we could do with an extra pair of hands."

Perhaps fate was lending a hand, for if the mistress had a headache it might be something Jessie could cure with a brew made from the lavender tops in the garden. She followed the housekeeper into the hall. It was a grand space with a neatly flagged floor. The dark, polished wood panels on the walls made her want to reach out and touch them. Colored light from the stained-glass window above the entrance filled the space. Gregor had told her this was where guests would arrive for parties and such, and it was most impressive. High up on the walls were numerous paintings, portraits of people, many of them with scowling expressions.

"Wait here," Mistress Gilroy instructed. She went into a parlor beyond, but left the door ajar. Jessie waited until the serving girl had picked up her load and scurried off, and then stepped closer to the door so that she might see inside the room.

Mistress Gilroy stood before a winged armchair, where a lady dressed entirely in black was sitting. A moment later the housekeeper came back to the door and gestured at her. "Come in. The mistress will see you."

Jessie hastened over and stepped into the parlor. It was a lavishly furnished room with images of birds and trees painted on the walls. She had never seen the likes. Comfortable chairs with well-stuffed seats and fancy side tables filled the place to capacity. To her immediate right as she entered was a tall cabinet with different-colored woods on the front, like a picture—the prettiest thing she had ever seen. Close to the fire, which was lit despite the fact that the room was unbearably warm, the mistress sat in her armchair, a delicate lace handkerchief clutched to her cheek.

As Jessie was led in, the woman of the house closed the large book on her lap. Jessie noticed that it bore a gold cross on the front cover, and she recognized it as a Bible. Ivor Wallace's wife wore black, looked unhappy and read the Bible.

"Good morning, ma'am." Jessie curtsied.

The mistress did not smile, nor did her frown fade. "Have you experience of working in a house this large?"

"Not so large, ma'am, but I am a good worker."

"It is not my usual way of conducting affairs, but I will give you a trial for one week. If you impress me, we will talk terms of employment. Is that understood?"

Jessie curtsied again. "Aye, ma'am, it is. I appreciate the opportunity." She was about to add that Mistress would not regret giving her this chance, but she thought she probably would, so she did not say any more.

Mistress Wallace and the housekeeper then discussed which jobs might be assigned to Jessie during her trial. As they did, Jessie became aware that someone was watching. She turned slightly and looked back toward the door out of the corner of her eye. A man was out there, observing.

Was it he, Ivor Wallace, Gregor's enemy?

When Mistress Wallace dismissed them and the housekeeper led her back into the hall, the man stepped out of the shadows and grasped Jessie around the upper arm with one hand. Her heart missed a beat. Tall and mean-looking, he was too young to be the master of the house, and was dressed in the garb of a servant. His bold stare bored into her relentlessly.

"Mistress Gilroy," he barked, holding Jessie as if she was an unruly child he had caught running about. "Who is this?"

His uppity manner led her to believe that he was perhaps the master's servant, because he held sway over the housekeeper.

"Jessie is on trial for a week. She will be helping out belowstairs. This is Cormac. He calls himself a valet, but none of us is quite sure what it is he does." There was sarcasm in her voice as she made the introduction for Jessie's benefit.

Cormac scowled at her, and released Jessie.

Instinctively, she backed away, staying close to the house-keeper. Cormac was a bad lot, and the way he looked at her made her uneasy. He continued to watch them as the house-keeper led her away. Jessie had a bad feeling about him, but she reminded herself that he was unimportant. It was only a matter of time until she would access the master of the house and begin her true work.

chapter Eighteen

Gregor soon discovered that it was painfully hard to pass the time once Jessie was gone. He paced the floorboards in his quarters and found himself made uneasy by the fact that the place seemed empty without her presence. As if that were not enough to grate on his nerves and make him restless, he could not settle for wondering about her progress up at the house and, more to the point, whether she was safe.

Cursing aloud, he knew it shouldn't matter to him. She was a whore whom he had hired to undertake a task. Nevertheless, it did matter. It mattered greatly. Pulling on his frock coat, he decided to pass the time at the ale counter instead.

When he got down there he found the place busy with land workers. Boisterous and red-faced, they had talk of rebellion on their lips as they conferred.

The curious excise man, Mister Grant, was also back from his daily visits and already seated at the counter. Gregor avoided him and his probing questions, and took a seat in a dark corner instead. He gestured for some ale. After the tankard had arrived, he remembered Jessie's strange comment about Mister Grant preferring men in his bed.

It struck him oddly, because Mister Grant was indeed engaged in a somewhat surreptitious conversation with a dark-haired man, a fieldworker by the looks of him. As Gregor watched, Grant touched the other man's hip, and they exchanged whispered comments.

It was not an unfamiliar sight to Gregor. His time at sea had proved that lust and indeed affection could develop in what most people would consider the most unlikely of circumstances. As an unworldly nineteen-year-old he had first witnessed two men in the act of mutual pleasuring and riding rump. Roused from his deep slumber by a sound different from the usual creaks and groans of the ship, he had cautiously opened one eye and caught sight of them.

One shipman had approached a fellow countryman in his hammock. At first Gregor had assumed they were engaged in some sort of fight, for it looked as if they were tussling, but soon after he realized it was a mutual exchange much more pleasurable. They had their hands down one another's breeches. They grasped each other's rigid cocks and worked them up and down, stopping occasionally to wet their palms with spit. That was a trick he himself had already learned, and it confirmed the true nature of the encounter. Quickly they both came off and then, to his utter astonishment, embraced. They did it gruffly, but as if they were man and wife.

During the exchange, one or two other slumbering souls lifted their heads to peer toward the noise, perhaps thinking it a rat, and then turned away, apparently not disturbed by this lewd act. Thus it was that Gregor had come to terms with such things. The following day he'd seen how the two men sought each other out, and then began to understand the ribald comments of the older men as they spoke about them.

The two men pleasured each other often, and another night as he lay on his side, half-asleep, Gregor caught sight of them again seeking each other out. This time they left their hammocks and withdrew to a corner where the light did not reach them, wherein one dropped to his hands and knees and bared his arse. Gregor had peered into the deep gloom where they had taken shelter, and witnessed the second man anoint his cock with spit and then drive it into the kneeling man's arse. Both men appeared to gain a great deal of pleasure from the exchange, which involved a lot of grunting and heaving and slamming together of hip and arse with breeches hanging down around their knees. Gregor himself had grown stiff and was forced to toss off his own seed beneath his meager blanket.

He subsequently thought upon it at great length and was sure he did not wish to join them, but he felt a certain sense of envy and recognized that he wanted to find some outlet for his own lust. Thankfully, he was guided by some of the older men when they reached safe harbor. There he was introduced to whores aplenty and had his eyes opened to the world and its infinite array of provocative pastimes. The fairer sex was indeed his preference, and he sampled it as often as he could, bedding women at every port.

Thankfully, he'd gained more direction and had soon risen among the ranks of the men he worked with, due to his ability to read and to understand maps. Fisticuffs were a daily occurrence over matters trivial, and often enough it was a reaction to the small number of men who kept close company with their own sex. Some found it unholy, others threatening. The more sensible turned a blind eye.

Gregor had discovered that most men were prepared to defend their own preferences in matters pertaining to carnal gratification, but were all too quick to point a finger at others whose tastes did not align with their own. Tolerance in such matters was the more sensible option, and he'd learned that at a young age.

That same familiarity between men was reflected here in

the staging inn in Fife, where the excise man and his companion exchanged secret touches before they drew apart and
the younger man left. Jessie was right, or so it appeared, but
how in God's name did she know?

Gregor attempted to shrug it off, but that, among other
questions about his unruly cohort, continued to haunt him.
Jessie was a canny sort and that was why he'd pursued her.
She was wily, sharp and observant, although sometimes she
was so hotheaded she barely paused to think. How did she
know Mister Grant preferred to bed a man than a woman?
Remembering the way she had looked that morning, he
mused again on the fact that she had gained entry to Balfour Hall with apparent ease. She'd said she had arranged it
to be so. How?

Many things about Jessie were a mite odd, and now that he
had a little distance from her and the task was under way, he
could not to stop thinking about her and her curious ways.
They called her a witch. They wanted to hang her for it. She
certainly had a bewitching side, but that was not what they
meant. Did she truly have some ability?

Moreover, why did thoughts of her fill his head? He had
never kept such close quarters with a woman for such a sus-
tained length of time. It must be familiarity that had brought
about this unusual state of concern in him. For the past several days they had been apart only when he had gone about
his business in the afternoons. She was present to greet him
when he returned, and there was comfort in that. He'd found
himself looking forward to the sight of her face while she
gazed upon whatever trinkets he'd brought back for her.

That was why her absence felt so odd. It was the nature
of the task, he told himself, because she was up there at Balfour Hall and he was not. They had agreed not to meet until
the following night, and none of his questions would be an-

swered before then. Soon thereafter, he gestured for a second draft of ale.

Gregor peered into his mug, brooding on what he had done. It ailed him so—even more than he'd thought it might—to have left her there at Wallace's mercy. Recalling the way Ivor Wallace had been, Gregor felt his gut knot at the thought that Jessie was there, and he had made her go. No amount of reasoning made him feel any better, in fact quite the reverse. All he wanted to do was fetch her back.

"I want to do this," she had stated as they parted. It was the money she desired. She was more sensible than he after their time together, or so it seemed.

"Excuse me, it is Mister Ramsay, is it not? Gregor Ramsay?"

Gregor jolted in his seat. It was the excise man, the one Jessie had said was their neighbor.

The man smiled and took off his tricorne, straightening his wig as he did so. "I knew it was you. I recalled just today when I was riding past Craigduff. I saw your father's old place up on the hill, and I thought, that is who it is, it is young Gregor Ramsay."

"No," Gregor stated, unprepared for an interrogation while he already had so much on his mind. "I do not believe I know you."

The man frowned. "It was a long time ago, aye, and I am older than you. I grew up in Craigduff, but my aunt took me in when my parents passed on. She has the cottage next door to your cousin, Margaret Mackie. I remember you and your father, Hugh, well. He used to bring you round to visit Margaret when you were a lad."

It was true. There was no denying that this man remembered him. And it was bad news, for Gregor did not want to be remembered in Craigduff—not yet, at any rate.

"I went away to work for the crown, when I had learned enough. I was sad to hear of your father's demise on my return."

Whether it was the mention of his father, or just because Gregor was tired of pretending, he did not want to deny it.

The excise man lifted his wig and rubbed his hand over his thinning blond hair. "I have less hair than you might remember."

"Forgive me. I denied the truth merely because I do not wish to draw attention." Mustering a suitable reason, he surprised himself by stating something that was actually the truth. "It is difficult for me when people mention my father." It was. It struck him then how cruel he had been to Jessie when she had done so in good faith.

"I understand." The excise man responded with a sympathetic glance.

"Please join me." Gregor gestured at the seat opposite, for he sensed it was company the excise man wanted most of all, and some company might take his own mind off Jessie. It would do him good to pass an hour or two with another soul instead of brooding over what might be going on up at Balfour Hall.

"I will, and I promise we will talk of other matters."

Gregor nodded. "Tell me what I have missed these eleven years past around the locality, and I will be in your debt."

Three mugs of ale later, Mister Grant's tongue was well and truly loosed. "Craigduff fairs well. The fishermen keep the village in good coin, and that will never change. It is the landowners who have struggled with the changes in Scottish governance."

"Landowners? Such as Ivor Wallace?"

"Wallace used to own much of this area, as I am sure you are well aware. However, his son has not managed things quite so well. Ivor Wallace had hoped to pass the reins to his son, but instead spends his time correcting his mistakes."

Gregor tried to piece this together with what Robert had said about Wallace. His old friend had described Forbes Wallace as a guard dog. That was perhaps what he saw—the son returning home if things were to change. "This has had significance on the size of their estate?"

Mister Grant nodded vigorously. "Some of the less fertile ground has already been sold off, and more of it is to go up for sale soon. I hear it's to pay the son's gambling debts."

Gambling debts, as well as the desire to support the battle for independence… Ivor Wallace needed money all right, and Gregor had it. The irony hit him, making him laugh into his ale. Perhaps fate agreed with his need for revenge. Perhaps God himself had spied Wallace's evil tactics and turned the tide.

"If only I had spoken to you before," Gregor murmured, amused. This information made him rest easier about the likelihood of land for sale. Now he only needed Jessie to find out which land was due to be sold. It occurred to him that he could have her out of there before the week was done.

Grant, who was now somewhat ale-sodden, smiled bleary-eyed at him.

The urge to ask him another question would not be quelled, even though Gregor wondered at his own sanity in asking it. "Tell me, Mister Grant, if you will. Something that made me wonder on my return. In Dundee there was talk of witches and burning."

Gregor paused.

Grant nodded, unsurprised.

"I thought such things were done with here in Scotland."

Grant nodded again. "There hasn't been a burning in

Dundee for many years, but still the accusations arise from time to time."

"Based on what—facts and evidence?"

"Rarely. Mostly it is hearsay. It is a sad truth about human nature, but many times an accusation is vengefully meant, and innocent people have suffered unnecessarily."

Those words made Gregor feel desperately uneasy. He ran one hand around the back of his neck and nodded, wishing he hadn't brought up the subject. Still, it was something he had not had the chance to speak with anyone else about, and his concerns had been building. "But do you believe it truly exists, witchcraft?"

Grant considered the question at length, his lips pursed and his brow furrowed. Eventually he replied, "Although I work with sums and coins and what is true and not true, I know that there are many strange things that we cannot account for in this world, and it pays not to put blinkers on."

He smiled, as if pleased with his own musings. The ale surely had him tonight.

Leaning forward, Grant tapped the wooden table with one finger. "Ask yourself this, Mister Ramsay. If there was no truth in it, why would the church warn so heavily against them?"

"They warn us against witches because they think they are evil and seek to bring down the church." Gregor could not think of anything less likely to interest Jessie.

"Aye." Grant appeared wistful. For a while he looked away, deep in thought, before returning to meet Gregor's gaze. "I saw a woman hanged and burned once. Up at Carbrey it was, a few years back." He shook his head. "McGraw was her name. They said she made another woman throw her bairns from the womb before they were ready, because she was in love with the woman's husband. Then the husband died quite suddenly, while she was being questioned. Poisoned, he was. It was a terrible affair."

Gregor frowned. "A horrendous crime on both scores, if it is true."

Grant nodded. "I see we share the same thinking on such matters. If it is true, it was indeed a terrible crime. But how does one prove such a thing?" He pushed his mug of ale away, as if he had had enough. "I cannot say if it was true or not, but I saw what they did to her, and I will never forget that."

Gregor's gut turned. For a moment he saw Jessie as she had been in the tollbooth, accused and facing trial. If he had not gone to her the same dreadful fate may have awaited her, as it had her mother.

"It is terrible what people will do to one another," Grant added, "in the name of justice."

"Justice," Gregor repeated, with some unease. For it was what drove him, too.

Jessie was allocated a small room in the top attics. The window was tiny and at the level of the floor, for the room was up under the eaves. She was grateful, however, that she did not have to share with another maid, a possibility that had been mentioned at one point. All the servants were very curious about her, quizzing her about where she had come from and who she knew in this area. Jessie had handled them well, but was eager most of all to make the acquaintance of the master of the house.

So far she had not seen him, although she'd heard voices raised as if in anger, coming from the parlor where she had met Mistress Wallace. That first night she retired with disappointment, but felt hope for the following day.

At first she could not sleep, because her thoughts kept running back to Gregor. She craved the pleasure of lying alongside him. But this separation was just as well, she thought, for she would have to do without him soon enough.

It did not help that the attic was stifling hot, and she had to lie atop the bed in her shift, casting aside the blanket. Eventually, she drifted to sleep.

She awoke sometime later when a man entered the room.

He held a candle aloft and she could see from his fine clothes that he was the master of the house.

Jessie sat bolt upright, staring.

Her thoughts scrambled as she tried to remember her purpose and act appropriately. She let out a stifled scream, not loud enough to wake everyone, but loud enough to inform him that she was horrified to find a man in her room.

She pressed herself back against the wall and put her hand to her throat. "Who are you? What do you want of me?"

The man gave a most lascivious smile. "I have come to examine my new serving girl. I am the master of Balfour Hall. You may call me Master Wallace."

"Yes, sire. Master Wallace. Forgive me. I am most astonished to find you here while I am in a state of undress."

Jessie tried to get a quick look at him before she lowered her gaze and cowered in her corner appropriately. He was a tall, distinguished-looking man with intense eyes. His hair was thick and wavy, silver peppered with dark strands. He had once been handsome, she surmised, although his character marred his good looks somewhat. There was petulance in the set of his mouth, and the glint of greed in his eyes.

"Stand up, girl, let me get a look at you."

Jessie did not expect to be meeting him this way, but Gregor had prepared her well.

Her mind ticked over fast, and as she rose to her feet she moved her hands. With her right forearm, she made as if to cover her breasts, squeezing them together beneath her thin shift. She pushed the other hand between her thighs as if to cover her intimate parts in reaction to his presence. He would believe her chaste, but his attention would be drawn to the places she touched.

It proved fruitful.

He moved his candle up and down, brazenly examining her.

Jessie did not like the man. She told herself that it did not matter. She had often serviced men she did not like, in order to fill her belly. This should be the same. But it wasn't. It felt somehow more uncomfortable to her.

Just then the door of the room creaked open, and Mistress Gilroy stood there with a candlestick. She had a shawl flung over her nightdress.

The mood altered quickly.

"Lurking, are we?" Wallace snapped in her direction.

The housekeeper stood her ground silently, and whatever small persuasion it was, Wallace lingered only a moment longer, and then went to push past her. Mistress Gilroy turned her face away, and as she did, Wallace paused and ran a finger along her jaw.

The woman closed her eyes, and Jessie was not sure if it was from pleasure or dislike. It was a curious exchange, and it occurred to Jessie that the housekeeper had chosen that room for her on purpose, because her own was close by and she would hear if the master came a-calling. There was some history between these two. Whatever it might be, Jessie was glad of the opportunity to gather her thoughts.

When the master was gone, Mistress Gilroy stepped into the room. "You are safe for now, my dear."

She acted friendlier than she had thus far, and Jessie nodded, giving her a weak smile.

"There is only so much I can do to protect you. If you honestly cannot find work elsewhere, be prepared to do whatever he asks, but mark my words—he can be a cruel man."

Jessie could have guessed as much. She was unsure how to respond, but Mistress Gilroy reached out and squeezed her shoulder, then took her leave.

Jessie let the darkness soothe her. That she would be able to get close to Wallace was undoubtable. The man was a leering seducer. She would not need to seduce him at all. At first she'd wondered at Gregor's choice in her, but he had been right to choose a woman who would honestly not be afraid of such a man. He had prepared her as an innocent, because that's obviously where Master Wallace's tastes led him. Soon she would have his ear, and Gregor would know everything he needed.

However, when Jessie sat down on her cot, the room seemed suddenly gloomier and more oppressive. There was barely a light at the tiny window by her feet, and it felt more cell-like than any she had known so far. Moreover, she felt as if she were back there in Dundee, scraping for her living, saving every penny she did not need for food or lodging. She had been spoiled, in between. Comfortable quarters and regular food. *And Gregor.*

His image burned in her mind.

Yes, it was going to be difficult from now on, because she had bonded with him. He only wanted her for this task, but she had grown to care for him far too much. Closing her eyes, she willed herself to be strong, but the feeling did not come. Hunching over her knees, she pressed her palms to her eyes, attempting to push down the knot in her chest. But it would not be quelled, and for the first time in many, many years, Jessie Taskill cried herself to sleep.

chapter Nineteen

"Begging your pardon, Master Wallace, may I enter in order to clear the grate?" Jessie stood just inside the doorway to the master's parlor and wiped her hands on the muslin apron she had been given.

Master Wallace was seated at a fancy table covered in papers. His head rested in his hands as he studied something there. Above the table rose shelves of boxes and books; it was a complicated affair with many drawers. He lifted one hand, which she took as a sign of consent.

She sidled past him slowly, clutching her brush and pail, but he scarcely lifted his head. This was no good. If she was to attract his attention, she would have to appear more interesting than whatever it was he was currently looking at. She cleared her throat. "I will try not to distract you from your work, Master Wallace."

He lifted his gaze and studied her for a moment, recognition flickering in his eyes. She noticed how the lace cuffs on his shirt were ink-stained, and he wore only a waistcoat, no frock coat. His silver-and-black-streaked hair was ruffled where he had rested his head in his hands. After a moment he nodded and gestured her toward the fireplace. At least she had forced him to take notice of the fact it was her, and not some other serving girl. That was a start.

She had begun the day much more determined, for her strange encounter with the master of the house looked more promising in the light of a new day. It was what she was here for, after all, and she could not let her attachment to Gregor make things difficult for her. After some lengthy self-chastisement she had scorned her tearful behavior of the night before, and strengthened her will. The faster she got on with it the quicker it would be over. She would grit her teeth, as she had so many times before, discover information for Gregor, and be out of this place quickly enough.

Thoroughly girded and prepared, she went about her duties with a fury. By midmorning she'd made sure that everyone else was occupied with work when it came time to clear the ashes. Mistress Gilroy seemed unwilling to let her attend to the task in the main parlors, but there was no one else available, and Jessie assured her she would do it and be quick about it.

As it turned out, she completed the clearing of the ashes and the laying of a new fire, and he had scarce made a sound other than to mumble over his papers. With the job completed, Jessie rested back on her haunches and put her hands on her hips. She'd arranged herself in a pretty pose and produced an excessive amount of wiggling of her hips and shoulders, but he had not lifted his head once to glance over at her. All that preparation and she couldn't manage to draw his attention away from whatever it was he was looking at.

This could become vexing.

She glared at his back.

Nevertheless, the night before had been a different story, and she reminded herself of that. The fact that he might be a night prowler occurred to her, but time was short and Gregor would appear that evening, expecting news of her progress. She was not about to sacrifice her meeting with Gregor to wait for Master Wallace to appear in her quarters with his wandering hands. This called for more desperate measures. Besides, she was curious as to what he was so fascinated with over there, and rued the fact that she could not read.

As she passed back across the parlor, she stumbled and set down her wooden pail. With a loud cry of dismay, she dropped to her knees and began sweeping the floor as if ashes had spilled on the rug near his table. "I beg your pardon, sire. Please forgive the disturbance. 'Tis terribly clumsy of me."

Ivor Wallace looked up from his papers and pushed the spectacles he was wearing down his nose as he observed her jiggling bosom.

She looked at him from beneath her lashes. "Please, sire, do not tell Mistress Gilroy about my clumsiness. I am on trial, and I hope to secure a permanent position in your household."

Jessie bit her lip as she wondered if her current position— on her hands and knees, with her rear end tilted appropriately and her breasts spilling from her bodice—might help in such a quest for permanent work. Apparently so, because Master Wallace shifted his chair away from the desk, abandoned his spectacles and rested his hands on his widely placed knees.

Jessie felt the urge to chuckle. He had positioned himself so that she might readily observe the strapping manhood he harbored inside his breeches. She took a quick glance and rounded her eyes, attempting to look shocked. Secretly, she congratulated herself for breaking his concentration.

"You are the new serving girl?"

Did he not recall her from the night before? Perhaps he had been drink-addled as he roamed the attics, prodding the serving girls at random.

She nodded.

"What is your name?"

"My name is Jessie, Master Wallace."

"Well, Jessie, I will not remark upon your clumsiness to Mistress Gilroy, if you come over here and do something for me."

Jessie hastened to her feet and wiped her hands on her apron. "What is it that you would like me to do, sire?"

Show me what we need to know. An enchantment whispered through her mind. She willed it to be so.

Ivor Wallace frowned as if confused. He considered her at length, his broad mouth pursed, his woolly eyebrows drawn low.

If it were not for the mean look about him he would be a reasonably handsome man, she decided, especially given his age. He was a cold, mercenary type, however, and that made her wary.

Pointing out a small set of wooden steps located near the desk, he beckoned to her. "Climb up there and reach for the rolled map you see on that shelf."

At first Jessie was disappointed, thinking her magic had not been inspired. However, she would get a look at what he was working on, and that was the important thing. Then, when she mounted the steps and reached for the rolled papers he had indicated, he moved. As quick as lightning he lifted the back of her skirt so that he could look at her legs while she stood there upon the steps.

A cold draft wafted up as far as her bottom, and she realized he had lifted her skirts and petticoat quite high in order to examine what Gregor had so often assured her were her delectable buttocks. Jessie had to keep her face averted in order not to laugh. Apparently she had managed to distract him after all.

For a moment she grappled for the appropriate response.

She froze, then grabbed up the rolled papers and hurried back down the steps, snatching her skirts free of his hand while she did so. Adopting a horror-stricken expression, she gazed at him woefully. "Sire, you shame me!"

He smacked his lips together in a most lewd way. "In good time you will know what true shame is. I will see to it myself."

Jessie managed to lower her eyelids and hang her head in an appropriate show of submission. Meanwhile, her thoughts shot to Gregor. More than ever, she knew why he had required a whore for this task. A less experienced maiden would have been out the door with a scream and halfway to Saint Andrews by now.

Master Wallace put out his hand and took the rolled parchment from her. A moment later he had the thing spread out upon the table, weighted at each corner with stones. She was just about to curtsy and leave when he gestured her closer. "Look at this, my dear. This is what your master owns."

Jessie stared down at the paper, once again annoyed at her limitations. "Beg pardon, sire, but I cannot read."

Undeterred, he pointed out the town of Saint Andrews at the top corner of the map, and some of the villages along the coast. She saw it then, which part of the drawing was land and which was sea. It was quite a clever thing. While she peered at it, her curiosity grew. Meanwhile, Master Wallace began to point out the extent of his holdings. There was a gloating quality to his demeanor, and it struck her how he wore his wealth with no regard to others and their status. Was he trying to impress her in order to have her bend over for him more readily? That was a possibility, but it only made her think how circumspect Gregor was with his wealth. She knew he had money and shares in a ship, but he only ever made a thing of it in order to illustrate a point or issue a sound promise of payment, not to fill a young girl's head with fancy dreams and expectations.

"It is a fine amount of land, sire," she commented, when Wallace looked at her expectantly.

Seemingly pleased, he put his arm about her waist and drew her closer. "It is indeed, and yet I am torn, my dear. I wish to support our quest for independence and have the English gone from Scottish soil. In order to do so I need to free funds, which means parting with my land. Either way, I lose something precious to me."

He shook his head wearily.

Jessie wondered briefly if Mistress Wallace was more interested in her Bible than in listening to her husband's pontifications. Meanwhile, he rambled on about grazing land and rough pasture and things that made little sense to her.

"Be grateful that you do not have such worries," he concluded eventually. "These matters press heavily upon me at the moment." He gave a sidelong glance at the swell of her breasts, as if regretful. "And distract me from otherwise more pleasant pastimes."

He patted her bottom with one hand.

Just then the door sprang open and Mistress Gilroy stood there in the doorway. "Jessie, are you done here?"

Jessie took the opportunity to step away and fetch her pail. She curtsied and took her leave. As she scurried out, she noticed that the housekeeper and the master of the house stared across the room at each other quite blatantly, and Mistress Gilroy looked most angry and disapproving.

Once again the housekeeper had taken it upon herself to protect Jessie's so-called honor. It was with some amusement that Jessie considered her reasons. Was Mistress Gilroy one of his conquests? Or was she secretly wishing she had been?

Either way, Jessie counted herself lucky. She had successfully gained his attention, avoided more of his groping and most important of all, she was able to confirm what Gregor had previously thought to be the case: Master Wallace was about to sell land. And she was in the right place to find out which lands, and when.

Gregor's mood was as heavy as if he was too far from land to aim for safe harbor and there was nowt but fouled water to drink. The events of the past few days—and nights—had left him somber, for they had made him think and feel too much. He lay on his bed and despised the fact that he missed Jessie's presence alongside him. The discussion he'd had with Mister Grant the night before did nothing to quell his desire to see Jessie. It should have, and yet all he could think about was being with her again and ensuring that she was safe and had come to no harm under Wallace's roof.

Gregor paced the wooden boards of his quarters until he could stand the waiting no more. Jessie was not due to leave the house and meet him until near midnight, but it was well before sunset when he rode to the nearby woodland to observe Balfour Hall from the hilltop. He secured his horse and then hastened to the edge of the forest, where he took cover in the long grass and peered down at the manor house.

Brooding on it, he was unsure which disturbed him most—the lurid images of Jessie and Wallace that assailed him, or his own reaction. His thoughts were a mess of guilt at having sent her in there.

He swung wildly between hope that his father would finally be revenged and self-ridicule over his concerns that a woman he barely knew, a woman of the streets who often showed signs of delusion, was safe and comfortable.

Who would comfort her if those fretful nightmares she had recurred? The thought of her alone in that house while the night made her return to that dark time made him feel crazed, as if the very notion of her fearful and unhappy was a dagger to his chest.

Eventually the sky darkened. Steeling himself, he moved to the appointed place—an old oak at the very edge of the well-tended gardens. There, he waited.

And waited.

The sound of creatures in the undergrowth attested to his absolute stillness, and yet the tension he bore kept them at bay.

Where are you? Scouring the building mentally, he wished her by his side. Finally, he saw a flash of white against the stone walls—her nightdress—as she emerged from the servants' entrance. It was hard to resist striding out to meet her. He steadied himself with one hand against the gnarled tree trunk, and checked the building to be sure that no one watched or followed.

Moments later, Jessie joined him under the canopy of summer leaves, which shaded them from the moonlight.

"Gregor," she whispered.

"Here." He grabbed her shoulders, examining her in what little light there was. With a weary sigh he silently cursed the passing clouds. He knew he should be glad of them for cover, but he could not welcome them when all he wanted to do was see her. "Are you safe?"

Even as he asked the question, he dreaded the answer. He had sent her in there with the task of seduction, and yet he found he could not bear the thought of Ivor Wallace touching her. What madness was this?

Jessie peered up at him. Her eyes searched his, and her upturned face in the shifting moonlight made his gut tighten, so earnest was her expression. Eventually she broke into a smile. "Of course I am safe."

Relief flooded him. Stroking his fingers along the outline

of her jaw, he savored the softness of her skin. So delicate, so feminine. The urge to hold her in his arms was almost over-whelming. "I feared that Wallace would gain the upper hand with you and you would be unable to leave."

She gripped Gregor's hand tightly. "You trusted me with this task. Please don't doubt me now. I promise I will find out what it is you need to know, and soon. My labor was needed and I am well placed in the household. Today has gone well."

It had gone well. Why did that make him feel angry? It didn't even matter that his enemy was close at hand, the man he had dreamed of undermining for these past eleven years. It was this woman that mattered, and when she moved closer to him, resting her free hand against his chest, he knew she'd infected his blood with a desire so strong that he was acting like a fool, and yet he did not care.

"Come, we will find somewhere away from the house where we can talk without being seen." She nodded toward a place where the gardens grew wilder.

He allowed her to lead him through the shrubs and bor-ders and into a more secluded area. As she moved through the undergrowth he heard her chuckle, and she glanced back over her shoulder from time to time as if to urge him on. How could she see where she was going? Gregor wondered. Especially here under the trees, where the scattered moon-light broke through only in patches? Following her blindly, he wondered at her strange talent. How was it that she sur-prised him still? Would he ever understand her fully, and why did the desire to do so unsettle him?

"No one from the house will see us here, but I must not be long away lest someone misses me."

He could barely respond, so eager was he to hold her in his arms. He stroked her cheek and she turned her face into it, kissing his palm. As they grew accustomed to the gloom, he was relieved to be able to see her more clearly.

"Why, Gregor, I sense you are concerned for me."

"I am. How have you fared?" He had to swallow down the urgent need to demand whether Wallace had touched her. That was the whole point, and he knew it was foolish to the point of absurdity to be angry about it happening.

"I have fared well. I have been given a week's trial, and have already gained the task of clearing the fireplace in the master's study. He pores over papers there, papers and maps. Today I learned that the maps are of the land he owns hereabouts. He rambles, and soon he will be telling me exactly what it is you need to know."

The information she imparted should have made Gregor happy, but he could scarcely hear it for wanting to know something else. "Did he put his hands on you?"

He could not help himself; the question was out before he even thought it through properly. When she shook her head, relief flooded him.

"There is a fire in the old man still," she commented, "but as yet he hasn't being able to claim his right to soil the newest serving girl."

She chuckled, which left Gregor feeling strangely adrift. They had been aligned in purpose, yet now he was not privy to everything that was happening—and he had to know.

When she saw his frown, she continued. "The housekeeper has taken it upon herself to protect me from the leering master of the house." Jessie rolled her eyes. "It is only a matter of time, but for the present moment I remain the new, pure and virginal housemaid of Balfour Hall."

There was wisdom in the way she spoke about the place, and her voice was filled with a gentle humor. It was only a matter of time, though? He had to fight the urge to suggest she leave with him now, before it went any further. They had come this far, so that would be ludicrous. But he had missed her presence, and his desire to couple with her was rising by the moment.

Moonlight bathed her suddenly, and it seemed to suit her so well. Her eyes sparkled and her hair tumbled to her shoulders most enticingly. Then she reached up and cupped his jaw, and there was a fondness in her eyes as she smiled at him. "Patience, Gregor. You have prepared me well and soon I will be privy to all the master's secrets."

Staggered by the way she looked, Gregor stared down at her. A desperate sense of need held him captive, and he balked at that. Claiming her mouth, he thrust his tongue into its damp warmth, unable to resist. Hot blood pumped through every vein in response to her, and he felt his cock lifting.

Jessie responded instantly and moved closer, her hands on his shoulders, her body warm and inviting against his. The need to be between her thighs grew even more pressing when he felt her tremble in his arms. Abruptly, she tugged on his hand and drew him down to the ground, where she lay back among the shrubs and gestured for him to join her.

He dropped to his knees at her side, eager to be united with her. The sight of her there, lying on the earth, with the smell of summer flowers all around them, struck him oddly. How true and right it seemed. It was so far from the place he had found her, and on the doorstep of his most hated enemy, and yet Gregor could not help noticing how fitting the setting seemed for her.

"Let me see you." The need he felt to reacquaint himself with her was overwhelming. As he pushed her nightdress up her thighs, he ran his thumbs along their soft insides, his cock hardening as he did so.

Jessie grasped the cotton hem. Half-sitting, she wriggled

it from under her, lifting it over her head and off, before lying back down. With her arms stretched overhead and the white garment twisted between her hands, she looked like a goddess in the moonlight. Her skin glowed and the flash of white fabric was like a torch held aloft in her palms.

Gregor bent over her, one hand resting on the ground at the side of her head to keep him steady. With the other he outlined her form, marveling at it. She was such a luxurious specimen of her sex. He had bought her for a cruel purpose, yet now he felt luck had been on his side when he'd discovered her. The desire he felt was growing more immense by the moment. His cock had stiffened and now it jerked, eager for the clasp of her. Never before had he wanted to be inside a woman so much.

"Oh, Gregor, your hands on me…" Her head rolled.

She did not need to say more; he felt it, too. "Yes, my sweet, I know."

The malleable flesh of her breasts lifted in response to his touch, the nipples growing hard under his fingers.

While he explored her he dropped a kiss on her throat, and another on her mouth. Unreservedly, her lips parted beneath his and the warm, wet cave of her mouth welcomed the thrust of his tongue there. Acknowledgment roared inside him. Jessie wanted him—she wanted him as much as he wanted her.

"Ah, that is good," she whispered, and abandoned the nightdress. With a happy sigh, she pushed her breasts together.

It was an offering he could not resist. Breathing in the now familiar musky scent of her skin, he bent to lick one nipple. Slowly he circled it, and when she moaned aloud he moved to the other, tenderly swiping its knotted peak with his tongue. When her hips lifted toward him, he shifted.

Wrapping his hands under her knees, he opened her legs and climbed between them.

The soft earth beneath his knees barely registered. The only thing he was aware of was her. He was finally there again, finally in that heavenly place. He kissed the soft curve of her belly, then moved lower, smiling to himself when she stroked his head and gasped.

He breathed over the mound of her puss, blowing on the feathery hair guarding her there. She moved restlessly, her body swelling up from the ground as her back arched. The scent of her intoxicated him, and for a moment he closed his eyes and just breathed her in, marveling at the way her fragrance seemed to dance among that of the foliage and the earth. With both hands he held her open, his fingers at the top of her thighs, his thumbs parting the plump, silky folds of her puss. Cursing the fact that it was too dark to see her well, he dipped his head and explored her with his tongue instead.

"Gregor! Oh, Gregor." Again her hands stroked over his head.

The pleasurable sighs she gave swamped his senses. His cock was hard to the point of pain, his ballocks high and tight, his spine throbbing. *Not yet,* he told himself. He had dreamed of this very thing the night before—dreamed of lifting her with his hands around her rump, and holding her open so that he could drink from her—and he would make it happen if it killed him.

With his tongue pressed against her hot folds, he ran it the length of her slit to her entrance, where her melting flow doused his tongue in nectar. He pushed inside, lapping at her. Her fingers clutched at his hair distractedly, her feet lifting from the ground. Without disengaging, Gregor shifted position. Draping her legs over his shoulders, he pushed his hands beneath her bottom and lifted her to gain better access, moving his tongue in and out of that glorious place, devouring her juices until she seemed close to her peak. Then he ran his tongue higher, to her swollen bud, circling it before stroking back and forth.

It was then that Gregor noticed he could see more clearly, for her body gleamed oddly. It looked almost unnatural, glowing like an insect he had once seen in the tropics, a thing they called a firefly. This had to be some trick of the moonlight, or its reflection on a nearby patch of water. Whatever the cause, it meant that he could see the ecstasy in her face. That she was pleasured by this was in no doubt, and the knowledge that he had made her so burned in his chest, his sense of pride and his need for her doubling.

Again he ran his tongue over her bud. Her body lurched. She cried out in her release and he lifted his head. Grappling for his breeches, he set his cock free and then moved between her thighs, ready to mount her.

As he did, the sight before him forced him to a halt.

Jerking back, he stared down at her, for he could not believe what he saw.

Her entire body was glowing, and when her head rolled and her eyes opened to the sky, he saw purple light flash in her eyes, just as he had seen at the Drover's Inn when she had ridden the horse without falling, despite her odd fear of the beasts. Gregor was horrified and yet compelled by the change he witnessed in her.

Was this her real nature? If so, all that had been said about her was true. He clasped her chin and turned her head from side to side, examining her.

Recognition flashed in her eyes when she met his gaze, and she quickly turned her face away. Her eyelids lowered and she let out a strange, mewling sound, one filled with regret. She had not wanted him to know.

Gritting his teeth, he silently cursed himself for his denial of evidence that had presented itself from the moment they'd met. Then he felt her pulling away from him, and knew he had to act on it. With his hand on her jaw, he forced her to face him. "Look at me, Jessie."

She shook her head.

"It is true what they said, isn't it? You practice witchcraft."

Her eyes flashed open. "I've done nothing bad, I promise you, Gregor. I know only a few spells and I have never hurt anyone."

She grasped him tightly, as if afraid he would turn away from her forever.

Yet it was he who should be afraid, and he knew it. He'd dismissed it as nonsense and trickery, and now he had to face the consequences. Gregor Ramsay recognized that for the first time in many years he felt fear, and yet the thing he feared was also the thing he desired above all else.

"Please, Gregor. Please don't cast me aside."

The eerie sound of an owl's call traveled close by on the night air. "I should. I should be done with this now." A chill ran the length of his spine.

She whimpered, and the light that had built around her began to fade. Her head rolled again, her body lifting to meet his.

His thoughts were in chaos, and yet so much that had happened began to make sense. He should not have dismissed it so readily. He should have listened to what they said, but he'd been swayed by the look of her. And now, after all that had passed between them, he could no longer deny that he'd turned a blind eye and a deaf ear because lust had taken him. As soon as he'd seen her, he'd wanted her. That was the truth of it. Rational thought evaded him as images from their time together flashed through his mind. That very day he'd wondered about it, yet still he came here wanting her, wanting Jessie Taskill.

"Have you used your craft on me?" he demanded.

"No, never." The conviction in her tone was reassurance enough, but she rushed on, vehement in her defense. "I have used it to aid your cause, yes, up at the house, but not to hurt or lead you. I could never do that." She paused, and he felt her holding back. "I am grateful for all you have done for me. You saved me from the bailie. I want to help you in your quest here. I would never harm you."

She clasped the collar of his frock coat and drew him closer to her. "Gregor, please, I need you. When we couple it makes me stronger. It helps me in my task."

The feel of her hands roving his back captured him. She was so lush and inviting beneath him, her hips lifting to his. The invitation was so strong and his cock was harder still inside a heartbeat, responding to her desire. His hips began to move again, the need to invade her sweet, succulent territory pressing, no matter the consequence.

Gregor felt the world spinning away, as if everything he had known and experienced was nothing in comparison to this moment where he found himself yearning to push inside this woman, this woman who was both a whore and a witch—a *condemned* witch. As the thought occurred to him and he recalled the baying crowd in the inn in Dundee, an urgent sense of defiance knifed through him.

I will not let it happen.

"God help me, I cannot resist you." He took his cock in his hand, directing it to her hot opening. He wanted her so badly that reason escaped him.

When he pressed against her and her body gave, his crown eased inside. The exquisite grip of her opening on his distended cock winded him. He was forced to pause, to inhale

deeply. Then she rippled beneath him and her sleek channel
embraced him, welcoming him in, and he pushed deeper.
Her cunt enclosed his length, tightening on him. There was
nothing like it, and for a long moment he savored the intense clasp of her body on his. Then he gave in to his need
to thrust deeper—to the hilt. *Jessie.*

Her name rang through his mind when his crown hit
home.

A gasp of pleasure issued from her mouth and her fingers
dug into his back, urging him on. He needed no such encouragement. Driving into her, he arched his spine and placed
a kiss on her pale throat. It was hot and damp to the touch,
and he licked her skin, tasting her.

"Ah," she cried out, "'tis as if you source the strongest
part of me and make me more alive than I have ever been,
more powerful."

He cursed again. It was the crazed stuff of dreams—drink-
addled dreams at that. "Madness, this is madness."

Yet his senses were full of her, and around them the night
itself seemed to hum with her radiance, as if the very air they
breathed had been affected by her. He could not deny what he
saw and felt, and all of it was because of her and what she was.
He sensed her heat spreading outward through the undergrowth, and it was as if she was in tune with the wild things
that lived there. Her eyes glowed. Her hair was flung back
against the ground, and before his eyes strands of it seemed
to plunge into the earth like roots of a tree. Her fingers, too,
melded with the earth beneath her, digging into the dirt in
time with his thrusts.

He lifted up onto his arms, probing deeper into that burning spot of hers. If this was his end, he welcomed it. Her
legs had locked around his hips, her heels bouncing on his
arse when he drew back. The position gave him deeper ac-

cess, and his cock arched inside her. Her cunt clamped hard on him. The pull on his sac was too good, and his ballocks were poised to spill.

"You do not fear me when we are like this, do you?" She asked the question, but there was certainty in her voice, as if she already knew the answer.

This was no ordinary woman, and he was all but enslaved to her. Even if he had not known it before, he knew it now. *How did this happen?*

"Aye, I do fear it," he blurted, as his body drove on, seeking more of her, seeking the ultimate pleasure in their mutual release. "But you are on fire, as if I dipped my wick into the most heavenly place that exists on this earth."

His words seemed to delight her. Her back arched and the fire that welled in her eyes coursed over her entire body and then lit the ground around them.

Her cunt clasped at his length and her head rolled from side to side and she whispered his name. The sound of it coming from her lips urged him on. With a flick of his head, he tossed off a bead of sweat that ran down his forehead.

She reached up and pushed his hair back, her thumb stroking him in between his brows. The gesture lit something in her eyes, and her cunt rippled around his length.

The dam had been breached. "Ah, sweet Jessie, you are magnificent."

She responded, but the words were garbled and he barely recognized them as Gaelic in origin. Her entire body trembled, her cunt milking him as if a warm, slippery fist held his cock.

Incandescent, she glowed as if the moonlight itself was captured in her release. As his seed poured into her and her warm thighs closed around his hips, he wanted nothing else than to be there, to savor that moment, and to see her so magically radiant and glorious at the very peak of their coupling.

chapter Twenty

Sated and somewhat stunned, Gregor rolled onto his back. A moment later he felt Jessie move against him, and when he put his arm around her, she wormed closer against his chest. With her ensconced that way—the way they had lain together on those nights back at the Drover's Inn—he found he was able to ignore the strange reality of this situation for a few moments and just hold her. He kissed the top of her head, and she gave a contented sigh.

Staring at the sky, he noticed that the moon overhead was huge, filling his vision. Was it always this way? He shut his eyes, unable to wrestle with the tide of meaning any longer.

Then the warm huff of her breath on his collarbone helped to anchor him, and the immensity of what had gone before hit him afresh, bringing with it a new honesty. Swallowing hard, he rubbed her back. He was not altogether eager to press forward and gain a better understanding of this situation, but he knew he could not avoid it any longer. He stroked her, embracing the woman he thought he knew, while inviting the woman who was new to him to reveal herself more fully.

Eventually she lifted her head. Silently, she studied him. "I am stronger now," she said.

It was not something he expected her to say, but he saw her

meaning reflected in her expression. Was it truly as she suggested, that some power had been granted her, brought about by what had passed between them? "Is that the way of it?"

She lifted one shoulder in a slight shrug. "I heard some talk of it when I was young, but I've been separated from my kind since then. I know very little of the craft, but I am learning."

She spoke cautiously, as if not sure how much more to reveal to him. Then she lifted her head and looked back at Balfour Hall. There was determination in the set of her mouth.

Gregor tightened his grip on her, hit by the sudden fear of what they would do to her if they discovered her nature. "Can you protect yourself through magic?"

She nodded. "In all honesty that is the only thing I have used it for, for myself. I have helped a few others, but I have been too afraid, because of what I saw them do to my mother."

There was a request for understanding in her eyes. There was also sorrow, and he recognized it was there whenever she remembered her mother's demise. He could not fault her for that, for it was how he felt about his own father's untimely death. "What is it that you wish to do with this talent of yours?"

She flashed him a glance, as if she knew he was not easily led. "Our magic is meant to be used for good, for healing and nurturing. Through it we embrace the seasons and call upon nature to enhance our time here on this bonny earth. Those who do not understand this tell lies about us and persecute us. When I was a child I did not use my magic for many years, and when I ran away I had to, to protect myself. In the work I do, I am lucky to have this gift, and I know that." She sighed. "I have kept myself clean and I have kept myself barren, but even these things make the other women wonder why my fate is so different to theirs. That is why they saw the truth about me, because the whispers were already being passed about that I was not like them."

Gregor nodded. He could see the narrow path she had to walk. To use magic to protect herself brought its own danger. Thankfully, she'd been able to keep herself safe. He stroked his hand down between her breasts and across the soft curve of her belly, where she was still naked and warm from their lovemaking. With one finger he caressed her, and her skin shivered under his touch. He covered her belly with his splayed palm. "You can deny a man's seed, here?"

She nodded. "I have been doing that particular enchantment for so long that I think maybe now I cannot ever change it back, and…" Turning her face away, she left her statement incomplete.

He sensed pain in her, as well as fear and loss. Something inside him yearned for that to be gone. He had thought her mercenary and tough, but beneath it all she was soft and womanly and craved the things she was made for—desire, affection, safety, a warm bed and a better life than she had been granted thus far.

"Hush now. Better things lie ahead. Believe in that."

"Yes, we must, for that is what keeps us alive." A moment later she drew his hand away from her belly and meshed her fingers with his. It was an attempt to divert him from where the conversation had led him.

"Terrible things happen to whores and their children." Her voice had changed, the vulnerability had gone, and yet he felt it still, for he would not forget that wishful, yearning note in her voice. "I have seen the bairns dying of starvation, and I have seen the women beaten and left for dead in the gutter. Or worse still, the pox." Jessie's pretty mouth tightened and she shook her head, as if unwilling to say more.

Gregor's thoughts clarified. He sat up, resting his elbows

on his knees. He pushed his fingers through his hair. "You will not have to return to that. I will double what I promised to pay you. You will be comfortable and you can start a new life in the Highlands."

Jessie sat up alongside him and covered one of his hands with hers. Mercifully, she held her tongue and nodded in agreement.

"The sooner you locate the information we need, the sooner you will be safe and my task will be done." He steeled himself. "Mister Grant, the excise man—do you remember him?"

She nodded.

"I spoke with him last night, and he informed me there will be a sale of land and cattle soon, and it is definitely Wallace who is selling. All I need you to do is to find out which land will be offered to the auctioneer, and I can bid on both it and the cattle."

Her mouth lifted at one corner and mischief flitted through her expression. "Which land would you like it to be, Gregor?"

He was about to respond and then paused, gazing at her, his ability to comprehend her talents sorely stretched. Could it be true? "You think you can hold sway over such a thing?"

"I believe so."

If she could influence the choice of land, all the better. Marveling at her, he simply stared, dumbfounded.

She shivered and reached for her nightdress and pulled it on. "You wish to reclaim your father's homestead, Strathbahn?"

The question pulled him out of his daze.

"Aye, I do." His heart was, however, heavy on that matter. "I cannot go back to Strathbahn, that much I know. But I would like to see a tenant happy there, making good use of the land. Bringing it back to what it was."

"Put your faith in me." She clutched his hand and lifted it to her lips, where she planted a kiss upon his palm. She closed his fingers over it, and he felt both heat and a deep sense of reassurance in the strange token. That she was not quite of this world he now knew for sure.

"I will put my faith in you, if you promise to protect yourself, first and foremost."

When she smiled, it made him want to keep her by his side. However, the knowledge that she could call upon magic calmed his reckless thoughts about forbidding her return to the hall. It was getting more difficult by the moment to imagine sending her back there, but if she could use her secret talent to protect herself and to influence what land would go on sale, that would hasten matters.

As they rose to their feet he held on to her with one hand around her waist. "Meet me at the same time tomorrow night."

"Yes, but wait for me close to the stables." She gestured to the opposite side of the hall, where stables and outhouses sprawled beyond the tall hedges. "There is less chance of me being seen from the windows if I stay close to the building. Be cautious in your approach."

She stepped away, her fingers still in his. As she peered up at him she broke into a soft laugh. "Why, Mister Ramsay, you look so serious. Be happy. We are within reach of your goal."

Her eyes flashed in the moonlight and then she flitted away, a fast-moving white streak in the darkness that held his attention until she vanished from sight, and long after.

Jessie raced along the wall toward the servants' entrance, then paused and rested her back against the cold, rough surface, catching her breath. It was the heady rush of their meeting as much as the run that had left her this way.

When she'd left this spot to meet Gregor earlier that night, she had expected him to be stern and cold, as he had been the last time she'd seen him. Instead he'd looked distraught, and he'd held her close. He had missed her. A fist clenched in her chest, then loosed and blossomed when he kissed and held her.

She could still see him now, his face and shirt visible as he stood among the trees, observing her return to Balfour Hall. Longing whispered across the space between them. Her breath huffed out in a soft laugh. It had to be her essence that made it so. She had marked him like a wild thing claiming its territory. The strange connection was fading even while she stared over at him, but it touched her deeply all the same.

Their lovemaking had been so poignant and so powerful that her magic had swelled and rippled all around them. Now she knew that it truly was Gregor who made her gift more rich and powerful. It was her union with him that had brought it about.

The fact that he had not turned away from her, that he had observed and accepted her in her most natural form, made her release the most overwhelming she had ever experienced. For the first time since she had been split from her kin, she did not feel alone. Never before had she been accepted, and never before had it mattered so much that she would be. At first there had been wariness in his expression, but he had thought on it, she could tell, and when he'd opened to her, oh, the release she felt!

I will treasure this for the rest of my days, however many they shall be. An image of her dead mother flashed through her mind, as it often did when she thought beyond the next moment. With one hand resting on her chest, Jessie stilled her breathing, and then forced herself to turn away and lift the latch on the door.

As she closed the door behind her and clicked the latch into place, a shiver ran over her. She pulled her shawl closer, but her senses warned her it was not cold that touched her now, but the presence of another.

The sound of her own breathing filled her ears. She barely dared turn around, and when she did, her heart sank.

In the darkness, a figure loomed.

Silently, Jessie willed Gregor to be gone, to hurry away from the grounds. If he lingered, discovery was a possibility. She would do everything she could to protect him from that.

"Well now," the man said from the shadows, "what would the new serving girl be doing outside at this time of night?"

Cautiously, Jessie stepped closer, blocking the way to the door. She knew the voice, and she steeled herself to engage with him lest he look outside instead. "I was after a breath of air, Mister Cormac, sire."

As she moved, he did, too, stepping into the fall of the moonlight from the window. It was indeed Cormac, and he was stripped to the waist, his naked chest gleaming pale in the dim light. His breeches were half-undone, and he held a glass in his hand. Not a servant's cup, no; it was one from the master's own shelf. When he closed on her, the smell of fine wine was heavy on his breath.

Drunk. Was it a blessing or a curse?

"A wild one, you are, Jessie. I knew it as soon as I saw you." He threw back the dregs in the glass and set it on a nearby table. Quick as lightning his hands moved to her neck, where he snatched up a skein of her hair and wrapped it around his fist, tugging on it.

It was a blessing, because Gregor would be safely gone by the time Cormac was done with her.

Pausing, he examined her expression. She knew what he sought there. She had met men like him before and knew that he wanted to witness her fear, to see her submission brought about for the sake of survival. Tugging hard, he jerked her head back. Her scalp stung, but the pain only strengthened her will. With his free hand he stroked her throat, then groped her through her nightgown, pulling it open so that he could view the dip between her breasts.

An enchantment leaped into her mind. Something that would distract him, a chair tipping over, or the bottle he had set down spilling. *I cannot risk it, not yet.* But his fingers on her breast made her stomach churn. Her lips moved, the words forming.

Then a voice from the corridor interrupted.

"Cormac?" It was a soft feminine inquiry. "Are you there?"

He had another woman warmed for the night already. Hope kindled in Jessie. He grunted, then threw an answer over his shoulder in the direction of the hallway. "Hasten back to my bed."

However, his gaze still raked Jessie as he spoke, and it lingered in the dip between her breasts, exposed by her nightgown.

Roughly, he bared her breasts. "Make ready for me," he called, even while he tore Jessie's nightgown fully open to examine her more closely.

Damnation. He would have her and then return to the woman who awaited.

"You will bring that wine you promised me?" The woman apparently had conditions.

Cormac cursed and let Jessie loose.

She staggered, clutching at her nightdress to cover herself.

He smirked and then reached for the bottle and the glass. "Later, Jessie," he promised, as he left.

Not if I have anything to do with it, she vowed.

In the shadows, she stayed quiet until his footsteps receded.

While she waited, it occurred to her that Gregor's masterful touch had spoiled her, and it would be hard to warm to another lover after him. That was a major fault for a woman who made her living by opening her legs to men who paid for the favor. She sighed. A moment later, when all was quiet in the hallway beyond, she made her way to her own quarters, and as she did she was begging good fortune to light her way and keep Cormac at bay until she had what she needed of this place. Once her purse was full she could indeed move on from the trade, just as Gregor had promised.

Meanwhile, she could not afford to be soft in the head.

Or the heart.

chapter Twenty-One

"Ah, Jessie." Master Wallace rose to his feet when she entered his parlor the following morning.

Jessie stifled her urge to sigh loudly or stick her tongue out at the master of the house. She had spent a restless night brooding over the contradictions she was currently facing. Gregor wanted her to leave soon, and she wanted that, too, but if she did they would soon say goodbye and part. Yet neither did she want to be here where threats of danger surrounded her and using magic could result in her being condemned once again. The thing that made her strong enough to press on was the sure knowledge that she could influence the master's list and that could benefit Gregor.

Wallace had a lecherous grin on his face and he was headed her way. The eyeful he had gained the day before had obviously whetted his appetite.

She dropped a curtsy. "Good morning, Master Wallace."

She hurried to the fireplace, where she knelt down and began to sweep out the ashes. Master Wallace was at her side within moments, one elbow resting on the stone mantel. His feet were widely planted, the buckled shoes close to her where she knelt on the floor. If she glanced up at him, she would get an eyeful of his breeches, which was exactly his intention. The man wanted her to peer at the spot where they were straining over his weapon, and she did so, briefly, for the thrill that would afford the old miscreant.

It was lucky, she supposed, that he had not come to her room the night before. Or if he had, it was while she was gone from there. That had worried her awhile, and then she realized he would think she was hiding from him, which would only strengthen her role as a novice when it came to matters of physical congress.

"How old are you, Jessie?"

"I am not certain, sire." That was the truth. There'd been no one around to tell her such things when she was a child. Deep in her heart, it was one of the facts she was hoping to discover when she went to the Highlands. Maisie would know. Maisie had been brighter than she and had no doubt kept count.

Wallace was talking again, and Jessie urged herself to listen.

"I wager you have many young men sniffing after you."

Here it comes.

"I do not know what you mean, sire." She afforded him a glance from under her eyelashes, delivering it with a puzzled expression.

"You are a shapely young woman, sturdy. You bait a man. There will be many who are eager to split your virginal crack with their pricks."

He was a real charmer.

Jessie rested back on her haunches but kept her eyes downcast. In the moment's hesitation that she thought an inexperienced woman might have after hearing such a blatant and lewd comment, she congratulated herself for pulling off the role she had been prepared for. "Please, sire," she bleated, feigning panic, "you make me afraid."

That he was attempting to shock her was obvious. Much

like the valet of the house, he wanted to see fear in her face and he wanted to break her. It was the way of most men, for it was the privilege of their sex. While she would not gratify Cormac, she was obliged to do so in this case in order to remain in the room and influence the list Wallace was preparing.

"I have given you nothing to be afraid of yet."

Jessie risked another glance up at him. There was an unsavory glint in his eyes, something that revealed his need to possess and destroy. She'd seen the likes of it before, and avoided such men if she had the option. Sometimes she could not, when Ranald was involved, but any whore who wanted to protect herself was wary of such a man.

"Oh, my," she blurted, and moved as if to wipe up a tear. She did not have long before Mistress Gilroy would appear, and she hadn't yet set her enchantment. If only he had stayed by the desk. It was where she needed to be.

Master Wallace reached over and grasped her hand. Pulling it away from where she dabbed at the corner of her eye, he drew it to the front of his breeches and forced her palm flat against the ridge of his erection there. "Is this what you're afraid of? Too large for you to take, p'raps?"

Jessie had the rebellious urge to declare that she had enjoyed much larger and he should be ashamed of himself for his lack of charm. Instead, she kept her face averted, wriggled and twisted and let out a squeal of horror. She knew what he wanted to hear and—reluctantly—she delivered it. "Oh, Master Wallace, that thing is monstrous large. Please do not make me touch it."

Much as she expected, the offending item swelled beneath her hand.

"I'll do more than have you touch it, my dear."

Just then the door sprang open and a cold draft blew

through the room. Master Wallace's grip on her hand loosened and she jerked away, snatching up her brush and holding it like a shield. If he tried anything else, he would be covered in ashes from the grate.

It was not, as expected, the housekeeper who entered the room; it was Mistress Wallace. Jessie saw her chance, lifted her pail and wandered away toward the desk.

"What do you want?" Wallace demanded as he turned to his wife.

She looked on her husband with obvious distaste, her mouth pinched, her eyes narrowed. "I have received word that Forbes will be here soon. You must promise me that you will make no final decisions until he arrives."

Both of them were indifferent to Jessie's presence, so she took the opportunity to cast her eye over the papers on the desk. The map was there, as were several other documents, two of which had wax seals and ribbons on them. Her eyes flashed shut, and she whispered her enchantment beneath her breath. In the same way her mother would lure a buyer's attention to the herbs and berries they had picked in the forest, Jessie drew attention to the land she named. *"Thoir an aire do Strathbahn."*

Once it was done, she busied herself retrieving several documents that had fallen on the floor when the door had opened. Now that the spell was laid, Master Wallace would have an overwhelming need to add Strathbahn to his list, if it wasn't already there. As Jessie tidied, she thought through what would happen next. There was only one way to determine it had been successful. That night she would need to take the papers to Gregor and have him read them. It would be simple enough. She could collect the documents from this room before she met him, and return them afterward.

She made ready to leave.

Meanwhile, Master Wallace had raised his voice to his wife. "I will do as I please."

Mistress Wallace had left the door to the hallway open, and Mistress Gilroy appeared there a moment later. Her eyebrows gathered when she heard the discussion, and then she glanced at Jessie and beckoned to her. Jessie lifted her tools and quickly joined her in the hall.

When the housekeeper shut the door behind them, the voices inside the room became even louder and more heated.

Mistress Gilroy pinched Jessie's chin between her thumb and finger and turned her face from side to side, examining her as she did so. "You look flushed, Jessie. Is it the master? Has he hurt you?"

Jessie saw her chance. "Begging your pardon, Mistress Gilroy, but the master…he makes me afraid." She pouted. "I know my place and I will do my best, but sometimes I would rather flee than have him touch me."

She was preparing the ground for when she did leave. If the housekeeper assumed it was because the master had frightened her off, so much the better. They would not think otherwise of her sudden departure.

"If you have somewhere else to go," the woman remarked, "I would not blame you. I wish I had done so, many years ago."

Somewhere else to go? Jessie considered the comment. The Highlands beckoned, as did the hunt for her sister and brother. Whether that was where her heart wanted to be was another question altogether.

That night Jessie made her way down the stairs from the attic rooms with even greater caution, remembering the master's nocturnal wanderings and her encounter with Cormac the night before. Cormac had lurked around that day, watching her while she went about her chores. She was ready to use an enchantment against him, if need be. It was a risky business and she would rather avoid making a show of herself with someone as wily as he.

The steep staircase was treacherous for her, making her dizzy and ill in her belly, so it was with a grateful sigh that she reached the hall. As planned, she crept into the master's parlor and located the papers he had been working on earlier. Cautiously she rolled them up, and with the bundle safely tucked under her shawl, she made her way through the hallway and kitchens, her heart beating ever faster.

If Gregor was out there, it meant he had not been angry or afraid during the course of the day. The night before, he had still wanted her, and there was tentative acceptance in the way he'd spoken to her afterward. Jessie knew how the harsh light of day could redirect a person's thoughts, and when she opened the door and stepped outside, she peered into the gloomy shadows over by the stables, desperate for sight of him. She saw nothing. A feeling of dread came over her. If he was not here to meet her tonight, he had abandoned her because of her craft.

Closing the door as quietly as she could, she made her way quickly alongside the manor house until she reached the corner. Again she craned her neck for sight of him. She was about to dart over to the stables when her skin prickled with awareness, and she found herself grabbed and drawn into the shadows. Her heart thundered when a hand closed over her mouth. For a moment she thought she may have been captured by Cormac. Then she felt tenderness in the embrace of the man who held her, tenderness and more.

"Ah, but you feel good," Gregor whispered against her ear, and then ran his lips along her earlobe, kissing its outline and making her dizzy with the rush from his hot breath on her sensitive skin.

The touch of his mouth was so intimate, so direct and so longed for that her whole body shivered with pleasure. Gregor had come despite what had been revealed the night before. First she melted against him, then twisted and turned in his arms to look at him.

He wore dark clothing and his head was bare. In the moonlight, she could see from his smile that he was happy. She clutched his shoulders through his frock coat, assuring herself that it was really him. When their eyes met she felt as if the stars grew brighter and the moon shone for them alone. *He'd come back.*

He stared at her for a moment longer, and then he claimed her mouth, kissing her long and hard, and shifting her up against the wall. She responded eagerly, her hands racing over him, her mouth opening under his. The thrust of his tongue against hers made her hips arch and her cunny melt.

"I thought you might not come," she said when they drew apart.

"You think I scare easily?" He shook his head.

She was pleased, but nevertheless felt uneasy about their current location, so close to the big house. "I hoped that would not be the case," she whispered.

He had her captured against him, with one arm locked around her back. He ran the fingers of his free hand through the loose tendrils of her hair. "How did you fare today?"

Jessie pulled the papers from beneath her shawl. "This will help you, I think, for I heard him discussing it and I swayed him somewhat while he made the list. I believe it shows the lands Ivor Wallace wishes to sell."

Gregor took the pages from her hand and turned them so he could read what was written there in the light of the moon. She watched as he scanned them and then nodded to himself with a half smile. When he looked back at her she knew she'd done the right thing. "This is most useful. You have done well."

Pride blossomed in her. It wasn't something that came her way often and certainly not through the genuine praise of others.

"Is this list for the auctioneer?"

She shook her head. "Wallace and his wife argued today. She said that he must show it to someone she called Forbes, but the master was angry about that."

"Forbes is Wallace's son. I understand that he attempts to have a say in the estate now, and that they are at odds."

"That would make sense. I heard some of the servants speaking in the kitchens, and they spoke about the master's son returning soon. Several of them grumbled about it. It seems he is even less well liked than his father."

Gregor nodded at the list. "Forbes could change this list before it goes to the auctioneer."

She shook her head. "No one can undo my influence there. Anyone who looks at the pages will want Strathbahn to be included."

The bemused expression on Gregor's face made her smile. When he rolled up the papers, she took the bundle from his hand. "I must return this to the cabinet before the night is out, or there will be trouble."

"Now?" He sounded unhappy about it.

"No, but soon." She glanced back along the path she'd come, and then up at the windows, to seek out any candles that may have been lit.

"What is it? Did someone see you leave?"

"No, not tonight. But we must be cautious." The thought

that they might be discovered made her feel quite ill. Gregor's enemy would attack him as an intruder on his land.

"Has something happened? Tell me." He examined her in the moonlight.

The concern Gregor showed softened her. "One of the other servants saw me going back into the house last night, but he knows nothing. I told him I was out getting some air." She nodded toward the stables and clasped his hand. "Come, we will find a more secluded place to talk awhile."

She urged him on with a tug of his hand and then led the way, darting across the courtyard and into the stables. She had meandered through the place several times that day and had located an empty stall beyond the horses, where the day's feed was kept.

However, once they were inside the door, Gregor attempted to take charge. He pointed at a ladder propped inside the entrance. "Here, up to the hayloft. We will be less likely to be discovered if someone comes."

"No, I cannot go up there." Just glancing up made her feel dizzy, and she swayed. The memories crowded in, and she squeezed her eyes shut. "I will fall."

"My God, that's what it is." He clasped her in his arms, steadying her. "I thought it was horses you were afraid of."

"I know."

"Why didn't you tell me?"

"Because you would think me a fool."

"You are no fool." Tipping her head back with his hand under her chin, he looked into her eyes under the faint glow of moonlight that reached inside. "Then the cart was no better than the horse?"

She shook her head.

"And this?" He lifted her in his arms, and for a moment her feet lost contact with the floor.

He was thinking about that first night, in the tollbooth in Dundee, when he'd lifted her against the wall to gain better access to her. Laughing softly, she thumped his chest with her fist. "If you hold me, it is not so bad."

That was the truth, but she had not even realized it was the case before she said it aloud.

He set her back down on the ground, but kept her close in his arms. "I wish you had told me."

The way he studied her made her want to explain. There was no reason not to, now that he knew about her magic. And he *had* returned. "It was because they made me and my sister, Maisie, stand on the pillars at the church gates while they stoned our mother. They thought it would teach us right from wrong. A man forced me to watch, holding me upright when I nearly fainted, to teach me of her evil ways and what became of people who attempted to cure others of their ailments."

"Oh, my precious." Gregor held her against him.

She clutched him close and rested her head on his shoulder. "Whenever my feet leave the ground I am put back in that place. My gut churns and the world spins."

Gregor's grip on her had tightened and she could tell he was about to respond. She shifted and rested her fingers over his lips, looking up at him. She could not bear it if he said anything. If he did, she would grow weak, and she didn't want that. "Please, make love to me instead. That makes me strong enough to fight the world."

He squeezed her. "I know. I saw it last night."

At her center, she ached for him. There in his arms she was sure she needed to couple, more than anything in life. Partly because it gave her the power to sail through the day and address its trials, to influence matters in the house and sway the master. Already she felt the fire kindling. The source of her magic was building within her, set alight by the sure knowledge that they would mate and it would nurture her power. However, she also wanted Gregor Ramsay for a much more basic reason—desire. This man fired her blood like no other had, and it was hard to imagine that it would ever feel the same with another. Soon this task would be done and he would be on his way back to his ship. In the meantime she was grateful for the opportunity of each and every moment they shared.

He nodded over his shoulder, and guided her away from the entrance and into the gloom. "If they knew what you were and that you had removed those papers from the house, they would show less mercy than the crowd in Dundee." With a sudden, swift move, he kissed her forehead. "I could not stand it if any harm came to you because of this."

"It won't." Grasping his hand, she led him to the stall at the end of the stable where hay was stacked for the horses' morning feed. "'Tis dark in here, but I feel sure you will find me," she whispered, teasing him.

On her hands and knees, she scurried away from him, only to feel him clasp her waist and hold her still. She canted up her skirts and petticoat, then swayed her hips, inviting him closer. When his fingers wended their way around her hips and grasped her bottom, she tossed back her head joyfully. "It was that, you say, that first caught your eye?"

"It was." He slapped her bared arse playfully, and then lifted her, stretching her knees wider and moving between her thighs. Her back arched and she swayed unsteadily while she waited breathlessly for his first thrust.

He seemed to be in no rush, however, for his hands outlined her bottom, squeezing the flesh possessively. "Ah, your delectable arse. How I missed seeing it these past two days."

"Please, Gregor," she begged.

"I intend to fill you, be sure of that."

Nevertheless, he tortured her for several moments longer by stroking her damp folds, keeping her waiting. The intimate act made every part of her sizzle and burn. When his hand cupped the swollen flesh of her nether lips and he squeezed, hard, she gasped aloud. Then he splayed her wide open. Jessie almost fainted. The extreme state of arousal she was in made her body flash with heat and her skin grow damp. She braced herself for his entry, desperate for it.

His fingers groped, exploring her cunny. The brush of his knuckles as he turned his hand, reaching inside her, let loose a ragged cry. "Ah, please," she blurted, "take pity on me."

"Hush, now, my precious harlot. I have the remedy for what ails you." He moved the blunt head of his erection along her slippery opening.

Oh, yes. She shifted her weight, leveled her head. The stiff fabric of her stays and bodice chafed at her breasts, and beneath her knees rough needles of hay tugged at her woolen stockings. But all that faded to nowt when he drove his length into her, stretching her open, filling her.

Dizzying light akin to shooting stars filled her vision. All she could do was pant for breath as the contact took her over. Then he rode her, in and out. Each time he filled her anew, she felt faint with pleasure. Her thighs shuddered. Her cunny swallowed his length each time, and then he pressed home and the blunt head of his rigid shaft massaged her deep inside, making her wriggle and buck.

"You are most eager," he commented, and there was humor in his tone.

His hand resting on her back did nothing to calm her. The stall had become increasingly hot, as if a storm was building. Beyond the wooden panels that separated them, the horses snuffled and shifted.

"I cannot deny it." Hot juices ran down her thighs. She shoved her fingers deeper into the hay bale. Her senses were so keen and sharp that each blade of hay seemed to connect with the wild tingling at her center, heightening her restless state. Her arms shook with the effort to remain upright, and her breasts felt unbearably crushed within her stays, the nipples rigid and stinging.

Then she felt his fingers stroking her most sensitive spot. He had bent over her back and reached between her thighs to rub her swollen nub, seemingly determined to bring her off while he held back.

"Gregor!" Her sheath tightened and she hit her peak. It was so sudden and all-encompassing that her forearms gave way and she slumped against the hay bale she had previously braced against.

"Can you take more?" There was amusement in his voice now.

He'd been holding back. That renewed her flame.

Struggling upright, she pushed him onto his back and climbed over him, straddling his hips. Need rolled through her when she stroked his bowed shaft. It jerked eagerly, and she found the surface hot and clammy from being inside her. She mounted him, taking him to the hilt. At first she could scarcely breathe, because it felt so good. Then she arched over him and found his mouth, kissing him fleetingly. Their fingers meshed, and she felt his encouragement in the squeeze of his strong hands.

She was powerful because of this.

His rod pushed up against her center, making her entire body hum. Quickly she worked him and they raced for the prize, moving urgently in rhythm until he whispered her name and his cock exploded inside her. Bending over him, she worked him still, grinding her hips from side to side as she kissed his face in the darkness. It was the last jerk of his cock that tipped her over the edge and melted her to him.

They rolled free of each other, then together again, facing one another.

"You are radiant, my sweet." He stroked her hair back from her forehead. "If you know magic like this, why have you worked as a whore?"

Instinctively, she bristled.

"I only want to understand you better," he added.

"I worked at other things. I was brought up by a family who feared me. Ran away when I was old enough to know how. For a time I lived in the woods and I was happy." Jessie sighed as she remembered. It had been a good time. Hard, but good. It felt right to be there so close to nature, but when winter came she'd sought help. A widow woman took her in, in exchange for work on her patch, doing things that she could no longer manage.

"Then I worked on the land, in exchange for a bed. Eventually I moved on." The widow woman had died, and distant neighbors arrived to pick her home clean, casting Jessie out as they did so. One of them had even accused her of making her employer sick.

"I made my way to Dundee, because that's where my father had gone."

"Your father? You have not mentioned a father before."

"I did not know him. He left before I was born, went to sea, by all accounts. My mother waited and waited for him to return, as he'd said he would, and eventually she told us we would find him, and went after him. Determined to locate him, she was." Jessie laughed softly. "Perhaps she couldn't face the fact he had left her with three bairns."

It was magic that had made him run. That was something they knew by instinct. Still, she had followed the trail south.

"When we came to the Lowlands, however, things changed. My mother's talent for magic and healing brought trouble."

Gregor drew Jessie closer and kissed her face.

For a moment she allowed herself to feel only that, the tenderness of his embrace and the succor he offered.

"What of your father?"

"Oh, I asked about him in every inn in Dundee, but none knew him, or at least none that would admit to it."

"I will ask, when my ship returns. If he is still alive I can help you find him."

Jessie pressed a finger to Gregor's lips. "I fear the moonlight has touched your mind and addled it," she teased. "If he is still alive, he will be a stranger to me. I have long since given up hope. The best I can do is return to the Highlands, where we were once happy and safe, and where Lennox and Maisie may be waiting for me."

"Your kin?"

"Maisie is my sister, and my twin. Lennox was several years older than us."

"Twins often have a bond."

She nodded, once again touched by Gregor's sensitivity on such matters. He was curious about her siblings, and yet he had said he had none. "Sometimes I feel her close to me, as if her thoughts and mine collide. I think she has fared better than I have, but I know that might just be hope and wishes leading my thoughts." Jessie pressed her hand to her heart when the familiar ache passed through her.

"And your brother?"

"He was a wild one."

"Wilder than you?"

"Oh, aye." Lennox sometimes appeared to her in dreams, and those dreams were always filled a dark sense of foreboding. "He had the gift even as a lad, and he played with it more than we did, learning fast." It had brought him trouble, as it had her, perhaps even more so. She pushed away the clouds that hovered, offering Gregor a smile. "It's been a long time now I've been trying to earn a purse to carry me back to my beginnings."

"And whoredom was the best way?"

Was that a note of disapproval in his voice? Now, after all that had gone between them? The notion intrigued her. Was he jealous, curious, or simply disapproving? The latter was not unusual; most people considered whores no better than vermin. Yet he had been much more possessive of her since she had left his side. The times they had met secretly at Balfour Hall were even more passionate than before. These two nights had been her happiest ever, yet the two of them were on a knife's edge. The threat of discovery lurked, her condemnation far too recent to ignore, and even when they were free of this task and Gregor's burden had been lifted, that moment would bring pain, because he would be gone. "You disapprove of whores, even though you use them?"

"I am curious about your reasons, that is all."

"People pay less attention to harlots, and wherever I went suspicion about my craft followed. Besides, I had run out of choices...there was no other option." It smarted, for she had pride, even though she'd had to bury it. She and Gregor were being honest with one another now, however, and Jessie saw no reason to pretend her life had not been hard.

But he was listening to her silently, and her discomfort about her confession grew. "Surely you cannot hate me for being a whore, when you seem to enjoy using me as such."

"No." There was regret in his voice. Why?

"If I had not been a whore," she added, "you would not have found me." She reached for him, wishing she could see him better in the gloomy stall, watching for his reaction. As she did, her heart beat a little faster.

He narrowed his eyes, but she could just see his faint smile. "You are a provocative woman, Jessie. Do you want me to be angry?" He rested his thumb against her chin, his mood thoughtful. "Or jealous, perhaps, the way I was when you dallied with Mister Grant?"

They were dancing around one another again, just as they had the night before, and she had to work hard to feign denial a moment longer. "Why would you be jealous? I am a servant to you, no more. You were annoyed about Mister Grant only because you had invested time and money in me. You need me to seduce your enemy. That's my task."

In a flash he was over her, pinning her down with the weight of his body. "Leave this place. I want you to come back with me now." He rained passionate kisses on her neck while he rocked his hips against hers. "I know enough already. There is no need for you to seduce Wallace."

Jessie smiled into the darkness and drew her lower lip between her teeth, her hips rising to meet his. "Why, Mister Ramsay, I think you are allowing your cock to think for you."

The laugh he gave was gentle. "Perhaps, but I hold the same opinion as my cock."

Closing his handsome face between her palms, she shook her head. "I do not have to seduce him in order to hold sway over him."

Gregor peered at her, then stroked his hand over hers, meshing their fingers. "Magic?"

"I have today influenced what he will sell. As you saw on the list, it will go to auction soon. If you want your father's land back, you can bid on it." She thought that would please Gregor, but his frown remained.

"It is dangerous, using magic. Word may have come from Dundee about your escape. Your name will be whispered."

It was true. A raw sense of clarity descended upon them. "No one has witnessed my actions, only the results."

Gregor's mood was somber as he considered her words. "Be sure that is how things remain. Promise me you will not use magic when anyone else is there?"

That was difficult to promise, since she might need it to protect herself. "Please do not fret, Gregor."

He was silent awhile, but his restlessness did not abate, as if a deep unhappiness pervaded his soul. "Has Wallace tried to touch you?"

Jessie drew a deep breath. "Scarcely. The will is there, but he has other concerns at the moment."

Gregor did not seem convinced. "There is no need to go back. You have brought more than enough information already."

"We do not know when the land will go to auction," she answered. "That information will help you, and then you will be rid of this need to avenge your father."

He considered her silently before he replied. "The date of the sale does not matter. I will wait close to Saint Andrews until it is time. I have told the auctioneer I will pay him well, and he will tell me when the time comes. Please, Jessie. You have more than earned your wages. Leave with me now and you can be on your way to the Highlands in the morning."

On her way to the Highlands.

A few days ago she would have grabbed the opportunity and would be making merry as she went on her way. Instead, the thought made her heart sink. If she were to leave in the morning, she would never see Gregor again. That time would come soon enough, she knew, but she wasn't ready yet.

Deep in her heart she felt it was not the right time, because she was just starting to learn things for him. *Or am I just blinding myself to the fact that I have grown to care for this man and cannot bear the idea of bidding him a final farewell?*

"His suspicions will be raised if I leave now." Stubbornly, she rose to her feet and straightened her clothing. "I will go back to the house now. I have to return the papers, or this auction will not go ahead at all. You know that much is true."

He gave a frustrated sigh and made ready to leave the stall. "I suppose you are right."

When they arrived at the entrance, she studied him in the better light. "I will keep my ears and eyes open, and meet you here tomorrow night."

There was a frown creasing his forehead. "Make ready to leave soon."

"Soon, yes."

"And you will not seduce him?"

She rolled her eyes. "No, Gregor, I will not seduce him, despite the fact that is what you spent so long training me to do."

Gregor's mood remained serious. In fact, he seemed almost woebegone as he considered her remark. "I confess that the idea torments me. Wallace is my enemy, and I would not wish him on any woman. In our short acquaintance I have come to realize it was wrong of me to expect that of you."

For some odd reason Jessie felt as if both tears and laughter were about to assault her. But when she saw his serious expression she quelled the laughter and dabbed at her eyes, blinking away the emotion. "I will be safe. Now let me finish what I promised I would do for you."

"You are a headstrong woman. I can tell you are set on this, but I would be happier if you left with me now."

"Those words make me stronger." Her heart brimmed. "Promise me this—that when we are done with this task you will hold me and kiss me while I wear my blue silk gown one last time, before we say farewell."

He snatched her against him. "The gown is yours." He kissed her mouth, softly brushing her lips with his. "I promise."

She melted into him, her head tipping back.

It was even harder to part than it had been the night before. They lingered there at the corner of the manor house exchanging long kisses, their fingers entwined, their bodies pressed together.

Eventually she drew away and placed her fingers to his lips.

The feeling of elation that had encompassed her slowly ebbed as she parted from him. When she reached the door, she glanced through the small windowpane, a feeling of trepidation rising. Inside, the kitchen was all in darkness. She'd told Gregor she was safe. Was she? Drawing a deep, steadying breath, Jessie opened the door and crept inside.

Once her eyes grew accustomed to the gloom she made her way through the passageways and into the grand hallway beyond. It was then that a feeling of extreme unease took hold of her. Squinting in the gloomy hallway, she looked toward her destination, the room with the cabinet, where the lists must be returned. Under her shawl, she gripped the rolled papers tightly. Then registered the fact that the parlor door had opened.

Cormac emerged. A bottle dangled from his hand, one he had purloined from the master's special supply that he kept in that room, no doubt.

Jessie stepped to the far side of the hallway, into the shadows, and flattened herself against the wall. Holding her breath, she listened. It was with a sinking feeling that she realized he was turning the key in the lock. If he took it with him, or hid it, she would have to use her magic, and that would take her longer to return the documents.

The soft scuff of stocking feet on the polished wood floor grew nearer, and she closed her eyes and muttered an enchantment. It was something she had never tried before—to slip into the shadows and be as one with them. With her finger, she drew an imaginary curtain closed in front of her. It was something Lennox had done, to scare them witless. There was no telling if it would work, and she forced herself to open her eyes, peer through the hazy cover and watch.

Something caught Cormac's attention, and he walked down the hallway quietly, glancing about as he went. When he looked her way, he peered directly at her, into the gloom.

Her blood froze.

A moment later he turned away and retreated.

He had not seen her! Jessie began to breathe again when she heard the stairs above creaking as he returned to his quarters. She had done it; she had mimicked Lennox's shadow spell. Her heart beat freely once again.

She could only hope Cormac was taking the bottle back to whomever he'd been with the night before, and not looking for her. The sooner she was done with this the better, for he would move on to her when he became bored with the other woman. His leering glances assured Jessie of that.

Once the sound of his movements had faded away, she darted over to the door and found to her relief that the key had been left in place. She entered the room and raced to the cabinet, where she replaced the papers. A moment later she was back out in the hallway.

As she made her way cautiously up the stairs, following in Cormac's tracks, she wondered whether luck had been on her side. Perhaps he'd been too drink-addled to notice her there in the shadows. Perhaps it was because her magic was growing more powerful and she had hidden herself well. If so, that was Gregor's doing. Her relationship with him was giving her what she needed to learn and grow her craft.

Love, she realized. *I love him.*

And it pained her deeply, because this man who had brought her so many precious things would soon be gone from her life.

chapter Twenty-Two

The following morning Master Wallace pounced before Jessie even got as far as the fireplace. She had barely stepped through the door when he grabbed her and had her pushed up against the wall.

The pail and her tools fell to the floor with a clatter. "Master Wallace!"

"Let me look at you." He jerked her chin to face him. There was whisky on his breath and his eyes looked strange, as if he'd had little sleep. "I came to you last night, but you were not in your room."

Jessie's gut tensed. "P'raps you came when I was doing a task for Mistress Gilroy. What was it you required me for, sire?"

If she continued to weave a web of lies, she might be trapped in it. She struggled to offer him a becoming glance, the way Gregor had taught her to. Why was it suddenly so hard to do what she had done so easily and so well in Dundee? If this were Gregor, it would not be hard, yet she could not force herself to pretend it was, especially knowing what she did.

'Tis a task. Gregor's happiness and my fee are my rewards.

Wallace's hands roamed her waist and hips. "I require you

to make this old man happy. Make me smile as I once did, Jessie."

The drink was talking here. He swayed against her as he grasped her breast through her bodice.

Jessie fought the urge to flinch and struggle out of his grasp. "How can I make you smile, sire?"

His face loomed closer, and then he sniffed her hair. "I knew a lass like you, a long time ago."

It was the last thing she'd expected him to say.

Again he grasped her breast, squeezing it roughly through her clothing. "She was a pretty woman, with soft skin." He lifted his hand and ran his knuckles over Jessie's cheek. "Always had a smile for me."

There was a wistful expression on his face.

Jessie forced a smile, hoping it would assuage him.

"Aye, that's it." His eyes grew sad. "What I would not do to see her again. Agatha was her name. Aggie they called her."

Jessie's attention sharpened. *Agatha*... The name sounded familiar and she scoured her memory to place it. Perhaps she had heard it in the kitchens. While Master Wallace rambled on about this woman, she turned her face away and flitted through the various conversations she had witnessed since she had been at the house. No, there had been no mention of anyone called Agatha. Still, it tapped away inside her mind—and then she remembered. Gregor had mentioned the name the day he'd taken her to Strathbahn.

She inhaled quickly, startled at the connection. Agatha was Gregor's mother! Jessie glanced at Master Wallace, who was smiling to himself, his thoughts faraway. Could it be a coincidence? Agatha was a common enough name.

Shifting so that she could get a better look at him, Jessie noticed there was genuine regret in his expression. He was talking about his sweetheart.

When he saw that she was looking at him, he smiled again. "How old are you, lass?"

How peculiar. He had asked her the very same question the day before. Was that the reason? Because he was thinking of his old sweetheart? Jessie's mind raced. She shrugged. "I am not sure, sire."

"Nineteen. That's how old Agatha was."

Am I nineteen? It was one of many questions that haunted her, estranged as she was from the basic facts of her early life. Still, her mind raced with curiosity about the identity of the woman he was thinking of. "Was Agatha a local lass?"

"From Craigduff, she was."

"Did you marry her?"

"No, oh, no. Alas, she married another, but I've never forgotten her." A wistful smile lingered around his mouth, and he stared down at Jessie's breasts with unseeing eyes as he groped at her, his actions undone by his curious state of mind.

The man was scarcely able to stand. Decisively, Jessie grasped his elbow and ushered him toward his armchair. Mercifully, he let her lead him, and when he sat down he slumped back in the chair. Jessie noticed that he looked somehow diminished. He mumbled beneath his breath and stared into the distance. A life of regret had made him this way, perhaps—a bitter man, greedy, unhappy and living on memories.

For a moment, she pitied him.

Then she turned away, went to the fireplace and completed her task with utmost haste. She left without a further word to him, for she was not eager to draw his attention back to her.

As she went about the rest of her duties, Jessie's thoughts raced. Had Ivor Wallace's dealings been driven in part by jealousy? Did he harbor a grudge against Gregor's father, because his sweetheart had married him instead?

The more she thought about it, the more she longed for

the hours to pass so that she could talk to Gregor and tell him about the discovery she had made. Would he be relieved to know the reason behind Wallace's actions? Would it enable him to forget what had happened to his father?

No, she knew him well enough now. Gregor's need for revenge ran deep, and it would not be assuaged by this. In fact, the news might only strengthen his cause. Nevertheless, Jessie could not shake the feeling that this had been Wallace's motive to destroy the happiness at Strathbahn—a long-lost sweetheart, and hatred for the man she had married.

Each day it grew harder for Gregor to keep away from Balfour Hall. He barely slept, because he knew it was wrong of Jessie to bring those documents outside. Despite the fact they had revealed so much useful information to him, he wished she had not taken the risk. What if someone had discovered her carrying papers about in the night? What if she'd been found as she returned them?

They would punish her. The thought made him murderous.

Restlessly he paced the room, refusing food when Morag brought it. When she lingered, Gregor eventually looked at her directly.

"Pardon me, Mister Ramsay. I was wondering, will Miss Jessie be returning?"

There was a wistful look in her eyes. Even the serving girl missed her presence. And why wouldn't she? Jessie had filled these rooms with life and spirit.

"She will, and soon." Aside from anything, Gregor did not think he could stand another day of this interminable waiting, wondering what in hell's name was going on with Jessie up at Balfour Hall. She would leave with him tonight even if he had to gag her and tie her to the horse.

Morag smiled, dropped a quick curtsy and was gone.

Gregor was disturbed by the girl's question, for it forced him to consider his own feelings on the matter. When he had first taken these rooms it was his life at sea that he missed, the boards beneath his feet, the roll of the ship and the adventure of never knowing quite what the day would bring. That lust for the seafaring life was all but buried in him now, because it was Jessie he longed for when he was not with her. It rattled him to find himself so concerned about a woman he had known for scarcely a week. She was a whore, a condemned woman who practiced witchcraft.

But it is Jessie.

How was it that she'd filled his life so quickly? He thought about her constantly, to the point of obsession. Wandering barefoot to the servant's room, where he had so cruelly locked her in, he stared at the meager furnishings. At first he thought the room bore few reminders of her presence, and then he spotted her old clothing folded neatly beneath the cot. Hauling the bundle out, he sat on the edge of the cot and handled the garments, remembering with a smile how fetching she had looked in the torn bodice, with her black hair tumbling over her shoulders and mischief in her eyes. Wistfully, he bunched the fabric in his hands. Resting his elbows on his knees, he buried his face in the garments.

Jessie, sweet Jessie. The lingering scent of her made him harden. Images of her in the splendor of release flitted through his mind. He recalled how she had been that fateful night when he'd first realized her witchcraft was real. Radiant and powerful, she'd looked like a goddess. Being inside her was magical enough, but seeing her that way—with her passionate nature so vividly apparent—meant he could not doubt her ability to work magic. She was far beyond everything he had thought she was, and he'd already decided she was the most lush, captivating creature he'd ever had the good fortune to encounter.

It was then that it occurred to him she could have left his room, just as she could have broken out of the tollbooth in Dundee. She'd told him that. Of course, he hadn't believed her. Now that he knew her secret, the pieces began to fall into place. He glanced about the servant's quarters. She could have left here at any point.

It was the promise of the purse that kept her here, he told himself.

Was it, though? The night before, he'd offered to pay her so that she could be on her way. But she'd insisted she wanted to see it through, to ease his sadness about his father. Compassion played its part.

She understood him, because her family had been torn apart just as his had. That made them both what they were—hardy, determined individuals, people who would survive no matter how bad their luck. Was this why he felt such a strong bond with her? Because they had this in common? Was this also why she understood his need to resolve things, to right the wrongs of the past? That had to be the explanation for the way he felt, which was positively wretched. He regretted that he had chosen Jessie, because he had put her at risk. She was vulnerable because of everything she was. *And I have sent her into a viper's nest.*

Gregor ground his teeth as he thought on it, cursing his poor choices. He was torn between a goal that he had spent eleven long years working toward, and concern for a woman he had known for just a few days.

As he sat there contemplating the situation, sunlight slowly filled the room. Something reflected the light and caught his eye. Between his feet, wedged between two floorboards, something glinted. He bent down to take a closer look. It was two shillings, by the looks of it. The coins were on their sides and had been pushed down between the boards.

Realization hit him: it was the two shillings he had given her in Dundee, when she had asked him to prove that he was good for his word. He had never once wondered where she had secreted the coins, but when he saw them hidden there, carefully concealed and covered over in dust, it made his gut ache. Every penny counted to this woman. She'd had to hide this bit of money as she would have had to hide her earnings, living with a greedy pimp and a bunch of other whores.

Gregor stood up, dropping her ragged possessions onto the cot. Jessie had suffered enough. From what little she had revealed of herself, he knew that persecution of one sort or another had haunted her all her life. If Wallace knew what she was, he would torment and persecute her, as well.

Gregor did not want life to be that way for Jessie Taskill anymore. Once he acknowledged that, he hated himself for the dangerous position he had put her in.

Within moments he was readying to leave. It was too early, yet he wanted to go up there and remove her from Balfour Hall before she put herself at any more risk on his behalf.

Jessie had refused to leave the night before, but he would hear no more of that talk. She'd set her sights on completing this task, and had convinced him she could protect herself, but he could not bear the uncertainty a moment longer. The urge to walk in, floor Wallace with a prize punch, and remove his woman overtook all his carefully crafted notions of subtle and devastating revenge, plans he'd spent years thinking up.

Gritting his teeth, Gregor made an effort to pace himself. If Wallace became aware that Jessie was connected to him, that would only bring more trouble her way, and Gregor would never forgive himself for that. With more than a little unwillingness he reminded himself that she would meet him at midnight. He would take her away from Balfour Hall then—even if she was kicking and screaming while he did so. With that in mind, he attempted to wait.

Time moved far too slowly. Never before had a day dragged by so interminably for Gregor Ramsay and by midafternoon he was on his way.

It was past sunset when he secured his mount in the forest above Balfour Hall. Staring down at the house, he tried to catch sight of her. That made him even more restless, and the urge to storm down there threatened to unhinge him. He could not take that risk. Instead he began to walk back toward the village, striding quickly to divert himself from doing anything rash.

By the time darkness fell he found that his feet had led him to the kirk and the small graveyard on the hill above Craigduff, where he'd spent his last hours years ago, before departing from Scotland. It was there he had watched his father's coffin being lowered into the grave beside his mother's.

He peered at the church, a dark profile against the night sky. When the breeze lifted and the clouds scudded away he saw a familiar path between the gravestones and opened the gate.

Moonlight scarcely lit the area, but his memories served him well and he wended his way through the graves to the exact place. His father had taken him there every Sunday after they attended the service, to pay their respects to his mother. Through each and every season they had come, and as Gregor thought back on it he could almost hear the congregation making their way home after the service, while he and his father stood there, their hats in their hands as they looked down at the grave of the wife and mother they still mourned.

Resting on his haunches, he rubbed his hand over the gravestone. His father's name had been added. There had barely been enough funds to buy the coffin, let alone pay for the burial, but he had sent his first wage to the stone merchant with a letter requesting the work be carried out. Gregor was glad to see that it had been done.

Mired in his memories, he was startled when he heard shuffling footsteps close by. With a quick glance over his shoulder he saw it was an old woman hunched over a stick, her head and shoulders swathed in shawls. She tottered and swayed and hummed to herself under her breath. Gregor assumed she was taking a shortcut through the graveyard to her home. He was several strides away from the path she was on, and estimated that if he remained as he was, she would not notice him.

Much to his surprise, however, she paused and then turned off the path, heading directly for him. She lifted her stick from the ground and poked his shoulder.

"Gregor Ramsay, is that you?" The woman peered at him in the gloom, and then broke into a toothless grin. "Well, I never. I thought it was you the moment I saw you by your parents' grave."

Bemused, Gregor stood up.

The old woman pushed back her shawl from her forehead and shook her head at him. "You do not remember me. I am your mother's cousin, Margaret Mackie."

Gregor was not sure which startled him more, that someone here remembered him or the fact that her face, although aged, was so familiar that he was swept back through the years. "I do remember you, Cousin Margaret. I was merely surprised that you spotted me here on this dark night."

She gave a gravelly laugh. "I did at first wonder if a demon was loose in the graveyard when I saw you there."

The laughing made her cough, and he realized how frail

she was. He crossed to her side and put a steadying hand beneath her elbow.

She lifted her stick again and pointed toward the village. "Walk me home, lad, and while you do you can tell me where in God's name you've been hiding yourself these past years."

Gregor had not been called "lad" for many years, and it made him smile. He wasn't altogether willing to head into the village in case anyone else recognized him, but he owed her this and more. Margaret had had a hand in his upbringing, in the early days after his mother's death. Besides, it would keep his mind off the interminable waiting until he could meet Jessie at the appointed hour.

Once she was moving Margaret seemed stronger, and her wit was every bit as sharp and forthright as he recalled.

"Have you a wife and children?" she demanded.

"No."

"Well, you'd better be thinking about it soon. 'Tis fine and dandy for a man to wait around before making his choice, but it is not fair on the bairns if he is too old to work to support them, after bringing them into this sorry world."

Margaret's concerns were so far removed from his own that her comments perplexed him. Gregor felt as if he'd been shunted back twenty years, when he had often accompanied her along this path to her home and she would attempt to fill his mind with womanly notions that he'd never encountered before.

"I worried about you to begin with, especially after you torched the house. I knew you weren't faring too badly," she continued, "because the stonemason spoke widely about the good sum you sent for his handiwork."

It hadn't occurred to Gregor that anyone would miss him. Apparently both Robert and Margaret had. He'd not done right by them, disappearing like that and sending no word, and he felt regret over his actions. "Those were my first wages aboard ship. I signed up to serve at sea, after the funeral."

"Aha, so the sea took you." They had reached the main street and she gestured at the houses as they passed, pointing out who was dead and who had wed and had bairns. She obviously felt he should be brought up-to-date on such things. At the door to her cottage she ushered him in and told him to sit at the table, announcing she had freshly baked bread, ham and a wee dram of the good stuff.

Gregor glanced back, toward Balfour Hall.

It was still too early, so he went inside.

The gloomy interior of Margaret Mackie's cottage was just as he remembered it, uncannily so. A fire burned in the grate, shedding enough light to see that her low wooden chair was in the same position, to one side of the fire, where she would be able to see the window from her seat. Next to it was the wooden stool he'd sat on as a young lad when he visited.

Margaret made him take the chair, while she continued informing him about everyone in the village. All the while Gregor yearned to be on his way to Balfour Hall—to Jessie.

Eventually the old woman sat on the stool, and studied him quietly. "You have a scar."

With a wry smile, he nodded. "I do."

"You've not come home to stay, have you, lad?"

"I think not, Cousin Margaret. I have a worthwhile life as a mariner."

"Why did you come back now?"

Lord, she was an inquisitive type. But now that she had started on him, he recalled that about her.

What could he say? "It was time for me to see the place again and stare it in the face." It was partly the truth, and he realized that now because Jessie had forced him to it. He regretted the way he had treated her afterward.

"After Da's death I fled. I thought I had to leave or I would continue to see that image of him...hanging there, every day of my life. As it turned out, the memory of it traveled with me."

"There's no escaping something like that."

They sat in silence for a moment, both of them remembering Hugh Ramsay and his untimely death.

"Now, Gregor, before you take your leave and disappear once more, there is something I need to say. Your mother would never forgive me if I did not take this opportunity to tell you something that she wished you to know when you reached the age of twenty-one."

Gregor glanced at the door yet again, eager to be on his way to Jessie. What nonsense was this that Margaret had to tell him? No doubt some sentimental message that his mother had left on her deathbed, something his father would have frowned upon. "Were you with her when she died?" he asked, humoring her.

"Aye, but I'd known this since before you were born."

Her cryptic comments barely distracted him from his need to get up to Balfour Hall and ensure that Jessie was safe. This was not what he'd expected to transpire this night, and he was beginning to grow impatient. Yet he knew that he owed his relative this time. Even so, he felt sure that any messages from his mother would be embellished by the romantic reflections of a weary spinster over the intervening years.

She reached for his hand and held it tightly. "This will come as a dreadful shock to you, but I believe that I am the only living person who knows this, so I must tell you now while I have the chance. Hugh Ramsay was a good man, and he brought you up well, but it was not him who was responsible for you coming into this world."

Her words made no sense. "Whatever do you mean?"

"Gregor, Hugh Ramsay was not your father."

Gregor shook his head dismissively. "Surely you are mistaken?"

She seemed put out and even insulted by that remark. "No, I am not. Don't forget that your mother and I lived together as sisters, before she was wed. When she fell pregnant, it was meself she turned to."

Margaret reached for her flask of whisky and poured another dram into the mug he held in his hand. "Your real father...well, he was off in Edinburgh plotting against the English by the time she found out. It would be weeks, even months before he returned."

She shook her head and the look in her eyes was distant, as if she had traveled back to that moment. "It was a dreadful time for your mother, God rest her soul. She didn't sleep or eat, fretting over it. I feared she would lose the child." Awkwardly, Margaret glanced his way, returning from her memories. "Hugh Ramsay had been attempting to court her for a long while."

Gregor's mind raced as he tried to come to terms with the news. He wanted to deny it, but at the same time he remembered how people would joke about the fact he stood a good head higher than his father by the time he was fourteen. They were close—no son could wish to be closer to his father—but physically they were very different. Hugh had told him to ignore it, and he had. Gregor had always assumed his characteristics were inherited from his mother's line.

"A young woman with a child has no other option, Gregor. She married Hugh, and she and I vowed that we would be the only ones who ever knew any different."

"Da did not know?"

"I think he may have guessed, but he was a good man." His cousin rested her hand on Gregor's arm. "He brought you up as his own." She considered him quietly for a long moment. "Sadly for him, your real father still wanted your mother, and he was a jealous man…a cruel man."

She paused, as if unsure whether to continue.

Gregor's blood ran cold as he began to see it.

"He made your father's life hell for claiming the girl he wanted. Even after your mother passed away, the hatred lived on. He wouldn't rest until he had taken everything your father had worked for."

Gregor's heart thumped wildly against the wall of his chest. His mouth had gone dry and he could scarcely swallow. It was Ivor Wallace who had taken everything they owned—Ivor Wallace who had poisoned the cattle and then tricked his da into signing the land away. She couldn't mean it.

"Hugh Ramsay was a proud man. He couldn't live with the fact that he'd lost it all and you had no inheritance. So he took his own life."

Gregor gripped the arms of the chair. "I am not Ivor Wallace's son."

Margaret met his angry stare with sad resignation in her eyes. He knew this woman well, and he knew that she would not lie to him about something as important as this. Unable to meet her gaze a moment longer, and sickened by what he had heard, he rested his forehead in his hands. "It cannot be. That man is immoral, greedy and cruel beyond redemption."

"Aye, and made bitter by his need for revenge."

Revenge.

Pain knifed through Gregor.

His eyes flickered shut and he pressed his fingers to his eyelids. He felt as if Margaret Mackie had held a mirror up to him. There in the reflection he saw it, and he was scalded by the truth. Revenge begets revenge. If Ivor Wallace had destroyed his father for the reasons Margaret gave, he was now carrying that same vindictive streak. His thoughts churned, and for a while Margaret's words went unheard. Eventually she fell silent, leaving him to his sorry thoughts.

Eleven years he had let the quest for revenge rule his life. He'd ignored his only kin in Margaret here, and his old friends, because he could think only of his enemy. He'd sent sweet Jessie in there, knowing how dangerous it could be for her, so fixed was he on retribution.

Jessie.

The thought of her became a single shining beacon in the chaos of his denial and despair, something worth fighting for in a life of ruined beliefs and broken dreams. He had to get her out of there. He had to make her safe.

Lifting his head, he quizzed Margaret. "Does he know that I may be his son?"

"No one told him." She eyed him cautiously. "Although he may have guessed there was a chance you were his. You came along very quickly after your mother wed."

That possibility did not make him feel any better. Gregor rose to his feet. "I want nothing to do with him."

"That does not surprise me. I have had many a year to think about this. I've little respect for Ivor Wallace, less each year as I have watched him become embittered and riddled with avarice. But I will say this...sometimes when a man loses the woman he loves, his reason is lost, too."

When a man loses the woman he loves...

Gregor rested his hand on her shoulder for a moment, silently vowing that he would make sure she was kept comfortable and not wanting for anything, and then he was on his way.

Outside the cottage, he cursed when he saw how far the moon had moved in the sky. It was late. The evening had escaped him as he sat there while history unfolded.

Jessie would think he was not coming.

She would go back into the house.

Gregor ran. He ran as fast as he could. Back through the graveyard he went, and across the fields beyond.

Finally, Balfour Hall loomed on the horizon.

The last thing in the world he wanted to do was set foot inside that house, knowing he was the blood relative of his most reviled enemy. But he had to, because Jessie was there.

chapter Twenty-Three

Jessie pressed against the wall where she could see the stables. To her left, the gardens and the hill that led up to the shadowy woods beyond were both within her sight. At first all was still, and the night was not too cold. Then the wind lifted and she wrapped her shawl more closely around her shoulders and huddled against the building.

Time passed. Clouds wisped across the moon, making it more difficult for her to judge how late it was. Her eyes began to ache from peering into the gloom, looking for him. *Where are you, Gregor?* It was a long while before she admitted to herself that Gregor had not come at the appointed time. Then she forced herself to consider that he might not be coming at all.

A tight knot of concern formed in Jessie's chest. Once again she scanned the gardens and the woods beyond for signs of movement. She saw nothing. She darted toward the outhouses and the stable itself, and checked inside. He was nowhere to be seen.

Fear for his safety was her first reaction. Perhaps he had been waylaid by a brigand, or maybe he had fallen from his horse in the forest. Or he might have had ill thoughts about her because of her craft. The last two nights she had not been able to stop herself from exposing the radiance of her magic when they coupled. It had been a revelation to him, and she was afraid he might turn his back on her after all.

As she stood by the stables, watching and waiting, she saw a flare of candlelight through one of the windows in the main house. Then another. They moved in quick succession, as if being carried. All had been quiet when she'd emerged from the hall. Now there was movement inside, at least two people. She could not risk waiting here in case someone saw her from inside the house and decided to question her. If Gregor came down from the forest now she hoped he would see the light and stay away.

Darting back toward the servants' entrance, she crept inside. To her dismay she saw that the kitchen door was open, and in the hall beyond, several candles had been lit. She'd barely stepped inside when she was grabbed and shoved along and out into the hallway.

It was Cormac at her back, she knew, but why was he pushing her out into the light? On the previous occasion he had lingered in the gloom with her.

As soon as she arrived in the hall she realized why. Another man awaited them there. He had his back to them, facing the sideboard, where he was busy pouring wine into a glass.

"Here she is," Cormac said, "the new serving girl, skulking about, up to no good by the looks of her."

Jessie tried to bolt, and her beloved blue shawl dropped to the floor, but Cormac had a tight grip on the back of her dress. Even though she twisted and turned she could not break free. He held her at her arm's length as if displaying her for the other man. Who was it, if not the master of the house?

"Well, well, if it isn't the Harlot of Dundee."

Jessie's head snapped around and she stared in disbelief at

the man who had spoken. It was not Master Wallace. It was a much younger man.

His cruel gray eyes raked over her and his full lips curled in delight, as if he was relishing the sight of the woman being held out to him. His face looked familiar, but for a moment she could not place him. Then she realized who he was. The last time she'd seen him he'd worn a wig and a heavily embroidered coat. Tonight his head was bare and his hair tied with a ribbon. His shirt was loose and hanging down over his breeches. The boots were just as she remembered, ostentatious. It was the man whose custom Eliza and herself were competing for on that final, fateful night in Dundee. This man had encouraged them to squabble over him, and Ranald Sweeney was all too willing to agree, knowing he would make money on the bets.

This was bad, worse even than if Cormac or the master of the house had come after her, because this man knew who and what she was. Jessie's skin flashed hot and cold as she realized the dangerous nature of her situation.

Cormac spoke. "You know the wench, Master Forbes?"

Forbes. This was Ivor Wallace's son, whom there had been much whispering about throughout the household. He'd been due to return, but she had taken little notice, because her mind was occupied elsewhere.

Cormac grabbed a handful of her hair and tugged on it, forcing her head back and her chin up. Pain shot through her neck. It was twisted badly, causing her to cry out. Her gaze darted this way and that as she tried to seek out the best route for her escape. She'd fled before with nowt but the clothes on her back when confronted with men who would rather force themselves on her and beat her than pay for what she offered.

Cormac peered at her as if he should know her, too, because his master did. "She's not from the village."

"No, she's not from the village." Forbes stepped closer and surveyed her as he did so. When his gaze shifted to her chest, he licked his lips.

"It seems I cannot turn my back on this place for a moment," he commented to Cormac, "what with the old man selling land behind my back. And as if that is not enough of a concern, I find he has brought a homeless slut under our roof."

There was disapproval in his tone, but Jessie could see he was secretly delighted. If the rumors she had heard were true and he was trying to take his father's place, he could use this against the master of the house.

He swigged heavily from the glass in his hand, draining it. By the looks of him and Cormac, they had shared plenty of spirits already. Forbes's petulant mouth was made even uglier once damp and stained by the wine.

"The Harlot of Dundee. Jessie Taskill is her name." He gestured at her with the glass before setting it down. "They are looking for you. They discovered you crossed the Tay. Word passes from mouth to mouth along the coast. It won't be long until it is the hangman's hand you feel."

There was loud thudding in Jessie's ears as images from her past shot through her mind. Her emotions were already unsteady because Gregor had not appeared, and they were fast coming unraveled.

Cormac's grip on her hair had not loosened and he peered at her again. "Who is she?"

"A dirty whore, and that's not all." Forbes sneered, but she sensed he was enjoying the situation, which did nothing to reassure her. "She has been charged with witchcraft. She was in the tollbooth awaiting the hangman, but somehow she escaped."

"Witchcraft?" Cormac let go of her and stepped toward his master, with whom he seemed on good terms.

Jessie edged away, her hands seeking the wall behind her. Again her gaze flitted to the doorway to the kitchens. Cormac blocked her path. That there were two of them would make it more difficult. She could use an enchantment, but what if they discovered she was working for Gregor? She did not want him to be associated with witchcraft.

"I've already made the acquaintance of our newest servant in Dundee," Master Forbes was saying to Cormac. He grinned her way. "I feel we must revisit our last encounter and bring it to its unfulfilled conclusion."

Jessie's breath was locked in her chest. She shook her head at him.

"I sponsored your actions that night in order to bed you, my dear. You owe me the rest of that performance, and more." He rubbed his hand over the turgid bulge in his breeches and then glanced at Cormac. "Take her into the dining hall and strip her."

No. I do not want this. At one time she would have flirted with such a suggestion, if only to keep a customer like him happy—anything to keep a violent streak in check. Not now. Not anymore.

Just as it had earlier that day with his father, her repugnance multiplied. *This is because I have tied myself to one man. This is because I have fallen in love with Gregor.* She did not want to be sullied by another, because she could not risk seeing disappointment in his eyes, the way she had that night when he had found her conversing with Mister Grant.

Cormac hesitated. "If she practices witchcraft, does she summon demons and the like?"

Jessie acted fast. She turned to him and hissed.

Cormac leaped away from her, walking backward with his hand raised as if to defend himself, his eyes wide.

Master Forbes chortled loudly, and then gestured at Jessie. "Get on with it, strip her."

Cormac stood his ground. "But…"

"She is only trying to scare you, man." He spat the words at his servant. Then he looked at her. "Eliza told me that you were good for a few herbs and such, but that you had no real power."

Jessie's chin lifted. Perhaps the scales were tipping in her direction. Eliza had never seen what she could really do, and now, after her magic had been nurtured and fed by physical, spiritual and emotional love, her talent was much more immense. The thought gave her strength. "And you chose to believe that," she responded, "when it is obvious that I had the power to escape the bailie before the night was out?"

Momentary doubt flickered in his eyes, and then his mouth tightened and he strode over to her. Grabbing her dress at the bodice, he shook her to and fro while he delivered a slap to her face with his free hand. "Insolent bitch."

The sting was nothing compared to the revulsion she felt when he began to drag her across the hallway. She struggled to escape, but he was a heavy, large man and he was determined to have her.

Cormac had gathered himself and reached for two candles, lifting them aloft as the small procession headed to the dining hall. There, Master Forbes pushed Jessie down on the long, polished mahogany table, holding her with one hand against her throat, the weight of his body crushing her thighs and hips.

She kicked and punched at him, but that only seemed to make him more keen.

"Cormac, quickly, hold her arms," Master Forbes instructed.

Magic was the only way. Even if it meant she was ousted. Being stoned to death, or even hanged, would be preferable to submitting to this brute.

Cormac set the candlesticks on the mantel, where their reflection in the mirror lit the room more brightly. Jessie squirmed and wriggled, looking for a way to escape, preparing to use an enchantment. At the far end of the room, a door stood open. She remembered passing through it as she went about her chores. It led into the library, where there was another door. She was in a state, and as she tried to whisper her trusted Gaelic protection enchantment, the words tangled.

Cormac had joined his master and grabbed her arms, pulling them over her head and holding them with his weight.

Forbes's grip tightened on her throat. With his other hand he ripped open her bodice, tearing the fabric to expose her breasts.

She screamed.

"Bitch." He forced her head to one side on the table and covered her mouth with his hand.

She struggled, attempting to bite him, but he was already pushing up her skirts. A sensible whore would get it over with, and she had done, in the past. Not this time. Instead she could only think of Gregor. Gregor would not want this. She was ready to leave and be gone from this house with its burden of guilt and cruelty. Her eyelids dropped. She whispered the words in her mind.

A moment later Cormac stumbled backward, and her arms were freed. She delivered a blow to the side of Forbes's head and then scrambled away from him.

He staggered, but still he blocked her path.

Instinctively, she turned and clambered onto the table on

her hands and knees. Her skirts were hampering her. The table was some ten strides long, but she would have to stand. Inhaling a deep breath, she got her feet under her then stood up. As she did, she caught sight of herself in the mirror.

So high up.

The realization sent her into a dizzy spin. She was right back there, back on the pillar outside the church, and she could hear the crowd baying for her mother's death, hurling stones at her collapsed body on the ground while they called her evil.

Maisie was too far away to reach, and Lennox had been thrown into the back of a cart, bound at wrists and ankles because he had cursed them so mightily that they were afraid of the lad and called him a demon.

"Lift your head and look at your mother," a harsh voice had instructed her.

But Jessie could not look at what they were doing to her mother. She had already seen enough of them, for they were pious souls turned into vicious animals.

"She's afraid!" It was Cormac.

The two men were closer still. She swayed. Cormac was pointing, his leering face split into a horrid grin. Beyond him, Forbes had lifted a poker from the fireplace and was walking toward her with it.

Cormac snatched at her ankle.

Master Forbes closed on her with the poker.

Cormac jerked her ankle, lifting her foot from the table.

The whole room began to spin.

Her belly heaved, and darkness descended.

chapter Twenty-Four

Gregor arrived at the meeting spot panting for breath, his lungs fit to burst. Jessie was nowhere to be seen. Scrubbing his hands through his hair, he glared at the moon and cursed. He hated himself for letting the time pass by.

With the utmost haste, he darted through the stables and outhouses. She had gone. He had let her down. The thought of her waiting here, and eventually returning to her quarters, no doubt confused about why he had not come, made his mood turn black. The night before she had been so grateful that he came. It was obvious to him that she'd thought he wouldn't, and no doubt this evening he'd proved that he was unreliable, when he had promised her so much.

He stared over at Balfour Hall. She was in there. Striding to the servants' entrance he opened the door and stepped inside the Wallace household. Where in God's name were her sleeping quarters? If only he had thought to ask.

But he would hunt her down.

He would shout her name from the rooftops if necessary.

The door beyond was ajar and he could see a hallway that was brightly lit. He proceeded in that direction. Before he entered the hall, he forced himself to pause in the doorway and listen. In the distance he heard the sound of voices. Men, two or more of them, shouting and laughing.

Something caught his eye. At his feet he saw a vivid blue shawl abandoned on the floor. He recognized it, and the sight made ice run the length of his spine.

A woman's scream rang out from beyond.

Jessie. Gregor bolted in that direction.

The noise led him, and when he reached the doorway and caught sight of what was happening inside the room beyond, he was all but blinded by rage. Jessie was standing on the table, staggering, her dress torn. Someone was taunting her, a poker held aloft in his hand. Pure outrage shot through Gregor.

It took immense effort to stifle the urge to blunder in, shouting and throwing punches without direction. His hand went to the dagger at his belt. Swallowing down the bile in his throat, he forced himself to gain the measure of Jessie's assailants. From his vantage point he could see that there were two of them. A large man, well dressed, and a slighter fellow.

The slighter one spoke. "Master Forbes, she will not put up so much of a fight when she falls."

Forbes Wallace.

Jessie wavered wildly, kicking at the man who grabbed her ankle. Her eyes were rolling and Gregor saw purple light flashing there. She was attempting to use her magic.

No, Jessie. Don't do it.

When he saw her faint, Gregor pushed the door open with such force it landed against the wall with a loud bang. The candles in the room flickered wildly and something fell from a table and crashed to the floor with the sound of breaking glass. He strode into the room.

As the man with the poker turned his way, Gregor grabbed the rod from his hand, taking him unawares. Turning it on him, Gregor delivered a sharp blow to the side of his head. The man staggered and then fell to the floor.

When Gregor caught sight of his sweet Jessie collapsed on the table with her dress torn asunder, and he realized their intention, his heart thundered.

The other man came forward, eyes flashing wildly, fists raised.

Gregor cast the poker aside and pushed up his sleeves, relishing the prospect of a fight.

He allowed his opponent to throw the first punch, for the man did not look much more than bone and gristle. When it came he ducked it, and meanwhile delivered a blow from beneath, landing it in his opponent's gut.

The man doubled over with a loud grunt, and Gregor followed through with a swinging blow directed upward, making contact with his jaw. His opponent staggered backward against a cabinet, where he slithered to the floor, out cold.

The larger man was rising to his feet again. Gregor allowed him to stand, because he looked forward to the prospect of taking them from under him once more. As he looked at him, Gregor's attention sharpened. He knew him. This man had been there that first night he'd seen Jessie, in Dundee. He'd been the customer who stood by while the betting went on.

"Forbes Wallace," Gregor said.

"Who the hell are you?" Forbes demanded.

Your brother. For a wild moment Gregor considered telling him, just to see the look on his face, but he could not stand to hear it said aloud. Any connection he had to the people in this house was something he wished to sever, forever.

"You're her new pimp," Forbes declared.

Gregor shook his head, then reached for the dagger at his belt, unsheathing it.

Fear flashed in Forbes Wallace's eyes.

Gregor grinned just to unnerve him, then stuck the knife into the wooden floorboards and lifted his fists.

Forbes's glance darted back and forth from him to the dagger.

"I will not fight an unarmed man," Gregor declared. "Now raise your fists!"

Instead of fighting fair, Forbes came at him, driving forward like a bull out of control, shoulder directed to Gregor's chest.

Gregor sidestepped and took him down by tripping him as he passed. With Forbes on his back on the floor, Gregor pounced, landing with his knee on Forbes's shoulder, pinning him down. The poker was within arm's reach.

The man bellowed in pain.

"So you prefer to wrestle? That suits me."

Once again Forbes's gaze darted to the knife. "Damn you!"

He will go for the knife, and then I will break his neck. Gregor grinned again and twisted his opponent's arm under him.

Forbes tried to use the chance, rocking in an attempt to dislodge him, one hand grappling toward where the dagger gleamed in the candlelight.

"Fight fair," Gregor ordered again, driving more pressure through the shoulder he knelt upon.

Again Forbes bellowed in pain. Using his weight, he wormed free and snatched at the dagger, dislodging it. It fell to the floor and he grabbed it.

When he rolled back, his expression triumphant, Gregor lifted the poker and knocked the dagger from his hand.

Astonished, Forbes bellowed for help and attempted to back away.

Gripping the poker, Gregor placed the tip under his opponent's chin, forcing him to lift his head. Then he peered into his eyes.

"What do you want?" Forbes blurted. "Name your price!" His lip was split and blood poured from it. On the side of his head a red gash showed from his earlier fall.

What is my price? Gregor wondered if he even had a price anymore. Justice? Nay, it was freedom he desired, freedom from the past.

He pressed the poker against Forbes's throat, feeling the urge to press down upon it with his entire weight.

"Gregor." It was Jessie's voice. A quick glance informed him that she had awoken and now stared in horror as he struggled with his opponent.

"Stay back," he instructed.

Once again he heard her speak, this time in Gaelic. The poker in his hand grew hot, the handle glowing.

She was trying to stop him, and she was using magic.

Dread struck him. If it was witnessed, she would be ousted. "Jessie, no!"

He forbade her with a glance.

"They will hang you for the crime," she warned, horror in her eyes.

The poker grew even hotter and he hurled it into a corner of the room. With his fist, he delivered a final blow to his opponent's jaw, stunning him.

Gregor rose to his feet and flexed his fingers.

Jessie had risen to her hands and knees but was still on the table, eyes wide, body shivering violently.

"Come, we're leaving." As he grabbed her in his arms and placed her safely on her feet, voices issued from the corridor outside and a door at the opposite end of the room sprang open. A man with a candle raised strode in.

Ivor Wallace. The landowner had aged, but Gregor knew him the moment he walked into the room.

"What goes on here?" he demanded, surveying the scene.

Meanwhile, a cluster of onlookers gathered in the doorway—an elderly woman in a nightdress, whom Gregor recognized as Mistress Wallace, and several hastily dressed servants.

Ivor Wallace's gaze shifted to Gregor.

Gregor felt the old familiar hatred well within him as he stared at this man who had destroyed everything in his world eleven years before. "I am Hugh Ramsay's son."

It was no explanation, but for Gregor it had to be said.

Wallace's head jerked in recognition, and as he did so Gregor saw it—the set of his eyes, the shape of his jaw and cheekbones, the heavy brows. As much as it made him sick to admit it, the likeness was there. This man was his father, and looking at him now, Gregor knew there was no denying it. Foreign emotions assailed him and he ground his teeth together. Secrets and lies had molded his history, and for a moment he hated them all, even his mother and Hugh, for destroying each other, for keeping the truth from him.

Ivor lifted his candle and stepped closer.

"You are Agatha's son?" As he asked the question, the taper in his hand shook, the flame flickering wildly.

He knew. The recognition that shone in his eyes revealed the truth to Gregor. Ivor Wallace knew he was his son.

He scrutinized Gregor, and as he did his expression changed. Hope flared in his eyes, a smile lifting his lips.

Behind him, Wallace's wife stifled a cry with her hand at her mouth, and then blessed herself with the sign of the cross.

She knew. They all knew, except him.

All the hatred Gregory had felt after Hugh's death came back tenfold. It was as if he was that angry lad who wanted nothing more than to fight this man with his fists, to force upon him some small part of what he deserved.

Then he felt Jessie shift at his back, and he moved his hand to still her. Once again it occurred to him that she was his beacon amid this chaos. Jessie was the only good thing that had come from this sorry mess.

Forbes had regained consciousness, and he wiped the blood from the corner of his mouth as he lifted himself on an elbow. "Keep away from the woman," he warned. "She is wanted by the bailie in Dundee under a charge of witchcraft."

Gregor steeled himself. Jessie was his only concern now. He grasped her hand, holding it tightly in his.

Concerned murmurs passed among the crowd gathered at the doorway, and several more heads peeked around the door before disappearing once again.

Coolly, he glanced at Forbes—his half brother. The man disgusted him. And when he looked again at his natural father, Gregor knew that he would finally be able to let go of his cause. The past would be buried in the past, where it belonged.

"Yes, I am Agatha's son, and I know who you are. But you will never see me again."

The old man's expression altered quickly, and he staggered. There was a broken, sad look in his eyes. Gregor saw the truth of it; he could not have hurt him more had he knocked him to the floor and torched his precious manor house.

He squeezed Jessie's hand and turned away.

At his back, he heard Ivor Wallace's voice. "You've turned out a fine young man, Gregor."

Pain flared in Gregor's chest. *No thanks to you.*

Holding tight to Jessie's hand, he forged a path through the small gathering and out into the hallway. The servants scattered, the mention of witchcraft putting wings beneath their feet, or so it seemed.

"I will send word to the bailie in Dundee," Forbes shouted after them. "I will inform him you are hereabouts. You won't get far."

Gregor's hand tightened on Jessie's. "Be ready to run, as fast as your feet can carry you," he whispered to her.

"I'm ready," she responded, and when Gregor glanced her way and saw the pride and affection in her eyes, he knew he did not deserve her.

If it was the last thing he did, he would make sure she was safely gone from here. No bailie or anyone else would set hands on her.

chapter Twenty-Five

Jessie could make no sense of what had happened, even though she tried for the entire journey back to the Drover's Inn. Gregor paused only to give her his frock coat to cover her torn garments and keep her warm. Then he hastened her through the forest to his horse, where he took her by the shoulders and apologized for the fact that she was going to have to climb up behind him once again. She did so willingly and clung to him for the duration. Her stomach churned as he urged the horse to gallop, and she kept her arms around his chest, fingers tightly knotted together.

Even through her distress, she sensed his thoughts were deeply troubled. She assumed it was her fault.

"I'm sorry, the master's son knew who I was," she blurted at the back of Gregor's head. "He was there that night in Dundee. You should not have come into the house. I have ruined it for you now."

"Hush, you have not ruined anything. It is over, and soon you will be safely on the road to the Highlands with your purse." For a moment Gregor rested his hand over hers and squeezed reassuringly.

Bewildered by his words, but soothed by his comforting touch, Jessie rested her head against his back. She didn't want to be on the road, not if it meant saying farewell. Sadness descended on her and her heart ached. For the rest of the journey they traveled in silence.

Back in his lodgings, Gregor was still quiet. Was it the strange, brief exchange between him and Master Wallace that had put him in this thoughtful, withdrawn mood? Ivor Wallace had seemed pleased to see him, and for a moment she'd thought he was about to apologize for what had happened in the past. Then Gregor had walked away. What of his need for justice?

He did not even pause to shut the door when they arrived back at his rooms. She did that, and then gathered water and a cloth and bathed his knuckles. He did not stop her, nor did he wince when she wiped the bloodied skin. Instead he sprawled in the chair. Her hands were trembling when she brought him his bottle of port, but he shook his head.

"Forgive me, Gregor. I have ruined things because Forbes Wallace knew me and what I am. But I have some knowledge, things that you must know."

"Everything has changed." He glanced at her and his expression softened. "Rest," he added, more gently. "You will need it. As soon as it is dawn you must be on your way. You must leave Fife, for word will be put about. You heard what Forbes Wallace said. He will inform the bailie."

Jessie stared at him, unable to respond, for his words sent a chill through her. She shook her head.

Rising to his feet, he went to his trunk and retrieved the purse he had promised her. He set it on the table. When she opened her mouth to speak, he held up his hand, silencing her, and then pointed at the bed. "I must think on what has happened," he explained.

Thwarted, she did as instructed.

Gregor did not sleep. Unhappily, Jessie watched him from

her place on the bed. After a while he rose from the chair and walked to the window, where he stared out into the night. To see him in such a resigned state tore her apart, for it was her fault he'd had to reveal himself at Balfour Hall.

Eventually she dozed awhile, wearied from the unhappy events of the evening. When she awoke, Gregor was sitting in the chair as before. The sun was beginning to rise. Beneath her breastbone she felt a gnawing ache.

Rising, she went to him and dropped to her knees by the side of his chair. With one hand on his arm and the other on his knee, she attempted to engage with him. "Gregor, please do not think harshly of me. I know I am of little use to you now, but you will still be able to continue with your scheme."

He smiled at her.

That warmed her. "There will be a way," she added. "I am sure of it."

He lifted his fingers and ran them down the length of her hair, absentmindedly. A moment later he laughed softly. Relief flooded through her and she tightened her hand on his knee.

"You believe in good things, Jessie. You reach for everything life might bring your way with such spirit. I think it is what drew me to you. The hope, the belief, the joy."

She did not want to talk about herself. She was making progress with him and she was not going to give in. "You believe in things, too. In justice."

He gave a wry laugh. "No, I have been a misguided fool."

"You are wrong. Why, just yesterday I found out things that may be useful to you."

Gregor rolled his eyes and again there was humor in his expression.

"All is not lost," she quickly added, wondering why his eyes had begun to twinkle as he looked at her. "Ivor Wallace spoke to me. Well, he rambled. He mentioned a name, and I remembered it. Gregor, he was smitten with your mother. That is why he hated your father so. It was not just greed on his part. It was a matter of the heart."

"Aye, it was." Gregor's smile was sad, and she noticed then that his eyes glistened. He took her hand in his. Kissing her fingertips, he whispered softly, "Sweet Jessie. It was revenge that Wallace sought, and that is not an honorable pursuit."

"Does it not help you to understand, knowing that he is an old man with regrets, a man who lives on his memories of the girl he should have married, but didn't?"

Gregor rested his head back in the chair and briefly covered his face with his hand. "It should be punishment enough. You are right there."

Jessie's emotions tangled. "Please don't be angry with me."

Again he kissed her fingertips. "Jessie, I'm not angry with you."

She wasn't convinced. Bravely, she pressed on. "Tell me then, what is it that troubles you so? Is it because I failed?"

"You did nothing wrong. Far from it." He gazed at her for the longest moment. "I learned something rather unpleasant about myself last night. I learned that the apple does not fall far from the tree." He scrubbed his eyes with the palm of his hand. "Eleven long years I have sought revenge. Revenge is something I was told was wrong, when I was growing up, and yet I have been driven by it. It's in the blood, you see." He met her gaze, but seemed to stare right through her for a moment. "What you have told me now has confirmed it. It seems that I have been seeking revenge on my own father."

Jessie's thoughts raced as she absorbed what he said. "Oh, Gregor." Now she understood. She huddled closer against his thigh and rested her cheek there a moment. "What a terrible shock that must have been."

He stroked her head, and for a moment she allowed her eyes to close, and absorbed that deep and silent connection between them. It had been a time of revelations indeed, but they would both come through it, and what she knew above all was that this rapport they had was worth fighting for.

"Everything that I have worked for," Gregor murmured, "my reason for living these past years, it all means nothing."

She lifted her head. "No. You found out the truth, and that is what you needed to know."

"Perhaps." There was pain in his eyes. "I hate that I am like him."

A soft laugh escaped her. "You are not like him, of that much I am certain."

That laugh seemed to work magic, without her attempting to do so. The pained look in his eyes softened.

"I pitied him yesterday," Jessie admitted. "Briefly. You are not like Ivor Wallace, but you needed to know the truth to make sense of what happened to the man who brought you up."

He squeezed her hand. He seemed more accepting, and she was glad of that. "I thought myself alone, and yet found I have a family, after all, one that I will never want."

It pained her so to hear that. She had no one, but secretly longed for loved ones that she could claim as her own.

He sighed. "The day is dawning. You must be on your way soon, my sweet."

She shook her head. "If I take that purse and leave this place now, where will you go?"

He lifted one shoulder. "I have months until my ship returns, but I suppose I will go back to sea when it does, if I am still needed. Perhaps there will be freedom in being adrift once more."

Months before his ship returned. Months she would gladly

spend by his side. "We have been good together," she said tentatively, "have we not?"

The expression in his eyes altered, desire glinting there, and her heart was mightily glad of it. "Aye, we have."

"Perhaps we make a good partnership. Perhaps we should stay together awhile longer." Her voice faded to a whisper, so afraid was she of putting that desire into words.

Gregor laughed softly and looked at her with fondness. "A vengeful blackguard and a condemned witch?"

"I suppose we are those things, but we are also a man and a woman, and together we can be more."

"You are no ordinary woman," he whispered.

Her heart sank, and then he lifted her chin with one finger and smiled into her eyes. "A woman, yes, oh, yes." His gaze covered her possessively as he spoke. "And a witch." He put one finger against his lips, holding that secret safe. "You have surely bewitched me, Jessie."

Her heart thudded wildly as hope rose within her. "You see it, don't you? Together we could build something better than either of us, something worth having."

"Perhaps." He seemed amused by her, and she feared he was only humoring her. "My fierce and prickly harlot…how difficult it must have been for you to state that aloud."

Startled as she was, it took her a moment to realize that he understood what she was saying. And more than that, that he understood her so well.

"Harlot of mine, you have made me feel again, and I hated you for doing so, that day at Strathbahn."

"Do you still hate me for it?"

"No. How can I?" Gently, he caressed her cheek. "I have not treated you much better than your pimp, sending you into that place."

Lifting up onto her knees, she moved between his legs,

her hands pressing against his chest as she looked up at him beseechingly. "I did it for you, because I have grown to… to care for you."

"I do not deserve it."

Jessie smiled. "Perhaps you don't. Perhaps I should be more cautious with my affections." She stroked her fingers down his shirt to the band of his breeches and then moved them from side to side. Instantly, she felt his response. He placed his feet a little wider, and the bulge in his breeches grew beneath her arm. His eyelids lowered, and his handsome mouth curved in an appreciative smile.

She tipped her head to one side. "This arrangement reminds me of our first encounter, in that cell in Dundee." She moved her hand over his swollen shaft through his breeches.

"It does?"

"Yes." She rubbed her palm up and down his impressive length, her own arousal building when she felt his cock leaning toward her, stretching the fabric. "In fact, I am compelled to make you an offer."

She looked at him from beneath her lashes and licked her lips. Brimming with ardent wishes, she carefully measured her words with him.

"An offer? Go on."

His response made the flame at her center flare. "If I pleasure you with my mouth, you will undertake a task for me."

"And that task would be?"

"Ah, I will tell you the nature of the task afterward, as you did me."

He laughed softly. "This sounds like a risk."

"I was willing to take the risk. Are you?" She lifted the lace that barely held his breeches closed, and tugged on it.

His lips parted.

She paused.

He nodded.

Jessie smiled and moved into position as she undid the laces and his cock sprang free. Her cunny clenched. "Oh, but I think you're ready for this."

"When it comes to you, Jessie, my cock is always ready."

Chuckling softly, she took his crown into her mouth and licked the underside.

His eyes narrowed and his teeth clamped together.

She moved her hands to his ballocks and lifted them, cradling them. When her tongue reached the base of his shaft, she squeezed and tugged on his sac gently. His cock jerked. The sight of it made her cunny clamp, and a trickle of hot juice slid down between her thighs.

"Jessie," he murmured.

For a moment her eyes closed, and memories flitted through her mind. The first time she had done this she'd had no idea what it would come to mean. It was a canny trick, to pleasure a man with her mouth, but she had come to adore this man and that part of him that pleasured her so and joined them together as she had never been joined before. She did not want that to end.

His hands locked over the arms of the chair, and she saw that the pulse in his throat beat fast.

"It is not enough," he muttered, and grasped her around the back of the neck, forcing her to stop.

Dismayed, she held his shaft in her hand and lifted her head. With the back of her other hand, she wiped her mouth. "Not enough?"

His eyes were filled with lusty intent. "I need to be inside you."

Her cunny melted. She could not withhold her pleasure and gave a throaty chuckle in response to his declaration.

Stroking his length, she flashed her eyes at him to let him know how much it pleased her.

With a low curse he stood and drew her up alongside him. Gratefully, joyfully, she kissed his mouth, cheek and jaw. With a heartfelt sigh, he lifted her off her feet.

She wrapped her arms around his neck, smiling up at him. He carried her to the bed and rolled her onto her back, pushing up her skirts as he did so, and climbing between her legs. His fingers roved over her mound until he found her swollen bud. "I missed you in my bed."

Those words thrilled her. "And I missed being here."

Even while he stroked her nub, making her moan and writhe beneath him, his cock stretched her open and slid into her slippery entrance.

Measure by measure, he filled her, until she felt him at her very center and she sighed with relief and clutched at him.

He buried his head at her throat, kissing her there while his hips worked his length into her in shallow thrusts.

She wrapped her legs around his hips and stroked his shoulders with her hands, hungry for every sensation.

To be united this way with him, after all that had been said and done, made emotions assail her. She blinked back the tears as her hips rolled to meet his, grateful for every blissful, breathless point of contact.

"Gregor, I am undone," she whispered, as her peak grew imminent.

He lifted his head and met her gaze. "Come to me, my precious harlot."

The muscles in his neck stood out as he worked her faster, chasing after her.

She cried out, joy spilling though her, and when she came, he would not let her look away as he pumped himself into her, making her entire body burn and throb.

Afterward, he rolled her next to him and she nestled there, gloriously happy.

"The task, Jessie?" he asked, when their breathing and heartbeats had returned to normal.

Say it, she urged herself. "That you will stay by my side and be my protector, as you were last night, for a while longer."

His expression remained serious. "I have taken my reward, so I suppose I must accept the task."

She was about to respond when she saw the twinkle in his eyes. "Does the task offend you?" she teased.

"It will be no easy undertaking, I am aware of that." He kissed her softly beneath her chin, breathing against her skin as he spoke. His hands covered her breasts, still sensitive, still trembling in the aftermath. "To be a protector, to a wild woman such as yourself…"

He sighed loudly.

She poked him, forcing him to look at her. "Gregor."

He laughed. "Of course I will assume the task."

"Would you…would you truly make your way to the Highlands with me?"

"Aye, Jessie. Why not? You are right in what you say. We turned out to be a good match. Last night all I could think about was pulling you out of that place, and I despise the fact that circumstances got in my way." His face tightened with regret.

"Hush. You were there for me. We are both safe."

He laughed. "I warrant it will be no easy task, but there is nothing here for me anymore, and my life at sea seems distant to me now. I may return to it one day, but you and I have become connected, and perhaps it is no bad thing that I find my land legs once more." He stroked her hair with one hand, and kissed her forehead. "Would you accept me as your protector, if I promise to do a better job of it?"

A disbelieving sigh escaped her, and she touched him with trembling fingers. "You *did* a good job of it."

Her mind raced over what had happened, and how he had forbidden her to make magic when she was so vulnerable. That he had stopped her exposing her abilities and risking her life meant more to her than the fact he had pulled her from her attacker's arms.

"Tell me, how long do you want me to be your protector for, exactly?"

Her hand went to her mouth and she swallowed hard, attempting to bravely state her desires. His eyes twinkled again and there was affection in them, too. He knew the state she was in.

"A long time," she ventured.

"That seems like a fair exchange, on one proviso."

Still unsure, she queried, "What is that?"

"I want you to be *my* harlot, *mine alone*. Do you understand?" Possessive demand flashed in his eyes.

Jessie's breath caught in her throat, her heart swelling. She nodded gratefully, blinking back her emotion. She was about to respond, but the sound of the door to the landing rattling interrupted them, distracting them both. Gregor frowned heavily and looked toward the door, as did she.

"We did not lock it," Jessie said, pulling her bodice into position.

Before he had a chance to say anything, the door was flung open and Morag bolted into the room. Both of them stared at her, finding her sudden and panicked appearance surprisingly out of character.

Morag closed the door behind her and waved her hands. "Hurry, you must be gone. The bailie is down there with a crowd of men and they are looking for a woman from

Dundee, a woman who practices witchcraft. They think she may be at a posting house along this road. Is it you, Jessie?"

Jessie's heart sank. "Yes, it is me they are after, dear friend."

Morag nodded, and smiled a curious smile. "I thought it probably was."

"Curses," Gregor muttered as he leaped out of the bed.

"Hurry now," Morag continued, "there is time to get away. I told them there were no women up here. Mistress Muir does not know that you came back. They plan to search the building, but they have started in the stables and outhouses."

"They will assume, of course, that I am a wild creature living with the animals," Jessie said as she hunted for her shoes, with no small amount of annoyance.

"You *are* a wild creature," Gregor commented, "but we must be gone from this place before they find out for sure."

"Aye, gather your things," Morag urged, "and I will show you another way out of here."

Gregor was already kneeling by his trunk. Opening a shirt on the floor, he threw his papers, the coins and parcels and several other items into it, tying the bundle in a knot. Jessie jolted into action and headed toward the other room for her clothing, picking up the purse from the table as she went. But Gregor stopped her. "Leave everything else."

"My blue gown! I cannot leave without it."

"I will buy you another if we escape this, and if you behave yourself I will buy you a wedding gown, as well. But let us leave this place, now!"

Jessie gaped at him.

Gregor laughed and grabbed her by the hand.

"The trunk and whatever is left in it is yours," he said to Morag.

She led them into an empty room farther down the landing, a small dressing room next to the door to Mister Grant's room, where she opened what looked like a cupboard and pointed inside.

"So this is how Mister Grant's lover comes to him," Jessie declared.

"Aye," said Morag. "Mister Grant pays highly for this room."

A tiny peephole in the stone wall let in enough light to reveal a narrow set of winding stairs that dropped steeply into the shadows.

"Oh, no," Jessie whispered. The stairs were barely wide enough to place her feet and there was no railing to hold, only the rough stone walls. It was so dark below that she could not see the steps.

Gregor did not give her time to think about it. "Stay behind me and put one hand on my shoulder as you follow. You will not be able to fall."

That he treated her fear with such consideration made her want to cry, but it also made her strong. "Go," she declared, clutching at him.

Down the stairs they hurried, and even though she was afraid of what might await them beyond, she was not as afraid of the steep stairs as she might have been, because of his guidance.

Morag brought up the rear, closing the doors as she went. At the bottom of the staircase Gregor paused. A narrow corridor led to a door at the back of the inn. Beyond that the stables were located.

From outside came the sounds of dogs barking and voices shouting. Jessie's heart beat wildly.

Morag listened and then nodded. "They are searching the outhouses. Turn quickly to the left when you go out there. If you drop down by the fence at the pigpen they will not be able to see you as you make your way out of the grounds."

Gregor paused briefly and gave Morag a hearty kiss on the cheek. Gathering herself, Jessie did the same. "Thank you, dear friend. Farewell!"

Gregor had his hand on the door handle.

Jessie was ready, ready to hide their trail by magic, and ready to take the road to the Highlands together. Gregor opened the door, holding tight to her hand. The last they saw of Morag she was dabbing her eyes with her apron.

They ducked down and scurried over to the pigpen, avoiding the outhouses. When they got to the end of the fence that marked the pigpen, they paused. A quick dash and they would be shielded by the stables as they made their way over the hill and to the open lands beyond, but for a short way they would have no cover at all.

As they hesitated, a man emerged from an outhouse carrying a musket. Within a heartbeat he would see them. Jessie tugged on Gregor's hand, and when he looked her way, she put her fingers to her lips.

Moving her hand, she whispered her enchantment, calling for calamity, and pointed into the pigpen.

One pig squealed as if startled, then another did the same and both ran at the wooden gate, flattening it. As they charged out of the pen, the man dropped his musket in fright and turned on his heel, taking cover inside the stable.

Gregor stared at the spectacle. His eyebrows shot up. Then he peered at her, most astonished, and shook his head in disbelief.

"Hurry, go now," she said, quelling the urge to chuckle.

Once they were well beyond the hill at the back of the inn and safe from discovery, Jessie began to laugh. She could not help teasing him about it. "Well, Gregor, I must confess, your face made me wonder if you regretted taking me on."

He frowned. "It will take some time to get used to this

ability of yours. I will have to become more familiar with it, I'm aware of that."

"You do not wish to take advantage of my abilities?" She acted most surprised.

He drew her against him as they walked, his arm about her waist. "Most of all, I want to take advantage of *you*."

Jessie's heart burned in her chest.

"Perhaps, with time," he added, "I will think of some uses for the magic."

No one had ever even wanted to understand her magic before. Anyone who had suspected it feared her. Such was the prevailing mood about witchcraft in the Lowlands. But they were headed to the Highlands, and he had promised to be her protector. She knew him well enough to know that he would not promise such a thing without considering it fully, including all that she was and had been.

Never before had Jessie felt safe. They were miles from anywhere with no horse or cart, and little to their name but for those odd stones and papers of his, but she felt safe and content.

"Did you mean what you said," she quizzed, "about the gowns that you would buy me?"

Gregor slapped her on the rump and smiled her way. "I'll need me a Highland-born wife, if I am to be accepted there."

"Aye." Jessie restrained her smile and responded most demurely, for he had taught her well in those lessons of his. "That you will."

★ ★ ★ ★ ★

Acknowledgments

I am indebted to Cindy Vallar, Jody Allen and Sharron Gunn for their knowledge and guidance on Scottish history, for their generous hearts and their willingness to help other writers with their research. And also to Beth Trissel, whose knowledge on herbal lore has been both an inspiration and an education.

My thanks go to classical Gaelic singer Fiona Mackenzie for helping me with my Gaelic translations, and for her wonderful and inspiring music.

Finally, thank you to Portia Da Costa, for her friendship, support and encouragement during the writing of this novel.

**Loving the enemy is one thing.
Trusting the enemy is quite another.**

New York Times **Bestselling Author**

CANDACE CAMP

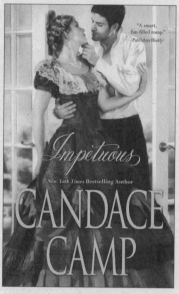

In the late 1600s, Black Maggie Verrere was engaged to marry
Sir Edric Neville in an effort to unite their two families. Instead she eloped to
America with another man, and the famed Spanish dowry vanished along with
her. The two families—the Verreres and the Nevilles—have hated
one another ever since.

Now, 150 years later, another Verrere woman seeks the dowry.
Cassandra Verrere has no hope of providing a future for her younger siblings,
or for herself, unless she recovers the treasure. Unfortunately her path to its
attainment requires the help of a Neville—the disarming Sir Philip. With an
ancient feud marking their lineage, Cassandra cannot imagine trusting him.
But the true challenge may be in trusting her heart not to fall for him.

Available wherever books are sold!

www.Harlequin.com

Revisit the enchanting Donovan clan from
#1 *New York Times* bestselling author

NORA ROBERTS

These fascinating cousins share a secret that's
been handed down through generations—a
secret that sets them apart....

Available wherever books are sold!

PSNR165TR

USA TODAY bestselling author

CHRISTIE RIDGWAY

introduces a sizzling new series set in Crescent Cove,
California, where the magic of summer
can last forever....

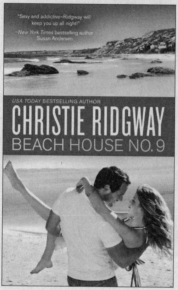

When book doctor Jane Pearson arrives at Griffin Lowell's beach house, she
expects a brooding loner. After all, his agent hired her to help the reclusive
war journalist write his stalled memoir. Instead, Jane finds a tanned, ocean-
blue-eyed man in a Hawaiian shirt, hosting a beach party and surrounded by
beauties. Faster than he can untie a bikini top, Griffin lets Jane know he doesn't
want her. But she desperately needs this job and digs her toes in the sand.

Griffin intends to spend the coming weeks at Beach House No. 9 taking refuge
from his painful memories—and from the primly sexy Jane, who wants to bare
his soul. But warm nights, moonlit walks and sultry kisses just may unlock
both their guarded hearts....

Available wherever books are sold!

www.Harlequin.com

PHCR740TR

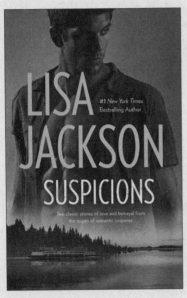